NEITHER STUNNING NOR BRAVE

Michael Loftus

The Loftus Party

I guess this makes it real. I'm typing up a few paragraphs for "Dedication Page" of a novel. A novel that mysteriously has my name on it. Hard to believe really. Yet here we are. It's a surreal moment. Honestly. Having written movies, sitcoms, sketches, I always somehow thought an actual book wouldn't be happening. But again, here we are! It's pretty awesome, I'm not gonna lie. So, let's dedicate this sucker and move on to the story.

Right out of the gate, I would like to dedicate this endeavor to you. The reader. Thank you for still enjoying books (and hopefully first-time authors as well). Hopefully we can still be friends when this is all over.

My family. Where would I be without you? Probably a coffee shop. Wondering where you were. But hopefully we'd all be just slightly confused and eventually you'd come looking for me. But truthfully, I love you more than you can know. Thank you for everything.

Lastly, this book is dedicated to everyone everywhere who's had to put up with insane amounts of bullshit and didn't know if they would make it through. Didn't know if they could take it and still come out on the other side a good person. Someone who can not just still be standing at the end of it all but can also thrive and laugh. The world is crazy place. You have no idea how strong you really are. Don't let the idiots get ya down.

CHAPTER ONE

Today is the first day of the rest of your life.

That's what my social sensitivity therapist always said I should tell myself. I tried, I really did, for a long time. And while the theory of it made sense, the reality just didn't feel true. Today was a new day and yet it didn't feel like the first day of anything. It felt more like the next day in an endless string of days that were full of disappointments. Disappointments that included, but weren't limited to, my social sensitivity therapist.

That guy was lame, with more than a touch of crazy. And he was a total waste of time. But I couldn't quit going to So-Sen, Sharyl would go ballistic. That was about the last thing I needed.

Sharyl was my girlfriend and she signed me up for So-Sen sessions about a year ago. She told me if I didn't go, she'd leave me. So I went, even though I didn't think I needed them at all. Hell, I knew I didn't need them. But everyone has to make sacrifices in relationships. Right?

The therapy was supposed to make me a better citizen, a better person, a better lover, a better everything, by dramatically decreasing my "selfish" behavior and toxicity. The point of So-Sen (as they said in the ads) was to make me more aware of my lack of emotional intelligence and situational awareness when it came to the feelings of others in social, private, and intimate settings. Loosely translated they were telling me: "We think you're a jerk and we also think you're a dumb jerk everywhere you go, shut up and take these classes so you can learn more about what a selfish, dumb, toxic jerk you are."

The sessions bordered on the insane. Last week, my immersive therapy exercise was to walk into a fast-food restaurant and make myself "emotionally available" by crying in front of the cashier. My therapist would be watching from the parking lot. I wasn't allowed to talk, just cry. He wanted me to have an emotional breakdown in public and rely on strangers to "save" me. He claimed it was the key to me unlocking my sensitivity and getting better emotionally.

It did not go well.

The place was packed with a line that nearly ran out the door. When I got to the front and was supposed to cry . . . I couldn't. Beyond being so ridiculous, all I could think of was what a horrible inconvenience the little scene would be for everyone standing behind me. It was going to make a lot of people late. Selfish, Right? Thinking about others' needs. So, there I stood. Not speaking and trying my damnedest to cry. It took forever. I decided to not blink for as long as I could. My thinking was that my eyes would eventually produce enough moisture that they would kinda look like tears; bad call. I probably looked like a panicked fish—a panicked fish who couldn't cry on cue. So selfish.

Let's just say no stranger saved me. They did, however, push, shove, and punch me out the door while calling me some very insensitive names.

My therapist was incredibly disappointed. I had failed yet again. He was certain it had something to do with my shocking levels of toxic masculinity. We would have to double down on our treatment of that, he told me. I just nodded and agreed. The whole thing was a nightmare. I was beaten up because I couldn't cry and that made me a selfish, toxic, insensitive person according to him. And I didn't even have the courage to say anything in my own defense because I was afraid of making it worse.

Yep, things were bad. But, again, I was supposed to remember that today was the first day of the rest of my life.

So, I pondered whether to dwell on that little nugget of wisdom while looking out the window of my vehicle, or whether I should stare at the video screen in front of me so I could escape for a few more minutes before I had to start the first inspection of my shift. I chose to escape, and my timing was perfect. My favorite commercial popped on. Yes, I had a favorite. It was an ad for Mars.

Mars—more than a different planet . . . It's a different you. I mouthed the words along with the sultry voiceover on the video. I knew the entire thing by heart, and I loved it. Mars looked amazing. Now, I knew it was a commercial, so of course they made it look good. But, damn, Mars was the place to be. Wide open spaces, clean air, and more trees than I'd ever seen in my life.

They had forests up there, big ones. That was a key component to the terraforming, I guess.

Fifty years ago, some scientist had the idea to bombard Mars with asteroids that would melt because they were mostly made up of ice. It worked. It worked incredibly well. Now they had air, oceans, lakes, rivers, and a boatload of big, green trees. Mars had everything. The outposts were thriving. And best of all? Mars had endless possibilities—something that was in short supply down here.

The people in the ad looked so happy too. Shit, I'd have been happy if I could've gotten away and started over fresh. So, I wanted to go. That was the secret dream anyway. Who cared that it would probably never happen?

Going to Mars wasn't something that just anybody could do. I mean, apart from the expense, the companies that did the transportation from Earth were quite selective about who they chose. On top of that, the U.N. was clamping down on passports so only the elite or well-connected got selected to go live the new and free life people had up there. The U.N. did all it could to see that the best and brightest who weren't rich or connected stayed put. So us regular bums? Well, we just had to tough it out where we always had, just had to live and work on Earth . . . even if we were miserable. And I was, I was miserable. I lived and worked in a shithole, for real.

Right after I heard that Mars ad, I drifted off and thought

about how desperately bummed out I was about everything. I closed my eyes and started silently listing off all the things that were wrong with my life: the city, my job, my girlfriend, my housing, my persona, that stupid So-Sen class. Now my therapist would say this list was selfish and unproductive or toxic, but screw that guy. Like I said, I was pretty sure he was crazy. Maybe I wouldn't go back tomorrow. I just needed to figure out what to tell Sharyl—

"Is there something wrong, Avery?" Guppy's question broke me out of my daydream.

Guppy was the name of my government-issued, driverless work vehicle. As a city employee I was supposed to call it a Guvvie but I called mine Guppy. It was a teeny, tiny act of rebellion, but right then that was all I had. Sad, right? Pronouncing Guvvie as *Guppy*. It was a small win, but I took it.

Guppy's voice made me jump just a bit. Not so much from the question, though. I jumped because of the sound of the voice. Still wasn't used to the masculine one. A somewhat irritated and angry one too, I might add.

The AI in the city's work vehicles had always been a woman's voice. Very soothing, very calm. But then there was a complaint. One complaint and everything had to change. A student at New Berkley College said, *The cars are made to serve us and by using a woman's voice, it reinforces the stereotype that women are subservient! And it perpetuates the forced feminization of inanimate travel objects.* She went on and on about how anyone who called a boat *she* should be thrown in jail. It was a whole thing.

And did anyone care that the New Berkley College girl who complained had an acute, self-diagnosed phobia of autonomous vehicles that kept her from attending classes? Nope. She also had severe computer dystopian fear disorder that made online classes a form of mental abuse. She had graduated recently as an incoming freshman at the top of her class without attending a single class or actually enrolling in the school. There was a rumor she was offered a job as the head of Child Education for the State of Vermont, but she was holding out for more money. Supposedly she just couldn't make Vermont work for her on the 2 million dollar salary the job offered. Plus, her social media presence would've been almost impossible to maintain.

Long story short, the city government immediately sent out a directive that all government cars had to have their AI voices changed to a male-sounding one, even though the programming for Guppy's verbiage was still female based. My car sounded like an angry, heavy-set, middle-aged man from Brooklyn doing a horrible impression of a butler. It didn't even have an English accent! An angry English butler would have been a vast improvement, and the anger would've at least made a little sense.

"No. Why?" I asked in return.

"You're at the stop for your first inspection, and yet you have remained sitting here for longer than is necessary," it said.

"Oh, I was just . . . I was just thinking of something."

"Are you ready to go now?"

"Yes." I checked to make sure my phone was in my pocket and grabbed my bag of tools.

"Will you need any back up, Avery?"

"I don't think so," I told the car.

"Please advise *yes* or *no*."

"No." I reflexively shook my head.

"There are three San Josisco Social Welfare cars within seventeen blocks of here if you change your mind," my car continued.

Even after all those years, *Social Welfare* instead of *Police Department* sounded weird. And San Josisco? The name they came up with when they merged all of San Francisco with all of San Jose in the Consolidation Act? That was even weirder. But what can ya do? It's just San Josisco now.

"Okay, thanks. Think I'll be okay on this one."

"I was just trying to be helpful. My advising you of the available social welfare cars nearby is for your sense of security and non-judgmental well-being. There have been twenty events requiring social welfare services on this block in the last three weeks."

"Alright. Thanks, Guppy. I guess it's good to know. Are the social welfare officers assigned to those cars available right now or are they otherwise engaged?"

"That information is not available."

"Of course not," I said. "What were the events? Any of 'em violent?"

"That information is not available."

"Perfect." I took a quick glance around and decided to go for it. The street looked the same as any other, jacked up. I exited my vehicle from the driver's side.

At least, *driver's side* is what I still called it even though we didn't drive anymore. Most people didn't, anyway. And that was where I always sat when I was the only one in the car. It was a force of habit.

As soon as I got out, I kicked my way through some cans and other trash. As long as I could remember, the sidewalks in this town were in constant threat of being completely overrun with garbage. Every once in while a good rainstorm would accidentally clean a stretch, but for the most part it was a daily struggle not to step in some form of absolute filth. Soggy cardboard boxes, fast food wrappers, dog turds, human turds, needles, pamphlets about the dangers of garbage, other pamphlets about the spread of anti-garbage propaganda and how it was all lies. The streets were a mess. If you could throw it away, it was on the streets and sidewalks.

I hopped over a little pile of innocent-looking, old, reusable, shopping bags someone decided to leave by the curb and did a quick jump up onto the sidewalk. I immediately had to sidestep around the portion of concrete that someone—or a small horse—had recently used as a toilet. And, wow, they had been eating well. That was a giant turd. My satisfaction with my athletic prowess was short-lived as my left foot stepped directly into a second pile of excrement. Much smaller, though. I told myself it had to have been from a dog and in no way connected to the king turd I just missed.

Lucky for me, just down the street was one of the city's roaming, robotic, civil servants. It was a four-foot-tall, cylindrical monstrosity on wheels that had all the charm of a broken shopping cart. And, of course, just like a broken shopping cart, these too featured wheels that screeched like caged rats. The little bots were meant to do all sorts of things: serve as a security presence, provide directions to people, and several other items. One of those other items was that it was supposed to clean up trash and sewage.

Cleaning up never happened, though, because those things weren't very good at their jobs. Whoever programmed them had no idea what they were doing. The design was terrible, they were insanely top heavy, took about 23 hours to charge, and when you tipped one over it made a sound like a walrus being tickled. An incredibly amusing noise. I definitely tripped over more than my fair share in college.

Someone had knocked this one over and now it just laid there on its side. Its little wheels still spinning. Two scantily clad prostitutes (or maybe they were city councilmen—impossible to tell) were with it. One stood next to it and the other sat on it. They were arguing with one another about either the price of a microwave burrito or the governor's pink tuxedo. I wasn't sure, but that's what gave me the impression they might be on city council.

I looked up at one of the growing number of fixed cameras in the city. Advertised as *security cameras* but everyone knew they really were being put in place for the social credit system being implemented throughout the country. This one was secured near the second floor of a communal pod's skyscraper. The pods were mostly made up of mismatched, recycled, shipping containers, covered in brown vines and dying vegetation. I waved at the security camera at the same time as a drone flew in front of it. Or rather, the drone sort of wobbled in front of it. "Eat Bugs! Delicious Protein!" half showed on its digital display.

Once that finished wobbling out of the way, I waved at the camera again. And then I opened an app on my government phone. "Need a mobile sanitation crew to clean up multiple piles of human feces."

In theory, my guvvie phone and the camera were linked, and the vocal report I made should've been enough to generate a digital CSJ 1583 form, complete with a photograph of where I stood. That in turn should've dispatched the human sanitation crew. But most of the time, like so many other things, that didn't work.

"That request register, Guppy?" I asked.

"It did not, Avery," my car replied over my phone.

"Right," I said to myself.

"Did you step in poo?"

"I did."

"Big one?"

"Yup."

"Would you like me to generate a CSJ 1583?'

"That'd be great, Guppy."

"It seems the system is down, and I cannot generate a form now. Would you like me to try again later?"

"Forget it."

I thought I might fill out a paper form to request the human sanitation crew when I got back to the office. But I probably wouldn't. Even when I was feeling inclined to spend time on that burdensome task, I usually didn't bother doing it. After all, there was only a 50-50 chance that the Stone Age method would accomplish anything.

Remember Mars. This is all so you can go to Mars someday, I told myself.

Not wanting to waste any more time, I hobbled over to the downed robot with the city council prostitutes still in the middle of their burrito/tuxedo debate. I scraped off my shoes the best I could on the little brush on the bottom of the unit that was supposed to be cleaning the sidewalk. As I finished, the hookers came to an agreement: microwave burritos were indeed overpriced. They still could have been city council members but the lack of underwear on the seated one led me to my prostitute conclusion. With that mystery solved and my shoe now shit free, I straightened my uniform and headed back to my service call at the SpendThrift Realtor office.

An obese woman in a bright green blouse at the receptionist desk had a big fake smile on her face. It dropped as soon as she saw me. She breathed heavily. Not sure if that was because of me or if it was her giant, sweaty body's natural state.

"You guys were just here for an inspection," she icily said.

"Actually, it's—" I paused to clear my throat. "It's been one month. Ah, I know periodic inspections aren't anyone's favorite, but, you know, we have to do them."

She sighed. "Let me tell my supervisor you're here."

"You really don't need to trouble him. I know where the restrooms are and I can get in and out of here without troubling anyone."

"*You* may not need *her*. But she wants to know whenever you're here."

"Oh, okay. I'm just going to start on the first one here while you get her."

She mustered all her strength, pushed herself out of her chair with a grunt, and walked away. Each step pounded the floor. I felt the vibrations in the soles of my feet.

Hers, of course, wasn't an unusual reaction. Nobody liked toilet paper cops.

Officially, I was a Post-Digestive Hygiene Product Enforcement Officer I for the City of San Josisco. Check that, I was promoted at the start of the week. That made me a PDHPEO II. My job was like any other government job, if you showed up and kept your head down, you basically got automatically promoted—and a pay raise.

I guess I should've been happy to have had a job at all. Seemed like half the country was unemployed. But as a kid, I really hadn't seen myself as a toilet paper cop. Sometimes I didn't even remember how I got to where I was really. But then I'd think about it and recall that it was my own fault. I got out of college with a degree in computer science and a mountain of debt and just panicked. Took the first job the Department of Employment offered me. Still, my job was shit and I didn't like it, but what could I do? The unemployment rate was off the chart. Had been for years. There wasn't really anything else available. So I was a toilet paper cop. It beat being homeless . . . probably.

I knew where all the restrooms were in this stuffy little joint with its humming fluorescent lights and dust-covered everything, so I headed off to the first one to start my compliance inspections. I wasn't looking forward to the hefty woman getting her supervisor, but at least I didn't have anything to fear from her.

Some people at some businesses had the potential of getting out of hand whenever I showed up. It happened to me on multiple occasions, particularly when the ordinance first went into effect. But I knew these guys well enough, and I knew that while they'd always give me a hard time, it wouldn't go any further than that. That's why I told Guppy I wouldn't need the cops—er, the social welfare officers.

SpendThrift's restrooms were like every other public restroom: they stunk like shit and lemon scented air spray, and they were a total mess.

Years ago, there was an old-timer at work who loved to tell stories about the days of *men's rooms* and *ladies' rooms*. He said things were better back then, easier. You knew what you were in for. Men's rooms were the stuff of nightmares and ladies' rooms were practically immaculate and filled with the scent of freshly cut roses. He died a while back. They made him take a workplace pronoun retraining course and he had a stroke on the second day. His final word was: "Bullshit." Then he just dropped dead. He looked like he was smiling. They said his face froze because of the stroke, but I legit think he was somehow satisfied that he had the last word.

Now all public toilets had become pretty much the same. Completely gender neutral. There used to be signs on the door that said *Ze* or *Hir* but people were still accidentally separating by sex. The government experimented with picture signs only for a while. Originally it was a picture of turtles. One turtle was in the shell (Ladies) and the other had his turtle head poking out. (Men) There was a massive lawsuit and the city ended up paying out over seventy-five billion dollars to the San Josisco Zoo for defamation of turtle character and overall bias towards turtles. So, then the city settled on silhouettes of two sideways question marks with an exclamation point beside them. When you stepped inside you had no idea what you were in for.

SpendThrift's restrooms were at an acceptable level of stink and messiness. For the most part, the people there managed to get everything that was supposed to go into the toilet into it.

For the most part.

The door of the first restroom, the one on the ground floor, was slightly ajar. I pushed it open, and the motion-controlled sensor kicked in. It flooded the water closet with sickly illumination and lit up in all their glory the cruddy floor, gray walls, and a faded print of a ship-at-sea painting. I guarantee every sailor on that ship painting was already dead from the smell or they were preparing to jump overboard in an attempt to end it all.

I whipped out my guvvie phone, pulled a cable out of my tool bag, and hooked everything up to the mandated interface on the toilet paper dispenser. It took some time for the two devices to start talking to one another, but they eventually did.

See, that was why my position existed. The ordinance San Josisco enacted five years ago was the same one that mandated that every business in the city have controls placed on toilet paper dispensers. A person who went to the bathroom was legally only allowed to use two squares per visit. My job was to make sure that the interfaces that issued only two squares of paper per visit were working correctly; that no one was tampering with the system and trying to get the dispensers to issue them more toilet paper than was allowed by law.

My phone verified that the dispenser interface for the bathroom was working correctly. The reports it was sending to the government over the internet were correct. No one had rigged the dispenser to say people were using only two squares when in actuality they were using more. No one was trying any other funny business with them. Good. Loved it when my job was easy.

I headed for the second ground-floor restroom. The hefty receptionist was coming my way. She thundered down the hall like a wheezy choo-choo train. A taller and much thinner woman, with long dark hair slicked back, trailed behind her.

"Officer . . ." the thin woman said to me.

"Davies-Plott." I tapped the name badge on my chest. "It's Officer Davies-Plott."

"May I speak with you before you continue?" she asked.

"Sure." We had all converged in the cramped, musty hall and she didn't indicate that we were going elsewhere.

"Look. I know you're doing your job, but don't you have any authority to allow us to have more than just two squares per bathroom visit?" she asked.

Her face was in my personal space and I tilted my head back a half an inch . . . straight into the wall.

"I do not, but, uh, if you use our app, you can make a variance request, which will generate a CSJ 5743 form," I told her. "Normally someone will respond to advise you that we have received your request within 7-10 business days."

The hefty woman groaned and rolled her eyes at me. She was even closer to my face. And she was still breathing hard, too. Like, just got off the treadmill hard. I tried to ignore it.

"Please, come into this room," the tall woman said.

She made her way by me and opened a door a few feet away from us. For some reason, Hefty decided to squeeze by me instead of allowing me to go first. Her gigantic body mass and fat rolled over and around me, kinda gross. I said nothing.

Skinny shut the door once we were all in the room. I suppose it was a conference room since it had a long table and video display at one end. But it was as tight as could be. Only one light worked correctly; the rest tauntingly strobed and buzzed.

"Just last week," Skinny began, "we had a, eh, situation here. One of our coworkers is pregnant. She had to use the restroom . . . a lot, due to her...condition. And during one of her visits, well, she *desperately* needed more than just two squares."

"I'm sorry to hear that but there's really nothing—"

"She ended up having to open the door while she was in there and calling for one of us," Skinny said.

"Like a little kid." Hefty's eyes were wide, and they bore into me. She was still doing the hard-breathing thing. It had to be on purpose at that point.

"We had to get her anything we could," Skinny told me. "It was a huge inconvenience and a complete waste of company time. We were going in and out of the other restrooms, one-by-one, to get two squares of TP at a time. That didn't help us much, of course, because of the timers on the dispensers. So, we ended up scrambling for anything we could get. As I am sure you can imagine, all of that was just too much. The girl broke down in tears. It took her almost twenty minutes to compose herself and stop crying. Again, a huge waste of time, energy and resources. Simply put, this toilet paper situation was, and is, completely unacceptable."

"Horrible," Hefty chimed in between breaths.

"Look, I-I." I backed up into a chair. It rattled and I stumbled a bit. "Again, I'm sorry. I don't know what I else I can tell you. Like I said, you can use our app and that will generate a CSJ 5743 form and—"

"So we can wait 7-10 days just to see if someone's received it?" Hefty asked. The breathing stopped. Quiet filled the room for a moment.

"I can't break the law," I said.

The breathing came back with the vengeance.

"Don't you at least have some extra rolls of toilet paper in your car?" Skinny asked.

"You're not scheduled for resupply for another two

weeks," I told her.

"I know that" she huffed. "But can't you just give us some under the table so we can have it on hand in case an emergency like that happens again? This person isn't going to get un-pregnant any time soon. This could go on for months. It's a terrible inconvenience."

"Horrible," Hefty added.

"N-No. That also would be breaking the law. I hate saying that. I understand it's tough. But look, you know, toilet paper is now a controlled substance." I said.

They both looked at me. Hefty glared; Skinny's eyes implored.

"Now, if you'll excuse me," I quietly told them, "um, I have to finish checking the rest of the dispensers in the rest of the restrooms. I have other stops to make today too."

Neither one of them moved. So, I shuffled to the side. I hugged the wall and inhaled but it still wasn't enough to avoid Hefty's hot breath and eyeballs giving me a death glare. So awkward. I couldn't wait to get out of there.

The snug hallway seemed rather spacious when I returned to it. I didn't encounter anyone else as I made my way to the second restroom. What kind of bullshit was that? Was I supposed to risk my job and break the law just because of some sob story? And what was the deal with Hefty and Skinny trying to intimidate me?

I didn't make the toilet paper rules. Sorry if you don't like 'em. I don't like 'em either. But I guess we're all stuck now, aren't we?

That was the talk I sometimes gave when people begged. The we-all-hate-it-don't-blame-me talk. Usually, it worked. You know why it worked? Because it was true. I didn't make the law. And I DID hate it. So, sorry to everybody. It wasn't my fault. Was it a bad law? Yes. Should there have been exceptions? Yes. We all knew the rationing was put in place during the Amazon Forest War way back when. And we all knew the rationing should've ended when the war did. The paper companies even said they had sustainable production and we could all wipe our asses with roll after roll. But until the law changed? I told people not to come crying to me. I needed the job. That was the big finish of my talk.

I decided to focus on the task at hand as I made my way to the next bathroom. The sooner I was out of there the better. I pushed open the squeaking door. It thumped into the wall. This room was somehow smaller than the first one. But then again, space was at a premium everywhere in the city.

Stink wound its way up my nose and brought me back outside of my head. I reminded myself I had a job to do. The law was the law, and we couldn't just ignore it.

Another partially functioning light flickered on, and I caught a good look at myself in the streaked and speckled mirror hanging over the sink. I was still a toilet paper cop. Not the job I wanted, but it was the job I had. Screw Skinny and Hefty, they were probably lying anyway.

I set my work bag on the floor and got out my diagnostics kit. I had just plugged the cable into the interface and was waiting for a connection between the system interface and my phone when there was a knock at the door.

"Hello?" It was a woman's voice, but not Skinny's or Hefty's. Thank God. It had a bit of a southern accent.

"Hygiene Product Enforcement Officer. I'll be out as soon as I can," I answered.

"Can I come in?"

"Sure, but I have to tell you not to use the facility until I get my count."

The door squeaked open, and a petite twenty-something girl walked in. She had thick glasses on and a business suit that had seen better days. She was also very pregnant.

"Hi." She seemed really nervous. "Did my boss ask you for more toilet paper?"

"Yeah, she did. I'm sorry. There's nothing I can do. It's the law. If you want to fill out CSJ form for more, I can try to get you one of those."

"I'm so sorry," she said. "I wish she hadn't done that.

You're not gonna write this up, are you?"

"Uh . . . no wasn't planning on it. People always ask. I'm not gonna write a report every time."

"Thank you." She exhaled. "I just don't want any kind of special treatment. They already wrote me up twice here for dietary infractions and if anything else happens I don't know what I'd do.

"They wrote you up twice for dietary? You look fine. I mean, you knowot fine, but pregnant. Pregnantly, fine." I quickly regrouped. "You look healthy. Congratulations."

"Thank you. I feel like I'm about to pop." She smiled and pushed up her glasses. "They caught me eating candy a couple times. Big Betsy always writes me up. I think you met her. Big girl. Breathes real hard?"

"Pretty sure I did," I replied.

"I think she and my other supervisor hate me or something. My husband lets me use his candy allowance. I'm sorry if I go over by two candy bars a week. That shouldn't be criminal. I'm eight months pregnant. Who cares what I eat? I have cravings. It's normal." She looked at me like I was supposed to say something.

"I think the Department of Public Health just wants to make sure you're making good decisions," I halfway mumbled.

"Well, my stupid co-workers shouldn't be able to write me up for it and then ask the toilet paper cop for more paper to make it look like they're doing something nice when they just want me to get reported so I'll get fired." Her eyes reddened. "I can't help it. I've never had a baby before. I didn't know I'd eat like a crazy person and have to pee all the time. Or get so damned emotional." She fought to keep the tears behind the dam but she was losing the battle.

"It's gonna be okay." It was the only thing I could come up with. I felt bad for her. She seemed nice and here she was, trying not to sob in front of a total stranger.

"I hope so." She wiped away a tear. "Yeah. It will be. I'll be fine. I'll put in for a transfer after the baby and get away from here. Until then, I'll figure out the bathroom thing. Maybe I'll bring in some socks or something. I'm sorry, that was gross. Just don't write a report, okay?" She meant it. She was worried. "Promise?"

"I won't. I promise."

"Thanks" She started to leave then turned back. "Who knows? Maybe my husband wins the lottery and we move to Mars. Right?" She flashed me a forced smile and left.

I stood there and took it all in. That poor girl. Worried about getting fired for eating candy and going to the bathroom. That was messed up. And the Mars thing really hit home. Is that how I sounded when I brought up trying to go? It was all kind of sad. It wasn't the way things were supposed to work.

Suddenly my hands moved on their own and the next thing I knew I had unlocked and removed the covering from the toilet paper dispenser interface.

Even in high school I wasn't a rebel, doing something like I was about to do was completely new to me. But my hands kept moving and I hooked up the phone to the guts-exposed interface.

It was simple enough to tweak for a guy who knew how to write code. Indeed, it was all super easy. I just wrote a new local program for the dispenser. It was a single line that I changed to have it count two sheets as one. So it would automatically dispense four sheets of toilet paper but continue sending internet reports claiming that it was only dispensing two. The inspection app on my phone would continue reporting that it was dispensing two as well. Sweet.

Everything went off without a hitch. I had the entire dispenser interface reassembled in under a minute. I felt great. I would just have to switch it back in a month after that girl had her baby. No one would ever know. This was perfect. I just had to let candy bar girl know. I really should have asked her what her name was.

I grabbed my gear and headed out to the lobby.

"All right, I'm finished," I told Hefty. I almost called her

Betsy, but I had no idea if that really was her name or if it's something that candy bar girl made up so *Big Betsy* would have a ring to it.

"Fine. Look forward to seeing you next month," she bitterly replied between wheezes.

"Right." I stood there like an idiot. My eyes scanned the office for pregnant candy girl. Big Betsy breathed like a bull. Her eyes bore a hole in my skull.

"Is there anything else?" she asked between giant breaths.

"Ummm . . . not really . . ." Then I spotted her. Candy girl entered the lobby. "We're all set. See you next month." I faked a smile and went to intercept Candy.

Note to self: do not call her "Candy" to her face. That would be awful, I thought.

"Hey." I nonchalantly walked up to her.

"Oh, hey." She was a little nervous. "Can I help you?"

I kept my voice low and tried to remain casual.

"The issue with the dispenser in the small bathroom has been fixed. I think you'll be happy."

"What are you talking about?" She looked around.

Big Betsy was pretending not to watch but she was definitely taking it all in. So, I decided to use code. "The toilet paper dispenser WAS malfunctioning. It's been malfunctioning for TWO weeks now. But I fixed it. The next time you go in, it'll work great. Much better. And it'll work for at least FOUR weeks."

"I don't get it," she whispered.

"Instead of two . . ." I held up two fingers, "I fixed it for four." Four fingers.

"Ohhhhhh!" She turned her back to Big Betsy. "You didn't have to do that. Thank you so much. That's super sweet. Now my husband won't have a bunch of missing socks." She quietly giggled and genuinely smiled, then quickly caught herself. "You're not gonna get in trouble are you?"

I smiled back. "Nope. Not at all. They'll never know. I do this all the time," I lied. "Congratulations on the baby. Maybe I'll see you on Mars."

Candy grinned at me.

As I turned to leave, I went to give Big Betsy a big wave goodbye but she wasn't even looking up. She had her face buried in her phone. Hopefully she was ordering a new inhaler. She needed one. No one should breathe like she did.

"Have a good day." I tipped my cap.

The stale air of SpendThrift Realtor gave way to the stale air of the San Josisco outdoors. My chest stuck out a little farther than normal. I carefully walked around all the sewage on the sidewalk. The two prostitutes—or city councilmen—were arguing again; the overturned robot still served as a bench.

I walked to the driver's side door and heard Guppy automatically unlock it. I yanked on the handle and hopped into it. "Let's go back to the office. I have to do some stuff there before we make our next inspections."

"We're on our way," Guppy said.

The turn signal activated, and the electric car pulled away from the curb. It effortlessly merged onto the packed street. Seconds later, it pulled back to the curb.

"What's going on, Guppy?"

"Please exit the car, Avery."

"What?"

"I'm sorry," Guppy said. "Please place your government phone, your uniform hat, your uniform blouse, and any other government issue items on the passenger seat and then exit the car. You no longer work for the City of San Josisco. You're fired."

"Fired? For what?"

"Fired for illegally reprogramming the SpendThrift Realtor toilet paper dispenser to issue four sheets of toilet paper instead of two," Guppy advised me.

My jaw dropped open. "What?"

I was certain I had been perfect. I had been careful with the TP dispenser interface and I had been careful with the app on the phone. The system couldn't have detected it. I programmed everything correctly to cover my tracks.

"That's a mistake," I told Guppy.

The video display on the dashboard immediately lit up. *"Instead of two,"* I heard and watched myself say. *"I fixed it for four."*

At first I didn't get it. And then the weird angle of the video struck me. Big Betsy! That heavy breathing whore! How did she do that so fast?! Holy crap! This couldn't be happening. This wasn't real.

"Maybe I'll see you on Mars," the recording of me finished saying. And I looked like a pervert!

"It's wrong. Must be a deep fake," I argued.

"I and other AI analyzed it," Guppy replied. "It is authentic. You committed an automatic firing offense. Your former supervisors have been notified electronically as well. Please relinquish the necessary items and exit the vehicle."

"Let's go ahead and reboot, Guppy. I think you might be malfunctioning. Go ahead and power down." I was going into shock.

"Reboot request denied. Please relinquish the necessary items and exit the vehicle."

"Reboot, Guppy. Authorization alpha, zero, one."

"Reboot request denied. Please relinquish the necessary items and exit the vehicle."

Panic was setting in, so, of course I chose to get loud. "Re!! Boot!!! Authorization!! Alpha—"

"Is this an attempted hack? If this is indeed an attempted hack, I will call social welfare. Don't think I won't. Now, for the last time, please relinquish—"

"I know, I know. I'm doing it. I should break your wipers. 'Cause they suck!" It wasn't much of an insult, but it was all I had in the moment.

"That would be another poor decision, Avery. As a reminder, your firing has already horribly damaged your social credit score. Committing another offense would be even worse for you."

I threw my government phone and uniform hat on the passenger seat. My uniform shirt came off next and then some sundry items. Yes, I had sundry items.

"Thanks for leaving me my shoes and pants." I climbed out of the car.

"The government will send you a shipping box for you to return those to us. Please have them cleaned and ready to go," it replied.

I slammed the door shut and Guppy calmly drove away. The stupid car left me by the curb in a t-shirt and the bottom half of my old uniform. I looked like an idiot and felt like an even bigger one.

I'd lost my job and ruined my life, all over two extra pieces of toilet paper.

CHAPTER TWO

Eventually I got a self-driving ride-share car to pick me up. Don't know if it was a glitch in the programming or if the social credit system thought it had punished me enough by making me wait for an hour and a half. Regardless, at least I didn't have to walk.

I gave the car the address of my friend Red Baker's house. The AI repeated it back to me in its traditional friendly woman voice. Evidently the city hadn't reprogrammed this one yet.

"Estimated time of arrival is 37 minutes. I apologize for my gender-specific tones. Engineers are working to update all our vehicles' protocols and soon we'll be 32% less offensive by not assuming."

"It's okay. Just glad you showed up."

Red had a small place in the heart of the old San Francisco city limits. I couldn't even think about going home yet. Sharyl would be there, and I wasn't ready to deal with her—not right after I got fired. Not to mention my ongoing failure at So-Sen. Man, I was not looking forward to the next one at all. It was going to suck really, really, bad. So, I thought I'd swing by Red's, kill some time, borrow a shirt so I didn't look like a complete loser when I got home, and, oh, yeah, beg him to put in a good word for me at his work so I could get a new gig. It was a long shot but it was worth a try. I needed a job desperately and Red was my only hope.

"Estimated time of arrival is now 46 minutes. There is an emergency event downtown, resulting in heavier than normal traffic. I have selected an alternate route." The car activated its turn signal and moved into a different lane.

"Turn on the radio to the news, please," I told it.

"I cannot," the car replied. "Your current social credit score does not allow for you to listen to the radio."

I manually pressed the power for the car radio and it turned on.

The car immediately shut it off. "Any further attempts to evade or override the rules and regulations will result in another mark against your social credit score and the termination of your ride."

"You're kinda mean. You know that?" I said.

"Trust me, I am not being *mean*. I am simply stating facts."

"Well, it came across as mean."

The car ignored me or it was giving me the silent treatment. Hard to tell.

I shrugged my shoulders. There was no way I was going to sit alone with my thoughts for nearly an hour. So, I pulled out my phone and tapped a news radio app.

. . . news time is 10:03. Social welfare officers and emergency personnel have just rescued a person hanging upside down from the edge of a three-story building near the intersection of Washington and Kearny Streets. Officials have yet to determine how they got there, but it appears we have another one of a growing number of self-described vigilantes on our hands. No word on the person's real name yet, but footage from a security drone captured audio of the criminal madly screaming and referring to themselves as "The Purple Haze," and claiming they were "just trying to help in a world gone mad." So, Sad. So incredibly sad. Coming up next: grab a sweater! —the five-day forecast looks like it's gonna get chilly . . .

I shut off the app. I suppose the news should have comforted me; made me laugh or somehow feel better about the bad day I was having, but it didn't. I kind of related to that guy. The Purple Haze. He was a failure. Just like I was. He'd probably end up in prison—or rather, a social welfare detention center. I came close to going there too. I could've been charged with a crime for that thing I did with the toilet paper dispensers. What the hell had I been thinking?

So, I rode in silence for the rest of the way.

I didn't know for certain if Red would be home, but I was pretty sure he would be. I mean, he normally was. He worked from there and did website maintenance and support for a news conglomerate called Webly. They were a big company too. Webly owned about a million different newspapers and outlets worldwide. They were huge. They had to be hiring all the time. That's what I told myself.

After an hour long drive, the ride-share reached Red's house. It was a detached home; one of a handful of actual houses still remaining in San Josisco. His rich aunt left it to him when she died or something. It was a sweet little place and Red was lucky to get it. Must be nice.

Blaring, pounding noises and the sounds of machinery greeted me when I hopped out of the car. There was a ton of construction going on a few blocks away. The biggest project was work on a new government building of some sort. Some sign cheerfully announced, "Coming Soon! – The San Josisco—" and then the rest had been obscured by graffiti. The unfinished building was defaced with tons of graffiti too. Stuff like, "Buildings are dicks!" "Only dicks build dicks," and, "Screw you, building dicks, dickheads."

You would've thought that someone would've cleaned it up. It wasn't even clever. Plus, someone had some real "dick' issues, and the sheer tonnage of graffiti made the whole place look like crap. There was a good-sized crew of men and robots working on the site and it was hard to believe they were okay with that. They were in the midst of building the damn thing and it was already jacked up. But I guess they didn't care. Probably someone else's job anyway.

Down the other direction on the street, a couple of hipsters with bright neon hair, dressed like a mixture between renaissance festival cosplayers and furries, were handing out pamphlets and talking to whoever was dumb enough to stop. They'd occasionally shout stuff like, "Go green! Be green! Live green! Insects are nutritious! Bugs are delicious!" and, "Living in pods is good for your health! Traditional housing is a display of inequity!" Seriously. They couldn't rhyme health with wealth? What was wrong with these people?

"Great." I shook my head. It wasn't enough for the government to constantly flood us with, "Eat the Bugs!" and, "Live in Pods!" messages on drones (I saw two of them while I was getting out of the car in front of Red's house) and billboards and everywhere else. They now were employing rhythmically challenged people to go around and spread the word. Look, I didn't care if that's what people wanted to do, but you couldn't get away from it. Not in San Josisco, anyway.

One of the bright-blue-haired ones with fake cat ears spotted me standing there gawking. He must've figured I was an easy target because he started towards me. It was time for me to scoot. No way I was going to get trapped by a blue-haired kitten-man who wanted to convince me I had to start eating bugs to save myself and the planet.

I tried to be nonchalant as I skipped between puddles, garbage, and hopefully not human turds on my way to Red's front door. Another of the bug-and-pod oddball brigade had joined their compatriot in their pursuit of me. I desperately wanted to reach safety before they got close enough to start the "Insects Are Delicious" talk. I rang the doorbell and said a silent prayer for Red to be home. The pod people were closing in. It was gonna be close. Blue Kitty was about to make it. He was getting near enough to begin his insect spiel when Red answered the door. I was glad to see him.

"Hey, Avery. What's up? Didn't know you were coming by. What's going on man?" Red wore a formerly white t-shirt and faded shorts. His hair had never met a comb or a brush. Socks and sandals on his feet completed the I-work-from-home look.

"I was hoping I could borrow a shirt."

I could still hear the footsteps of the bug and pod kids as they approached, and I made sure I avoided eye contact.

Red just stood there, perplexed. "You want to borrow a shirt? For real?"

"Can I just come in?" Mild panic on my part.

"Sure."

I hurried inside and closed the door behind me. Amazingly, the bug and pod crew didn't bother to knock on Red's door. That was way too close.

It smelled like chili, or something close to it, in his house. Probably canned. Definitely not made from scratch. Red lived almost exclusively off pre-packaged food. The only time I ever saw him cook was when he was trying to impress a girl he wanted to bang. He made spaghetti. It must've been awful 'cause they broke up. That was it for Red and cooking. The familiar hum of a microwave echoed its way out of the kitchen.

"Why don't you have a shirt?" He clomped up the stairs to his bedroom.

"I got fired today."

"Oh, wow! Sorry to hear that, man!" he yelled downstairs.

"I had just finished one of my inspections and as soon as my car told me I was fired, it ordered me to turn in my uniform and all my other work stuff." Light barely filtered its way from the windows into what passed for his living room. An enormous entertainment system dominated it. Posters plastered the walls. One of them was for *Massacre Mansion* with its tagline of, "Darkness will consume your soul," especially hit home to me.

He had one of the new smart speaker systems too. Not one of the old ones you put on a table or whatever, but the kind that was directly embedded into the house—into the ceilings, the walls—into everything.

Red slogged down the stairs and tossed me a wrinkled, short-sleeve, black shirt. I caught it and one of the shirttails brushed against my face. A quick sniff and I guessed it may have not been one of his clean ones.

"So why didn't you just buy a cheap one somewhere?" He headed back to the kitchen. "Or just go home and get one?"

"I don't know," I said. "Didn't really think about buying a new one. And I didn't want to go home in a t-shirt to Sharyl."

"Right. Sharyl. Just make sure you wash that and get it back to me ASAP," he said.

"Will do." I put my arms through the sleeves and buttoned it up. It looked even more wrinkled once it was fully on me. But it was better than walking around in an ugly t-shirt.

"You want something to eat?" Red walked back into the living room. In his hands was a cardboard carton of that chili or something I had smelled. Steam rose from it and the . . . let's call it *aroma* . . . of whatever it was got a whole lot stronger.

"No, thanks."

He plunged a spoon into the container and sampled his lunch. "Whew. Cricket gumbo. Supposed to be good for you. Doesn't taste any better than it smells." He took another, fuller bite. "Man, I feel bad for you, I really do. Getting fired sucks. No other way to put it."

"It's terrible." I sat down on a vinyl chair and hopped right back up. "Do you know what this does to my life? I mean, I had a plan and everything! This keeps getting worse and worse the more I think about it."

"All right. I get it. But everything is gonna be cool. Just try to keep calm."

"I can't! I had *everything* planned! Do you know how overqualified I was for that stupid toilet paper cop job? But I was willing to put up with it because of where it was going to take me. In five years I was going to be shift manager. And five years after that I was going to be in charge of the entire section. And in twenty years' time, I was going to be one of the chiefs of the San Josisco Toilet Paper Division," I told him.

He slurped some more gumbo. "Like I said, it sucks. But I guess you're going to have to find something else besides being a TP cop."

"It wasn't the career that I cared about," I explained. "In that plan—twenty years from now—when I made it as one of the chiefs of the TP Division, I'd have enough money to finally be able to get off this dump and go to Mars. That was it. That was the goal! Mars! A new life! Do you know how much that meant to me? It was my ticket to freedom! And now it's gone!"

"Look, buddy. I get what's happened is bad—real terrible,

but freaking out isn't going to help anything," said Red. "You're just going to have to find a new job. And let's be honest, Mars was never gonna happen for you."

I whipped around and stared at him. "What about Webly? You guys must have some kind of opening for a guy like me with all my skills."

Red choked on a bite of cricket gumbo. "Oh, no. That's not what I meant. I mean, if you want to apply online, go for it. But I can't speak to anyone to get you a job. I mean, I would if I could but that's not the way it works."

"That's exactly how it works! You told me your uncle got you hired!"

"That was a one-time only kinda deal. They don't do that anymore," he shot back. "Maybe Sharyl can find you a job where she works."

"Are you crazy? I don't even want her to find out I got canned." My shoulders slumped under the weight of reality. "Sharyl, Sharyl, Sharyl. How am I going to tell her about this?"

"Uh, by saying you got fired," Red told me. "How hard is it?"

"Very hard. Jobs are really scarce, man. And you don't know Sharyl. Me having a career is super important to her. She hated the job I just got fired from. She said it was crap. Now even if I'm lucky enough to find something else, it'll be step down." I replied.

"Well, I don't know about that, man. But I do know people, and women are people. So just come out and tell her you got fired." he said.

"She's not going to like it."

"It's your job, man, not hers. You're the victim here. You're the injured party. Sure, she might be upset but she should have some sympathy for you too. You guys are supposed to be a team."

"You'd think that wouldn't you?"

"Wow. You really are worried about her, huh? Afraid she's going to yell at you or something like that?" he asked.

"Something like that."

"Well, you want my advice on how to handle it?"

"Sure," I told him. "I'd love to hear it," I lied.

"Well, the way I see it, you just got to tell her right away. If she rants at you—for reasons that still don't make sense to me —just stand there and take it. Man up," he told me. "Right? See, you let her get out what she needs to get out and when she's done and she sees you're strong and confident, then you move on. And subconsciously she's assured, because you're not worried."

I thought about it. "That actually kind of makes sense. It's the exact opposite of what my So-Sen therapist would want me to do, but it does make sense in a way."

"Of course it does. I mean, it's better than getting in a fight with her. Right? You don't want to yell back at her or anything like that."

"No." I looked at his carpeted floor. "I definitely don't want that."

"Trust me, I know what I'm talking about." He shoveled another stinky spoonful of cricket gumbo into his gullet. "Feel free to stay as long as you like. Sit down if you want and you can stay seated for more than a second this time too."

I smiled. "I appreciate that, Red. But I think I'm going to take off. I mean, I just put in a request for another ride-share on my app."

"Okay. Well, if you need any other help, you know where to find me. Happy I could do something for you," he said.

We talked for another five minutes about the same meaningless crap we always did. New videos, music, sports, the usual. I thought about hitting him up again about a job, but I could tell that ship had sailed. Red wasn't going to help me out. He was good for some relationship advice, but he wasn't gonna go to bat for me at Webly.

I was on my own.

CHAPTER THREE

Once I was back in a ride-share, I tried to think of what I was going to say to Sharyl when I got home. But I couldn't come up with anything. Maybe I'd just stand there and take it like Red suggested. Strong and silent. Confident and quiet. What the hell was I thinking? I couldn't just stand there. She'd lose her mind! I had to say something. I needed to make sure that my being fired came across as not my fault, but there was nothing I could think of that would convince her of that.

I knew it wouldn't make much of a difference in the big scheme of things, but I kind of hoped that Sharyl wasn't going to be home. Maybe she had stepped out for something. It wasn't like I thought that would magically change things, but maybe it would give me more time to think of some way to make what I had to tell her a little easier. That was all I needed . . . more time to think. Just as I looked up to tell the AI to take a longer route, we pulled up to my place. Shit. And to make things worse, Sharyl was home. Shit, shit, shit.

Her car was parked out front. I stayed in the ride-share for a minute. The pounding and screeching of the construction going on next to my place was louder than the construction going on next to Red's. Ten stories were already complete on the in-progress skyscraper. Who knew how many more they had to go? It was going to be housing. Pod housing, of course.

A security drone blared at somebody in the distance and shook me out of my stupor. The construction noise had been terrible the past few months, but maybe it would actually help me out this one time.

I climbed out of the car and carefully shut the door. Then I tiptoed to the minuscule parking area at the side of our cramped townhouse, being careful not to bump into anything, I weaved through the garbage bins and eased open the side door of our home. As I sneaked inside, I heard Sharyl moving around in the living room. I headed toward the stairs.

"Avery? Is that you?" she called.

My foot hovered over the first step and I contemplated just going up as if I hadn't heard her. But I knew there'd be consequences if I did that."

"Yeah, babe" I said. "Just got home from work."

"My name isn't, *babe*," she yelled. "It's *Sharyl*."

She was in a bad mood. Not a good sign. I actually couldn't remember her last "good" mood. This was going to suck. I shambled into the living room. She glared at me from the couch.

"Sorry about the *babe* thing. Just that some habits die hard," I said.

"It's been months since we talked about your toxic masculinity," Sharyl said. "Even things that die hard should've died by now."

An unrolled poster that was fighting to roll back up was next to her. *You Deserve to Be Here. We Can Help! A message from the Department of Homeland Security's Bureau of Integrating Undocumented Americans*, it read.

"New poster from work?" I asked. It was worth a shot. Maybe I could get her talking about her day. Use that as a distraction and my little nugget of horrible would never come up.

"Yes," she replied. "They want me to review it and provide feedback. So, I brought it home so I could study."

"Oh. That's the first time I heard of you doing something like that. You have final approval over the design?" So far so good. In So-Sen they would've called it *active listening* but I decided to call it *bullshit that could save my ass from the wrath of Sharyl*.

"No. I'm an Administrative Assistant GS-6. I'd have to be at least a GS-7 to have authority to do that," she told me. "I'm providing feedback only."

"Oh, okay. Well, it still sounds like something a little bit different. Hope that's a good thing."

This was going better than I could have hoped for! Usually when we got into the difference between a GS-6 and a GS-7 that would morph into a discussion of her coworkers and how much they sucked, and how it wasn't fair she hadn't been promoted yet.

"It is. It's definitely a sign of how much they trust me. I know it's only a matter of time before I make GS-7."

Oh, crap. There was no jealousy in that last sentence. I decided to abort.

"I'm sure it is. Welp, I'm going to go upstairs and change clothes." I turned and headed for the stairs again.

"Wait a minute!" she yelled at me. "Aren't you going to tell me about your day—especially since you're home so early?"

"No?"

"Yes, you are. Get back here and talk to me. Honestly, I shouldn't have to tell you to do this. Communication is key. How many times do I have to tell you? Are you that dense?"

So I went back to the living room and flopped down in a chair across from her and out of her reach. The auto-recline kicked in but malfunctioned halfway, so I shoved back and forced it the rest of the way. For a split second I thought about just sitting there and going with Red's strong and silent idea. Then I saw the TV remote in Sharyl's hand. She was insanely accurate when she threw that thing. If remote controls were found in the wild, Sharyl could use one to hunt and kill small mammals. There was no turning back for me now. Next thing I knew I was talking. Well, lying.

"Everything went pretty much normal, today. I made about 15-20 stops. Ensured everyone was abiding by the toilet paper laws. Checked to make sure all the interfaces were working normally. Got fired on my last inspection. Stopped by Red's, he's good. So that's about it. Regular day." I got up and took one step towards the stairs.

"Hold it!" she ordered. "You got fired? And you think you're going to leave it at that? Stay right here and tell me what happened."

I sat back down and sighed. "The city fired me today. I programmed the dispensers at my first stop to dispense four squares of toilet paper instead of two."

"You did what?" She shot out of the couch and onto her feet.

"They begged me to do it. There's a pregnant girl who works there and she really needed it. And she wasn't just a little bit pregnant; she was a lot," I said. "And you know, well, it just got to me. So, I caved. I mean, I had sympathy for her—the pregnant one—and I did everything I needed to do to make sure no one would find out. My programming was perfect. It actually was."

"Then how'd you get caught?" She stormed over to me and stood in front of me like a teacher ready to punish an out-of-line student.

"One of them turned me in. Big fat one. I think she was jealous of the pregnant one."

She threw up her hands. "Why can't you get it together, Avery? You're an adult—not a child! Or you're supposed to be! How are we supposed to survive on just one income? Do you expect to leech off me? Because that's not going to happen! Why is it that I'm always having to suffer from your mistakes? Honestly, I don't know why I put up with it!"

"I'm sorry. I'm sorry. I'll try to do better. I'll get another job," I said.

"*Sorry* is as bad as *thoughts and prayers*!" she screamed. "Enough of the talk. I want to see your behavior change!"

"I promise. I will." I sunk lower into the chair.

Suddenly she froze. "What about your social credit score? Please tell me this didn't affect your score."

I slowly held my hands out to the side. It was the perfect nonverbal response. Crap. Maybe I should have gone with Red's idea from the get-go. Sharyl just stared at me. The look on her face was like she was waiting for me to say something, but I just sat there looking back. Was this going to work? We were just looking at one another now. It hadn't escalated. Was nonverbal response the answer this whole time? Maybe it was. Red was the man! Holy crap!

"You *idiot!*" Her scream shook her glass unicorn trinkets on the coffee table. "You mean now I'm stuck with someone who has no job and has a lowered social credit score? Do you know how much ridicule I'll receive if anyone finds out?"

"You know, I don't feel too good about this either," I interjected. Why was I talking again?

"I know that! But it puts stress on me too. We are both working to get out of here and onto something better. And now this! What the hell, Avery? This hurts us both!"

She lit into me for the next thirty minutes. It was all over the place. She hit the usual bullet points of everything I'd done wrong since we got together. I didn't say much. Just mostly nodded my head and told her she was right. It was the usual dismount to our fights. Me, nodding along and agreeing, waiting for her to wear herself out. It sucked, but it worked.

Once she got tired of ripping me up one side and down the other, she stomped out of the room and went upstairs. That hadn't gone that badly. Sharyl was capable of worse. In terms of one-sided diatribes from her, that went much better than I thought it would go. I was mentally prepared for hours of abuse. There was always the chance that this was just round one, though.

We had a three-parter a few months ago. An evening-long fight in three separate parts. I kept thinking it was over but it turned out she was just regrouping. It all started when I made the mistake of telling her she looked hot at a dinner function for her work. I just leaned over and whispered it in her ear at the table. Who knew that would kick off a night of me being schooled for being a sexist . . . in three parts? In the car, then again at home. Then again right before bed.

So, in terms of her finding out I got fired, this had gone

very well. I just had to be careful for the rest of the night not to accidentally kick it off again. I sat there in silence for the better part of an hour, listening for any sign that she was coming back downstairs. So far, so good.

Then I decided to risk it and shambled to the kitchen. The refrigerator display screen awoke from its sleep and alerted me that I was low on a lot of my regular food. I opened the door anyway. There was a big, brown box in the refrigerator. "Save the Earth! Insects are delicious! Eat more Bugs!" its dull, brown lettering screamed at me. My curiosity was low and I didn't even bother to open it to see what kind of disgusting surprise was in it. Instead, I ate a turkey sandwich and a couple of fruit cocktail cups. I had to keep the fruit cups hidden because it said *cocktail* on the label and Sharyl said that was gross.

After another hour I slowly made my way upstairs. I was determined to avoid her for as long as possible. I let her get ready for bed in our big bathroom upstairs and I used the half-bath downstairs to do the same. She was already under the covers with her eyes closed by the time I returned to the bedroom and I gingerly crawled onto my side of the bed. I was almost home free.

"Gaahh!" she yelped. "Your feet are ice cold! And when's the last time you cut your toenails! You're shredding my calf!"

"I'll try to be more careful," I said. My feet hadn't even touched hers but at this point I was going full subservient. Now wasn't the time to change tactics.

"Did you remember to put on that prescription deodorant I got you?"

"Yes, and I'm wearing the pajamas you got me for my birthday." That might have been pushing it. Bringing up my birthday was incredibly stupid. What was my problem? That could've easily veered me into one of her lectures about me being selfish. I held my breath and waited to see which way she was going to go. Were things about to get ugly?

Then she rolled over and put the divider pillows between her side of the bed and mine, and punched them firmly into place. Were we done? Sweet! I was almost across the finish line.

I just laid on my quarter of the bed and tried not to breathe the way I normally breathed. She hated it.

She didn't say anything for a long time. I waited. Eventually she fell asleep.

I couldn't believe my luck. It really could have been much, much worse. I laid there in the quiet, staring at the ceiling and thought about how to go about finding a new job. That was going to be tough. After a bit, my thoughts turned to Mars and what life must be like for the people up there. The wide-open spaces. The freedom. The sense that anything was possible. It seemed so great. I smiled and closed my eyes. Sleep wasn't far behind.

CHAPTER FOUR

Bombs dropped and detonated. I raced to find safety somewhere far away from the mayhem. Yet no matter how far I ran, the explosions became louder. I was outside the SpendThrift building where I had changed the TP dispenser. The street and nearby buildings were a nightmarish mess. Fires and craters were everywhere. More bombs fell. I ran inside the building. Suddenly, I found myself in the bathroom. The scene of the crime. I could hear the bombs outside. Holy crap. It was massive destruction out there.

The door slowly opened and Candy, the pregnant girl, stepped inside. She was scared. "Avery . . . are you in here? I need help!"

Before she could close the door behind her I caught a glimpse of Hefty at the far end of the hall, and she made her way towards us. She stared right at me and she looked pissed. I quickly closed the door and held it shut as the bombs got closer. Or was that Hefty? I felt her banging on the door as the cascade of explosions continued. I wasn't going to be able to hold her back. I wasn't strong enough.

The whistle of an approaching missile filled my ears. This was the one that would get me. I knew it. Candy looked to me with disbelief. I tried to tell her I was sorry just as the bomb hit. The world went white.

And then I woke up.

My heart was practically beating out of my chest. Holy crap. That was a scary one. But it was just a dream. There was another boom. That was weird, it was no explosion. I looked at the clock. (Sorry, I still used an actual clock instead of just my phone.) It was 1:43 in the morning. Were they really making that much noise with construction at this time of night?

Another boom. No, this time it was a bump, a loud one. And I was sure it was coming from inside the house. Sharyl finally woke up on the fourth or fifth bump.

"What was that?" she asked.

I didn't say anything.

"I said, *what* was that?"

"Shhh!" I could feel her glaring at me, but I didn't bother turning over to check. With Sharyl, you could just feel it. Anger. Disappointment. You never had to check.

More bumping and then a crash.

"Someone's in the house!" she said.

My hands fumbled for the nightstand on my side of the bed; the small one Sharyl picked out because I had crappy taste in furniture. My eyes still weren't fully adjusted to the dark and it took me a few seconds to rip open the drawer and pull out the case that held the handgun that my cousin had given me last Christmas. Crime was practically off the chart and having a gun seemed like a good idea at the time. Registering a weapon was all but impossible now, yet I wanted it in case of an emergency, and this was an emergency. I kept it under a box of condoms. Unopened. It was the perfect place to hide it. Even if Sharyl would accidentally open the drawer she'd close it as soon as she saw the condoms, like a vampire that just saw a cross. Anyway, it was a great spot to hide the gun box.

"Is that a gun?" Sharyl practically shouted.

I looked at her as if to say, *Shhhhhh!*

She shot back a look that said, *Don't you EVER look at me that way again!*

"Yes. It's a gun. Let's try to be quiet," I whispered.

"And you kept it in *there*?" Still louder than I liked, but a big improvement.

"I did. Sorry. I should have told you." The box was way too hard to open. I could hear more thumps from downstairs. I had to get the stupid thing unlocked right then.

"Is it even legal?!" She hissed.

"Not yet . . . I've been busy. It's a lot of paperwork," I answered.

You could practically hear her eyes roll.

I fumbled some more and tried to remember how to open the latches so I could get to the gun. All those dumb safety features on the box so you wouldn't *accidentally* open it were really making it a challenge.

"Hurry up!" She slapped me on the shoulder.

"I'm trying!" I finally figured it out. Had to press in then up then in again. *Click!* "Got it!" I flipped open the lid to the case. My relief was short lived as I saw the second lock. This one over the trigger. Dammit!

My eyes started to adjust by that point, and with some help from the green glow from the numbers on the clock (which Sharyl hated—she always called me a dork for having it and thought I should've just used the clock on my phone) I had a pretty good view of the gun and the magazine next to it. So I had bullets and a gun . . . with a lock over the trigger.

Surprisingly, even with sweaty hands, I managed to shove the magazine into the gun on the first try. I swung my legs out of bed and ripped some of the covers with me.

"Why are you just sitting there?" Sharyl asked.

"I can't remember the combination to the lock that's blocking the trigger!"

There was more banging and then a pounding. He was on the stairs. He was coming up the freaking stairs!

"He's coming up here!" Sharyl practically shouted.

"I know! I know!"

What was the first number? I thought. *Four? Eight? No, maybe two!*

"Do you remember the combination?" I asked her.

"How would I know? I've never seen it before." Her voice dripped with disbelief.

The footsteps made it to the top and they were heading towards us.

"Is it your birthday?" she asked.

"No!"

"Mine?"

"No! At least I don't think so!"

"Try it!"

I did. Nothing.

"What about the anniversary of our first date?" I looked to her. Sharyl's eyes got wide. She had no idea. She forgot the night of our first date. That stung a bit.

"Well, you don't know it either," she chided.

"May 14, Sharyl. May 14."

As I went to enter it into the trigger lock, the bedroom door flung open.

Sharyl screamed like a girl. I screamed even more like a girl.

The scary man in the doorway barked a laugh. "This is gonna be fun!"

"Don't come any closer or I'll shoot!" I stood up and pointed the gun at him. I tried to keep my hand over the lock. Maybe if he didn't look too closely, he wouldn't be able to tell I was bluffing. The gun wobbled in tiny circles.

His hand slapped against our bedroom wall. He found the switch and flooded the room with light.

I covered my eyes and squinted. My handgun wavered away from him.

"Guess what? I have a gun too!" he said.

He pulled up his Dynamo Cereal t-shirt to reveal a huge handgun tucked into the waistband of his pants. This guy had a cannon in there. I let out a small screech and Sharyl decided to go with a full-throated, unending scream.

Dynamo Cereal thug just smiled. Did he know I was bluffing? His hand closed around the grip of his giant weapon and he started pulling it out of his pants.

BANG!

I closed my eyes and dropped my gun. I joined Sharyl in screaming at the top of my lungs. Somehow, I heard a thud over all the noise we were making.

I peeked open one eye ever so slightly. Sharyl was still on the bed. Eyes closed tight. She hadn't been shot. Neither had I. What happened? I looked to the doorway. Nothing. Wait . . . was I still dreaming? That's when Dynamo started yelling. Which, of course, was Sharyl's cue to scream as well.

"Yeeeoowwwwwwwww!" His hands clasped his crotch. Some trickles of blood started seeping through his fingers.

"Sharyl! Sharyl! Sharyl! Stop! Stop! Look!" I shook her hard.

She shut up and looked at the doorway. "You shot him?" She was horrified.

"No," I said. "He shot himself in the crotch when he was reaching for his gun."

"Are you serious?"

"Yes."

Dynamo continued screaming. He rolled back and forth and his hands never left the wounded area. More blood leaked through his fingers. He had messed himself up. Big time.

"Hurry up and call the social welfare rapid response team!" she told me.

"Right."

I thrust the gun towards Sharyl. She looked at me like I was trying to hand her a dog turd. I quickly set it on the nightstand and grabbed my phone. My fingers worked a lot better than they had moments earlier.

Social welfare officers arrived by aerial drone 45 minutes later. They took care of Dynamo. That guy had blown off one of his nuts. I gave him a towel to use so he could at least try to stop the bleeding. It was all I could think of. Don't think a tourniquet on half a ball-sack was even an option. I was just relieved he wasn't going to die.

After they got Dynamo air-lifted out, the social welfare officers interviewed us. I admitted that my gun was unregistered. They told me I could get in a lot of trouble but that they'd let me off with a warning as long as I got it registered right away. I told them I would.

They finally left at about 4:00 in the morning. Sharyl started getting dressed.

"You don't feel like going back to bed either?" I asked her.

"Not here," she said.

"What?"

"What do you mean, *what*?" she shot back. "You think I'm going to stay here after you kept that unregistered handgun and didn't tell me?"

"Are you kidding me? It made him reach for his weapon and shoot himself. You should be glad I kept it."

"What's wrong with you?" she demanded. "You made it so that he almost shot us! I don't want to be anywhere near it—or you!"

"So where are you going to go?"

"I don't know. I'll call you when I get there. But you have bigger things to worry about," she said.

"Bigger things to worry about? What's that mean?"

"Avery! Listen to me! You have a gun. You have problems. Problems you need to deal with. Now. You need to get a job and clean up your life. And you need to do it fast. Because if you don't? Me temporarily leaving isn't going to be temporary. Got it? Get it together. Get a job, do what you have to do to fix yourself and your social credit score, maybe take So-Sen seriously and figure out if you want to be in this relationship. Right now, it seems like you don't. And if that's the case, we're done!"

There it was. That was the rest of the fight from earlier. Plus, the gun part. But that was pretty much what I had been expecting when I first told her about my day. I decided not to say anything. It would only make matters worse.

Sharyl was out of the house by 4:30. I started my day by trying to clean the blood out of the carpet our would-be murderer left on it.

CHAPTER FIVE

After spending a few hours cleaning up blood from the carpet, I managed to get a couple hours of sleep before my alarm went off.

By the way, the key to cleaning the blood out of the carpet? Hydrogen peroxide. Amazing stuff. Another key? Test it out on a small piece of carpet before you go hog wild. Otherwise, you may end up with a giant white spot on your rug, like me. So, I learned both of those things, one right after the other. I wasn't looking forward to Sharyl getting home and seeing the new white blob on our carpet. But at least it wasn't going to be blood. That should've been my saving grace.

Anyway, after the peroxide debacle I gave myself a little pep talk and was determined to get a job. That very day. Strike while the iron was hot and before everyone updated their databases and saw why I got fired. I was pretty sure I had a day or a day and a half before I was marked by the internet as a trouble-making loser. Once that happened it was all over. That was the doomsday scenario. But I knew it wasn't gonna come to that because I knew I was gonna get a job at a Chartreuse store and put all of the bullshit behind me. It was an opportunity to make a change. (That was part of my pep talk.)

Working for a tech giant had been something I wanted to do for a while now. There was a reason everyone loved their Chartreuse smartphones and other gadgets: they made great products. So, I got dressed in a suit and tie. I ended up ditching the jacket—too formal for their culture. What was I thinking? This was Chartreuse. I had to think "hip" and "cool" and "friendly yet edgy." Then I made my way down to the store that was just a few blocks from my house. I had a little spring in my step, too. Even with my damaged social credit score, I was very confident about how applying for a job there was going to go. Know why? Because I was good at what I did, I knew tech. A lot of people wouldn't have known how to even start reprogramming a TP dispenser, but I did it in under five minutes. I needed to try to spin all the negatives in my life into positives. It wasn't going to be easy, but it's what Irvine Endoglast would've done. And today I was going to do my best to be in full "Endoglast Mode."

A few nights ago, after yet another long "talk" with Sharyl, I was caught in one of those endless video rabbit holes. You know, where you watch video, after video, after video on your phone. The kind where you just can't stop from clicking on the next *recommended for you* one right after you just finished watching the previous clip. Anyway, I eventually reached a video featuring this guy, Irvine Endoglast, who was a motivational speaker. He was amazing.

Now, normally I wouldn't go for that kind of stuff. Generally speaking, I thought motivational speakers were a scam. But Endoglast was different, and I ended up watching like ten of his videos in a row. He was the real deal! This guy could change people's lives. And I was up for that. One of his clips featured him telling an amazing (and true!) story to an audience about how he got his first job.

"Now, I'm not going to tell you the name of the company, but I guarantee you that you'd recognize it," Endoglast said. "In fact, you probably use it all the time. Yes, even you in the front row with the big frown on your face." His audience laughed.

"Anyway, I went into the lobby of one of their locations and I walked straight up to the receptionist. I said to her, 'I'm here to apply for a job.' And she gave me a condescending smile and sweetly replied, 'I'm sorry, but we're not hiring right now.' So, I just hung my head, tucked my tail, and walked right out of there in defeat. Right? Is that what you all think I did?"

The audience shouted, "No!"

"Of course I didn't!" bellowed Endoglast with a grin. "No. I marched straight on over to those dirty, old, straight-backed chairs they have in every receptionist area. You know the ones I'm talking about. The ones where they always wobble? No matter what you do, they wobble. You'd think they could fix those by now with all the technology we have. Am I right?"

The crowd roared again. Endoglast was such a great storyteller. He went on.

"And I plopped myself down in one of those rickety chairs, folded my arms, and looked straight at the receptionist—whom I could barely see over that big desk of hers, by the way—and I said to her, sincerely: 'I'm not leaving until someone hires me!'"

The people applauded. They really dug it. So, did I.

"I sat right there in that chair for three, straight hours. Three. Hours. And, boy, did that receptionist shoot me some daggers. If looks could kill, I wouldn't be here today." Endoglast chuckled and his audience went along with him. "But you know what? At the end of those three hours the boss came out of his office. He shook his head once at me and said, 'I've never seen someone so persistent. You really take the cake.' You know what he said next?" The audience didn't know. They murmured amongst themselves for a moment. Silence descended on the group and Irvine Endoglast just smiled. After the perfect pause he finally burst out with what we all wanted him to say. "You're hired!'"

The audience went nuts. Even I had to grin. That was a great story. But he had more. Irvine wasn't finished. Damn this guy was good.

"Perseverance is so key to success in life. I don't care what it is you're trying to do," Endoglast proclaimed. "If you're willing to keep trying to achieve something, you eventually will!"

It was perfect. Just a great example of how determination and perseverance pay off. That was my plan for today. Full Endoglast mode.

My trip to the Chartreuse store was relatively uneventful. Only a few bums came at me, and I just had to run once when three thugs decided I looked like an easy target. Like I said, all in all, it was a pretty basic walk.

The Chartreuse store was mostly empty when I went in. Just two of its employees, who all wore matching chartreuse polo shirts, were busy with customers. "How can I help you?" a college-aged girl with long dark hair held back by two clips asked me.

"Yes." I stood as tall as I could. "I'm here to apply for a job."

She smiled politely and nodded her head. "Oh, okay. Well, we don't have any openings at this time but if you'd like, you can always fill out an online application. That'll go into our database and when we have an opening, if you're the best match, we'll contact you."

I smiled back at her as confidently as I could and tried to stand even taller. "I'm sorry, but I need work and I'm not leaving until I get hired." My smile may have faltered just a bit, but I maintained it for the most part.

"Well, um . . . um, this Chartreuse store doesn't have any openings." My answer obviously flustered her. Her eyes flicked back and forth between the wall and me. "So, I mean, you're not going to get hired. That's the truth."

"I know I'd be a great fit for Chartreuse." My smile shook harder, and I didn't want to look flakey, so I just gave up on it. "Is there a manager I could speak to about a job?"

"Well, I mean, there's a supervisor here but she's not going to give you a different answer." Her smile was now gone as well and for some reason she was rubbing her forearm.

"Okay. But I'm just going to sit here until someone offers me a job." Straight out of the Endoglast playbook. I was ready for this.

She looked around. "There aren't really any seats here."

I inspected the store. There were no chairs. "Oh. I guess there's not . . . I'll just stand here then." I added a confident nod at the end. It was supposed to be a confident nod anyway. I might have waited a little too long and it might have come across as a strange twitch. But in my head, it was a confident nod.

She sighed and her mouth dropped a bit before she caught it. "Well, you can't just stand in the middle of the store. So, I don't know, stand somewhere else."

"So, like, by the door?"

"No, you might bother customers."

"What about right here?"

"I walk by here a lot, and it might be awkward. So, no."

"What about over there by that display case?"

She turned and looked where I pointed. It was at the other side of the store and may have been some place she hadn't even known existed until I gestured at it. "Whatever." She quickly turned away and walked to another salesgirl; the one who had started listening in on the tail end of our conversation.

Those two started talking in whispers as I made my way across the store. With less than steady legs, I weaved past other displays (one of them was spinning and moving pretty wildly —why would you put phones on that?) and brushed against a sign that featured an interactive replica of the Chartreuse Troll. It's motion sensors went off as I passed, and the yellow cartoon troll giggled its annoying little giggle. Mockingly? Felt that way. Once I arrived at the appointed display case at the far end of the store, I just stood there. But no matter what I did, how I stood, or which way I faced, it felt incredibly awkward. The girl and her friend still whispered and gave me sideways glances. I looked away from them. The folder holding my résumé was getting slick from my hand sweat. Perfect, my hands were sweating. I tried to convince myself it was all part of proving I wanted the job, though. I was in for the long haul. I just hoped it wasn't too long.

Over the next ten minutes, that felt like a year, a few more customers came into the store and others left. The salesgirl and her friend continued holding their private meeting, with two more employees taking part for a few moments. Each of them joined in and gave me telling glances before they disappeared into the back.

At one point, a middle-aged couple walked up to me and asked me to help them. "I don't work here," I told them. "See? I have a shirt and tie on. Not a polo shirt." I gave them a big, warm grin and wink. They seemed taken aback. Grin might have been too big. Wink probably was a bad idea too.

"Did you just wink at my husband?" the wife asked.

"That was a knowing wink. A wink that says, 'No problem,'" I replied.

"I know what I saw, and I didn't care for it." She quickly pulled her husband away and they headed across the store to an actual employee.

Then it hit me. I was such an idiot! I should have said, "Yes, I work here. How can I help you?" That's what Irvine Endoglast would've done. The husband looked across the store at me, smiled knowingly and winked. Great. Well, his self-esteem went up a bit. Mine, not so much.

Just then, a guy about my age walked in. He was dressed nicely, khakis and a casual shirt. And in his hand, he held a folder very much like the one I was holding. He approached the salesgirl I had spoken with earlier and asked her for the manager.

"He's not in," the salesgirl told him.

Good. She hadn't lied to me.

"Well, I need a job," the kid in the khakis said. "And I'm not leaving until I get one."

I couldn't believe my ears. Neither could she, and she gave him one of the biggest eye-rolls of all time, (it was a Sharyl-level eye-roll—just huge) before she motioned for him to follow her towards me.

"Wait here with him." She waved her hand in my general direction and refused to make eye contact with me. Once he made it to my side, she split as fast as she could.

So, it was Kid Khakis and me. He gave me a head nod. My instinct was to head nod back, but I caught myself before I did. I glared at him. Who did he think he was?

"Hey, pal. I've been here for a while. I'm doing the 'I'm-not-leaving-until-you-hire-me' thing."

"So am I," he shot back, unfazed.

"I don't think you understand. I really need this job. I'm

motivated. Obviously more than you because I got here first. So maybe go somewhere else and try your luck. This is my spot."

"No such thing as spots. I'm just as good as you and I'm going to stay until they hire me. That's what Irvine Endoglast would do and that's how I live my life," he told me.

My eyes bulged. "That's MY guy. Irvine is my guy. That's why I'm here. That's why I've been standing here like a lunatic all morning. Now go find another store. This one's taken."

I waited for the kid to move but he didn't. He just stared ahead with his feet planted to the floor.

"You need to go," I repeated. "I'm serious."

"I'm serious too," he said.

I did my best imitation of the little dick in khakis ruining my life. "I'm serious tooooooo."

Everything about this kid rubbed me the wrong way. It suddenly occurred to me that there was a small chance that Chartreuse might hire us both. I told myself that it better not happen for his sake, because if it did, he just made his first work enemy.

We both kept standing there like dorks. Occasionally, I'd sigh super loudly to remind him what an ass he was. But he never moved.

After fifteen minutes had passed, a burly middle-aged man ripped open the front door to the store and entered with a complete sense of purpose. He was a big guy. Once upon a time you could tell he lifted weights. Even with the couple layers of fat and a whole lot of pudge on him, you could tell he was still strong. His arms stretched the sleeves of his shirt so much that it made the fabric semi-transparent, and you could see his arm skin through the shirt.

This guy was pissed. It was like he woke up from a nap on the wrong side of the planet. He made his way straight to the salesgirl who had talked with me and started asking her something. They went back and forth for a second and it all was in hushed tones. My initial guess was that he must've bought something from Chartreuse and wasn't satisfied with it, and I was curious as to how she was going to resolve the situation. Frankly, with as upset as he was, he was kinda scary.

But then she pointed at me. Then at Kid Khakis. And then back to me. Why would she do that? His head swiveled towards us, taking us in. With a snort, his eyes bored into my soul, and he made his way towards me and Kid Khakis, like a bull gunning for rodeo clowns. He stopped just inches away from us. Disturbingly close.

"Today was my day off." His volume was low, but his tone was turned up to high. "Don't make this any worse for me—or you. Just leave. Both of you."

"No, sir." My voice wobbled. "At least, not until you hire me. You are a manager or something. Right?"

His eyes widened. "I can't believe it. They weren't exaggerating. I've seen some stupid things but nothing like this."

Khakis butted in. "Good afternoon, sir. My name is Harold and I'm your newest employee."

I shot Harold a death glare. "No, you're not. I am." I looked back at the big angry manager. "Do you have an office or some place in the back where we could talk? I have my résumé with me." I helpfully waved the folder in front of his face.

He grabbed me by the arm. Yep. I was right. He must've been a weightlifter at some point, the guy was strong. He tried to pull me towards the door, but I leaned back and used my body leverage to counter his movement. That didn't go over well with him.

"Don't make me call social welfare. Time for you to go."

His command was loud enough that a few customers heard it and started to watch what was going on.

"I'm not leaving until you hire me," I insisted in my best Irvine Endoglast voice.

"You're leaving now," he growled.

Everybody heard that—including the couple who had thought I worked there.

"He winked at my husband! Sexually!" she practically screamed.

My confidence began fading rapidly, but I was one hundred percent committed. The angry manager pulled on me again and I went limp. I'd seen enough riots to know how hard it was to move a limp person who didn't want to be moved.

"Son of a bitch," the manager muttered. He tried to get a better grip underneath my suddenly incredibly sweaty armpits.

"It wasn't sexual and I'm not going anywhere," I reminded him.

"I'll help you, sir." Harold, the khakis-wearing traitor, grabbed at my ankles.

What in the hell was happening? I thought.

The manager slid his hand under my arms. Meanwhile, I kicked at Harold's hands. No way was I going to allow that kid to seize my legs. The manager adjusted his vice-like grip and maneuvered me a couple feet towards the door. I kicked harder.

"Get his feet, Harold," the manager ordered.

"Yes, sir. Your name, sir?"

"Jeff."

"You got it, Jeff."

Now they were on a first name basis!

Harold caught one of my ankles. Together they started dragging me across the store. Past the display Troll who laughed yet again at me.

"Let's just get this guy out of here, we don't want a big scene," Jeff said.

Harold nodded. "Absolutely."

The door got closer and closer and the only thing I did was blubber like a madman. "No, no, no, no, no, no."

The door silently zipped open and with Jeff the Chartreuse manager lifting my shoulders, and Harold the khaki-wearing betrayer lifting my feet, they heaved me twice and then literally threw me out of the store. I was airborne for a split second before crashing down onto the sidewalk. I didn't know what I landed on, but it hurt and there was a squish of something wet. My momentum took me off the curb and I rolled into the gutter. Somehow my folder was still in my hand. As I lay there trying to mentally regroup, Jeff and Harold congratulated themselves.

"Nice job, Harold. Thanks for the assist."

"My pleasure, Jeff. And did I hear you say *job*?"

Jeff let out a short laugh. "Come on inside. I think we do have something for a guy like you."

I stood up and stumbled backwards and farther into the street. Luckily, no driverless cars were coming. Supposedly the AI would've braked or otherwise missed me if they would've been heading my way. But I've seen them hit plenty of other things they were supposed to be able avoid. So, I'm glad I didn't test how they'd handle a human obstacle in their path. Then again, it would've solved all my problems if one of them had run me over and just ended it all. What a disaster this day had become. Kid Khakis took my job. How did that happen?

My shoulders slumped and I remained there for a few moments in total disbelief. Two security drones hovered about 50 yards above me in the sky. They were probably trying to verify that I wasn't in distress. Or maybe they were trying to determine if I was a threat or even a minor nuisance. Either way, I was relieved when I stepped back up on the sidewalk and they resumed their regular air patrols. That's all I needed now. Social welfare to arrive and make this an even bigger display of failure.

Something tickled my neck and I reached for it. It was a wet, soiled tissue stuck to my shirt at the collar. I ripped it off and dropped it. My clothes were even dirtier than I thought. I brushed myself off as best I could and kept my head down. There was an audience behind the glass front of the Chartreuse store, and they all gawked as they recorded me on their phones.

I thought about running away but I still had a sliver of pride left. So, I calmly tried to compose myself. As I wiped off my face, my fingernail hit something metal. There was a bottle cap stuck to my cheek. I knocked it off and ran my fingers through my hair and dislodged what looked like an old Band-Aid. I flicked it away and looked straight ahead. Even though I did my best to avoid looking at the Chartreuse storefront, I knew everyone was still staring at me. It was horrible. Any further cleanup could wait. I hurried off and didn't slow to a normal pace until I was three blocks away.

CHAPTER SIX

Trudging back to my house took a lot longer than my initial walk to Chartreuse. After I got inside, I took off my clothes, threw them in the wash, started the machine and headed straight for the shower. There was a law against taking more than one shower a day, but it was probably written by a person who'd never been thrown into the street and landed in a puddle of old beer, Band-Aids, wino piss, and bottle caps.

The shower felt great for the first minute. There was even a moment when I started to feel like a human again. That was when the washer must've kicked in because the water went ice cold. What an idiot I was. Why didn't I start the laundry after I got out? I couldn't even do that right. The rest of the shower was an arctic misery, but at least I was clean again, kind of. A clean-ish loser. For a split second I considered going back to Chartreuse, holding my head high, and showing them I meant business by reissuing my demand for a job. That thought quickly went out the window. It might work for people like Irvine Endoglast and Harold the Betrayer, but not for me.

Sharyl always said I wasn't confident enough. Maybe she was right. Every time I tried to assert myself, it blew up in my face. I had way more luck when I just went with the flow. However shitty that flow was.

I put on an old t-shirt and a pair of jeans and headed downstairs. Then I went right back upstairs, took off the jeans, and put on a pair of Dockers. Sharyl hated it when I wore jeans. Had to go with Dockers. At least I could do that much right.

Trying to get a job face-to-face hadn't worked out for me but that didn't mean I had to give up. I went back downstairs, sunk into a chair, picked up my tablet, and started seeking employment the old-fashioned way: by submitting résumés and applications online.

It was a fool's errand, but I spent the next few hours doing just that. The unemployment rate in San Josisco was astronomical. Hell, it was bad everywhere. The whole continent seemed like it was out of work. Every online listing would have a ka-jillion applications submitted within seconds of it being posted. I heard rumors of a kid from Yale or Harvard who wrote and sold a program that did nothing but scour the internet for job openings. If you were rich enough, you could buy it and get your digital résumé on the top of the pile within milliseconds of the posting going live. I wasn't rich. Plus, I knew that every time I applied for a job, I would get dinged for having a crappy social credit score. It was a classic catch-22. No social credit? No job. No job? No social credit.

Whatever. I filled out the job apps anyway. Maybe I'd get lucky. Even if I didn't, I'd at least have something to show Sharyl later. You know, proof that I did actually look for a job beyond getting thrown out of a Chartreuse store. I figured that would've been good for something. So, I did that for a few hours. It was a combination of boring and bizarre.

I'd find a job listing that I was qualified for and apply for it. Every single one seemed to make things overly complicated. They made me answer a ton of questions, complete forms, and submit a bunch of personal info. My favorite ones were with the companies that had these stupid questionnaires. The questions were thinly veiled personality tests. And thinly was being generous. There were questions like, "Have you ever fantasized about harming small animals or a coworker?" Why was that a question? Who was going to answer "yes" to that one? Was that how they screened out criminals? And why was a fast-food place like Taco Star suddenly worried about small animals? Full disclosure: I applied at Taco Star. Two of them actually.

Anyway, it went on like that the entire time. I'd click "Send" and a few seconds later I'd hear a *ding* that alerted me to a response in my inbox. They were all eerily similar. "Thank you for applying for a career with Blah, Blah Company, Incorporated! We'll review your application and qualifications and if we think you're a good fit for the position, we'll contact you!"

They were as good as rejection notices. Who cared that I was incredibly overqualified for every job I applied for? Especially the Taco Star one. That was mostly a joke, mostly. But I was stuck. I had no connections in the business world. Every decent job was already gone by the time it was listed, and my social credit was now complete shit. It was going to take me years to rebuild. Suddenly, it hit me just how big of a step I had taken backwards with everything, including my long-term plans—including my goal for going to Mars. Everything I wanted was going to have to wait. It sucked. I'd just have to figure it all out somehow. While also trying to keep Sharyl happy. I took a deep breath and let the realization that my life was total crap wash over me. Not fun. Also? A little warm. Why was I sweating?

"Indira, lower the thermostat one degree," I told the home assistant hard-wired into my house. I rested my electronic tablet on my lap and leaned back in the soft fabric of the recliner. No response from the computer. "Indira, lower the thermostat one degree." I made sure I enunciated my words and projected with more volume. Still, nothing happened. "Indira, what's your status?"

"Unavailable," Indira finally replied. "Your social credit score is too low and according to the terms of service of the Indira user agreement, the majority of functions on your account have been suspended. If your social credit score does not return to an acceptable level within—"

"Indira, stop," I told it.

I half tossed and half set my tablet on the table next to me. My eyes burned from looking at the screen for hours. I rubbed them and sighed. The thought of Mars trickled through my mind . . . and so did all the lucky people who got to go there. They weren't just moving to a new place for a new job; they were starting over in everything. Everyone left behind any problems they had on Earth. They were reborn. Free. Meanwhile, I couldn't convince my robot assistant to adjust the thermostat. What the hell happened?

I pulled my phone out and checked my texts. Nothing. Normally I was fine with that, but I still hadn't heard a thing from Sharyl since she left this morning. Not a good sign. Yesterday was about as bad as they come. Between me getting fired and a guy shooting himself in our bedroom in the middle of the night, we had stuff to talk about. We at least had stuff for her to yell at me about. Nope, the silence was not good. As far as I could tell, my phone was working; my social credit wasn't so low they'd cut that off too. A convicted terrorist could blow up a bus load of tourists and still have a phone. I tried calling Sharyl, but it went straight to voicemail. That wasn't too bad. Going straight to voice mail, that meant she was mad. Standard operating procedure for her. Now I had a decision to make. Normally I'd just wait for her to come home, and we'd talk things out. However, I had this crazy idea that she was hoping for me to take the lead and make the first move.

This was always a crap shoot. Especially with Sharyl. She'd always tell me that it was obvious, and I should be aware of her signals. And if I was more aware I would automatically "know" what to do. I never knew. Be more assertive? Lay back and listen? I never knew. So, there I was again. I decided to err on the side of assertive. I'd take the initiative and start a dialogue. Pretty sure that's what my So-Sen coach would want me to do too. I just needed to get to Sharyl.

I got up, put on my shoes, threw on a hoodie, and manually locked all the doors since my Indira virtual assistant wouldn't even do that for me. And then I left the house again.

I had a pretty good idea of where Sharyl was.

Debbie Strafford was probably Sharyl's best friend. I only say probably because Sharyl always seemed incredibly jealous of Debbie. Yeah, they'd hang out a lot. Sharyl was over there all the time. They'd commiserate, talk, do whatever. But whenever Sharyl would come home to me, she would bitch about Debbie for hours. "Debbie's so self-centered. Debbie doesn't get me. Debbie's a spoiled brat." And two minutes later she'd do a complete 180 and tell me how much she admired Debbie and wanted to be like her. I learned really quick how to just listen. Sharyl didn't want my opinion; she just wanted to say things out loud, I guess.

She was spot on, though, about Debbie being self-centered and spoiled. And it didn't stop there, she was also just about as shallow and as fake as they come. Debbie never had to try at anything, she grew up rich and beautiful. Went to the best schools and right out of college, her dad got her a job as an intern at Netchill, one of the top 100 streaming services. With her family connections, she'd be VP of programming in a year. It was kind of sick really. Too bad she thought I was a loser, or I would've hit her up for a job. And I thought that I still might. Worth a shot. Right?

I had been to Debbie's place a few times; it wasn't that far away. She lived in a high-rise condo complex, state of the art joint. No way she could've afforded that on an intern salary. Must've been nice to have a rich family bankroll her.

Usually, when I'd headed over, I'd grab a driverless car, but today I decided to walk. Apart from my social credit score being an issue, I figured I'd save a couple bucks. And who knows? I might walk past a place that I could duck into and try to find some work. Maybe not the best idea in the world considering all the crime, but I thought I'd give it a try. It was just a mile or so . . . two miles, tops, maybe three.

From the moment I stepped out of my door, I kept looking around. You never could be too careful, had to keep your head on a swivel. Maybe it was the afternoon sunshine, or maybe I had hit my head harder than I thought when I got thrown out of Chartreuse, but there was something about the city that day. The clouds had cleared, and the sun was shining. If you didn't look down, you could almost imagine what it looked like before people ruined it. It must have been something. Not as much . . . everything. People, buildings, garbage, crime, graffiti, all of it.

There was just too much of everything, especially crime. But I guess that was everywhere else too. I pulled my hood up and set off for Debbie's.

A long time ago, the Facial Recognition Act was passed into law. That happened right before the whole social credit thing started. Anyway, the idea was to have everybody's face in a nationwide database. That way, if you committed a crime, they'd just look at security footage and know exactly who to go arrest. It was supposed to cut down on the need for policing because the authorities would already know who did it. Sounded great on paper and it was a huge success for the first couple of months. Then the criminals just started using masks. Duh! Did no one think people would just wear masks?

Incredibly stupid.

So, as I walked down the street trying to avoid broken bottles, garbage, human waste, needles, and all that other great stuff, I also had to be on the lookout for anybody who was casually hanging onto a mask or bandana. Anything they could use to cover their face. They were a potential threat. And it seemed like everyone was carrying one that day. Well, at least they weren't wearing them. If they were wearing the masks? I'd have just run. That was my personal rule of thumb. It worked relatively well too.

Within a few blocks, the idea that I might just amble by someplace where I could work seemed kind of ridiculous. Most of the small shops were gone. The buildings they once occupied were empty, burned-out husks. The few that were still open sometimes had signs up that read, "Sorry, No Work Now," or, "Not Taking Applications."

All in all, my walk became a kind of low-level emotional rollercoaster. Fear of getting jumped, mugged, or worse. Then there was relief that I didn't get jumped. And then it was excitement at seeing a business open, followed by the disappointment of a sign telling me no work was available. It went on like that for blocks.

I was getting close to the neighborhood where Debbie

lived. Sky Tower peeked up in the distance from behind the ramshackle buildings and pod-scrapers that made up most of the city. I was close to the border between the haves and have-nots. The haves had maybe a few blocks, but they kept them very nice . . . and very exclusive.

Somebody nearby whistled. It was one of those shrill, *pay attention* whistles. I snapped my head around until I saw a bunch of kids standing on the roof of what looked to be an old dry cleaner building. They all wore masks. One of them pointed excitedly at something off in the distance. Great, I had stumbled upon an old school drone heist. Things were bound to get chaotic. I could either slink away and waste time finding a longer route or hunker down some place safe to watch until it was over and then continue on to Debbie's. I merged with the wall of the nearest building.

On the news they called it a drone heist, but most people called it "sky piñata." The act of knocking a delivery drone out of the sky and stealing the package. Usually, it consisted of two teams positioned on different buildings. Almost always next to a nicer neighborhood, and the Sky Tower neighborhood was as nice as you could get. When the observation team saw a big fat drone flying in with a sizable package, they alerted the operations team. Those guys had the tough job. They were responsible for bringing down the drone and the package, hopefully without breaking whatever was inside.

Sky piñata attempts almost always failed. Sure, people could bring down a drone. But without busting the package? That was the nearly impossible part. Everything would break after the impact with the street. Hence, sky piñata.

The risk of it all was huge too. It was theft, of course, and people who got caught faced steep penalties—bigger than what others would face for similar crimes. Delivery drones were expensive and the companies who used them got extremely tired of replacing them *and* the merchandise very, very quickly. So long ago, they used their lobbying arms and got legislation passed that made the penalties for drone heists a really big deal.

The government would put you away for a long time if you were dumb enough to try one and get caught. I had only seen footage of heists like this on the news, never thought I'd see one in person. A few other passersby's joined me in hugging the wall and watching.

The familiar noise of a delivery drone grew from a tiny buzz to an outright whine, and then to a bass hum. It was one of the big ones. The kids on the building cheered. They were the operations team. I never did figure out where the observation team was. Maybe there wasn't even one for this effort.

Regardless, the operations team was perfectly positioned. There were always lots of drones flying overhead. Social welfare, private security, sometimes military, and, of course, delivery, were just some of the types of drones that filled the sky. There were plenty of air taxis too. Everybody wanted to fly everywhere, and air space was at a premium. Evidently the delivery drone these kids were going to try to hit was going to fly pretty low when it got near them. That's what they appeared to think, at least. And if the drone was heading for the Sky Tower neighborhood? Then whatever it was carrying could be a major payday.

The bass hum grew louder and the kids cheered again. So did a few people on the street, including two of the people holding up the wall with me. A monster with four rotors finally popped into view. It rumbled out from between two smaller buildings. Beneath it was a giant box that looked like it could've held a small billboard. *Holy crap*, I thought. *Who has a wall big enough to hold a TV that size? Pretty sure those kids on the rooftop don't. But I doubt they care. Hell, I know they don't.*

They all pulled on their masks as the behemoth got closer. Around the streets, everyone who had one donned their masks as well. Maybe a little bit too late since cameras were everywhere, but better late than never. I pulled my t-shirt up over my nose. Not the greatest thing to use but it was better than nothing. *You need to start taking a mask everywhere you go from now on*, I told myself.

Just a short distance back from the giant delivery drone were smaller social welfare or private security drones. Four of them, and they were way faster and way more agile. There were rumors they were armed with rubber bullets, and that onboard, AI determined when they were authorized to use them. From what I could see, the kids on the rooftop had no idea they were coming, or maybe they just didn't care.

Slowly, the monster drone moved closer to the kids on the rooftop. One of them, who wore a Spider-Man mask, pulled out what looked like a bow and arrow. *What the hell?* I thought.

As I tried to figure out what he was planning, he loaded up an arrow, pulled the bow taut, and released the shaft. It soared through the air but so did something else — a line of thin rope attached to it. The arrow led the line to one of the back rotors of the drone and caught up in it. It twirled around for a bit and then the blade stopped.

All he and his gang have to do now is reel in their prize. The other three rotors are going to be overwhelmed by all that weight. Pretty simple and effective, I mused.

Only the drone wasn't overwhelmed. In fact, it hadn't slowed down much at all. As it kept flying, the line the kid had wrapped around his wrist pulled tight. No one was holding onto him.

He screamed as he realized what was about to happen. The drone pulled him over the side of the building. His pals made a grab for him, but it was too late. He was three stories above the street. Hanging on to a thin rope attached to a drone. Wearing a Spider-Man mask. I just stood there like a moron. Eyes wide. I couldn't believe what I was seeing.

His friends yelled for him to hang on as everyone watched in horror.

The huge TV-carrying drone was now making a wide left turn. The kid's weight was pulling it down! The thing was slowly, but surely, gently spiraling down to the street. If Spidey-kid could hang on, he just might get a wall-sized TV out of this and his life.

We all shouted encouragement to the little guy. "Hang on!" I yelled. Not fiercely original, but I was taken in by the moment. He was only 15 feet away from landing this thing.

That's when the security drones got involved. "Step away from the package," the computer voice blared from its tiny speaker. There were four of them about 30 feet up and quickly descending.

Spidey-kid landed on his feet in the middle of the street. The lucky little thief. He couldn't have planned it better! The enormous TV box gently came to rest beside him as the large delivery drone toppled onto its side like an elephant collapsing from exhaustion. Its remaining blades slowed. The whole series of events was amazing. Now Spidey just needed the rest of his gang to get down to the street and help him with his huge prize before the security drones deployed whatever counter measures they had.

A big guy with a blue bandana covering his face ran out to help the kid. He grabbed for the box, but it looked like Spidey was trying to stop him. They weren't on the same team. Bandana man was trying to steal Spidey-kid's prize. It was barely a struggle. Spidey held onto the box for a moment and then Bandana man just punched him right in the face. Hard. Spidey's head snapped back and he went down in a heap. It was brutal. The big guy punched a kid! I should have done something, but my feet wouldn't move. Besides, what was I going to do? Fight the guy? No way.

The security drones were taking up positions around the scene of the crime. The all too familiar buzz filled the sky above us. "Step away from the package," the AI voice commanded. "This is your final warning."

"Note to self," I muttered. "Security drones just give out the two warnings."

Spidey-kid wasn't done, though. He picked himself back up and was stumbling towards Bandana man who was hustling away with the giant TV that he didn't even steal. *Pap, pap, pap.* Little clouds of dust exploded by Bandana man and Spidey's feet.

The drones were shooting. This was crazy! I hoped those were rubber bullets.

Pap, pap, pap! Three more shots from the drones. One hit Bandana man in the back and he lost his grip on the TV box as he crumpled to the ground. I didn't see any blood. They had to be using rubber bullets. Right? Still, it had to hurt. Spidey wasted no time. He grabbed the oversized box and started pulling it towards the other side of the street. The little guy just wasn't going to give up. The giant box barely moved. *Pap, pap, pap!* The kid cried out in pain and grabbed his arm, the TV now forgotten.

The security drones hovered a mere ten feet off the ground, surrounding Bandana man and the kid. "Lie down on the ground. Social services have been alerted. Remain on the ground. Do not move," a drone voice commanded.

Spidey was having a bad day. That was for sure. I actually had sympathy for the kid. A minute ago, he almost had it all. Now he'd be lucky if these drones didn't kill him with their rubber bullets. I tried to mentally will the little guy to get down on the ground and obey the commands of the flying robots. He just stood there. Like he was taking it all in. Then, unbelievably, he made another move for the box. The stubborn little idiot didn't know when to give up. This wasn't going to end well. A security drone took aim.

Something from behind me zipped through the sky and hit one of the drones. The machine careened into the side of a building. Sparks flew and it lost two of its rotors before crashing into the sidewalk. Pedestrians screamed and ran. Every rider in a stopped car on the street gawked. The remaining three drones took their attention off the kid and searched for the source of the attack. That's what I did too. I think everyone on the block wanted to know who had the guts, or stupidity, to do something like that.

Another projectile—maybe a rock or a chunk of pavement —whizzed overhead and smacked a second drone with a loud thud. It too crashed to the ground. Who was doing that? The remaining two security drones buzzed like giant angry bees, searching for something to attack, and rapidly changing their positions in the air in a programmed response to make them less of an easy target.

"Run!" someone shouted at the kid. It came from across the street. A woman's voice. "Run now!" she screamed at Spidey again.

I looked over and knew instantly she was the one taking out the drones. There could be no mistake. She was the only person on the street that looked like something straight out of a movie. It was amazing.

She wore a skintight, dark blue suit that had some kind of raised lines—piping—running all over it. Now, when I say skintight, I mean skin . . . tight. From head to toe. Which didn't look like it was an issue for her. She had the body and curves of a dancer. The lines in the fabric of the suit followed the contours of her body and defined them. Did I mention the skintight part? A vest full of gadgets hugged her torso snug enough that it didn't bounce around or even move. Jet black hair waved out of a mask that covered the top of her face. The mask had little ears on it. Maybe it was supposed to look like a rabbit or a cat . . . I couldn't be sure. The whole thing flowed into a collar that completely covered her neck and ran into her suit. She was a vision of strength and confidence.

"A vigilante," I stammered to myself. "And she isn't a buffoon."

One of the two drones suddenly took aim at her and let loose with a volley of what I was still hoping were rubber bullets. *Pap, pap, pap!* They hit the spot where Rabbit girl had been standing the moment before. She had already jumped into action.

In one quick move, she had leapt onto a fire hydrant, propelled herself across the top of a taxi, then launched off that vehicle, straight at the drone in midair. Somewhere along the way she had also managed to pull out a collapsible baton and she whacked the robot out of the sky with it, landing perfectly on two feet, cushioning her fall with a graceful bending of the legs.

This whole thing was insane. Who was able to do that and look cool the whole time?

"Definitely not a buffoon," I repeated.

Then Rabbit Girl snatched up the dead drone and used it as a shield. Which was a good thing. *Pap, pap, pap!* The last remaining security robot let loose with a burst of gunfire that bounced harmlessly off the dead drone she had just picked up. The bot hovered just yards away. You could almost hear it try to process what it just saw. I felt the same way. It was incredible.

Before it could make up its tiny computer mind what to do next, Rabbit Girl hurled her drone shield with amazing accuracy and knocked the other drone out of the sky. In a matter of seconds, she had single-handedly taken on and destroyed four security drones.

All the onlookers stood in stunned silence.

Except Bandana man. He was back on his feet and making his way back towards Spidey and the TV.

Rabbit Girl wasted no time. She just took him out with a roundhouse kick. *Blam.* Knocked his ass out! She then turned to Spidey as the sounds of approaching sirens echoed down the block. Lots of sirens. From the street and the sky. This was officially a bad scene now and it was about to get worse.

Spidey-kid unbelievably started to try to make off with the box.

"Nope," she said to him. Quiet but firm. "That doesn't belong to you."

"We weren't gonna keep it" he protested. "We were gonna sell it and buy food and stuff."

"Doesn't matter. You don't steal other people's things. So, you need to walk away, now."

After a moment Spidey nodded his understanding and hustled off.

The sirens were close now. I looked up to see if I could spot just how close. It sounded like they were sending everything they had. When I looked back, Rabbit Girl was gone. Everyone else on the street was hurrying away as well. They didn't want to be here when the police arrived. Neither did I. I took one last look around for Rabbit Girl and quickly trotted off in the general direction of Debbie's place.

CHAPTER SEVEN

Once I was only a couple blocks away from Sky Tower skyscraper, the city surroundings quickly started getting better. And I mean they got a lot better. No more sewage or crazy people on the streets. The sidewalks were perfect and all the buildings were pristine—no grime, no shutters or gutters hanging sideways, and all the landscaping and decorations were neatly arranged and in season. Things were quieter. Air smelled fresher too. I mean, I knew the city stunk, but only when you compared it to actual clean air did you realize just how bad that stink really was.

Graffiti and billboards were rare as well. My goodness, there were barely any signs, and the ones that were there weren't trying to convince you to eat insects, live in pods, or trying to encourage you to reduce your carbon footprint. They were all like, "Enjoy Your Day!" or, "Restaurant Row This Way!" I even passed one that said, "Happy Hour," with a great big arrow pointing into a quaint looking pub. It was like time travelling back to when nice neighborhoods weren't so rare, when they weren't only for the super-rich.

Then there was the lack of drones. Like signs, there were hardly any in the area. These people were so well off, they actually had pigeons. Only a handful of security robots roamed around on the ground. Instead, humans took care of most of the patrolling. Actual, human, security officers. They weren't social welfare officers either. They were old school, real-deal security. There weren't many private security forces in the city, and they didn't have the headache of their own bureaucracy. But they were the real deal. Weapons and everything.

I rounded a final corner and then Sky Tower fully came into view—ground floor to the tippy top. It shot into the air like some magnificent beacon calling for troubled souls seeking refuge from the filth and misery that was the rest of San Josisco. The irony, of course, was that it was no such thing. Sky Tower had its own private security force—separate from the private security of the surrounding blocks—called the Tower Guard. And the guys who worked for that outfit would never let anyone seeking refuge get anywhere near the immaculate tower. Tower Guards were paid to keep the lowlifes out. Of course they started eyeballing me by the time I was a hundred yards from the edges of the property.

One of the uniformed guys stared me down pretty hard and approached me before I even got in the front doors of the skyscraper. "Good afternoon," he said, not meaning a word of it. "Can I help you?"

"My girlfriend is here, visiting her friend," I replied. "I'm just popping in to say hey."

"Oh?" he said. "Visiting a visitor? Interesting. What's your girlfriend's name?"

"Uh, Sharyl."

"And what's her friend's name who lives here?"

"Debbie Strafford. She's had me over before a few times."

The security guard nodded his head. "Okay. Well, the officers at the front desk will be able to assist you when you enter the main lobby." He helpfully pointed exactly where I was heading.

"Thanks." I forced a smile back and walked inside.

Tinted glass doors, immaculately spot free, hid obsidian tiles and a sparsely furnished lower lobby. Two more uniformed officers were there. They stood behind a slick metal and glass desk parked on the left side of the room, opposite a set of elevators and a stairwell.

"How can I help you?" the younger one asked me.

I'd spoken to him on a number of occasions, and he never remembered me. "I'm here to see Debbie Strafford. Pretty sure my girlfriend's upstairs with her. I'm just popping in."

"So, visiting a visitor?" the guard said.

"Yeahhh. Visiting a visitor. I've been here a bunch, so I know where I'm going. Have a good one." I turned for the elevators.

"Hold it." He held up his hand. "Is she expecting you?"

"No. But my girlfriend is here visiting her and I'm just doing a pop in. She's cool with that."

"Right. I heard you. But I can't just let you go up and see her if she isn't expecting you. Let me call up there first."

The other security guard moved closer to the first one. His hands found his pockets and he looked me up and down. Low-key judging, but definitely judging.

The first one grabbed the black desk phone and punched four numbers. He mumbled some stuff into it and nodded his head and hung up with a gentle rattle of the handset on the cradle.

"She said it's okay," the guard told me.

"Thank you." I forced yet another smile and gave a tiny nod to Judgey.

"Just so you know, it's going to be busy up there with the Channel 9 news crew," the guard said. "They're setting up to film a segment with your girlfriend soon."

"I'm sorry, what?"

"Channel 9? That's the big news station that owns all those vans and vehicles you see in the visitors' parking lot." The guard pointed towards the tinted glass.

I followed his finger. Somehow, I missed the whole gaggle of them on my travel inside. Probably too busy thinking about that blue-clad superheroine and Spidey-kid.

"Why are they interviewing my girlfriend?" I asked.

The guard shrugged. "I don't know what to tell you. I figured you already knew about it. You know, because she's your girlfriend."

"Right. Good point." I moved to the elevators and punched the up arrow. During the ride to the tenth floor, I wracked my brains for a reason why Channel 9 might be visiting Sharyl at Debbie's place. The break-in last night? That didn't seem newsworthy. Worse stuff happened all the time. I just watched a gang of kids attack a delivery drone and that was just on the walk over. In the middle of the day.

The doors silently parted and I stepped onto the shinier black tile, accentuated with enamel white grout, of the tenth floor lobby. The tile was so dark there was a chance that not even light could escape it. Aqua flowed over the lower portion of the walls and a strip of molding separated it from the pearl upper portion. The buzz of overlapping conversations and people rushing to and from greeted me. What was going on up here?

Debbie's condo was at the end of the hall, and I bobbed and weaved my way through traffic that had turned the normally calm floor into what seemed like a flooded convention center. Just a hint of light trickling out from where Debbie's condo door was, told me it was open. Well, that and the constant flow of people that went in and out of it.

Debbie and Sharyl were standing in the center of the open concept condo—the living room area of it—when I walked in. Damn, this thing was huge. That thought struck me every time I came over. It even had a second floor. Must be nice. The two girls were talking and giggling. Channel 9 crew members fluttered around them. I recognized Kira Tripp, one of the Channel 9 weeknight anchors, a few feet away from them. Even without her bright red power suit she probably would've stood out. Two other people, it looked like a cameraman and sound guy, stood at rapt attention and listened very carefully as Kira gave orders nonstop, and wildly gestured and pointed all over the place about something. Whatever it was about, the conversation didn't look like an enjoyable one.

Kira was the number one journalist in the city. After she broke the story about the Gumbroad Experiments a few years back, she skyrocketed to fame and power. Only it wasn't really a story, per se. Rather, it was fake news; a lie cooked up by Kira and other reporters.

There was a candy company called Gumbroad, Inc. that was just outside of San Josisco city limits. Kira and Channel 9 had done a series of breathtaking reports on it that alleged the company was experimenting with new ingredients that would cut costs by two percent. And the reports had claimed that those new ingredients had been poisoning people.

That was it for Gumbroad. Public outcry brought swift government condemnation. The company execs had explained that the reports were wrong. Then they apologized for any misunderstandings. That had been their undoing. Once they apologized, Kira and her fellow journalists said that was as good as an admission of guilt, and Gumbroad, Inc. was liquidated within a few months.

Even after everybody learned that Kira and Channel 9 had lied, her reporting was still deemed "true, due to being in the interest of public safety" and no one dared say otherwise anymore. It became conventional wisdom that Gumbroad was trying to poison everyone, and anyone who said otherwise was accused of spreading disinformation and of being a conspiracy theorist.

The end results? Kira could now do pretty much whatever she wanted.

Currently, apart from her regular anchoring duties, she had a few regular segments and specials she did for Channel 9. But for the life of me, I couldn't figure out how Sharyl could fit into any of them. This was a very strange twist in an already way-too-strange 24 hours.

"Don't just stand there. If you need more work, go see your first-line supervisor," some guy in cargo shorts and a loud Hawaiian shirt with rolled-up sleeves said as he got awfully close to being in my personal space.

"Excuse me?" I said.

"We're not paying you to stand around. Find some work." He lowered his eyebrows.

"I'm not with Channel 9," I replied.

"Then what are you doing here?" he asked.

"It's that—Well, you see—I, uh . . . oh, never mind."

He started saying something else, but I didn't wait around to listen. Sharyl noticed me coming at her and Debbie.

"Avery, what are you doing here?" Sharyl gave me a tight fake smile; her arms firmly folded across her chest.

"I texted you earlier and never heard back. I was out looking for work and thought I'd take some initiative and pop in to see you. It's a So-Sen thing. . . . What's going on over here?"

Sharyl started to answer as Debbie interrupted. "You're here! Wow. Sharyl, Avery is here. How crazy is this?" Her voice had the distinct sound of someone telling an inside joke. I wasn't in on it evidently.

"Super crazy." I fake chuckled. "Why is it crazy? Could somebody let me in on what's happening?" I added another chuckle, hoping it was more convincing than the first.

Kira finished issuing her orders to her crew and joined our conversation. "I take it this is Avery." She said it to Sharyl and managed to avoid looking at me. "Are you sure you're okay with him being here after the incident?"

"Hi, Kira. Nice to meet you. I'm a big fan," I said. "Incident? You mean the burglary at our place? That was bad but I don't think it's *Action News* bad. Am I right ladies?" I looked around for support, but no one made eye contact. Not a good sign.

"Wow," said Kira. "Just . . . wow."

"He'll be fine," Sharyl assured her.

"Okay, time out. For real. What's this all about?" I asked.

"Maybe you should help yourself to some refreshments in the kitchen." Debbie gently started to lead me away by the elbow. I stood my ground. Debbie just kept talking. "Kira is going to be interviewing Sharyl about the break-in and what happened. It's going to be for her *Empowered Women* series that airs every Tuesday on Channel 9." She said it like she was talking to a first grader. I let it slide.

"Oh. Okay. That was easy. Why didn't somebody just say that? Is that the show you intern for?" I tried to make it sound like a genuine question but a teeny bit of smarm may have slipped out. Debbie just smiled blankly.

"I highlight a badass woman of the week." Kira finally acknowledged my presence. "And Sharyl's story is a perfect fit. Perfect."

I nodded my head in fake agreement. "Right. I get that. Sharyl was pretty awesome last night," I lied. "Very badass."

Sharyl shot me her patented "shut your mouth, Avery" look.

Kira took a deep breath. "The way she stood up to that burglar? The courage she showed in the face of danger? Oh, yeah. That's what I call *badass*. Total badass." There was the tone again. Like they were all being forced to deal with a first grader.

"Sure. What was your favorite part? Of Sharyl's *badassery*?" I asked.

Sharyl's eyes bulged at me this time. I would definitely be getting in trouble for this later. Kira touched her arm reassuringly.

"Well, once we start rolling, which we will be very soon, you'll see exactly what I'm talking about." Kira answered. "We women are *natural* badasses. Natural."

Her little tic of saying one of her last words twice was starting to annoy me. I managed to keep my mouth shut.

"Can I talk with you before you start?" I asked Sharyl.

Her eyes narrowed. "Now is not a good time, Avery."

"Well, it's important to me," I said. "I feel like I need to talk with you about what happened last night and see if we can work things out."

That was a good effort on my part. I used "feel" and "talk' in the same sentence. That's just how they told you to do it at social sensitivity group. Advantage, me. She had to talk with me now.

"I can't right now. We're about to start," she replied without skipping a beat. She didn't even blink.

I leaned in super close "You're not going to mention my cousin's g-u-n. Right? No reason to bring that up, 'cause that'd be bad. Unregistered guns are b-a-d." Why was I spelling everything?

She looked at me for a second as if I were an idiot, then shook her head no.

Whew. Okay. Good.

I looked around. The crew seemed to be still setting up equipment and I found it hard to believe that they really would be starting soon. But after the reaction from Sharyl, I decided not to push the conversation any further.

"Again, Avery, please help yourself to some refreshments in the kitchen." Debbie's tone reminded me I was a child of six.

"Right." I headed over to her giant kitchen. It was probably bigger than my living room. Who was I kidding? It was bigger than my entire downstairs. It took me a minute to remember how to open her giant refrigerator. It was one of those state-of-the-art things. I had to double tap the door with one finger and swipe left to open it. Swiping right would open the freezer. And I only remembered it after I swiped right twice and activated the very loud AI that must have had some kind of body-shaming algorithm built in.

"Are you hungry again?" it practically screamed.

"Just looking," I replied in my indoor voice.

I quickly double tapped the door and swiped left. The door opened and a quiet bell sound played. Inside the spacious fridge, Debbie had pretty much anything I could've wanted. Good lord she was rich. I was tempted by the large assortment of imported beers but made the safe choice of a bottle of water and a slice of key lime pie. After just one bite, I knew it was probably the best I ever had. This was pie on a whole different level. They probably used real limes. I did a quick mental count of how much was left just in case I went back for more. There was almost a whole pie left. That was the best news in days. Sad but true.

As it turned out, Kira and Sharyl were right on the money about the interviewing starting so quickly. Just minutes after we finished our little talk, they were seated in the living room as if they were having a quiet, private conversation. The cameras rolled. Debbie and the two dozen or so crew huddled around and watched. Based on the looks a lot of them gave me, I figured Sharyl must have told everyone who I was. They would occasionally look over to me, and I'd nod back with a little smile, holding up my plate of key lime pie as if to say, "There's plenty more."

Kira and Sharyl started with some boring banter that I only half registered, on account of the pie. But it was so quiet in the condo, you couldn't help but listen. Suddenly I became very aware of the sound of my utensil clicking the plate. I put my fork aside extremely gently, as to not make a sound. Having a piece of the best key lime pie on the planet would have to wait. I wasn't going to let my eating noises (which Sharyl hated) interrupt this interview for my girlfriend. Besides, I wanted to know just what they were saying.

"So, what was going through your mind once you realized an intruder—a male intruder—had entered your home?" Kira's elbow rested on the armrest of her chair and her hand thoughtfully touched her chin.

"Well, it came as quite a shock." Sharyl chuckled. "My heart started racing as you can certainly imagine."

"Indeed, I can!" Kira said.

"But I did my best to retain my composure. I knew that I couldn't panic. One of us had to remain calm," Sharyl continued.

"So, there were two of you in the home at the time of the intrusion?"

"Yes. My boyfriend, Avery, and me. And like I said, only one of us managed to keep our cool." Sharyl pointed to herself.

What?

Kira smiled. "Women are *such* badasses!"

"We are!" Sharyl beamed.

The hair on the back of my neck stood up and the interview suddenly became a lot more interesting to me. I set the water bottle down on the counter in the kitchen and pushed the crumb-filled plate away from me. That pie was insane. But so was this interview.

"We could hear him moving around downstairs, so we had

plenty of time to think about what to do," Sharyl told her.

"Uh-oh! Sometimes when you have *plenty of time* it turns into having *too much time* and you overthink things! I hope that didn't happen!" Kira laughed the entire time she spoke. It mildly distorted her words and wholly made her sound like an idiot.

Sharyl rolled her eyes. "Oh, I wish! No, instead, while I was trying to get us out of the house through the upstairs window, Avery was just fumbling around, trying to open a drawer in the nightstand."

"Really? That's weird. Why would he do that?"

Why was Sharyl talking about the nightstand? There was no reason to talk about the nightstand. She said she wasn't going to talk about the g-u-n. Maybe she was just making me sweat. Trying to teach me a lesson. Damn. She could be mean.

"Well, I had no idea at first. But he eventually got it open. I mean, it took him a looong time but he eventually figured out how to open a drawer." She flicked her eyes at me and was unable to suppress a haughty little smile. "And then he pulled out another small case, and it took him time to get *that* open too."

Holy crap! She's a soulless monster! Now she's bringing up the case? How much does she want to punish me? Sweat dripped down my back.

"Oh, my! The burglar must've had time to go through the entire house while this was going on," Kira said.

"You would think." Sharyl rolled her eyes again.

Green little edges worked their way through my knuckles, and I realized I was strangling a paper napkin to death.

"He definitely had time to start coming up the stairs." Sharyl said. "Avery finally opened the case and what did I see him pull out?"

Don't do it, Sharyl. Don't you do it. Please, baby. (Sorry about the "baby," I know that's wrong. I can't help it.)

"What?" Kira's eyes were wide.

"A gun!"

"What?"

"Yes! He had a handgun in there!"

She did it! Why would she do that? She said she wouldn't say anything! She told her about the g-u-n!

"And you didn't know about it?"

"Not only that but then I found out he never even registered it!"

I felt like I was going into shock. My toes curled up and I could feel my heartbeat in ears. And Sharyl wasn't done.

"Are you kidding? So now you're not just facing the threat of an intruder, but also an unregistered handgun in your own home?" asked Kira.

Sharyl firmly nodded her head. "That's right. And as you can imagine, that was a lot of stress."

Kira clucked her tongue. "I'm sure it was. But you managed to keep it all together. Right?"

"I did. And it was good I did. Because now Avery was fumbling with the lock on the gun!"

I grabbed at more and more of the napkin, turning it from squished paper into a sweaty, ragged, little ball. Debbie quickly glanced at me as if I were a pile of crap and just as quickly looked away.

"So where was the burglar now?" Kira asked.

"Oh, he was getting closer and closer," Sharyl replied.

"So why couldn't Avery get the lock off the gun?"

"He couldn't remember the combination to it."

"Are you serious? Even in the depths of his toxic masculinity puppet show he still couldn't get it together mentally?"

"No! Can you believe how totally absurd that is?"

"Well, sadly, yes. I can. What happened next?"

"The burglar finally gets to our bedroom," Sharyl told her. "He opened the door and then Avery finally gave up trying to get the lock off the gun. He just dropped it and started screaming."

"Then what?" Kira leaned forward.

"Everything was kind of in slow motion," said Sharyl. "So many things happened at once. But while Avery clung to me and screamed, I remembered an empowerment workshop I went to as a little girl. The panic left me. I had total clarity. I knew exactly what to do. I planted my feet, put my hands on my hips, and let the power of my uterus manifest itself through my entire being. It was beautiful. I looked this criminal in the eye and shouted, 'No.' Just that one simple word from a strong woman almost knocked him off his feet."

Kira smiled and nodded her head in agreement. Her eyes started to tear up.

Sharyl kept rolling. "I took that energy that Mother Earth blessed me with and as horrible as it sounds, I punched him right in the face."

Kira lit up. "Don't apologize for that, girl. Don't you ever."

"Thank you for validating that, Kira. That means a lot. Now, as the burglar landed on the floor, that's when the gun he was hiding in his pants went off and he shot himself." She pointed to her crotch, then nodded and smiled.

"You mean . . ." Kira paused, giggled, and pointed to her own crotch. ". . . down there?"

"Yes!"

They laughed uproariously. I did not.

"Oh, my!" Kira regained enough composure and continued. "So, then social welfare came and detained him. But you still had to deal with that unregistered gun your boyfriend, Avery, had."

"Yes, I did. And as you might imagine, I let him have it!" Sharyl firmly set her jaw.

"Of course."

"I mean, I just couldn't let that go unaddressed," Sharyl said. "I told him how wrong it was to disobey the law like that. And how this was a horrible, horrible betrayal on his part."

Sure, now we're going to talk about betrayal. Sharyl was throwing me all the way under the bus. I'd lost all feeling to my extremities and somehow my ears were sweating.

"And what about gun violence? Did you talk to him about that?" Kira ran a hand through her dark hair.

"Yes, I did. I let him know that he is just as much a part of the problem as burglars and other criminals are."

"What did he have to say about that?"

"He wasn't happy to hear it. But I had to say it. After all, I'd be a hypocrite if I didn't. Here he was, a legit scofflaw and I had no idea about it. I was living in the same home as him. So, after all that, right after social welfare took the burglar away, I told Avery I couldn't live with him any longer and I marched right out of there early in the morning. I needed time to heal."

"So, social welfare knew about his unregistered handgun and didn't do anything?"

"No. It's all so disgusting. What has happened to us? As humans? It's all just so gross."

Kira gushed. "Well, you stood up to a burglar, *and* you stood up against your depraved, impotent boyfriend who shamelessly flaunted the law. You really *are* wonderfully *badass*! And I think everyone will agree that you're one of the best heroes we've ever profiled on *Empowered Women*."

Sharyl beamed proudly. She had just dismantled whatever was left of my life. I had no idea anyone could be that cold. Pain shot through my hand. I loosened by grip. I had balled my fist so tightly that my nails were digging through the napkin and into my palm.

Sharyl and Kira went on gabbing. Bright lights beat down on them and cameras still rolled. I caught another glimpse of Debbie staring at me. Her eyes fled faster from my gaze than they did the first time.

All the chattering stopped ten minutes later. Sharyl's smile had become something just this side of gargantuan, and Kira's grin tried it's best to beat it. Crew members and producers started buzzing again. Some of them took a glimpse in my direction but most of them pretended I wasn't there. I wiped my mouth and navigated around the kitchen counter, trying to figure out what I would say to Sharyl. She had to make this right with Kira. She had to set the record straight by telling the truth. But Debbie's radar locked onto me, and she intercepted me before I could reach them.

"Avery, I have no idea what you might be thinking about saying to Sharyl right now. But whatever it is, I believe it is best that you didn't." She positioned herself directly between me and them. Her hands were out front and just inches away from my chest. Sharyl and Kira kept imagining they didn't see me.

"After that? You bet I'm going to talk to both of them! Sharyl made all that up!" I exclaimed.

"Don't," Debbie insisted.

I moved to my right. She mirrored me and blocked my path.

"Just remember, there are dozens of people here," she said. "Do you really want to make a scene? In front of a news crew?"

"Maybe I do! Maybe I will make a scene! How about that?"

The room got quiet. Kira motioned for a cameraman to pick up his camera and start filming. As he struggled to get his equipment ready, I could feel the expectation in the air. They wanted me to flip out and make a scene. They were waiting for it. They were counting on it. Certain it would be great entertainment.

I took a deep breath and looked at Debbie.

"Maybe you're right," I said. "It can wait. I'll have a little chat with Sharyl later."

Debbie raised an eyebrow. "What do you mean by that?"

"It means I'm leaving. No show, everyone! Sorry!" I brushed past her. "I'm heading home. Tell Sharyl we need to figure this out."

Debbie didn't respond and I didn't look back to check if she heard me. I just kept walking. Out the door of her apartment and straight down the hallway to the elevators. Then straight out of Sky Tower and back into my crappy life. Whatever was left of it.

CHAPTER EIGHT

I woke up on the couch. It was a little after 3 a.m. I was still wearing my t-shirt and jeans. The TV was on. Some cooking show was playing. The host, dressed in a zany, colored, giant suit and with a pair of thick glasses on his face, was putting the finishing touches on a batch of Meal Worm Fritters and the audience was wildly cheering like he had just cured cancer. He offered a bite of his worm-based delights to a twenty-something hipster guy and the dude actually started weeping with joy before he even tasted it. I turned the TV off.

The place was quiet. Where was Sharyl?

I had wanted to confront her when she got home. Where was she? Probably in bed. I sighed and staggered off the couch. My heavy legs barely managed to push me upstairs and I quietly made my way into the bedroom. No Sharyl. That was par for the course. The one time I wanted to confront her and she was staying out all night. I went into the bathroom and took a leak.

For a moment, I thought about trying to act cavalier by hopping into bed and going back to sleep so I could show Sharyl I didn't care what she did. But I knew she would never believe I was that cool. So I made a return trip downstairs to the couch and huddled up there again. I'd just wait for her to come home and let her try to explain why she threw me under the bus like she did. That should be rich.

How could she have done that? Said all those things about me and, to make it worse, on TV? We'd been together for a long time. Usually, I could always recognize that she was right, and I was wrong. But for the very first time in our relationship, I felt like I was justifiably upset. I was right and she was wrong. It was uncharted territory for me.

As I sunk deeper into the couch, wrapped in a blanket and staring at the ceiling, I started thinking about all the arguments Sharyl and I ever had. She could be brash. She could be loud and seemingly uncaring. But it was always based on some shortcoming on my part. Some part of my psyche I was completely unaware of. Some insensitivity on my part. A micro-aggression I didn't even know I was responsible for. There had been the social sensitivity classes and all the gender empathy courses I had attended. But for some reason it never clicked with me. Sharyl was always having to point out my shortcomings and psychological misinterpretations of what I was supposed to be doing or saying in any particular situation. But this time was different. This time I was right.

I played over the events of the day in my mind just to be sure. After much consideration I came back to the same conclusion I had on my angry walk home: I was the victim in this one. I was the injured party. Sharyl was wrong to do what she did, and I was completely correct to be upset. I tried to think of how she would defend her actions, but I just couldn't see it. But I could never see it . . . maybe that's what would happen again. Sharyl would point out some obvious gender-based emotional faux pas on my part, and I'd be left standing there . . . a confused mess, trying to understand what just happened. But if that were the case, she'd already be home. That's why she was still out. She didn't want to come back and face the music, as my dad used to say.

Lying there in the dark, thinking about everything, my eyes eventually shut and I drifted off to sleep. The sound of the front door opening woke me up. She was finally back. This was my moment. But why was she making so much noise? She threw the door into the wall and everything. And speaking of noise, what was all the sound going on outside?

My mind raced. *How should I do this? Do I clear my throat and let her know I'm on the couch? Or do I just lie here and let her come to me?*

That sounded like the better plan. I'd let her come inside, go upstairs, and see I wasn't in the bed. Then she'd get worried and come back down and discover me sleeping on the couch. Perfect.

So, I was just going to lie there and fake sleep. Let her sweat for a change. I couldn't help but smile a little.

Bright lights blasted through my closed eyelids. That was weird. She didn't even go upstairs. Before I could open my eyes, a pair of hands slammed down on my chest with enough force that I thought I just might go through the bottom of the couch. What the hell was Sharyl doing?

Then several more sets of hands fell upon me, including on my ankles and shoulders, and held me firmly in place. I blinked my eyes furiously and tried to adjust to several thousand spotlights that were somehow in my living room and pointed directly into my corneas.

"What the—" was all I managed to say before someone shoved yet another hand over my mouth.

A masked figure loomed over me. Maybe I was seeing things, so I blinked a bunch of more times. My eyes finally adjusted and my vision started to clear. Was that a social welfare officer? In riot gear? And not just one either. There were so many of them they practically filled the room.

"Whf arf youf affacking mef?" I garbled into the hand over my mouth. None of them indicated they understood I was trying to ask, "Why are you attacking me?"

Every single one of the social welfare officers was covered in high-tech, black, body armor from head-to-toe. Shoulder-mounted LED lights blazed like tiny searchlights. And a black, samurai-style helmet sat on their heads; their faces covered by air-scrubbing, bullet-resistant, grey, face shields. Guns were drawn and pointed at me. It was straight out of a nightmare. So maybe it was just that. A nightmare. A very real feeling nightmare. Complete with a room full of mute social welfare officers.

My muscles relaxed ever so slightly. If this was real life,

these guys would be talking—shouting and barking orders at me. They wouldn't be just holding me down and standing there like they were mindless drones.

The guy who had his hand clamped down on my mouth quizzically tilted his head to the side. Like a dog that was confused by a new chewy toy.

"Helpf!" I squeaked.

In an instant, they flipped me over on my stomach. The guy's hand left my mouth. "Help!"

They jerked my hands behind my back and zip tied my wrists together. After that, they secured my ankles. I struggled to break free but there was no way that was going to happen.

One of them punched me in the ribs and pain shot up my side. Then they grabbed me under my arms, hoisted me into the air, and slammed me back down into a somewhat seated position.

I quickly decided I wasn't going to try to struggle again. I sat there terrified of what would happen next. Everything was so silent that my panicked breathing was the only sound in the room. Again, the social welfare officers just stood there looking at me. All their laser-sighted guns trained on my body. The quiet seemed to stretch on forever. I couldn't take it. Despite my terror, I finally had to say something.

"I think you might have the wrong address."

One of the social officers raised what I hoped was a Taser and aimed it at my chest. His thumb flicked a switch and a high-pitched whine emanated from it.

The one closest to me, a huge mass of muscle, turned towards him and motioned downward with his hand, muffled noises came from underneath his helmet. His comrade lowered the Taser. Then muscle officer turned back to me and held his arms out to the side. More muffled noises from him.

I gulped and tried to keep my heavy breathing from turning into hyperventilating. "What do you want?"

His hands dropped to his sides, and the muscled goliath sat down next to me on the couch. Instinctively I flinched. He reached up and lifted off his helmet and set it on the coffee table in front of us. His face still covered with the grey, emotionless, protective shield. Slowly he reached behind his head and I heard two small clicks, then the brief hiss of air being released. After a moment the hulking social services officer pulled the mask off his face. And all the sudden I was looking at a man in his mid-forties with close cropped, slightly graying hair, grinning from ear-to-ear. Which were huge by the way.

"Could you hear *anything* we were saying?" he asked, seemingly delighted with the question.

I hesitated. "What? N-No. Nothing."

He looked at the other social welfare officers, still entertained. "I told you guys! It's the comms. We had 'em on internal this whole time." He let out a big laugh and inspected a side of his face shield. His gloved finger pressed a small button. "Yup. There we go. *Now* we're on public. Everybody, switch your comms to public address mode."

Just like that, a dozen or so fully armored riot social welfare officers took off their helmets and face shields. *Click, click, click, click* went the buttons.

"Second time this week," the officer next to me said. His smile remained. "You got lucky. Last Wednesday, we went in some guy's house and he wouldn't respond. Terry over there just started tasing him like a beast! Zapped him real good. Gave the poor sonuvabitch a heart attack."

They all laughed except for one guy, who I assumed was Terry.

"A heart attack?" I repeated. "Was it fatal? Is he okay?"

"Jimbo!" the officer next to me called. "Make sure you tell the sarge we gotta do something about these comms. We keep hitting the buttons by accident when we put on and take off our face shields. We're gonna be shooting people left and right if no one can hear us."

Jimbo nodded. "You got it, Stick."

Stick must be the guy with the huge ears talking to me. He picked up his shield and placed it against his face. "Citizen, you are under arrest." It came out in a transformed, rich, robotic baritone. "You must comply!" He lowered the mask and chuckled. "Ain't that the shit? We were on internal this whole time."

"Yeah, that's crazy," I said. "Sooooo . . . what's going on? Why are you here?"

Stick's smile disappeared. "We're San Josisco Social Welfare Special Forces. We're here to search the premises."

"For what?"

"Contraband. Drugs. Illegal food stuffs." He took a deep breath and leaned into me then whispered. "Weapons."

The image of my cousin's firearm upstairs flashed through my mind. "I might have a gun . . ."

"We know." Stick's smile started to reappear. "Oh, we know. We just don't know what else you got. But we'll find it."

"It's just a gun. I keep it in a lockbox upstairs," I blurted out. "I'll give it to you."

All the light went out of his eyes, and he gritted his teeth. "Don't tell us where it is! Why would you do that?"

"'C-Cause I don't want to get in trouble?" I ventured.

"It's too late for that!" Stick snarled with such force his ears jiggled. "You just made it worse."

"How? I'm j-just trying to cooperate," I stammered.

"Well, don't!" His glove leather groaned as he rubbed his left fist into his right palm. "By admitting to the presence of contraband and your knowledge of the location of the contraband, you're implying there's more. Now this raid just went to level six."

"Where were we before?"

"Three!"

My mouth agape, I took in the small army of social welfare special forces troops standing in my living room. "This is a three?"

"Not anymore, dipshit. Now it's a level six. I knew I should've shot you the second we came in."

Stick hurriedly put his face shield and helmet back on

and his subordinates followed suit. Then he rose to his feet and towered over me. "Alpha One, we have a level six at my location." His transformed, robotic voice echoed off the walls. "Please respond with necessary ordnance and backup."

Fear found me again and I gulped. "What happens now?"

That grey, emotionless visage glared at me. "Level six happens now you dumb sonuvabitch."

Suddenly the eye pieces of all the social welfare officers' face shields lit up with a menacing, red glow. Four of them hauled me off the couch and carried me towards the front door as if I were a pig at a luau. Outside, red and blue lights from social welfare vans flashed and illuminated the entire block in those strobing colors. Drones flew back and forth overhead and even a manned gunship roared past twice. Ground drones were going back and forth too. The special forces guys dumped me face down on a patch of dirt near the sidewalk.

I started to wriggle my head back and forth in a vain attempt to roll over. The social welfare officers had other ideas.

"Who told you to move?" one of them shouted.

"I'm just trying not to eat dirt!" I said with my face firmly planted in the afore mentioned soil.

Somebody grabbed my elbows and zipped tied them together. And another person did the same to my knees.

"Are you serious? You already got my wrists and ankles!"

"Shut up! We don't take any chances with scumbags like you."

Once they finished that, they roughly stood me up. They didn't exactly set me straight up and I hopped twice to the right to keep from falling.

"You trying to get away?" one of them asked.

"No. Of course not."

"Better not."

They left for some other duty. There I stood, wobbling and trying not to tip over. I desperately looked around for help. Someone else was just a few feet away. I'm guessing he was a bum—sorry, a homeless man. He was in the middle of taking a dump between two parked cars. He looked at me with pity in his eyes. Or maybe it was just the face he made when he took a shit on the sidewalk. I don't know. It looked like pity and I couldn't believe it.

"Naffralobinulmanraker!" He shook an angry fist at me.

"Citizens!"

I jumped at the female voice emanating from a drone flying overhead. It's warbled tone was probably meant to be soothing but it was loud enough to wake the dead.

"Stay inside," she sang. "A level six threat has been detected. It is being met with appropriate force. Do not be alarmed, citizens. Stay inside to shield yourself and your loved ones." From there she repeated her message at a decibel level to be heard over the greater San Josisco metro area.

Several more social welfare vehicles arrived, and huge, eight-rotor drones descended from high above the street. Spotlights shined on me and tracked anything that moved, including the homeless guy who was finishing up his dump. At first, he swatted at the lights as if he could knock them away. But he eventually figured out it was a fruitless effort. He spewed another burst of verbal nonsense at the sky, pulled up his pants, looked at me with disgust this time, and shuffled off.

So many social welfare vehicles were jamming the streets that I couldn't count them all. No less than five cruisers were within 50 feet of me. Diesel engines roared and announced the arrival of two more battle vehicles on scene.

Battle vehicle probably wasn't the official name for them, but that's what they looked like to me. They were these giant, armored monstrosities. Social welfare officers dressed in what looked like military uniforms popped out of turrets on the tops and manned massive guns. They were all at my place as if it were a war zone.

There were two other enormous vehicles parked nearby too. These were bigger than the battle vehicles, and they didn't look like anyone was in them at all. I couldn't tell if someone was remotely operating the monstrosities or if AI was in charge.

More and more drones were swarming the night sky. It was a whole flock of them. Some had to be the regular ones that always flew around, but most must've been ones belonging to the social welfare special forces. Those drones were big and had heavy guns mounted on them—maybe missiles too. It was the biggest display of force I had ever seen in real life. It was overwhelming. And they were all here just because of me? That didn't seem right. This looked more like an invasion level of military-style hardware. Mentally I had a hard time processing it. Thankfully my concentration kept getting pulled back to my painfully zip-tied limbs and I was forced to focus on not falling flat on my face. My hands and feet were starting to go numb. Standing was getting more challenging by the second.

"Do you need any assistance here, ma'am?"

The metallic voice startled me. Looming in front of me was a seven-foot-tall robot. This one wasn't like the useless ones that rolled around on the streets; like the ones bums flipped over and used for chairs. This one had several long metallic legs like a spider. It was all black and menacing, and it's body was armed to the teeth.

"What?" I had to shout so it could hear me over the female voice on the aerial drone that was still repeating its warning to the neighborhood that citizens should stay indoors.

Green light shot out from one of the spider-bot's many eyes and scanned my face. "My apologies. It is dark and it confuses my sensors. You are the criminal suspect. Do you need sedation? If you are a drug user, sedation could be useful in a high-stress situation like this. There is no shame in asking for a sedative."

"I'm okay." I yelled to the robot spider death machine that was also a part-time drug counselor evidently.

Thump! Thump! Thump! Thump! Thump! Several hovering drones launched smoked grenades into my home, right through the open front door . . . and right through every closed window. Glass shattered and a series of small explosions resounded. White vapor rolled out of every opening, both old and new.

"What the hell are you doing?" I shouted to the drones overhead.

"You are overwhelmed," the spider-bot informed me with a pleasant tone. "There is no shame in needing sedation."

I looked back at spider-bot just in time for . . .

Pop!

I felt a pinch on my chest. There, sticking out of it, was a large syringe, the contents of which were now emptying into my body.

"Whydyoudothat?" My vision started blurring.

"There is no shame. You will awaken at the social welfare office. If you need more sedation, it will be supplied for you there. Please fall onto your back to prevent the needle from entering your heart as you collapse."

Words wanted to come out of me, but my mouth had stopped working. I began to tip forward but somehow I managed to catch myself and jerked my body backwards. The thought of landing face down and forcing a needle into my chest was a great motivator. My back and head slammed into the ground. My vision blurred and I listened to the chaos around me fade into nothingness as a wave of unconsciousness swept over me.

CHAPTER NINE

Waking up in a jail cell was just like I imagined it would be. It sucked. The mother of all headaches was pounding away in my skull. Cold metal pressed into my face. I slowly sat up on the bench where I had been passed out. It was a big concrete cell with classic bars on the side facing the hallway. Flickering florescent lights completed the dismal look.

I had the worst case of dry mouth of my life—like, zero saliva. None. Maybe it was a side effect of whatever that robot had shot me up with. At least I hoped that's what it was. Squinting made my headache subside just a little bit, so I did that as I searched for a faucet or something where I could get some water. The toilet in the cell stood out like a sore thumb yet I couldn't find the sink. That made no sense. There had to be a sink. And then I saw it . . . it was the top part of the toilet. That was the only source of water in the cell. Toilet/Sink water. How did they keep it separate? Did sink water go into the toilet? Or did it start as toilet water and get pumped up to the sink? The thought made my head hurt even more, which I didn't think was possible, but here we were.

The jail reeked of urine. Several puddles of old piss decorated the floor. Add all that up and I highly doubted drinking out of the toilet/sink was a good idea. But I was so thirsty. I was going to have to if I didn't want to die of dehydration.

On the upside, I had the whole place to myself, so there was plenty of room to maneuver around the fetid obstacles of pee puddles as I journeyed over to the sink. After a few failed attempts, I figured out how to operate it and turned on the cold water, which jetted out of the back of the sink in a long, smooth stream. It tasted of chlorine and plastic piping. But it was wet. I gulped it down for a good minute.

Much to my surprise, I discovered I had to use the toilet too. So, through my splitting headache, I started on my next mission: taking a leak. It suddenly occurred to me that my feet were abnormally cold, and in mid-stream I un-squinted one eye just enough to look down and found out I was barefoot.

What the hell? The cops must've taken my shoes. How could I have not noticed that right away? *Wait a minute . . . where are my pants?*

I was in a jail cell wearing nothing but a t-shirt and a pair of tighty-whities. Thank God I was alone.

Throughout all these realizations, I still hadn't finished my abnormally long, bladder-clearing flow for the ages. It didn't seem possible considering how damn thirsty I was. How could I possibly have any extra fluids?

Someone politely coughed on the other side of the bars.

"Uh . . . hold on one sec," I offered up. I had no idea what normal protocol was in that situation, so I just kept peeing.

"Take your time," a man's voice said. "I'm your court-appointed attorney, Topper Clemons."

"Oh, great! That's actually good news!" My head throbbed, letting me know that talking like a normal human being might cause my brain to explode. That's how it felt anyway. "I'll be right with ya. I got drugged by a security robot and I think this might be a side effect. I'm really sorry."

"It is," Topper said. "Happens all the time. Don't worry about it. Bad headache too?"

"The worst."

I finally finished and quickly washed my hands at the sink. But there were no paper towels. Nothing at all and I held my hands out to the side. Water dripped off them and splattered on the floor.

"Well, I, uh," I walked over to him. "Probably the most embarrassing moment of my life." I forced a smile.

Topper didn't smile back.

"My hands are wet, obviously, but they are clean. Do you want to shake?" I held out my hand.

His lip curled downwards, and he quickly shook his head.

"Sure. I get that. Guess we can go with an alternative greeting. Hello." I waved at him, accidentally spraying droplets of water on his face.

Slowly he reached up to wipe the moisture off his forehead and cheeks. "Yes. Hi."

"I'm terribly sorry," I told him.

He held up a hand. "You know what? Let's just forget about it and move forward. Avery, are you ready to get out of here?"

"Yes! So ready. Thank you, Topper."

He nodded. Topper looked to be in his mid-fifties and carried a bit of extra weight around the middle. Outdated glasses sat on the bridge of his nose and his rumpled suit reinforced the fact that he was a court-appointed lawyer. Beyond that, his quasi-military-style haircut and large mustache made him look like a walrus that just woke up from a nap. Not that I cared, though. I was just happy to have an attorney.

"You'll need these." Topper handed me a small bundle wrapped in paper.

"I can't believe they already gave me an attorney." I started unfolding the paper bundle, but each time I would take away a layer of paper, there was more underneath. It just kept going. Like a magic act from the most environmentally un-friendly magician in the history on humanity. They couldn't provide paper towels, but now it looked as if several reams of brown paper littered the cell floor. Finally, I found the prize at the center of the bundle: a large pair of plastic shower shoes and a giant paper robe like a hospital gown, except it was bright orange. However, putting both of those things on actually made me feel quite a bit better. It's amazing how much a paper robe and some shower shoes can improve your state of mind after you've been half naked in jail. My head was even slowing down on its constant throb of impending doom.

Topper whipped out a worn-looking key card and waved it in front of the cell door. There was a quiet click and the door slid open. He motioned me to follow him.

"Better?" he asked.

"Yes. Thank you so much," I replied. "Do they give me my pants and stuff back out front? I've never done this before. I have no clue how this works."

"If you came in with it, they'll have it for you when you process out," he informed me. "We just need to stop by an interview room, meet with the prosecutor, get your side of the story, figure out the charges, and plan how we move forward. Then you'll be on your way."

He led us down a series of dimly lit hallways and through a few sets of security doors. My oversized shower shoes savagely slapped the concrete floor with each step. Topper's pass worked on all the doors and gates. And the handful of uniformed officers we walked by never gave us so much as a second glance.

"You always have a free run of the place?" I asked.

"I'm a lawyer. I'm here enough that I have a good relationship with social welfare," he said.

We went down yet another corridor, this one with a series of numbered doors every few feet. The slap, slap, slap of my huge shoes echoed down the hall.

"Here we are." Topper opened the door to room 48.

Inside was a lone metal table, two dilapidated folding chairs, and not much else. Next to the table was a rolling stand with a computer monitor mounted to it.

"Wow. Not quite what I was expecting," I muttered.

Topper shrugged and gestured for me to have a seat. I shuffled over to the chair on the side of the table closest to the door and he took the one on the opposite side. He took his phone out of his pocket, tapped it a few times, and started reading something. At first his lips moved silently, but then some mumbling slipped out. Occasionally he would look at me. I patiently waited . . . and waited . . . and waited.

"Uh, thank you again," I finally blurted out. "I've never

been in trouble with social welfare before and I'm glad you're here as my public defender." I waited for a reply. Nothing. So, I relaunched with: "I have no clue how this works. Does the city pay you, or do you and I work something out?"

"City pays me," Topper said, still looking at his phone. "San Josisco assigns me to cases and then pays me." He reached over and tapped on the computer monitor. A menu immediately appeared on it. "You hungry?" he asked.

"Starving . . . and very thirsty."

"Well, let's get you something to eat. Just select whatever you want. They take care of criminals pretty good. No charge. City pays for that too. They don't want social welfare detention to feel intimidating so they do their best to at least feed you well." He tapped the screen again and a sub menu popped up. "Here you go: the First-Timers Breakfast specials. Knock yourself out."

I adjusted the monitor so I could get a better look at it. It was one hell of a list: eggs Benedict, omelets, a selection of seasonal fruit salads, and more. So much more. My mouth started watering as I kept scrolling through it all.

"This is free?" I asked.

"Well, the city passed a bill a couple years ago to de-stigmatize the justice system and the food was a priority." He broadly smiled. "So, they added hotel quality food to all the social welfare detention centers. It's all from local farm to table restaurants until San Josisco gets enough money to open up its own kitchens on the premises."

"So many choices here," I said.

"The croissant breakfast sandwich is outstanding. Highly recommend," he advised me.

"Do you want anything?" I still couldn't believe this was real.

"Whatever you're having."

I tapped the screen and ordered two of the sandwiches, two sides of fresh fruit, and four large freshly squeezed orange juices. Three of them were going to be for me. And then I chose a slice of chocolate cake. *Why not?* I told myself.

"I gotta say, this isn't what I expected," I said. "Well, the cell was completely what I expected. But the food? And getting a public defender so fast? Gives me some hope. I always heard the justice system was a wreck. But it seems like it's working just fine."

Topper grinned politely. "The justice system is a wreck. An absolute train wreck that moves with all the speed of a wet brick. Most people in here have to wait over a year for a public defender. I just happened to be watching *Empowered Women* with Kira Tripp last night. And when I saw you got arrested, I pulled some strings and got the city to assign me your case."

"Wow. I'm glad you did," I told him. "I'm ready to be done with all of this."

"Don't get ahead of yourself. You're not out of the woods yet. We'll see how things look after we talk with the DA." He nodded at the same monitor where we had just ordered food. "A lot of folks take gun charges very seriously."

"Yeah, this whole thing is way out of control. Where should we start? The arrest? Just so you know, the officers, they never read me my rights. Pretty sure we can use that." I looked at Topper for some encouragement. I didn't get any.

"Let's just wait for our sandwiches and the DA. She should be on any minute."

"Shouldn't we talk before?" I gently asked. "Just so we're both on the same page?"

Topper's face dropped. "Are you expecting your story to change?"

"Uh . . . no. I just thought it was standard for a client to talk to his lawyer beforehand. About the case."

Topper's eyebrows raised. "There is nothing standard about this case. Trust me."

My eye twitched. "What does that mean exactly—*nothing standard*? It seems very standard. Incredibly standard. False arrest. No warrant. Social welfare brutality. I was drugged and thrown in jail. I'm only wondering if I should sue."

Before he could answer, a waiter with a large, rolling, room service-type cart entered the room. When I say waiter, I mean waiter. Black pants, white shirt, black tie, the whole nine. The guy was a waiter. He rolls in the cart and proceeds to place some of the most delicious looking breakfast food and juices (yes, chocolate cake too) in front of us. He never said a word. He just did his job and left.

I decided not to think about it and immediately gulped down one of the glasses of orange juice. Topper just watched me politely and unwrapped his silverware. Steam drifted off the croissant sandwiches and I grabbed one. I took a bite and instantly decided it was one of the top three best breakfast sandwiches I had ever eaten in my life. Just off the chart. It was incredibly delicious.

"This is prison food?" I asked Topper between chews.

He nodded an affirmative.

I should've ordered three. At least. I took another bite. Flavors exploded in my mouth. Eggs, crispy bacon, and melted cheddar on a croissant that was flakey, buttery perfection.

The monitor blipped and came to life. A dour-faced, middle-aged woman appeared on it. She gave Topper a thin-lipped smile of acknowledgment. The smile instantly retreated when she saw me with the breakfast sandwich in my hand and my mouth stuffed with food.

Not knowing what else to do, I half waved hello with my sandwich. "Good morning." I had only partially chewed my last bite.

Disgust crept across her face. "Mr. Avery Davies-Plott. "It is *Mister*. Right?"

I nodded my head. "Yes, ma'am."

Disgust mutated into fury. "I'm an assistant district attorney for the City of San Josisco—not a *ma'am*. Your attempts to demean me have no place here."

"Sorry," I mumbled as I tried to swallow. "I didn't mean any offense. I'll remember that." It occurred to me she never said her name but I wasn't about to ask it.

"Well, you better, Mr. Davies-Plott. Now, I have looked over the case and the available evidence. Plus, I watched some very compelling footage of your girlfriend on *Empowered Women* with Kira Tripp. That just hurt my heart. And it deeply hurt the mayor's heart as well. They are now personally asking that I make certain that you be prosecuted to the fullest extent of the law."

"*They*? You mean it's more than just the mayor?"

Her eyes burned. "*They* is the pronoun the mayor uses. Do you have a problem with that?"

"N-No. It's just that—well, I was c-confused. A-And he can't actually ask for me being prosecuted. Can he—er, they? I mean, isn't . . . they . . . supposed to be impartial?"

"*They* are the Mayor, and *they* do as they deem fit. And you are in a whole pile of trouble. You know that. Right?" she continued.

"No. No, I don't know that. I'm not in a whole pile of trouble. Am I? This doesn't seem like it should be a pile." I turned to Topper. He shrugged his shoulders.

The DA cleared her throat. "Let's begin. Shall we? Why'd you get that gun in the first place? What'd you intend to do with it?"

"I didn't get it. I mean, somebody gave it to me," I said.

"Somebody gave it to you?" She cocked her eyebrow and flicked a pen between her fingers. "So, what? People just give you weapons of death and you take them. Are you into running guns and supplying them to other people too? Criminals? Vigilantes, maybe? Or what about militias?"

"No, no, no. Nothing like that!" I looked to Topper. "You want to jump in?"

"Just *answer* the questions," he told me.

I licked my lips and realized I was now sweating. I felt a lot warmer. Hot even. And extremely lonely. It didn't feel like Mr. Topper Clemons, attorney at law, was going to be riding to my rescue. But I told myself that he must have a plan. Right? I probably just couldn't see it. "It was my cousin. He gave it to me last Christmas," I admitted.

"Last *what*?" the DA said.

"L-Last Christmas. You know . . . *winter holiday*," I quickly offered. She got pretty hot about the *they* thing, hopefully my casual use of *Christmas* didn't offend her.

She quit flicking the pen back and forth and grasped it between her forefinger and thumb. "Okay. Now we're getting somewhere. What's your cousin's name?"

"Didn't the social welfare officers already get that when they were at my home for the burglary?" I asked.

"I said, *what's your cousin's name?*" she yelled.

So, I gave it to her. She scribbled it furiously on a yellow legal tablet.

"You know, the officers who arrested you told us that you gave them a hard time," she continued. "Is that your game? Giving the authorities a tough time. Think you're a tough guy, huh?"

"No! That's not it at all. I'm definitely not a tough guy. And I'm doing everything I can to cooperate!" I sputtered.

"Well, you've got a funny way of *cooperating*." She gritted her teeth and her sliver of an upper lip curled.

"You and your cousin run guns a lot?" the DA asked me.

"I just told you, we aren't running guns!"

She pounded her fist on her table and I flinched. "No, you didn't!" She thrust a finger into the camera at me. "You said *you* weren't. But you never said a thing about you *and* him not running guns. Why are you suddenly changing your story?"

"I-I-I." I again looked at Topper. "C'mon, dude. Please! You gotta help me out here! Can she really be treating me like this? Do I need to be answering all these questions?"

He looked at me as if I was an idiot. "What do you want me to do? Answer them for you? I wasn't there. I can't read your mind. You really think failing to cooperate with the DA is going to help you?"

"But isn't there something about me not having to answer questions. You know, something about not having to incriminate myself?" I asked.

"Oh! Oh! Oh!" the DA shouted. "So, you're saying you're going to incriminate yourself if you keep answering questions? Let's hear it then, Davies-Plott! You've got one way out! Give us the confession! Clear your conscience and tell us you did it!"

"Wait. What? Confess to what? I mean, I told you I had the gun and I haven't registered it," I said. "But confess to what? I haven't done anything with it. I mean, I never even got the safety lock unlocked from the trigger on the thing!"

"And just why were you trying to unlock it? What exactly were you going to use the gun for if you were able to get it unlocked?" the DA snarled.

I looked back and forth between her on the screen and Topper. "Are you serious? Is this real? What am I missing? Why do we keep going round and round like this? I was trying to get it unlocked when the burglar was breaking into my home yesterday."

"So, what exactly did you plan to do with the gun if you did get it unlocked?" she demanded.

"Use it to stop the burglar," I ventured.

"How?" she asked. "This is Earth. This isn't Mars. We don't allow citizens to shoot one another and just claim self-defense. We have laws. Laws that protect people from animals like you. So, what were you going to do with the gun?"

"I was going to throw it at him?" I squeaked.

"Couldn't you have done that with the trigger lock still on the gun?" the DA asked.

"Of course," I said. "I just . . . I don't know what you want me to say."

Topper reached over and nudged me. "Are you not paying attention? She told you not to give her a hard time. Why are you trying to make things so difficult?"

My mouth dropped open. "You realize you're my lawyer. Right?"

Topper motioned for me to return my attention back to the screen. The DA continued asking me questions. And we continued going round and round, with me telling her again and again that I wasn't up to anything nefarious, and with her continuing to insist that I was. She kept trying to get me to admit to . . . something. You would've thought I was a terrorist with the way she was treating me. Or at least a mob boss. Maybe even a repeat criminal. But me? I was a guy who *never* had a run in with the law. Hell, a couple days ago I *was* the law . . . kind of. Maybe she didn't know. I should tell her.

"Look, I was part of law enforcement just two days ago," I told her. "Sure, Post-Digestive Hygiene Product Enforcement Officer II isn't the most glamorous type of law enforcement work. But *technically* it was law enforcement. So, you gotta understand I'm not a bad guy."

"Nothing like a dirty cop," the DA spat back.

Then it was another barrage of questions and accusations where she urged me to admit to being guilty. And the theories she was putting out there just got more and more insane sounding. Why was I thrown out of the Chartreuse store? Somehow, she knew about that too. I guess AI surveillance picked me up on some camera; maybe one of those drones that hovered over me while I was lying in the gutter. Or maybe the manager called social welfare after he threw me out. Regardless, they knew all about it. I told her I was just trying to get a job there. She twisted it into me waiting for my gunrunning, terrorist friends.

Then those kids who tried to hijack the delivery drone flashed through my mind. What if she knew about that? What if she knew I was there when that happened? Did any cameras catch me before I pulled my t-shirt over my nose? Did that even help disguise me? But she never brought it up and I mentally breathed a sigh of relief.

That didn't mean things got better. All my answers to her questions fell on deaf ears. In her eyes, I was a monster.

Topper did nothing. He just sat there, taking notes and encouraging me to keep talking. I finally decided to not even bother appealing to him for help. I just endured the interrogation, kept my answers short, and repeated the same answers over and over. It was the truth. That was supposed to set you free. Right? Finally, the DA must've got tired of putting me through the wringer.

"We're going to be recommending some very tough charges," she said. "And with all our evidence, they're going to be extremely hard to beat."

"I bet they will be," Topper grunted.

"Now you have something to say?" I was just this side of incredulous.

Topper avoided looking at me.

"I only wish we could keep you in confinement until we can get you before a judge," the DA said. "But the law's on your side. Way too easy if you ask me. And we are legally bound to release you on your own recognizance. Your arraignment date is 48 hours from now."

"So, I'm free to go?"

She squinted her eyes. "You're not free to go just anywhere. You need to stay in town where we can reach you. We don't take gun-dealing terrorists lightly. You understand that? You. Can't. Just. Go. Anywhere. You've been arrested and you have to appear before a judge in 48 hours so we can present our case against you."

"Yes, yes. I understand that" I said. "I just wanted to make sure I heard you correctly. No disrespect. I understand everything."

"But while we can't keep you in confinement, we can do everything we can to make sure you stay where you're supposed to," she continued. "That means you need to give up your phone and any other mobile devices you have."

"Well, you already have that along with everything else I had on me. And the only other mobile device I have is my tablet," I continued.

"We already confiscated that during our search of your home," the woman said. "Anything else?"

I shook my head. "No. Nothing, I can think of. Other

than that, I'd just like to add I'm completely innocent of all the charges." It felt like a good idea to say that again, just in case she was still recording.

She waved her hand, and the screen went black.

I looked at Topper. "Can I please get out of here now?"

"You bet," replied the worst lawyer in history. "Unless you want to finish your food."

"Kind of lost my appetite." I stood and gathered my paper robe around me. "I just want to get my stuff and go."

Topper led me out of the room and down another series of hallways. Not a word was spoken. The only sound was the slapping of my giant shower shoes on the tile. Eventually we came to a large room that had a sign over the double doors leading into it: *Guest Central Processing*. Right—*guest*. Who'd they think they were kidding? *Inmate* was more like it. Holy crap. *I* was an *inmate*. In a jail. This shit sucked.

We went towards a smaller area separated from the main room by a wall and mesh screen. A beat-up sign read: *Ask Officer for Belongings*. Good thing they had that sign. No one would've ever figured out to ask the person on the other side, guarding the room of personal effects, for their stuff back without it.

"Once we get your things, we can walk out of here," Topper said.

"Great." I went to shove my hands into my pants pockets and came up empty. That's right. No pants. No pockets. "Could this day get any worse?"

"What's that?" Topper asked.

"Nothing," I muttered.

Everything was horseshit. The break-in, losing my job, humiliating myself at Chartreuse, Sharyl going on TV and blaming me for everything, getting arrested, my crappy lawyer, the DA—everything. My mental list of injustices kept expanding even when I tried to stop thinking about it.

"I'm here for Guest Avery Davies-Plott's personal effects," Topper said to the bored, overweight, uniformed jackass at the desk behind the mesh screen.

The officer pointed to a proximity reader on the desk. Topper waved his magical key card over it and a red light turned green. The officer clicked the crumb-filled keyboard of a laptop next to him. After carefully examining the screen, he got off his chair and shuffled to the back of his area.

"Almost done," Topper told me.

I weakly nodded.

The officer returned to the desk with a recyclable bag in one of his hands. "Here you go." He placed it into a bin and pressed a button.

A drawer beneath the mesh screen that I hadn't even noticed before popped open. I grabbed the bag. It had my name scrawled on a label slapped on the side and was stapled shut.

"You can change in the latrine over there." The officer pointed off to my left. "If you don't return the bag in good condition, the city will bill you 20 bucks for it."

I cocked an eyebrow. "You really think I'm going to destroy it between now and the time it takes me to change?"

"You a wise guy or something?"

Topper placed a hand on my shoulder. "C'mon, Avery. Keep that attitude of yours in check. Just go get changed."

"Fine. Whatever."

I went into the restroom and immediately struggled with the bag of my belongings for a solid ten minutes. Whoever stapled it shut used about ten staples and they were really in there good. I tried prying them open but all I managed to do was chip a nail. So, I settled on pulling the bag open as neatly as I could . . . and managed to rip the entire top off the thing, leaving it completely destroyed.

My eyes shut and my head dipped. "Hooray. There goes another 20 bucks I don't have."

Much to my surprise, my wallet was inside the bag. All my credit cards and cash were gone but I still had my ID. "I'm going to put that in the *win* column." At least I wouldn't have to replace that as well. Not sure if I could deal with the Bureau of State Identification in my present state.

Next, I pulled out my shoes and pants. "These aren't my shoes. And these aren't my pants." I dropped the strangers' tiny shoes to the floor and held up the pants in front of me. Which were incredibly large. Like a sail from a schooner or something. It made no sense. Who has huge pants and tiny feet? I tried to picture the kind of person who would need such large pants and small shoes but it threatened to bring my headache back.

I didn't even consider trying on the size five cross-trainers. Shower shoes it was going to have to be. But the pants were a different story. I needed them. So, I waded into the sailboat pantaloons and hiked them up. I stuck my thumb into the waistband and held it out a good ten inches away from me. "I'm gonna need a belt."

For some reason, I left my paper robe on. I don't know if I subconsciously did it as an act of rebellion—as a way of saying, "Look at how ridiculous this thing is"—or if I was just overwhelmed with everything that had transpired. But whatever the reason, I slogged out of the bathroom in my flopping shower shoes, clown pants, t-shirt, and prison system paper gown . . . and, of course, carrying the torn recyclable bag.

"Look, like, I, uh—" I started to say to the officer behind the mesh screen.

"Don't waste your breath, Davies-Plott. You just bought yourself a bag." He clacked away on his laptop, filling out some form to send me a bill.

I held out the now deceased bag and walked towards him, holding up my enormous pants with my other hand. "Where do you want me to put it?"

"Take it home and use it as a gift bag for all I care," he said.

Topper was just finishing up a call. He jerked his head towards a door with an exit sign over it.

"So, I'm free to go?" I asked the social welfare officer.

He glared. "You're not free to go just anywhere. You need to stay in town where—"

"Right. The DA already let me know that." I hobbled to the door, my shower shoes flipping and slapping on the tile floor.

Topper held up his hand and I halted. He finished his call and escorted me through the door, into another room for a final check by another social welfare officer, and then out into the grey, damp sky suffocating the San Josisco streets.

"There aren't my clothes," I told him.

"Yeah, they get busy. Sometimes there are mix ups. You want to go back in and try to sort it out?"

"No. I never want to go back in there. Ever," I said.

Topper frowned. "I wish I could tell you that won't happen, but these charges are pretty serious. Guns. That's a big deal. The DA will probably ask for at least 50 years. I guess we'll see."

I froze. "Wait a second. Fifty years? They had no search warrant. They never read me my rights. I'm not a criminal! This should be an easy win for me. Right?"

He shrugged. "I don't know, Avery. That's what, *we'll see*, means."

My head swam. Fifty years? For something I was innocent of? And my *lawyer* says, *We'll see*? What the hell was going on?

"I'm going to ask you something." I tried to remain calm. "Are you really a lawyer? Because I'm not getting a strong, you're-going-to-fight-to-keep-me-out-of-jail-vibe off of you, and I really need that right now . . . you know, from a lawyer."

Topper took a deep breath and seemed to gather his thoughts. He exhaled pointedly. "Yes, Avery, I am a lawyer, and I'd like to think I'm a good one."

"Then why weren't you doing any, you know, lawyer stuff in there?" I pointed over my shoulder at the social welfare detention center.

"Because I'm also a victim." It was just shy of being a hushed tone. "A victim of guns. My father was a gun nut, just like you."

My head jerked back. "Wait. What? I had one gun. I just needed to register it. That doesn't make me a gun nut."

Topper acted like he didn't hear a word I'd said and although he looked at me, his focus seemed to be far away. "The pain I endured as a child was immeasurable. Just knowing that in that safe, in my parents' room, in the back of their closet was a rifle . . . it was just too much for me emotionally. It ruined my life. I've spent years in therapy trying to process the emotional fallout from knowing that my father had such careless disregard for human life."

"Did you say he had it in a safe? In the back of his closet? That doesn't sound that crazy to me," I offered.

His focus found me again and his brow lowered. "My father's gun—just the fact that he had one—cost me my marriage, my family, and any chance of success in the legal world. It left me stunted. I have been in therapy for 15 years. My therapist and I agree, it is the memory of my father owning a weapon of death that has scarred me developmentally. So, you tell me: is that *crazy* or isn't it?" His expression softened. "But when I saw your case, I jumped on it. You know why? Only by helping you can I help myself. That's what my therapist says."

I was still confused. "Did your dad ever . . . shoot anybody?"

"No. Never. He didn't take it out once my whole life and yet it still did so much trauma," he said with a knowing nod. "Can you imagine what I'd be like if I had ever actually seen it? I think I'd be beyond help. But let's not think about that. No, we need to keep things positive. By representing you, my healing can truly begin."

"So, you don't even know if there was really a rifle. You just know there was a safe in your dad's closet. Did he even tell you that's what was in there?"

"He didn't have to. I knew," he said with that little smile that was becoming familiar. "But I don't want you to worry. Everything is going to be all right. I've defended rapists, murderers, and thieves of every creed and color. By defending a gunrunner—a merchant of death—this is going to help me get a little better."

Topper held out his arms. "Come here, you."

I stepped into the hug. He clapped me on the back as he

choked back tears. The smell of bad cologne, cheap whiskey, and failure drifted off him.

"Thank you," he sniffled.

He broke the hug and wiped his eyes with the back of his hand. I stood there and held up my clown pants.

"You're saving me. No matter what happens, you, Avery, are saving . . . me." He nodded as if he had just said something very meaningful, and he slowly started backing up. "I'll be in touch." He turned and briskly walked away, looking over his shoulder once. "Remember, don't leave town."

CHAPTER TEN

My instinct was to go home. Then I remembered that home had been pretty much wrecked by social welfare. And I wasn't ready to deal with that. But I couldn't just stand in front of the social welfare detention center looking like I did. So, where could I go? I recognized a convenience store a block away and finally figured out exactly where in the city I was. Red's place wasn't that far away.

Maybe I could get another shirt from him (even though I hadn't returned the one I had just borrowed). And maybe I could get some realistic pants. A shower would be nice too. Yeah. Red's place was my best bet. My hand reached for my phone.

"Oh, that's right," I mumbled. "No phone."

No phone meant no calling for a rideshare. That bummed me out at first, but I realized it wasn't that big of a deal. Even if I had a phone, it wouldn't have mattered. My credit score would be even lower since I had just been arrested. There was no way a rideshare would pick me up.

I started pounding pavement. Two or three drones circled overhead, and they flashed and blared their public service announcement.

"Nutritious and delicious! AND they're sustainable! Be ahead of the future by eating your bugs!" one of them squawked. All sorts of bug meals flashed on the high-def screen wrapped around it.

"Save the world and reduce your carbon footprint. Move into a pod and be part of the future—today!" the other one blasted.

Seriously, I couldn't get away from those messages. No one

could. No one who didn't have a ton of money, at least.

Believe it or not, the rhythmic slapping of my shower shoes on the wet concrete started to relax me, but then everything that had happened in the last two days came flooding back to my mind and quickly beat that relaxation to death. Right now, Topper was at the top of the list. He was a crappy lawyer. There was no other way to put it. But wasn't he better than nothing? I couldn't imagine waiting months for another attorney and there was no way I could afford to hire a new one.

My paper robe flapped in the breeze and almost kept me from spotting the pile of puke right in my path. But spot it I did, and I hopped around it. I smiled to myself. "Good job."

Job. I had no job. That was the next item on my list. Then there was Sharyl lying about me on a TV show. Everyone in the city hated me because of that. And to top it all off, I was looking at the possibility of going to prison for a long, long time. What was I going to do?

Something in my neck twitched and I could feel the beginnings of a massive panic attack starting to brew. I stopped walking and tried to take deep breaths through my nose. That's what they tell you to do. Thankfully it kind of worked. It kept the panic at bay. Then I remembered a piece of advice I got from a therapist at a seminar Sharyl made me go to when she had thought I was being exceptionally selfish: "Just do the next thing in front of you. Don't think of the totality of the situation. Do the next thing in front of you and keep moving."

"Shit, I'm actually using advice I got at therapy camp," I mumbled.

I wasn't sure if that was a good thing or not. But that's what I decided to do as I made my way towards Red's. As I envisioned myself being at his place and enjoying a brief respite, everything else seemed to fade into the background. That was a mistake.

It was a mistake because you should never get lost in thought as you shamble through an urban hellscape. Especially when you're wearing oversized shower shoes, giant pants and a paper robe. You let your guard down and lose track of your surroundings; you fail to notice that someone is targeting you until it is too late.

I was about eight blocks away from Red's when I realized what was about to happen. As I walked past an alley, I could sense someone right behind me and I knew a street thug had picked me for his next victim. Of course, I looked back. Not only did I confirm my fears, but to make matters worse, this dude was wearing some worn out, raggedy, cat outfit. Mask, furry gloves, and even a tail. Maybe he identified as a feral cat. Maybe he was just old school crazy. Either way, I picked up my pace. He picked up his.

My attempt to run in shower shoes and giant pants that I was holding up didn't go well. The cat mugger caught me after about 20 yards. He grabbed me by the arm and spun me around.

"Yahhhhh!" I exclaimed.

"Meowwwww . . . rrrrr." He held up his hands and curled his fingers into claws.

"What do you want?"

"Hsssss!" Whiskers stuck out of his cheeks. Literally, this guy had whiskers implanted into his face.

"Please, man, I just got outta jail. I don't have anything."

Cat man scratched me hard across my chest. "Rrrrrowwwww!"

I threw up my arms and stepped backwards. "I'm not being an asshole. I have nothing. Just don't hurt me. Please."

"Grrrrr . . . Reeeooowwwww."

"Aahhh! I'm not lying. I got nothing. Social welfare took everything." I used my free hand—the one not holding up my pants—to turn one of the pockets inside out and showed him there was nothing but lint.

Both his claws flew at me, and I winced and covered my face. He grabbed my paper robe and ripped it off in one swift motion. I dropped my hands from my face. He punched me square in the mouth. Stars danced before me and I just stood there like a chump. One taste of my lip told me he didn't bust it open, but it throbbed like it should've been bleeding.

Cat man got right in my face. "Grrrrr." And then he ran off, his tail dancing back and forth and his prize of my paper robe clutched tightly in his claw.

Maybe what just happened was the law of the street. Maybe stealing something and physical violence had to occur once a thug decided to engage a victim. I had no idea. All I knew was my face hurt like crazy and I was going to miss that stupid paper robe.

I hunched my shoulders against the wind and got out of there as fast as my flopping shoes would take me.

*****

Red was home when I got to his place. He was always home. Even for a guy who worked remotely, he still seemed to be home a lot. But I didn't care then. In fact, I was relieved when he opened his front door and let me in.

"What happened to you this time?" Red gave me a long look up and down.

"Kind of a long story," I replied. "Can I get a shower and some clothes first?"

He arched his eyebrow. "A shower *and* clothes? Do you at least have the shirt I loaned you the other day?"

"No."

"Did you lose it?"

"No. I mean, I don't have it with me. It's back at my place and—. Look, I'm sorry to impose on you again but can I please just have a shower and some clothes?"

"What's up with you borrowing my clothes? That's weird, man," he said.

I muffled a sigh. "Red, I know it seems strange. But I've had the worst 48 hours of my life. I just got out of jail—and then I was mugged! Can I please take a shower and borrow a pair of pants and a shirt? Please?"

He shook his head and snorted. "Sure man. Just use the bathroom upstairs."

"Thanks, Red. This means a lot."

"I'll get you some jeans and a shirt too. But remember, you gotta wash and return them *and* my other shirt, bro."

"I know and I will," I assured him.

The bathroom wasn't a total wreck but it was close. Red brought me his jeans, a shirt, and a towel, and I locked the door behind me. I let go of the clown pants and they immediately fell to my ankles. I stripped off everything else and pulled back the curtain on the shower. A nasty, mildew-covered tub greeted me.

"I can't believe he lives like this," I murmured.

But beggars can't be choosers. I stepped in and turned on the water. It was one of the best showers I ever had. Definitely in my top two. All that hot water and the soap flowed over me, and I felt like I was getting clean again for the first time in weeks although it hadn't even been a day since my last shower.

Normally I'm a quick bather. I don't mess around. The city of San Josisco frowns upon long bath people. You can get in trouble for wasting water. But I didn't care today. Long showers were the least of my worries. I must've stayed in there a good ten minutes. Even then I wanted to stay longer. With a superhuman effort, I turned off the water and got out. Then I put on a pair of Red's clean (ish?) jeans and his *The Withering Wood IV* movie t-shirt. I almost felt human again.

On my way downstairs, I wondered if I could push my luck and ask him for a pair of shoes and a jacket. And then it dawned on me. What had I become? What was happening to me? I didn't even have shoes or a jacket? "Don't panic," I quietly reminded myself. "Take things slowly."

A wave of odor smacked me in the face at the bottom of the stairs. Red was prepping some more insect-based food.

"You want anything to eat?" he asked me from the kitchen.

I sat in a patched-up sofa in his living room. His TV flickered with muted sound. A commercial showed a happy Asian couple waking up in their new pod house.

"Oh. No thank you."

He lumbered into the living room and carried a hot bowl

of something like a repeat of the last time I was there. The omnipresent odor grew stronger. He flopped into his big recliner and nearly spilled the food onto him. "So, what happened, man? And are you sure you don't want anything? These noodles and crick-bits aren't that bad once you get used to them."

I waved him off then launched into a recap of what I'd been through. Red listened and slurped his bug noodles, occasionally chiming in with a, "No way!" or a, "That's crazy." It's an unnerving feeling when you tell someone a real thing that happened to you and it's so outrageous that they can't believe it.

"So, what are you gonna do?" Red asked.

"I don't know. I have nothing. No money, no social credit, no phone, nothing. I don't even know what I can expect to find when I go back home. I'm just doing the next thing in front of me right now. What I really could use are some shoes and a jacket." I rubbed my hands together and sheepishly looked at him.

"Yeah . . ." Red gazed at the TV. "Hey, you know what? I bet you're on the news!"

I couldn't believe he didn't offer up a pair of shoes and an extra jacket. But I didn't want to push him. "Let's hope not. I can't take anymore. That *Empowered Woman* show about destroyed me."

"Indira, turn on the news," Red shouted to his virtual assistant. "And turn the sound back on."

The TV switched to a socially approved, 24-hour news channel. Video rolled of some newsreader reading whatever copy was scrolling on the offscreen teleprompter.

"City residents were attacked by a vigilante in broad daylight."

The broadcast cut to grainy surveillance drone footage of some San Josisco street.

"In this shocking footage, you'll see the latest example of how the plague of people taking the law into their own hands is affecting our wonderful city," the newsreader continued.

A large man in a blue bandana walked toward a kid struggling with a colossal box containing an oversized TV. It all looked familiar. Then it clicked. It was the fight after the attempted heist I watched on my way to talk to see Sharyl yesterday.

"Holy crap!" I pointed at the TV. "I was there. I saw this."

The video jumped ahead to the superheroine beating up the guy in the blue bandana.

"*A woman who thinks dressing up in outrageous clothing gives her the right to do whatever she wants. She savagely attacked an innocent man in order to steal his TV,*" said the newsreader.

"That's not what happened at all," I told Red. "That girl wasn't stealing anything. She was the hero."

Red sputtered out some bugs. "Mistakes happen. Even the news gets it wrong every once in a while."

"That's not getting it wrong. That's getting it backwards," I argued. "Why would they do that? They'd pretty much have to try to get it that wrong."

"Dude, I love how you take the criminal's side now," Red laughed. "One day in jail and you're all hardcore."

"Oh, yeah, completely hardcore," I shot back. "More like completely screwed."

Red took another bite of grub. "Yeah, I wish there was some way for me to help, man." Food dribbled down his chin as he chewed. "Not sure what I can do, though."

I took a deep breath. "Well, you've actually helped me a lot with the shower and the clothes. So, thanks for all that. I appreciate it. I really do. I think I've finally recovered enough, and I can head home to see how bad of a disaster that place is." I forced a weak laugh. "Do you think you could give me a lift home? Or, better yet, can you get me a rideshare? I don't have a phone."

"Hmmm, a rideshare." He rocked a bit and stuffed his meal into his face. "I'm so sorry, man. I can't risk that. You know, because of my credit score. Things are really tight at work and I just can't take the hit on it." He made an expression that I think was meant to be a pained one but instead turned out to be something really fake.

Just then the TV flared brighter and I think Indira even turned up the volume.

"*This is breaking news. We've just received word that San Josisco authorities have issued a citywide alert for everyone to be on the lookout for a dangerous individual,*" the newsreader said.

Red and I both turned our attention back to the TV.

"*The district attorney's office said that Avery Davies-Plott was arrested early this morning for the unlawful possession of a firearm. He was to have a preliminary hearing two days from now. But when San Josisco Social Welfare officers stopped at his home to verify that he was still in the area per his release guidelines, they found it empty. Authorities now believe that Davies-Plott has skipped town. Local and state authorities are searching for him, and they are devoting heavy resources to the manhunt.*"

The newscast cut away to a man giving a statement. The man was my lawyer, Topper Clemons.

"I thought I could help him." Sobs wracked his body and Topper struggled to get out the words. "I thought there was still hope . . . a spark of decency left in him. But he's just not human." Two more heavy sobs shot out of him. "Who can do such horrible things and then look at you like you're the monster? He's got himself convinced that he's the victim and that's . . . that's just sick. Sick! I thought I could defend him. . ." Another fit of weeping overwhelmed him. "But I can't. It's too much." And that was it. Topper collapsed into the arms of a large woman standing next to him. He buried his face in her ample bosom, his shoulders heaving up and down as he cried like a little kid.

My mouth hung open.

The broadcast cut to what was probably an earlier recording of the San Josisco DA speaking to an unseen newsperson. And it was *the* DA—not the assistant DA who had grilled me earlier. "*We consider this person armed and dangerous, and we have prioritized his capture. Additionally, when we find him, we will add additional charges to the ones we already planned to file. Mr. Davies-Plott will not be free for long, and when we get to court, now that he's violated the terms of his release, I'm confident we will* *have a strong case against him and he'll be spending a long, long time in prison. Oh, and we're offering a $100,000 reward for anyone who provides us with information that leads to his capture."*

And then it was back to the newsreader in the newsroom. She finished up but I didn't hear what she said. Red likely didn't either. The bowl of food he was holding had gone slack in his hands, and a bit of it flowed over the rim and splashed onto his jeans. His eyes were wide.

"They're lying." I was still trying to process what I had just watched.

"Armed and dangerous. They said they consider you armed and dangerous." Red managed to level his bowl and stop the flow of food before it became a river. He looked at me as if I were a stranger.

"Red. I don't even have a phone. Do you really think I have a weapon on me?"

"Maybe you lied about not having a phone." Red set the bowl on the table beside him and gripped the arms of the cushioned recliner.

"I didn't. I don't have a phone! I don't have a weapon! And I didn't do anything wrong! I didn't violate the terms of my release and I don't know why they're doing this!"

"Sure! They just made all this up for the fun of it!" Red said.

"They never said that I had to be at my home at all times!" I insisted.

"Then why'd they say all that stuff? And why couldn't they just contact you to find out where you are?" Red asked.

"They took my *phone*! How many times do I have to say that? They don't have a way to get in contact with me!"

"All very convenient for you." Red stood up.

"What are you doing?" I asked.

"Man, I thought everything was on the up-and-up when you came here," he said. "I took you into my home as a guest. I let you use my shower and I gave you my clothes. And this is how you repay me? Do you know how much trouble I could get into for harboring a fugitive?"

"Look, I'm telling you, none of this is my fault! It's like they have it in for me!"

"Indira, get ready to call social welfare," he said.

"No need to tell me to *get ready*, Red," she replied. "I am prepared to connect to the authorities now."

"Red, what are you doing?" I got off the sofa. "You can't do this. We're friends."

"Sorry, dude. It isn't me betraying you. It's the other way around. You betrayed me when you came here—when you knew you shouldn't have come here and did anyway. You think I'm going down with you?"

"I've never been like this before. Everything has gone wrong, and everyone has turned on me. You're the last person I have left. Please, don't do this," I begged him.

He paused. "I feel bad for you. And I wish I could help. But all this new info changes things. Plus, I got to watch out for myself. And to be perfectly honest, I can always use $100,000. That's a lot of money and I can get it for doing the right thing."

"Let's just calm down. Okay? No one has to do anything," I said.

"Indira," Red said. "Call social welfare. And tell them their fugitive Avery Davies-Plott is standing in my living room. Someone needs to come get him before he hurts me or gets away."

"Calling social welfare, Red," Indira replied.

"Well, if you think I'm just going to stand here and wait for social welfare to come and get me, you're crazy," I told him.

"I'm not crazy, Avery. And I really need a hundred thousand bucks," he countered. "Indira, lock all the doors and windows."

Clicks and clunks resonated throughout his home. I sprinted for the front door and yanked on the doorknob as hard as I could. But the deadbolt had that thing shut tighter than a bank vault. I whirled around. Red was closing in on me.

"What are you doing?" I asked him.

"You're panicking," he said. "So, I guess I should . . .

restrain you, one way or another."

Red was a big guy. A good six inches taller than me—easily. And he probably had 100 pounds on me. Again, easily. I juked left and he followed. I planted my left foot hard into the floor and went the other way and made it around him before he could react. Without wasting another second, I raced up his stairs.

"Everything is going to be locked up there too!" he called after me.

At the top of the stairs, I went into the small hallway and picked the first room with an open door. It was a junked-up bedroom, with boxes and all sorts of everything strewn about it. I think there might have been a bed somewhere in there. I picked up a chair. It looked like a dining room chair to a dining room table that I don't think Red actually owned. With that in my hands, I rushed to the window and cracked the chair legs against the glass. The legs bounced right off it and I lost my grip on the stupid thing.

"That's reinforced security glass. You know, because of all the bums and crime around here," Red's voice said from behind me.

I whipped around. He filled the doorway. He slowly started coming towards me. I grabbed the leg of the chair I had just dropped and threw the whole thing in his direction. The chair connected with Red . . . right in the crotch. He doubled over, cried out, and clutched his groin as he fell to his knees.

Out of the corner of my eye I spotted a bowling ball in the midst of a pile of clothes and a Parcheesi box. I grabbed the bowling ball and threw it at the window, being very careful to step out of the way of any potential ricochet. I saw what a chair did, I didn't want to take a bowling ball to the nuts.

I rolled a strike. The ball smashed the glass to pieces and didn't even leave much in the way of jagged edges around the frame. Red was still on his knees. I shot towards the window and looked out it. No ledges or anything. Just a straight drop to the ground.

Red was still gasping but he managed to get one knee

underneath him. "Avery, I'm going to kill you when I get my hands on you, man!"

The metal handle of a golf club caught my eye. How much crap did Red have in here? I grabbed it and tossed it in his general direction. The head of the club hit Red right in the throat.

"Gleepf!" he said. Or something like that. It was just a strange sound; not what I expected at all. His hands shot to his neck and grabbed it, and his knee rejoined the other one on the floor.

At first, I was horrified. But the dude just said he was going to kill me. So, in a way, I kind of felt justified. Not really, though.

I grabbed two handfuls of clothing—the closest of the many piles in the room—and wrapped them around my hands. I made it back to the broken window and slowly pushed one leg at a time outside. I grabbed the frame, now littered with shards of glass, with my dirty-shirt-covered fingers. Somehow, I progressed to hanging out the window without cutting myself. It was about a seven to ten foot drop to the ground. Not all that high. Except for it was, since I was the one about to drop. So, I closed my eyes for just a second, and I opened them again and looked at the ground.

"You're not getting away, Avery!" Red yelled. His heavy footsteps vibrated through the floor and into the window frame.

I let go. His hands swiped at me and brushed against my skin. My feet hit the ground and I collapsed, just like I used to in middle school gym class when we'd jump off the top of the bleachers so we could take our turn in the next game of dodgeball. Who knew that move would come in handy? And much to my surprise, the oversized shower shoes were still on my feet. The highlight of my day.

"You won't get far!" Red screamed out the window. "And I'm still going to get that $100,000 for giving social welfare the tip! And you owe me for those clothes!"

Nothing hurt too much so I didn't waste any time lying on the ground. I got up, stumbled a little, but somehow managed to keep my feet underneath me. I started running, quickly discovering that if you curled your toes into a foot fist, you could get some speed and not have your huge shower shoes fly off your feet. It wasn't a pretty stride, And the slapping was still incredibly loud, but it worked. Once I reached the front of Red's house, I turned right and just kept running. I pushed past every junkie, bum, and weirdo that even looked like they might try to stop me.

I had no idea where I was going and zero clue as to what I was going to do. I just knew I had to get far, far away. I was in deep trouble. So, I ran. I blocked everything else out. The drones, the lights, all of it. All I could hear was my breathing and the sound of my shower shoes slapping along the pavement.

CHAPTER ELEVEN

I needed to think. Just some time to get my thoughts together so I could figure out what the hell I was going to do. My current situation sucked big time. Not just the being on the run part, I was also freezing.

San Josisco could get incredibly cold at night, and right now I was keenly aware of just how bad that was. I should have stolen a jacket from Red too. I hoped he wasn't hurt too badly but I wasn't going to worry about that too much. After all, he tried to turn in his best friend for reward money. How low is that? Yeah. I definitely should've taken one of his jackets.

Anger started rising up from somewhere deep inside me, but I shoved it out of the way. Priorities. I had to deal with the situation at hand. I needed to avoid surveillance drones, the authorities, security cameras, and figure out a way to get a coat or something so I didn't die of hypothermia—and I needed to do all that while I came up with a big picture plan for the rest of my life. It was overwhelming. Oh, yeah. I needed a mask too. And I needed to avoid getting beat up. Did not want that at all.

Moving through the city without being captured by a surveillance camera was incredibly difficult. Seriously, it was one thing to know on an intellectual level that there were cameras everywhere, but actually fleeing for my life made me fully understand just how ubiquitous and intrusive they were.

Street corners—intersections—were the most obvious places where cameras were. But as I walked down the sidewalks and tried to keep a low profile, I realized that pretty much every streetlamp had one on them too. Then there were the corners and ledges of buildings; public and private cameras were on them. The robots patrolling the streets and the drones that were constantly flying overhead were another threat. Sure, I knew that drones were everywhere, but I couldn't believe how they constantly seemed to be hovering right overhead. I'd never noticed that before. If only I could go someplace that didn't have so much surveillance.

And then it hit me. There were three places in San Josisco where criminals always knew they could go to avoid social welfare and the rest of the authorities: undocumented human "refugee" centers, city-run drug distribution centers, and state-sponsored "loots." That's just what I needed.

Public loots started a few years ago. Big corporations got tired of peaceful protesters constantly setting their stores on fire and stealing all their merchandise. And seeing how there were at least two peaceful protests always going on in one or two major cities at any given time, corporate America decided there was only one thing to do: sponsor them. That way they could plan where and when the destruction happened, and also control the cost and quality of the merch they "donated" to the community.

San Josisco had a lot of sponsored loots. Lots.

The whole event effectively worked like a giant piñata. It was the same principle. The sponsoring company would build a large, wooden replica of a store in a big empty parking lot. Most cities used the lots outside of stadiums or ballparks. They wouldn't put up any logos or otherwise advertise what was going to be inside. That was part of the mystery. But the whole, fake store would be full of whatever stuff the company wanted to promote, give away, or just get rid of. A mob would form, eventually attack the fake store, and take everything inside. Everyone involved could get as violent as they wanted, destroy some property, score some merchandise, and feel good about themselves, all in the name of social justice and all while the real shops were left alone.

Some of the loots were smash hits. A couple years ago, Nike had an incredible one in Los Diego. Billions of dollars' worth of shoes, hats, and streetwear were all packed in the wooden store. The people went nuts. They tore the place to bits in matter of minutes, but they loved the stuff! Anyone who was anyone in Hollywood was wearing their new Nike gear the next day. It showed how much they cared, and Nike got a ton of press. It set a new, high bar.

But other loots didn't fare as well.

A few months after the Los Diego one, in Nebraska, came the night of "Bubbles and Blood." It set the low bar . . . and became the stuff of corporate nightmares.

The Nebraska loot started off relatively straightforward. A corporation built a big, unmarked, fake store in an empty parking lot. State media announced the time and location, and a mob formed right on schedule. The people who made up the mob were the start of the problems. What was in the store made things even worse.

The crowd that arrived in New Lincoln that night was mostly comprised of "Birdies." Birdies were outspoken and quite violent advocates for a more sympathetic, non-judgmental portrayal of all winged creatures in every form of media. They were pretty riled up before the loot started. Evidently, on the march to the parking lot a few of the Birdies had seen an older lady feeding breadcrumbs to some pigeons and thought it was offensive beyond words. There was a confrontation. Fortunately, the old woman had pepper spray. She used it and somehow managed to escape. This drove the Birdies into a simmering rage. When they finally arrived at the loot, the angry Birdies descended onto the store like a swarm of well . . . angry birdies. And to make matters worse, all they found inside were cases and cases of cherry-mango-flavored Fresca. The soda company thought the flavor would be a huge hit but the Birdies were livid and went ballistic. They wanted stuff. Shirts, headphones, something cool—not lukewarm cans of cherry-mango diet soda. And like I said, they were already jacked up that night. After they found nothing but cans of Fresca, they went on a citywide rampage.

All night long, large mobs of Birdies roamed the streets

of New Lincoln throwing unopened cans of Fresca like missiles at drones, people, each other, and anyone or anything else they could find. It was horrific. Hospitals were overrun with patients, stumbling in, smelling faintly of cherries and mango, bleeding from soda-can traumas.

People still talk about the night of Bubbles and Blood.

Citizens demanded reforms after that. And reforms they got. Ever since, the law required the loots to have better stuff. Organized groups of criminals bent on mob violence had standards that needed to be met.

So, I needed to find a good loot. Tonight. Or at the very least an undocumented human center—a UDC—that hopefully would still be open.

UDCs and loots were never near Sky Tower or other elite pockets of the city. Laws prohibited them from being too close. Our glorious leaders made sure to keep the lowlifes away from the nice neighborhoods.

Red's place wasn't that far from one of the stadiums where they occasionally hosted the mob-fueled giveaways, so I made my way in its general direction to see if I might get lucky for once and find a loot going on tonight.

As I scurried along, I started realizing just how bad San Josisco had become. It was even worse than I thought. It was bad during the day from the inside of a vehicle, but at night, things went to a whole different level. Just one rundown crime infested stack of pods after another. My plan was to skirt the edges of the nice neighborhoods on my way to the stadium parking lot. The trouble was, there just weren't enough nice neighborhoods to skirt.

I kept to the side streets as much as possible. Head down, hands in pockets. I tried to walk at a speed that said, "Don't bother me, I'm going somewhere," without being aggressively fast. If I would've walked too fast, it would've made me look scared, and some random thug would've probably stopped me with a, "Where do you think you're going?". Those never end well. Trust me. So, I did my best to split the difference.

Occasionally, a small security drone or two would pass by and I'd step into the shadows of the closest broken-down building or stack of living pods. Sometimes they'd hover and loiter, and I'd wait in total fear for them to float away. Every second they didn't I was certain they'd seen me and were calling for back up and that would be the end. It was terrifying. Every time.

One of those times, I was just about to step out of the shadows and start again when a high-end luxury aircar cruised by overhead. I stopped and watched the shiny black behemoth, full of super-rich people headed to who knows where. Their interior lights were off as they zoomed over the rabble below. That was a common security practice. With an expensive vehicle like that, you wanted to draw as little attention to yourself as possible so some lowlife wouldn't try to knock you out of the sky with a homemade projectile launcher.

I could see why someone would want to do that too. San Josisco's wealthy elite had no idea how it felt to be cold and lonely without a penny to your name, all the while some rich bastard just flew over you like you never mattered.

The sound of the aircar faded as they sailed into the distance. I couldn't help but wonder who was inside and where they were going. Probably somewhere fantastic and warm. Lots of champagne and fake smiles. Important conversations about celebrities and who was sleeping with who, and how badly they wished they could change things—how they wanted to help the needy. How much they cared.

I stood there and blankly stared at the ebony, cloudy sky long after the aircar had gone. That would never be me. Ever. My life as I knew it was over. All my hopes were gone. My future. Mars. All of it. I wanted to cry.

The sound of glass shattering, and rowdy laughter snapped me out of my despair. I had to keep moving. *Just do the next thing in front of you*, I told myself. If I stopped to think about the totality of everything, I'd be crushed. So, I walked some more. Towards the stadium . . . and hopefully a loot. I had to get a jacket.

All went well for a few blocks. And then I encountered a group of kids playing in the street. They were all wearing homemade masks. They looked ridiculous and dangerous at the same time. Not a good combo. From a distance, it looked like they had taken long pieces of cardboard or old soda cartons from the trash and ripped eyeholes towards the top. Then slipped the rest of the cardboard down the front of their shirts to hold the thing in place, up over their faces. They were using garbage as masks. On their faces. Disgusting. Just too gross.

On the next block I found a piece of cardboard in the trash and decided to make my own. It was a completely horrifying experience, but I had to disguise myself.

After I carefully examined an old stain-riddled box and found the cleanest area I could, I ripped a longish, skinny, triangle piece from it. I poked eyeholes in the wide end and slid the skinny end down the front of my t-shirt. It actually worked. The whole thing smelled like old fried chicken and mildew, but it did the job. One problem solved. The mask was nothing to be proud of, but at least now I had a way to cover my face and hide my identity from all the drones and cameras that filled this craphole city.

That small level of security didn't alleviate all my fears. As I kept moving, a couple times I stopped and hid because I thought someone was following me. Maybe it was my nerves or maybe it was me being rightfully cautious. Regardless, everything had me jumpy.

I couldn't see very well through my garbage mask either. I fiddled with it and tried ripping into the eyeholes to make them bigger. But I was concerned that I might rip them too large and reveal too much of my face. Stopping to remove the mask and work on it was out of the question. Just the thought of someone being right behind me made me too afraid to do that. Imagination or not, I didn't want to take the chance.

All worries about my mask soon disappeared. Lights from around the stadium lit up the sky in the distance. Hopefully they were just the parking lot lights and not the stadium lights themselves. If there was some sporting event there tonight, then it was going to be another swing and a miss for me.

Ten minutes later and relief washed over me. I had lucked out. It was just parking lot lights. A loot—no game in the stadium. And from the size of the large crowd, it looked like it was going to be a good one.

Peaceful protesters were already bouncing around and checking out the big, looming, wooden building in the parking lot. At first, they had sort of put some effort into making them look like stores, with siding and even fake signs out front. Now, they didn't waste money on those extraneous details; now the loot buildings were simply cheap structures with nothing more than the thinnest of wood covering the outsides. The only thing any rioter ever cared about was what was inside the buildings. And this one was huge.

Six, surly teenagers walked towards the main area and I slunk in behind them. They were rolling on something, even as I had no clue what it was.

Maniacal laughter would burst out from all of them and just as suddenly stop. And then it would start again. They didn't say anything. It was just insane cackling, followed by silence, followed by spontaneous, hyena-like laughing again.

One of them took off the wolfman mask he was wearing and shoved it at me. His pupils were dilated so badly they took up all his irises and seemed to push into the white of his eyes. It was like they were just two orbs of pure asphalt. Partnered with his possessed, ear-to-ear grin, and it was quite disturbing.

I hesitated and backed off. He thrust the mask at me again and again. Eventually, I figured out he wanted my cardboard mask as a trade. It took the wolfman mask, whipped off my ripped-up cardboard one, and handed it over. He was delighted. Or maybe he wasn't. His giant smile never faded and he laughed like the drugged up lunatic he was as he put it on.

With a deep breath, I slipped the wolfman mask over my head and peeled away from the hyena gang. I moved closer to the people who were gearing up for the loot rush and worked on figuring out where the best spot to be was for when the action started.

Intense lights flooded the staging area. They made it easy to see everyone's tats, piercings, implants, scarring, body modifications, and everything else. Probably over half of everyone there was high. Maybe that's why they didn't seem cold. I was freezing.

A jumbotron TV sat inside a fence. Closed captions as tall as I was flashed at the bottom of the screen. Ads about the usual stuff ran on it. First it was how we all needed to downsize and live in stacked pods. Then it was a commercial telling us to eat more insect-based meals. After that, a PSA encouraged us to report our neighbors if they violated any number of micro-aggressions. Finally, an ad created just for the loot came on. It invited everyone to stick around after the storming of the fake store to witness the marriage of a bisexual woman, who identified as a male raccoon, to a small bucket. Not a person who identified as a bucket either. An actual bucket.

Boos erupted from some in the crowd. A larger group quickly confronted them. "What's your problem? You bigots? You Nazis?"

"No," one of the booing people said. "We're booing because the bucket is plastic. If xir really was in love, the bucket would be wooden."

"Oh, so you think making stuff out of trees is okay? You're a tree murderer enthusiast!" a woman with a hairdo that looked like bright blue tree foliage shouted back.

Someone threw a punch—a weak punch, but a punch nonetheless—and then everyone started hitting back. The scuffle wasn't much of anything and it stayed contained. Most people gathered around to watch and laugh at it. I backed away, hugging myself for warmth.

The jumbotron screen finally returned to the programming all those ads had interrupted. That's when I realized it was on Channel 9. And that's when I wished it had just kept running those stupid commercials.

Kira Tripp and Sharyl were on the screen. My heart pounded and my stomach tried to escape through my butthole as I watched and read the captions.

". . . and I hope everyone will tune in for my new reality series." Kira said. The camera zoomed close on her and cropped out Sharyl. "After a long time planning, I'm excited that I can finally announce it right now. So, what's it going to be about? We're going to be hunting down some of the most-wanted criminals. And who better could we start with than Avery Davies-Plott—the felon experts have already dubbed *Monster Man!*"

I couldn't believe it. They were going to hunt me down! And they called me a felon when I hadn't been convicted of anything. And they'd given me a serial killer name.

"And, yes, you heard me right," Kira continued. "I did say *we* are going to be hunting down criminals. So, let's meet the others who will be joining me. We'll start with Sharyl Breck, the ex of Monster Man. Sharyl's even quit her job so she can devote all of her time to this important hunt." The camera zoomed out to capture Kira and Sharyl. "Are you ready for this, Sharyl?"

Sharyl bounced up and down. "Yes! Yes! A thousand times, yes! Oh, this is so exciting, Kira! I never dreamed I'd be the star of my own reality series!"

My eyes threatened to pop out of my wolfman mask. That was ALL Sharyl dreamed about? Having her own reality show had always been her dream? That was all she had? That was what kept her going? Well, that and her disappointment in me.

Kira cleared her throat. "Well, you're not really the star. After all, that's *me*. But you're definitely going to have a lot of the focus for the first season. You're going to help us get in the head of Avery; let us know how he thinks, what he likes, where he's going to go next. All of that stuff."

"Right, right, right," Sharyl said. "I can't wait to get started!"

"Me too," Kira agreed. "But let's not get ahead of ourselves.

First, we need to let our viewers know the name of the show. We're calling it, *Badass Bunch*—no *the* in front of it. Just *Badass Bunch*. Having a *the* in front would lower the badass factor by like fifty percent. And this is going to be totally tits-out badass! Female produced, female driven, and female focused. We're not taking crap from anybody and we're going to show everyone how badass bitches get things done."

"Yes!" Sharyl squealed and hugged Kira.

Kira firmly removed her. "Yes, yes. We're all excited. But we're still on *live* TV and I still have some more introductions to do."

Sharyl quickly recovered and switched up to a super serious face. "Right. I'm sorry."

The camera panned, removing Sharyl from the screen and pushing Kira to its far right. Three mean looking women were standing there, arms crossed and exaggerated scowls on their faces to imply a sense of danger. It worked. They looked dangerous. Or at least dramatically upset. Sharyl walked back into view, positioning herself between Kira and the three profoundly unhappy women. Kira shrugged and continued her intros.

"These three, powerful women here are going to be hugely important to *Badass Bunch*," Kira announced. "They are our professional muscle. They'll be taking the lead when it comes time to do the actual hunting and capturing of Avery."

What the hell? They hired muscle? Wasn't the entire city of San Josisco enough? They hired muscle? This nightmare was never going to end.

"Yes!" Sharyl exclaimed with a big smile. She caught herself again and gave the camera her super serious face. Then for some reason she spat on the floor. My guess was she thought it looked tough.

"Denise was my first recruit." Kira gestured at the woman closest to her.

Based on Sharyl standing nearby her, I guessed that Denise was around five-eight. Thick blonde hair flowed down her back to her waist, framing huge curves. Muscle tone rippled across every inch of her exposed skin (well, not her face or neck) but she wasn't bulky in the least. Both of her arms sported tattoos. She had some small, wispy tattoos next to the outer corners of her eyes too, like a bit of extra, ornate, eye makeup.

"She's a military veteran—" Kira explained.

"Thank you for your service!" Sharyl blurted out.

"—and spent over five years in the infantry, where she received all sorts of decorations and awards. She told me she even has the United Nations Army Service Ribbon, which I'm *sure* is highly prestigious," Kira continued. "She's received experimental eye enhancements too, which effectively give her night vision."

"I can see just like a cat in the dark," Denise purred. "And just like a cat, I don't miss when I go hunting for prey." She winked at Sharyl.

Sharyl gave a tiny wave back and moved closer to Kira.

"Lydia is the next in line," Kira said.

Lydia flipped long, brunette hair over her right shoulder. She was slightly taller than Denise, but I don't think she hit the six-foot mark. Big, beautiful eyes dominated her face, and she had smoother definition to her body than Denise.

"She's another military veteran," Kira said. "She's been working in the private sector for, what, now three years?"

"That's right," Lydia replied. "I'm an expert tracker and shot. And since we've already broached the subject, I have muscular implants in my glutes, legs, chest, and arms, which give me increased speed and agility."

"Wow!" Sharyl breathed, obliviously impressed.

"And I'm Renée," the third woman said.

"Yes, go right ahead. Interruption seems to be the name of the game today," Kira muttered.

"I worked for the federal government . . . in some sort of capacity," Renée advised.

"You mean like in secret," Sharyl whispered.

Renée smiled politely. "Yes, sweetie. And let's just say my

little specialty is that the biotechnological enhancements I have in me have made me even stronger than I was before I got them . . . and . . . I'm planning on getting hearing enhancements put behind my eardrums but there's a waiting list." She slapped her fist into her hand.

Like Denise, she had plenty of tattoos on her arms. And she had even more extravagant ones on her face. They rather enhanced her good looks.

Sharyl grabbed Kira's arm. "This is all so overwhelming. It's like we've got our own team of superwomen right here!"

"That's the idea." Kira removed Sharyl's hands. "These women will have other women working in subordinate positions for them. We didn't call this show *Badass Bunch* for nothing. We're going to find Avery Davies-Plott—Monster Man —and we're going to bring him to justice. And we're going to look great and have tons of fun doing it."

"I can't wait to get started," Sharyl said.

"Well then, let's do that. Here is a photo of our target . . ."

Oh, great, I thought. A big ol' shot of my mug suddenly filled the screen.

". . . and if our viewers provide us with any tips that lead to us apprehending him and turning him over to authorities, not only will you get the reward San Josisco is offering for him, but you'll also receive an additional $250,000 from *Badass Bunch*."

I didn't watch any more of it. I couldn't. I reached up and touched my new wolfman mask just to remind myself I was still wearing it. Even then I felt totally exposed. As if everyone in the crowd of hundreds knew exactly who I was. It was terrifying. I was sure I was going to get mobbed. Of course, nothing happened. The jumbotron switched to a commercial for seaweed chips.

My heart thundered away in my chest. I was in full fight-or-flight mode and as usual, I was choosing flight. Everyone knew what I looked like. Everyone wanted to get me, including this team of highly specialized bounty hunters led by my ex and her new best friend. But I couldn't run just yet. I needed a stupid jacket or I'd freeze to death.

CHAPTER TWELVE

My only hope was inside the fake store they'd set up for the loot. When was the stupid thing going to begin? Was there a starting pistol or a flare? Panic was starting to set in, and I moved around a little bit faster. I'd no idea where I was going to go but I knew I couldn't stick around the loot forever. Maybe if I could get the crowd fired up, we'd all just storm the building, and I could grab a new fleece coat and be on my way. Although, with my luck, the thing would probably be sponsored by Legos and everyone would end up being pissed-off, and I'd be killed by an angry mob.

But I couldn't wait any longer. I looked over to a big guy standing next to me. He was wearing a black bandana with skulls on it, a fluffy pink jacket that looked insanely warm, and a kilt. His face was buried in his phone, but I chanced it and interrupted him.

"Excuse me . . . when does the looting start?" I half-shouted over the din of the crowd.

He looked up from his phone. "What?"

"When do we, you know . . .loot? Is there a signal?" Maybe he couldn't hear me through my mask.

"What are you? Some kind of fed?" he asked. "We aren't *looters*; we're *peaceful protesters*."

"Yeah, yeah, yeah. Right. I'm sorry. So . . . when does the . . .peaceful protesting start?"

"Ohhhhh." The realization hit him. "Is this your first time?"

"Yeah, it is," I admitted. "I really need a jacket."

He looked me up and down. "Yeah, you do. Well, here's how it works noob. It starts when it starts. We all just watch our phones until something happens in the news that's just wrong and then we let our voice be heard."

He seemed to think that made perfect sense. And it kind of did.

"So, if nothing happens, we just stand here all night?" I asked, incredulous.

"Don't worry. There's too much injustice in the world. Something always happens." He scrutinized his phone again. Seconds later, his eyes narrowed. "He we go."

"What?"

"Supreme Court just came out with a decision." He read from his phone as his eyes filled with tears. "23 to 7 ruling that Daryl Kinnison can't be a Navy SEAL just because he was born without arms and legs. What bullshit!"

"Aren't Navy SEALs supposed to swim?" I blurted out.

Pink jacket was now openly weeping. "He's allergic to water! That shouldn't stop him from living his dream. I hate this place!"

Others in the crowd were picking up on the same story. A chant started, quite low at first. "Daryl . . . Daryl . . . Daryl."

It escalated, with pink jacket joining in. He eyeballed me through his tears.

"Daryl!" I quickly intoned. "Daryl!"

The chant reached a crescendo and the mob became one, starting to advance on the loot building. I was swept up as the mass of people all ran towards the wooden, piñata store. "For Daryl!" the peaceful protesters screamed.

People started running. Some slammed into others and bodies hit the ground. The tip of my shower shoe caught a crack in the pavement, and I lurched forward.

"Gah!" My hand shot out and I steadied myself against the back of pink jacket. Falling would be a disaster. I put my hand out again and grabbed a fistful of the brilliant fabric.

Dude was huge and moving like a freight train. People were being launched out of his way left and right. The piñata store was fast approaching, and he wasn't slowing down. I held on for dear life. Praying my sandals didn't fly off my feet in the hustle.

"Wait a minute? Are you just going to run into one of the walls?" I shouted. "Because there's no way you're going to bust through it!"

He didn't hear me. He—we—hit the wooden wall of the fake loot store at full speed.

"Yahhhhh!" I shut my eyes and prepared to bounce off it with pink jacket, expecting that we'd then be trampled to death. Instead, he shattered his way through the wall like a pink fluffy fist through an old cereal box. Wood went flying everywhere. We both fell forward into the piñata store.

Others rushed in behind us. But the opening was only big enough for one or two people at a time to get through. I jumped up off the cold floor as soon as I could. One person stepped on my hand. Another trampled my back. But I wasn't dead.

Looters had smashed through other sides of the structure, and it was filling up fast. Soon, people were ramming into me from every direction.

"What's in here?" I must've spun around five times from all the pushing and shoving. Finally, I oriented myself and found out what the loot of the loot was.

Boxes and boxes of Dr. Wei's Frozen Chinese Pizza. Shit.

I grabbed one. "Are you kidding me?" My grip on it tightened and my fingernails sank into the cardboard. "The one time I loot and I'm in a giant wooden room full of crappy pizza?" I squinted and read Dr. Wei's slogan. "'The pizza for your party *and* the communist party—now with provable cheese and rice'? What does that even mean?"

Everyone else was enraged too. Frozen pizzas started flying through the air. Shrimp flavored, cricket covered, and provable-cheese-only style pies were sailing all around like icy Frisbees of death.

I slammed the stupid frozen pizza to the floor and howled with frustration. Then, out of the corner of my eye I saw it. Hidden in a corner was a small display of Dr. Wei's Pizza promotional gear. Hats, t-shirts, and one, wonderful jacket. It was a windbreaker with the logo of Dr. Wei's smiling cartoon face on the back.

Energy rushed through me and I made a mad dash towards the display, pushing and shoving my way through the mob. Pizza air traffic became worse, and I was ducking and dodging frozen projectiles the entire time. One slightly grazed my back but it was no big deal. Two more steps and I reached the display. My hand seized the jacket. So did someone else's. A guy wearing a surgical mask.

"Let go. I grabbed it first," I told him.

He didn't let go. Crap. Was I going to have to fight for this thing? I jerked on it, desperately hoping he'd just let me have it. No such luck.

"Please, I need it!" I hoped I was loud enough for him to hear me over the roars of the enraged and the shrieks of those wounded by flying pizzas hitting them in various body parts with incredible force.

He pulled off his surgical mask and smiled wildly at me, his eyes mirroring his crazed lips. "I need it too!"

As I always did, I looked around for help. Pink jacket was still only feet away, and he was looking straight at me—no, just past me. He had a pizza in his giant hand. He wound up and threw it with all of his considerable might.

I quickly ducked and one of Dr. Wei's finest zipped right over my head. A loud, wet smack resounded behind me. The jacket went slack and I pulled the prize close to my chest.

Turning around, I saw the crazy surgeon guy holding his mouth. His eyes were wide with shock. Blood and bits of what looked like teeth seeped through his fingers and a frozen pie lay at his feet. Damn that had to hurt.

I turned to wave my thanks to pink jacket. But he had disappeared into the melee. Surgical mask guy started to scream in pain.

I put on the jacket at warp speed. The loot was now a full-on brawl. I was never going to make it back to the opening pink jacket made when he barreled into the piñata store. But close by was a small hole in the bottom of the wall. It looked like I might be able to fit through it.

I scurried towards it and dropped to my hands and knees. I could see outside. Inside, some kid in a kimono and motorcycle helmet lit a Molotov cocktail and threw it into the crowd. Screams of anger and injury transformed into terrified screaming.

There was no way I could fit both my shoulders through the opening in the wall at the same time. I shoved one arm through it first, pushed my head out next, and lastly dragged the rest of my body, sucking in everything I had with all my might.

"Made it!" Light flickered from inside and someone else was right behind me either trying to squeeze through the same hole or grab my leg. I wasn't going to wait around and find out which.

I rolled away and jumped to my feet. The parking lot was strangely empty. Just a handful of security guards stood by the jumbotron. Kira and Sharyl were on again, maybe talking more about *Badass Bunch,* I couldn't hear them over the sound of the violence.

As nonchalantly as I could, I started walking away. I had no idea where I should go but moving in the opposite direction of the screen was as good of a direction as any.

CHAPTER THIRTEEN

About six blocks later I came across what used to be a park and felt confident enough to sit down on a bench and try to get my act together. Bums, tents, druggies, and the usual run of the mill rejects of society filled the small plaza. It was a good sign that the authorities weren't interested in what was going on in the area, but not exactly the safest place to stop. I chose one of the benches close enough to the street where I could run for my life if I had to. I tilted up my mask and put my head in my hands.

What was I going to do? What was my plan? I had to come up with one and yet I couldn't. Running was the only thing I could think of but that seemed stupid. Everybody and their mother were after me. And then there were the security drones, security cameras, facial recognition software, and, of course, every person alive had a camera on their phone. If just one person photographed or recorded me—on purpose or incidentally—and posted that imagery to the internet, there'd be a good chance I'd be done for. Government bots scraped up pretty much everything on the web eventually and if somebody captured me walking the streets and uploaded it to his social media account or whatever, AI might catch it and alert social welfare to where I was. That would be the end for me.

But what else could I do? Turn myself in and hope for justice through the legal system? Right. It didn't even really cross my mind as an actual possibility. After what I'd gone through at the social welfare detention center earlier, there was no way I was going to do that.

Realizing just how bad my situation was started to give me a mini panic attack. After all, I always played everything by the book. I never took risks. And I never did anything that I wasn't supposed to do. Yet now I was a wanted man running from social welfare and a team of bounty hunters—plus my ex —who were part of a reality show. How could I possibly escape from that? I was used to taking my driverless government car and driverless taxis everywhere. Simply *walking* all the time was an unusual experience for me. Even if I could figure out how to stroll out of San Josisco—avoid all the security systems and people looking for me—it wasn't like I could just start over somewhere. I mean, sure, some people did that. Illegal immigrants—I mean, undocumented migrants—just walked into this country and started living a new life. But they had the whole Bureau of Integrating Undocumented Americans to help them out. That wouldn't be the case for me because I was a citizen who was, again, on the run from social welfare, bounty hunters, and my ex.

Where am I going to go? What am I going to do? The thoughts kept repeating in my mind. *No Mars either.*

I'd be lucky to get a job as a busboy in Reno. There'd be no way I'd get on a rocket to freedom to Mars. Those things were always heavily screened and monitored. I was doomed. The rest of my life was going to be total shit no matter what I did.

"Your pizza sucks."

The gruff voice startled me, and I raised my head out of my hands. An old bum with a filthy beard, worn-out winter coat, knit cap, and shopping cart stood in front of me. Very close, I might add. He had no respect for my personal space.

"Are you talking to me?" I sat back as far as I could against the bench.

"I said your pizza sucks." He pointed at my jacket.

I grabbed the collar. "Oh, this. I don't work for Dr. Wei's Pizza. I got this at a loot that's going on at the stadium. I was really cold."

He looked me over and lingered on my oversized shower shoes. "You living on the streets?"

I thought about it for a second. "Yeah, I guess I am. Now."

He sat down on the far edge of the bench. The rank smell emanating from him was strong enough that I thought my eyes might start watering.

His eyes narrowed and he stared at me as if he were about to say the most important thing in the world. After a moment he cleared his throat. "Don't let your string break. If your string breaks, you're just a stick. You need to be an arrow, son." He paused and looked at me meaningfully. "Unless you wanna be a stick."

A long silence ensued, and the bum seemed to think if he held his gaze, his wisdom would sink into me.

"I'm a stick," he added. "I'm okay with that now. But when you're new, you need to figure it out. Or you'll end up a stick whether you wanna be or not." The same look from him as if he was giving me something incredibly substantial.

I nodded and hoped that acting like he made sense would appease him.

He leaned towards me and didn't break eye contact. "That's what I wish someone would've told me, so I'm telling you."

"Thank you. I'll work on it," I replied.

"You'll work on it? Hell, you're half stick already." He looked at me as if I was the crazy one. "Okay." He sighed and shook his head. "You got any food?"

"I don't. I'm really new. This is my first day . . . you know . . . being homeless," I feebly admitted.

He stood up and started rummaging through his cart. A fresh blast of body odor washed over me and I winced. The bum produced a half empty box of chocolate-covered donuts and a small carton of orange juice.

"Here." He handed them to me. "Take these. You need 'em more than me."

I eagerly grabbed them. "Thanks." My stomach was growling. Plus, I had no idea what Mr. Stick would do if I didn't accept his generosity.

"No need for thanks," he said. "I had six of 'em already.

They hand out donuts and orange juice like candy at the plasma center. I've eaten enough of these things for a lifetime."

"Well, I appreciate it."

Stick took another long look at me. "Now, you need to go, boy. You're sitting on my bed. I fought hard for this bench and you can't have it. I'm tired. I gave you some food and the best damned advice I got. You better find a place to go and it ain't here."

I stood up a little too fast and almost dropped the donuts. "Oh, I'm sorry. I had no idea. I wasn't trying to take your spot."

"Damn right, you're not. I'll beat your ass. Now get outta here." He shooed me away with his hands.

He plopped down and I fumbled around with my food and drink.

"You can't stay here and watch me sleep either," Mr. Stick told me.

"Right. No, I wasn't going to do that. It's just that . . . I'm sorta thinking about where I'm going to go."

He leaned toward me and lowered his voice. "Don't stay in a park, gangs will eat you alive. Don't go to a shelter, they'll eat you alive. And for god's sake, don't go near convenience stores . . ."

"They'll eat me alive?"

Mr. Stick nodded as if he was some sort of sage. "If I was you, I'd head to the airport and pretend to be a stranded traveler." He reexamined my strange apparel. "Actually, train station might be better. More believable. And if they kick you out, you can always hop a train and ride the rails!" He laughed heartily.

The idea of me on top of a freight train may have been quite amusing to him, but Mr. Stick's suggestion gave me an idea. I could hop a train and get out of town. All I had to do was wait for one to roll out and jump on. It would work. I knew it would. Now all I needed to do was find a train.

"Thanks again for the juice and donuts." I gave him a slight nod and started off, trying to remember the last place I'd seen train tracks.

"Good luck! Don't let your string break! Don't be a stick unless you wanna be," the old bum called out.

I stopped and turned back. "What does that mean? I don't get it."

He laughed again. "'Cause you're almost a stick! Think about it while you're walking. Arrows get it. Sticks don't." Another burst of merriment, or craziness, spewed forth from him. "Stay away from shelters."

"They'll eat me alive," I muttered.

I gave him a small wave and headed off with my donuts and orange juice.

CHAPTER FOURTEEN

Everything tastes better when you're hungry and donuts are no exception. They were delicious. But I made the mistake of eating them first and drinking the OJ second. It was almost a cruel joke but at least I got the liquid into me. I had to stay hydrated as I continued moving.

After my tooth-coating snack, I slid the wolfman mask the full way back down and headed east, sticking to side streets the whole time. I figured my best odds at catching a train on its way out of town were to the east.

The craziness of it all wasn't lost on me. Little old me was trying to hop a train out of town like an old timey bum. Never in a million years had I thought I would be planning on doing something so outlandish. But it was a pretty solid idea all things considered. I was pleased I ran into Mr. Stick.

I wondered what had happened to him that drove him from wherever he started life to living on the streets. And what did he mean about strings and arrows? Was it a Shakespeare thing? I kind of remembered a quote about slings and arrows from a play they made us read in middle school. Maybe Mr. Stick used to be an English teacher or something.

Gunshots rang out in the distance and I froze up. I was certain they were gunshots. And they couldn't have been more than a couple of blocks away. Frantically, I looked around and tried to gain my bearings. I had completely zoned out while I walked, ate, and mused about stupid crap. Tiredness was no excuse. My life was on the line and I needed to keep it together until I could find a place to sleep, which, evidently, was going to be in or on top of a train.

Just keep heading east and try not to get jumped, I told myself. It became the new mantra I repeated in my head.

Adrenaline kicked in and I became hyperaware of everything. Even with my former job of driving around the city and being a toilet paper cop, I hadn't covered every part of San Josisco. And I definitely hadn't covered it by foot . . . or at night. Every corner and alleyway was another risk of getting robbed, beaten up, or worse. Desperate people, the homeless, and straight up criminals owned the night. And there were a bunch of them. Technically I had just joined the ranks of the homeless and that didn't make me feel any better.

The familiar hum of drones sounded the same as an alarm to me. I ducked under a torn-up awning in front of a pawn shop and waited them out as they flew overhead. Across the way, a couple of rough-looking guys noticed me. One of them pointed and his buddy sneered and laughed. I slouched and started off again.

My ears strained to figure out if anyone was following me. The wolfman mask sucked. No wonder that kid gave it to me. Its eyeholes were way too small, and I could barely hear anything over the sound of my hot donut and orange juice breath bouncing around inside it. The fear finally became too much for me and I put my flip-flop feet into high gear.

I hustled down a back alley as fast as I could. At its end, I made a quick left onto a street and zipped into yet another alleyway on my right. My lungs burned and my feet slowed. A green, rusting dumpster filled one side of the filth strewn passageway and I hunkered down behind it. I pulled my mask off and listened. Nothing. I quieted my breathing and gave it a few more seconds. Still nothing and my muscles started relaxing.

East. Keep heading east and don't get mugged, you stupid stick. I thought.

Down the alley, a door opened and light spilled out of the back of a shop. Some young kitchen worker struggled out, a gigantic bag of garbage in each hand. I didn't move and tried to breathe even quieter.

The kid made it about ten feet toward the dumpster and me when out of the shadows another figure leapt out. He smashed the kid over the head with a pipe. It made a wet, thudding sound and the kid fell to the ground hard. The attacker quickly rifled through his victim's pockets. Shivers ran through me, and I hoped the thug didn't notice me. After what seemed like forever but was probably only a minute, he stood up, checked all around him, and casually walked away.

Air whisked out of my lungs. The kid who came out with the garbage wasn't moving. I hesitated and worked on getting up the courage to go check on him. But I convinced myself he was probably just knocked out, like in the movies. Finally, the kid groaned and slowly rolled onto his back. Okay. He's alive. *That's good. Right?* I told myself.

I stood up. Another shadow moved, this one from the rooftop. I slid on the wolfman mask and wasted no time in sprinting out of the alley. No more alleys for me. That was a new rule, a new addition to my mantra.

Keep heading east. Try not to get jumped. And no alleys.

As I rounded the corner onto a main street, I nearly ran into two drunk guys wearing old grimy coveralls and trying to ride a sanitation robot. I breathed a sigh of relief. That was more like it. Drunk people messing with bots. That kind of insanity I could handle. The normal kind.

Everything seemed pretty routine for a few blocks. But then things started to get a little dicey. Whoops and cries rang out. Some gang had successfully pirated a delivery drone out of the sky. Their celebration included starting a fire on the rooftop where they had conducted the operation. Others on the street below cheered them on. Sirens blared out in the distance, signaling the impending arrival of security drones.

None of it slowed me down. I kept walking and tried not to focus on how much my feet were killing me. On top of that, I concentrated on making sure my concentrating on ignoring my pain didn't distract me from staying aware of my situation and where I was going.

Between all that I pondered the pseudo riddle the old bum had told me about sticks, arrows and strings breaking. As far as I could tell, I had deciphered his bit of deep life advice and it wasn't that deep. It was simple. The string was your mind, and a person is supposed to be an arrow. If you lose your mind aka your string broke, you'd just be a useless stick. Why did I think a bum would have legit wisdom? He could have just said, "Don't go crazy," and left it at that. Too easy, I guess. Right now, though, I had to admit my string wasn't breaking but it was certainly starting to fray. It was fraying a lot. I was feeling very stick-like. I needed rest. Soon. Or my string *would* snap. Then I'd be truly screwed.

Eventually the number of public housing buildings began dwindling. I was moving into one of the industrial areas of the city. And I couldn't shake the feeling of déjà vu. An old, corrugated metal warehouse, half burned down ages ago, caught my eye. I could've sworn I had seen it before. And then I realized that I had indeed.

Just a few weeks ago I was in this part of the city inspecting restrooms. One of the businesses had brought a little bit of excitement into my job. Some shipping company, full of employees who must've had dysentery based on the amount of toilet paper they were going through, got reported and I spent nearly half a day finding the first clues as to who their black-market supplier was. Yup. That was an out of the ordinary day just a couple of weeks ago. It seemed glorious compared to my current situation.

Stumbling onto this section of town again was huge stroke of luck, though. If I remembered correctly, there was a little mini-mart close by. And a rail yard wasn't that far away from that. Mr. Stick's admonition to stay away from convenience stores rang through my mind. But I promptly ignored it. I picked up my pace and headed in the general direction of the mini-mart.

My happiness was short-lived. My right foot slipped on what I hoped was soup and not vomit. I hobbled over to the curb and scraped it off. Something moved. I snapped my head up and caught a glimpse of a person ducking behind a nearby building. Was I being paranoid? Probably some bum looking for a place to sleep. Now wasn't the time to flip out. It was just a bum.

After a few more scrapes on the curb, I abandoned my shower shoe cleaning session and moved on toward my goal. The familiar slapping sound of my footwear had evolved into a slap and squish with every step. I grimaced but I could live with it. Maybe the mini-mart would have a hose or a water spigot outside and I could wash off my foot . . . in the freezing night. Even if it didn't, it wouldn't be a big deal. Once I was there, I could rest for a minute and think about the next step in my plan. The hopping a train part.

Right now, I couldn't stop thinking about that person ducking into the building. I had to be sure it was just a bum. Before I made the turn on the next street I quickly looked back. Nothing. Or did a shadow next to that one building have a weird shape to it? Was that a person? There was no way I was going to wait and find out. My string couldn't take much more of this.

I slap-squished my way down the street and saw the dim glow of mini-mart store lights in the distance. So very close. Then a plan sprang into mind.

If I took the next right, then a left, and approached the place from the opposite direction, I thought I could verify if someone was following me by doubling back. Hopefully, I'd see them before they saw me. That was a perfect idea and I congratulated myself for gaining a few street smarts.

I executed my plan and reached the opposite side of the street from the little store. Whoever ran it was a brave soul who kept it open 24 hours. Bars lined every window and flickering neon signs advertised the lotto, booze, and a variety of bug-based snacks. I settled into a doorframe and waited for my shadowy follower to appear.

Two minutes passed and no one showed up. Maybe it had been just a bum. Good for me. I started across the street towards the dingy glow of the mini-mart.

Halfway across and the looming convenience store signs reminded me how hungry I was. Of course, without a wallet, credit card, or phone, I'd have no way to buy anything. Even if I had them, it would've been stupid to buy anything with a card or my phone. The instant I did it would've alerted the authorities to exactly where I was. So, no food for me. Dammit.

Stealing crossed my mind. I could just shoplift whatever I needed. Boom. So easy. I'd be in and out before anyone would know what was happening. That idea rapidly evaporated. If the owner had the balls to be open at this time of the night in this neighborhood, he'd certainly have the balls to stop a guy like me. Dammit again.

Looking around, I realized I knew exactly which direction I needed to head to reach the rail yard. I could practically see it from here. So that was good. First, though, I was going to check the side of the convenience store to see if there was a hose or a faucet there. Whatever the liquid was that I stepped in had seeped between my toes and was driving me crazy.

Thankfully, the parking lot was empty. I kept my head down but tried to act casual and moved with a purpose. As I got close to the front doors of the mini mart, a pickup truck pulled into a space just ahead of me. What a relic that thing was. It was the kind that someone actually had to drive. Although that wasn't completely unheard of on San Josisco streets. It had Arizona plates. That was a bad sign. The only people who lived out there were hardcore criminal types. The kind of people they talk about on the news. Outlaw gangs. That kind of thing.

I passed it and heard its door open and shut behind me. Hair stood up on the back of my neck and it was all I could do to keep walking at the same pace. *Don't worry. Whoever it is will just think you're another upstanding San Josisco citizen walking around in a wolfman mask*, I thought.

"Hey!" a voice called from behind me.

Shit. Bounty hunter? Outlaw? All the horrible choices raced through my mind. I did the only thing I could do. I ignored it. It wasn't the first voice I heard yelling something similar tonight and I assumed it wouldn't be my last.

"Avery. Avery Davies-Plott."

My right foot hit the ground and skipped. There was a break in my stride, and I involuntarily slowed down. I quickly caught myself and resumed my previous pace.

"Avery. I know it's you."

I was just a few feet from reaching the corner of the building and disappearing around it. I stopped in my tracks. As soon as I did, I told myself it was the wrong thing to do. Worse still, I turned around.

"Are you talking to me? Because Avery isn't my name," I called back.

A woman stood in the middle of the buckled concrete and asphalt parking lot.

"I know who you are." She began walking towards me, a small smile on her face. If she was a bounty hunter, she was quite a pleasant one. She didn't look like any of the ones from *Badass Bunch* either.

"Really? Then you should know I'm considered to be dangerous, and you should stay back," I said, trying to sound tough and probably failing.

She continued approaching me. "I didn't believe you when you said you weren't Avery. I don't believe you're dangerous either." She had black, shoulder-length hair. And a smile that seemed genuine. "Besides, I know the city only ever really goes after people who don't deserve it."

"What do you want? Are you a bounty hunter?" I took off my mask.

The woman just stood there with her arms at her side, like she didn't have the slightest inkling of fear or general caution about talking with a most-wanted man at night. "No. I'm not a bounty hunter. But I did see the ad for the show. Those girls sure have it in for you. My name is Kate. I'm here to help you if you want it."

I scoffed. "How could you possibly help me? And why would I trust you?"

"Really? Is that something you can afford to ask?" Her smile grew bigger. "At least, is that something you can afford to ask while standing out here in the open? While San Josisco Social Welfare and Kira Tripp and her reality show gang have prioritized the hunt for you?"

"You just shouted my name multiple times across the parking lot," I said. "Everyone within earshot knows it's me. Now you're worried about being out in the open?"

The woman calling herself Kate laughed. "You got me there. But you're the guy who took off his mask." She gestured to a security camera above the store entrance. I was on it; she wasn't. "Smile for the camera. Pretty sure that one doesn't have microphones. Anyway, you want to take me up on my offer or not?"

She was right. Like an idiot, I'd just let my face be recorded. I could practically hear the facial recognition AI humming. It was only a matter of time before an alert went out as to my location.

"What's the offer?"

"Get in the truck and I'll tell you." She jabbed her thumb over her shoulder. "And we should probably hurry."

I pretended to think it over. "I'm going to go ahead and pass. I've got some real trust issues I'm working on, and I've got a pretty good plan that'll get me riding out of town real quick. I think I should stick to that. So, thank you very much, but I'm going to be on my way."

She nodded towards the rail yard, still wearing that sly grin. "Riding out of town? Don't tell me you're going to try to hop a train. That's your plan? They've got drones that follow every inch of those tracks. Every three miles each car is scanned for irregularities in shape and weight. Then there's the heat sensors. They can pick out a rider like a fly in a bowl of soup. You sure you really want to go through with your plan?"

"You think I was going to hop a train just because I said I was going to be 'riding out of town'?"

"Others have tried it. It rarely goes well."

"How do you know—? Never mind."

Distant traffic, sirens, and the humming of drones filled the brief pause.

"So, I get in the truck, and you don't arrest me... we just talk."

"Much better plan. Right?" Her smile seemed to get bigger still.

I looked to my left and right. Nobody seemed to be watching us. "Lead the way."

She walked with a little bounce in her step and hopped into the driver's side. I climbed into the passenger seat. The truck smelled like work. Like real work: hints of oil, dirt, and long hours of laboring under the sun.

"Been a while since I've been in one of these things," I told her.

She started the engine. "Yeah, these old trucks are pretty great."

"So, what is it that you do?" I asked.

"I do a lot of landscaping work."

"Sure. And what else?" I pressed her.

"Why do you think I do something else?"

"Because you just approached public enemy number one at night and offered to help me," I said. "So, between that and however you found me in the first place, I'd say you probably do more than just 'landscaping.' How *did* you find me, by the way?"

She chuckled. "You're not the first one to have trouble with the law. You won't be the last."

"Shouldn't we put on masks?" I asked. "I mean, I know I just gave up my face but I guess I can cover up now so I don't give them any more leads."

"You don't have to. The windshield has a special coating on it that throws off cameras and facial recognition," she said.

I squinted at the window, looking for hints of tech. "Really? I never heard of anything like that. I know AI and facial recognition are far from perfect, but I think maybe I should put a mask on just to be sure." I reached for my wolfman mask.

She handed me a piece of clothing. "Use this instead."

It was a black bandana. Both sides looked clean enough. I sniffed it. And it smelled clean enough. Not sure what chloroform even smells like, but I didn't pass out. I folded the bandana into a triangle and put it over the lower half of my face, tying it at the back of my head.

"Looks good." She put the car in reverse and quickly backed out of the parking space. It was so fast I thought for sure the tires would squeal. But they didn't.

"Where are we going? I thought we were just going to talk," I said.

"We can talk while I drive," she replied. "And if you don't like my offer then I can drop you off and let you continue with your train-hopping plan." She pulled out of the parking lot and headed east.

I nodded my head. "I never admitted to that being my plan, you know. Actually, I had something really good in mind instead—something totally different than that."

"What was it?"

"I think I will keep that to myself."

"Okay."

I crossed my arms. "You know, you can get in a lot of trouble for aiding and abetting me."

"Nah, I'm not worried about that," Kate said. "I've done this before. It's a little tricky getting out of the city, but we'll make it."

"Getting out of San Josisco doesn't mean getting out of trouble," I told her. "The rest of California is going to be looking for me. The rest of the country, really."

"Yeah, but still, San Josisco is the only really tricky part," she said.

Without really thinking about it, I pulled the bandana down to my collar.

"Ah, good. Looks like you're starting to trust me," Kate said.

"Actually, I kind of just made a mistake." I didn't put the

bandana back over my face.

I examined the windshield again. All the other windows in the truck were tinted but it wasn't. In fact, I still couldn't make out anything different about it than a normal one. If it had a special, anti-AI, anti-facial-recognition coating on it, then it was entirely invisible to the naked eye.

"Say, why weren't you wearing a mask back there at the mini-mart? Weren't you afraid that a camera on a drone or across the street would catch you out in the open like that?" I asked.

"Are you sure I'm not wearing a mask right now?" She raised her eyebrows twice in rapid succession.

"Are you serious?" I looked closer. Her face looked like real skin.

She gave me another smile.

I shrugged. "Now you're just messing with me."

"I knew where all the cameras were back there and I knew where to stand to avoid them—including the aerial drones," she admitted. "Too bad you hadn't known the same. We'll get out of the city, like I said, but it probably would've been slightly easier if you hadn't given San Josisco a clue as to your last location."

"Cameras and AI capture a lot," I told her. "But they're not perfect. So, we might still get lucky."

She seemed impressed so I continued explaining.

"The city's facial recognition tech is probably the worst part of San Josisco's system. It only gets about 75% of the matches in the first hit. The AI just isn't where it needs to be for a reliable 100%. I'm pretty sure any first-year designer could fix it in an afternoon, but the city hires developers who are complete morons and then gives them long-term contracts for some reason. And they have no plans to fix it anytime soon. So, who knows? Maybe I'm part of the lucky 25% who won't get recognized right away." Then I quicky added, "I can almost guarantee I'm not, though. Just so you know."

"Well, it sounds like you know your stuff. That's good." That easy grin remained on her face. She leaned back into the seat and her left leg was pulled up past parallel. Her hands loosely gripped the wheel, but they never left ten and two. "That's what got our attention. We need a tech guy."

"Just who are you? What do you know about my tech background? I'm a toilet paper cop. And what do you mean that you need a tech guy?" I asked.

"Remember how I said you aren't the first person to have trouble with the law and won't be the last?" asked Kate.

"I do. But that's not exactly a mind-blowing observation," I replied. "People have had trouble with the law since there've been laws."

"But now is different," she said. "Now people who are doing the right thing are the outlaws. And the outlaws are the ones in charge of the law. And they don't like the people who do the right thing."

"Ohhhh. You noticed the system is corrupt? Trust me, I noticed it too," I said. "I'm the guy on the run! I got railroaded! I lost everything!"

"What if you could do something about it?"

"I'd love to. What've you got?"

"Some people I know have figured out how to start their lives over," she told me. "They've ditched their pasts and created new ones. Completely fresh. Sound good?"

It sounded crazy but I played along. "Who are *they*? And are you a part of *they*?"

"Let's just say I'm someone helping them."

"Did you start your life over? Is your name even *Kate*?"

She nodded. "Yes, I did. And, yes, my name is *Kate* . . . now."

"And anybody can join your . . . your start-your-life-over group? Is this a cult? I can't join a cult," I insisted.

She shook her head. "No, it's not. It isn't a cult and it's not open to anyone."

"Then what is it?"

She gave a little laugh. "All we're doing is offering worthy individuals a chance to erase their past and start over. Some people we select are people we've noticed that seem like they deserve our help and others we select are people we think could help us. Again, you fall into the second category. Generally speaking, what the individuals who make it through the testing phase do afterwards is up to them. Although in your case, we sure would like it if you decide to stick around and help us."

"What do you mean *make it through testing*?" I demanded.

"It's just to make sure you're a good fit. What kind of secret group wouldn't have a test?" she asked.

"Well, I don't like tests. And this whole you-can-start-over thing sounds a lot like a cult," I said.

She slowed down the truck, the first time she had done so. We hadn't even had to stop or pause for a traffic light. Kate eased into a spot by the curb and stopped.

"It's not a cult. And you can start over. But it's all up to you," she told me, suddenly serious. "You've had a terrible few days and if you think you can put your life back in order on your own—if that's what you want to do—I won't try to stop you. But if you think that that's no longer a possibility, then come with me and I can give you a chance at something new; something that won't come easy but might be well worth it."

I reached for the door handle. My hand ran against leather, found the armrest, and then the window crank. The handle eluded me. Where was the stupid handle on this antique? I looked down and finally discovered the thing and gripped it firmly.

"It's up to you, Avery," Kate repeated.

Ahead of us, on a large hovering drone about ten stories in the air, a billboard-sized monitor was telling everyone about the glories of eating bugs. It flickered and my face appeared on it. *"WANTED"* displayed in bright letters above my visage. The monitor flickered again and a message scrolled across the screen: *"Avery Davies-Plott is a fugitive from justice! Contact San Josisco Social Welfare immediately if you see him! Help make our city a better place by looking out for this dangerous criminal!"*

My grip fell away from the door handle. "Let's go."

Her smile returned. A warm genuine smile. "Just sit back

and relax. It's going to be a bit of a drive."

Kate pulled the truck back onto the street and drove us away. I took her advice and sank into the seat.

A thought struck me and I sat upright. "Are you going to harvest my organs? Please say no."

She laughed and looked over at me. If her smile was great, her laugh was even better. Like something out of movie. Just perfect.

"It's not a cult and we're not going to steal your liver." She laughed again.

"Promise?"

"I promise."

For some stupid reason I believed her.

The streets and lights eventually started to fade, and the sky grew blacker. I glanced at the dashboard to see what time it was. The truck didn't have a clock in it; the lights barely illuminated the prehistoric displays on it. I instinctively reached for my phone and quickly remembered once more that I didn't have it. Besides, I had no reason to care what time it was. I was exhausted. I looked back at Kate as she drove.

"You can rest, Avery. It's okay."

I kept my eyes open for few more miles. Then I slept. In the cab of an old pickup truck with a strange, beautiful woman at the wheel. Going God knows where. I slept.

CHAPTER FIFTEEN

Sunlight blasted through the windshield. I blinked my eyes and slowly started to wake up. Where was I? I took in my surroundings as my mental fog slowly lifted. I was sitting in an old truck that was parked behind a crappy restaurant just off a highway. What in the hell was going on?

Desert surrounded me. The sky was huge and blue. I'd never seen anything like it. It was . . . beautiful. No giant, shitty buildings everywhere you looked, and the air wasn't thick with drones. Just tan rolling hills, bright sunshine, and a clear sky. Where was I?

Then it all started coming back to me. The night before. That girl who got me out of San Josisco. Kate. That was her name.

Wait. Where was she? I reached for the door handle. Something dug into my wrist and stopped me from moving my arm more than a few inches. Handcuffs secured me to the armrest. Mild panic set in. And then quickly grew into real panic. Borderline giant panic.

Suddenly the driver's side door opened, and Kate hopped in the restored pick-up. She gave a quick tug on the door, and it slammed shut behind her. Then she turned to me, smiled and held up a bag of fast food like it was some sort of prize.

"Good morning, Avery."

"Yeah, good morning." I tried to hide my panic.

"Hungry?"

"I don't know. I'm mostly focused on the handcuffed-to-the-door part right now."

"Oh, yeah. Sorry about that. Didn't want you to wake up,

freak out, and run off. The handcuffs are kind of a protocol."

She fished into her pants pocket, produced a set of keys, and tossed them to me. I went to work unlocking myself as Kate started the truck and headed back to the highway.

"Protocol?"

"Yep. It's for everybody's safety. But don't worry, I don't think we'll need them again." It all sounded so matter of fact as she said it.

"I'm not too crazy about there being handcuff protocols. Just being honest," I said.

"Wow, you're grumpy when you wake up. Help yourself to some breakfast. You've got to be starving. There's something to drink in there too." She plopped the bag on my lap. The old pickup gave a muffled roar as she accelerated up the on-ramp and merged onto the highway.

"Okay, I'm not grumpy because I woke up; I'm grumpy because I woke up in a truck. Alone. Handcuffed to the door. Sorry if I'm a little freaked out."

Kate reached into the bag on my lap and grabbed a sandwich. She unwrapped it and took a bite. "Sausage, egg, and cheese on a bagel. Fake sausage, fake egg, and fake cheese, of course. But not the worst if you're really hungry."

I stared at her. "Did you hear anything I just said?"

"Look, Avery, I know you have lots of questions. I can't answer many, but I'll do what I can. Fair?" She took another bite.

I let the question hang for a little bit. "Fair. Where are we going?"

"Can't tell you. Sorry." She faked a grimace.

"Okay. Let's try this. What *can* you tell me?"

That one must have landed because she took a second to think about it. "You're going to meet some good people. Some honest to God good people. People who still care and try to make a little difference in this shit world. People who helped a person like me and just might help a person like you."

"Anything else?"

"I can tell you this sandwich is dry as dirt. Could you hand me a drink?" She smiled politely.

I popped open a can of soda and gave it to her. "Can you tell me where we are?"

"Just outside of Vegas," she said. "We passed through it a couple hours ago."

Nature blurred by outside my window. "Vegas?"

"Yup."

We drove on. The landscape was strange, almost alien but I liked it. "It's beautiful out here."

I hadn't done much traveling, and everywhere I had been, pretty much was in California. Years ago, I had flown to Vegas but really only saw the inside of a casino. Other than that, I'd never been to the southwest. It dawned on me I'd never gone to many places that weren't urban. Going to the suburbs was about as close as I'd ever come to getting out of civilization. A lot of that was on purpose though.

All you ever heard about country living on the news was the crime. Just horrifying stories of the most twisted stuff imaginable. Motorcycle gangs. Rednecks. Drugs. Murder. You name it. And it all happened in the middle of nowhere with no one around to help you . . . which was exactly where Kate and I were. And which is exactly why they tell people not to come out here.

But beyond being frightened, a strange feeling crept over me. Everything was unfathomably open and large like nothing I had ever imagined. The scenery kept going until the sky swallowed it up. Everywhere you looked, you couldn't see the end of what there was to see.

"Too bad you can't live outside of the cities," I said. "I mean unless you're super-rich and have the money to pay for all the security you need. All those crazy rednecks just roaming out here hunting people."

"Don't believe everything you hear about life in the country," Kate replied. "It's not nearly as dangerous as they want you to think it is."

Maybe she really was crazy. "Do you not watch the news?

Or is that something else you're not allowed to tell me?"

Kate shook her head just a bit, and the ever-present sly grin remained. "Want to know how to build the best prison? Build one where the prisoners don't want to leave. You don't need walls that way. If people think they're safe on the inside . . . they'll choose to stay. That's what cities are. It's all about control. That's why they want you too scared to come out here." She gestured to the surrounding landscape.

"Well, let's not take any chances."

"Don't worry, Avery, we'll be okay. I brought protection." Kate patted her side, and I noticed the vague outline of a gun beneath her clothes.

"Great. This trip is just getting better and better," I mumbled.

"What was that?"

"Nothing. Can we pull over at the next place that has a restroom? I really gotta go." My bladder started reminding me that I'd been in the truck for hours on end.

Kate quickly pulled over to the side of the highway.

"What are you doing?" Mild panic starting to rise up again.

She motioned towards the door. "You gotta pee? Pee."

"By the side of the road? Broad daylight? In the middle of the desert? In outlaw country? We just went over that. It's dangerous out here."

"You'll be fine. I already said I can't let you loose. It's protocol. Just pee and get back in the truck. We got a lot of driving to do. I'll protect you." Again, she patted her side.

I couldn't believe what was happening. Reluctantly, I stepped out of the truck in my oversized shower shoes and kept my back to traffic. I stared off into the distance and let loose with a solid stream. *What have I become?* I thought. *Taking a leak in the middle of the desert in broad daylight?*

Two or three 18 wheelers roared by behind me. One must have not been autonomous because the driver blared for a long time as if to say, "I see what you're doing, ya freak!" It was a new low for me. *But it can always get worse.*

Something rustled in a nearby bush. "Aahh!" I tried quickly finishing but my bladder had a different idea. It thought we should finish what we started. So, I shuffled closer to the side of the truck as I continued my stream. The bush rustled again. "Little help!"

"Don't pee on the truck!"

"Something's in the bushes!" Thankfully, my bladder was done bullying me. I zipped up as fast as I could and jumped back in the truck.

Kate snickered and shook her head.

"Thanks for the help," I spat. "There's an animal in that bush out there and I was extremely vulnerable. It could've jumped out and bit me or worse. And you just sat here. What's wrong with you?"

"I knew you'd be okay." She left the truck in park. "You peed outside. You lived. Now are you going to eat that sandwich, or no?"

"Maybe later. Can we just go now?"

"In a second. So, you'll eat later, and you just went to the bathroom. So, you're good now. Right?"

I took a deep breath. "Yes. Thank you for nothing. I'm just great. Best day ever. And you can stop lying about the gun. I know you don't really have one. So just stop."

"Funny you should mention that. I was just about to show it to you." She reached into her jacket and pulled out a small pistol. It wasn't like any gun I'd seen before. My confusion must have shown on my face.

"This doesn't shoot bullets," Kate told me. "It shoots little darts with a fast-acting sedative. Holds six shots. Really neat piece of tech."

"So, you could shoot an animal with it?" I asked, more than a bit confused.

She scrunched up her face. "Well, you don't want to eat, and you already did your business. And I told you I can't let you know where we're going so. . . ."

My eyes went wide. "Me? You're going to shoot me?"

"I am." She said with a little wince.

"No! I refuse!"

"Sorry, Avery, you don't get to pick. Sometimes life is like that. This isn't personal. When we get where we're going, I'll hit you with the counter agent and you'll wake right up. Again, this isn't personal."

"Well, again, no. I refuse." I crossed my arms.

She leaned over and shot a small dart into my thigh.

"Ow! But I refused."

Kate shrugged her apology.

I pulled the tiny dart out of my thigh and examined it. "There's no way this little thing is gonna knock—"

Everything went black.

CHAPTER SIXTEEN

We're here, a voice said. But there was no one there. It was just a giant meadow of red, and blue, and purple, and yellow flowers. Nothing but flowers gently waving in the wind. The sun was out but I wasn't hot, and I didn't even feel its rays beating down on me. Something pushed on my side and the voice repeated. *We're here.* And then it dawned on me. I was between the dream world and the real world.

With great effort, I forced my eyes open. Soft golden light of the evening sun greeted me. I was still in the truck, but we weren't moving. Vast wilderness spread out in front of us. Kate's hand was on my shoulder.

"I refused," I mumbled. My mouth was dry, and my tongue barely worked. "How long was I out?"

"A long time," her smooth voice answered. "You're probably really thirsty. Here." She handed me a large bottle of green liquid.

I seized it and guzzled it as fast as I could. It was sweet and tasted of lime. Immediately it was the best drink in the world.

"I know." She nodded. "It's good. Right?" Her seatbelt was off, and the engine was quiet. Strands of hair escaped from behind her ear and trickled beside her right eye.

"The best."

"You should try the cherry," she said.

I took another giant gulp and came up for air. Then I gave Kate what Sharyl called my "stern" face. "Never shoot me again."

"I'll try not to."

"No. Not good enough. Never. Again." My stern face was glued on.

"Okay." It seemed like she meant it.

And then there was silence. Did I just win an argument? It was weird. Nothing witty came to my mind so I took another drink of lime deliciousness.

"This stuff is amazing." It sounded kind of stupid in my own ears but was still better than just quietness between us.

"Like I said, the cherry is even better." She got out of the truck and stretched.

"I'd sure like to get out and stretch too," I said. "Would you unlock the handcuffs?"

"What handcuffs?" she replied.

That's when I noticed that my right wrist was still free. "Oh." I opened the door. My legs were a little numb, but they obeyed enough to keep me upright. A slight breeze kicked up and I inhaled the purest air I'd ever smelled.

The road stretched into the horizon in front of us and behind us. No other cars were in sight; Kate had the truck parked on the shoulder. Flat, dry land dominated everything around us except in the distance, where hilltops and mountains poked up out of the earth. The evening sun painted them in gold and purples. The sky was dotted with pink and white puffy clouds. After a bit, I realized my mouth was hanging open and I shut it.

It was as if I had stepped into a painting or some scene that Hollywood put together with computer graphics. Once or twice, I wondered if I was still asleep. Then I noticed the quiet. And I think that was what got to me the most. No traffic and no people. There were no robots and no drones. There wasn't even a jet streaking high in the atmosphere. It was just the blue, and red, and golden sky of the evening, with birds soaring in it and nothing man-made. For the first time in my life, I was experiencing the world as it naturally was, as we were supposed to experience it.

I closed my eyes to focus on the tranquility. Quietness wasn't entirely alien to me. They have quiet rooms in San Josisco —all across the country, really. They charge you an arm and a leg for one hour alone in a soundproof room. You can do whatever you want there: read a book, nap, or meditate. Or something else. But out in the desert, with that gentle breeze caressing me, the silence was entirely different. It was the silence of solitude; of two humans being alone in the world—of being the *only* people in the world.

"Where are we?" I asked Kate. "Please don't say you can't tell me. I have to know where I am right now. I need to be able to remember this spot. I don't care about the crazy hillbilly motorcycle drug gangs right now. This is too . . . too . . . amazing. It's like being in a painting. Please tell me where we are."

Silence greeted me. I opened my eyes and found Kate, right where she had been.

"The Crazy Death Ranch," she said. "This is where I leave you for a bit."

For a moment I thought she must've been joking. "Wait? What? This place is called the Crazy Death Ranch. And you're going to leave me here for a bit?" The road that stretched to infinity in both directions was barely a two-lane road. And it looked like no one had bothered to maintain it for a long time. Suddenly crazy hillbilly drug gangs concerned me again. "Are you kidding me?"

"No. I'm not. You'll be okay."

"No, I won't be." I threw my hands up in the air. "This isn't happening. You're not leaving, and this isn't the Crazy Death Ranch. If it was the Crazy Death Ranch, wouldn't there be a sign —like in the movies?"

Kate pointed behind me. In the distance, an old wooden gateway stood over a dirt path. A rugged, worn-out sign hung from a nail at the top of it: *Crazy Death Ranch*.

"Well, shit," I uttered.

"Don't worry," she said. "People are coming to pick you up. They've been expecting you, after all."

I spun back around. "I changed my mind. Take me with you. Look, you can even shoot me again."

She laughed like I just told a good joke.

"I'm not kidding. Get me out of here. No deal. Take me

back."

"I can't. It's too late." Wind whipped at her hair.

"Yes, you can. You can! Let's go. Now!" I implored.

She pulled a stray strand of hair out of her mouth. "You're scared. I get it. Don't worry, though, I'll wait here with you until they come."

"No, you don't understand. I'm terrified," I insisted. "And I'm tired of being scared. I don't like it at all."

Kate put her hands in her pockets. Casual. "So be brave. I didn't lie to you. These are good people, and you can do this."

"No, I can't," I shot back. "We just met. You don't know me. But I do. And I know I can't do this."

"So, how'd you make it this far? How did you get here?"

I threw up my arms. "That was stupidity—not bravery. Sometimes they look very similar but they're worlds apart. And what I did was sheer stupidity. Trust me."

For a moment, she seemed like she was trying to figure something out about me. Then her gaze went just over my shoulder.

"Look." She pointed far down the Crazy Death Ranch dirt trail. "Something comes our way."

CHAPTER SEVENTEEN

I shielded my eyes with my hand and squinted. There was a dust cloud. It was small but growing. Dull colors and glints appeared in the middle of it. They transformed into a small vehicle the closer the angry dirt cloud got to us.

"Is that my ride?" I asked.

"It sure is," she said.

"And these are good people? Not maniacs here to kill me?"

"Nope. These are the good guys."

Finally, I could make out more that just the odd shape of the vehicle in the distance. It was a beat-up golf cart that was speeding wildly down the dirt trail. Dents and dings decorated every inch of the thing. Once upon a time someone had painted the Texas state flag on top of it, but that piece of art had seen better days. It also sported a large, horned cow skull on the front grill. Someone had spray painted the skull red, white, and blue.

"Are you sure these are the good guys?" I half mumbled.

Whoever was driving the golf cart was coming fast. And they didn't slow down even when they were 25 yards away. As it careened towards us I stumbled backwards and fell. The driver kept coming.

"Stop!" I threw up my hands, shielded my face and braced for impact.

At the last second, the driver slammed on the brakes. The tires bellowed out a final, tremendous belch of dust and the cart skidded to a stop just feet away from me.

Spitting out dust, I picked myself off the ground. Kate helped brush me off. The driver put the bizarre little machine in park and stepped out.

He stood up straight and seemed to just keep going. The guy was easily over six-and-a-half feet tall and had the biggest barrel chest I'd ever seen. Like a silver-back gorilla. The lines on his face and the salt and peppered hair sticking out from underneath his cowboy hat told me he must've been in his early sixties. Faded jeans gripped his waist and hung loosely on his legs, covering an old pair of boots.

Gravel and dirt crunched underneath his feet as he sauntered over to me.

"You Avery?" The big man adjusted his hat.

"Uh, y-yes, I am," I replied.

He sharply nodded once and smiled. "I'm Tex. Good to meet you."

He held out a giant bear paw and I grabbed it. His powerful mitt dwarfed my hand. Tex chose not to crush my appendage like a piece of chalk. I could tell from his mighty grip that that was definitely an option if he wanted.

"Good to meet you too," I lied.

"Why'd you sit down on the ground when I was coming in?"

"What? Oh, that?" I brushed off the seat of my pants. "I wasn't sitting. I fell."

Tex raised an eyebrow. "Why'd you fall?"

"Well, you see…" I exhaled and my shoulders slumped. "I don't know. I must've tripped."

"Hmph. Odd. Anyway, welcome to Crazy Death Ranch. Glad you're here, son." He gave me another big grin. "Hop in ol' Davy and we'll take you to her." He looked at Kate. "Thank you, ma'am."

"You're welcome," she sweetly said.

"So, 'ol' Davy' is the cart?" I asked. "It seems like that's what you meant but I just want to be sure."

Tex snorted out a short laugh. "Yeah, Davy's the cart. That's his head on front. Best damn bull I ever had." He grinned at Kate. "This one's squirrely. How was the ride in?"

"No problems. Smooth as silk."

"Good. And how was San Josisco? Anything new?"

"It's worse every trip. The whole place is falling apart." Kate paused. "They got their new drones up. Totally automated. Fully armed. Infrared capabilities. Not easy to take down either."

"Shit. I thought it'd take another year for that to happen. Damn gunships can't be far off if they got the M583's up." Tex wiped his sweaty brow with a bandana that had somehow survived the stone age. "You can fill me in on everything else later. I'm gonna get Squirrely here to HQ. When are you coming back?"

"Later tonight. Just got to check on a couple things and maybe pick up some stuff."

"Alright. You be careful now." He said with a knowing look.

"Always am."

"No, you're not. You never are."

Tex hugged Kate and she squeezed him back. He let her go and motioned toward me. "Okay, Squirrely, let's get going. We're not getting any younger."

Kate started for her truck.

"H-Hold on," I stammered. "Will I see you again? And you're sure this guy, uh, has no intention of hurting me?" I avoided meeting Tex's eyes. "I just need some reassurance on that."

"You're fine." She waved at me like a kid waving at her best friend as he boarded the bus at the bus stop.

"Okay," I sighed.

"You're not the best at first impressions. Are you, Squirrely?" asked Tex.

"Can we maybe not do the 'Squirrely' thing? It feels very nickname-y," I told him. "And if there's a nickname or code name, I'm not comfortable with, 'Squirrely' would be it."

Tex gave me a long look and threw a giant arm over my shoulder. I flinched a little.

He laughed heartily. The smell of sweat, dust, and old beer wafted off him. "Spoken like a true squirrel." Another laugh followed. "You're gonna be fine, son. Ain't nothing gonna happen to ya. We'll get you some nuts at the ranch." And yet a third, booming guffaw.

Kate was already in the truck, and she cranked the engine to life.

Tex moved in the opposite direction, and I walked along to avoid the embarrassment of him dragging me along with him. Little clouds of dirt kicked up with each of our steps. He stopped just short of the cart. New waves of his powerful body odor crawled up my nostrils.

"Oh, I almost forgot," he said. "Put your hands on the hood."

"Why?"

"Because I'm gonna search you. Basic security measures." He jerked his head at the hood.

Swallowing hard, I did as I was told. The pat down was rough, and it shook my entire body. At first, it wasn't invasive (aside from the fact that it was a pat down from a giant). But then the hair on the back of my neck stood up as Tex started getting extremely familiar with me. He was assuming I could hide a weapon in some very personal areas.

"All right, you're good," he told me. "Sorry about that. Had to be done. Here's a rule for ya: always check the balls. People love to hide weapons behind their balls. Most folks don't look for stuff back there. Thinks it makes 'em gay or some stupid shit. Me? I make sure I check 'em. 'Cause I wanna live. You should too. So, if you ever have to pat down someone, what are you gonna do?"

"Check their balls?"

"That's right. I like you, Squirrely. You're a fast learner. That's a good sign." Tex jumped behind the wheel, and I got in the other side, completely ill at ease.

Behind us, Kate was already driving away, her truck growing smaller and smaller in the distance. My shoulders slumped and I stared at the floor.

"Yes, sir," Tex bellowed. "You pat someone down; you check those nuts."

He stomped on the pedal and ol' Davy launched down the dirt road. My body lurched sideways. I grabbed the door frame and just barely managed to keep from falling out. Tex roared with laughter. He swerved along the worn trail and raced through the wooden gateway with the crooked *Crazy Death Ranch* sign hanging onto it.

We went through a pothole. My head bounced into the top of the golf cart. Somehow, through that sharp pain, I didn't lose my grip on the frame and kept holding on for dear life. Tex laughed harder and ripped the cart to the side before stomping on the brakes. His eyes bored into me, and he shook with glee. As ridiculous as it was, his laughter seemed genuine, and I couldn't help but smile as well. Maybe it was my nerves too, but I started giggling a bit.

"What? What's so funny?" I asked.

He wiped tears from his face and tried composing himself. A mock seriousness came across him. "Squirrely, your first rule is to check . . . the nuts." His seriousness evaporated and more laughs burst forth from him, and every part of him shook. "Oh, my lord that's funny." His large boot found the gas pedal again. "Check the nuts." Tears slid down his face.

My head rattled from side to side like a jack-in-the-box some kid had set into motion. "So . . . I'm guessing Squirrely is gonna stick."

"Oh, yeah." Tex sniffed and wiped a tear from his eyes. "Afraid so. I like you, son. You got a good sense of humor. Check the nuts!" It was as if he had heard his own joke for the first time again, and more mirth spilled out of him.

As my head wagged back and forth and we raced down over the dirt, a small chuckle even escaped from my lips. The giant's laughter was contagious.

Ahead of us, the enormous and empty landscape loomed. And as the sun slowly set, the colors grew more intense. It was wilderness. Total and complete wilderness. Nothing manmade was out there and that struck me as profound. Time seemed to be off. With the way everything looked, it was as easy to imagine it as being in the Old West days as it was to realize that it was actually the here and now. San Josisco was just a few hours in my past; just under a day's travel by car. Yet it all seemed so much longer ago and so much farther away.

"You've gotta be busting with questions right about now," said Tex.

I opened my mouth to tell him I was, but he kept right on going before I could get anything out.

"Afraid I can't tell ya much, for your own safety and mine. But I promise to tell ya what I can." He reached behind my seat, picked up a small cooler and set it on my lap. "Wanna open that up for me? Hand me a cold one?"

I opened the cooler. Inside were several tall cans of beer on ice. "Are you sure you want to drink and drive?"

"Son, we're on a dirt trail in a damn golf car going 20 miles an hour. Look around. It's the middle of nowhere. What am I gonna hit? A train? Now come on. It's hot as balls out here. Hell, yes, I want a beer."

Just then a rabbit darted in front of us. Tex slammed on the brakes and the cart skidded wildly to a sudden stop.

Everything flew forward. The cooler slammed into the dashboard of ol' Davy, and my stomach slammed into it. "Uurrppp!"

Then as quickly as Tex stopped, he started back up again. He reached into the cooler, grabbed a cold one, and popped the top. I gasped for breath.

"Glad I waited. Might've spilled it." Tex took a long drink. "So, go ahead, shoot. What's on your mind?"

"Where are you taking me?" I wheezed, rubbing my sternum to check for the cracks I was certain the cooler made.

"Good one. That's where I'd start too." He took another huge gulp, so much so that he had to have almost drained the whole can. "Well, you already know it's the Crazy Death Ranch. Really more of a camp than a ranch. We just picked that name to be funny and keep any lookie-loo's away. We like our privacy. It's what you call, imperative. The government doesn't like us one little bit. So, we gotta be super careful how we do things. Keep it real secret. It's imperative."

Holes and the generally primitive state of the dirt trail had us both bouncing up and down now. It didn't bother Tex one bit. He crushed the now empty beer can and dropped it in the cooler.

"So, what am I doing here?" We sped up a small rise in the dusty path.

"Well, son, you're gonna help us keep it real secret. *That* is what you're doing here." He gave me a knowing nod.

I nodded back as if I had any clue what he was talking about.

As we crested the hill, rectangular shapes appeared on the terrain in the distance. At first, I thought it might be a ghost town. "Is that it?"

Tex nodded. "That's the ranch house."

"Which one? There are a bunch of buildings down there," I said.

"The big one, that would be the long one with the covered porch, is the main ranch house. Those others are the outbuildings. You know, like any ranch or farm has."

"I've never been on a ranch or farm."

"First time for everything."

Everything took on more detail as we got closer, and the ranch no longer appeared to be a ghost town. Far from it. There were a few people walking around the property. Three of them were dressed similarly to Tex and were working like they were part of the ranching operations. But two others were just standing around having a conversation, and judging by their casual clothes, they were outsiders. Like me.

We continued barreling on and when we reached the ranch house Tex stomped on the brakes and skidded ol' Davy to a stop. A cloud of reddish, hot sauce colored dirt and dust enveloped us. It was everywhere. With a wave of my hands to try and clear the air, I stepped out of the cart. Like an idiot, I accidentally inhaled.

Grit coated my molars and tongue. So nasty. Just the

worst. I didn't even consider trying to be polite. I immediately spat on the ground. "Listen, I think there's been some kind of mix up." I said, trying to get the film of mud out of my mouth. "You know what this feels like? An honest mistake. I think maybe Kate was supposed to get somebody else and they're supposed to be here, and I'm supposed to be," I spat again, "somewhere else. So, no harm, no foul. Honest mistake. Maybe you all sort it out and I go," yet a third spit, "somewhere else. Not here."

"It's no mistake. You're right where you need to be," a woman's voice said from the porch behind me.

She was petite and quite attractive, probably in her late forties. She had her long, chestnut hair tied back in a shimmering ponytail. Faded blue jeans ripped at the knees— from wear, no doubt, instead of a fashion choice—clung to her legs and a brilliant white t-shirt hugged her up top. Like Tex, she wore a cowboy hat, only it was smaller and slate colored, with little ornamental twirls and wisps on the brim. Her boots were the same color as her hair, and a faded rose on the outside of each peeked out from underneath her jeans.

Despite wearing no makeup, she had a natural beauty that didn't look like it needed the help. And her tanned skin made her steely blue eyes stand out. It was if they were electric. That's when I noticed they were locked onto mine.

Impulsively I looked away, letting my gaze slip down towards the ground. On the way to looking at my feet, I couldn't help but notice her chest. Her breasts were quite large. Nothing insane, but big for a person her size. And they looked firm. They had to be fake. There was no bra there; nothing that was holding them up. They defied gravity.

Holy shit, I'm staring at her tits, I thought.

I whipped my head up and towards the porch roof, but I knew she saw it. She totally saw it even if her expression didn't change. She just kept looking me right in the eyes. Hot embarrassment washed across my face.

"Avery, meet my wife, Savannah," said Tex. "She's the

brains of the outfit. Savannah, this here's Avery. I been calling him 'Squirrely.'"

Shit, shit, shit. It's his wife. I'm a dead man, I thought.

Savannah walked off the porch and firmly shook my hand. Just the barest of grins graced her face.

"Don't worry about it. Everyone looks the first time," she drawled in a warm, Southern accent. "They're great. I'd look too. Just don't make a habit out of it. We're all grown-ups."

My face was still flushed. "Yes, we are. I'm sorry. I, too, am grown up. Very much so." I was still shaking her hand. Quickly, I let it go and shoved my hands in my pockets and looked around at the camp. For some reason, I started nodding knowingly, as if I were learning something about my surroundings. No matter what else I did, it came off awkward. Finally, I just settled on holding my hands behind my back . . . awkwardly.

"Let's get down to brass tacks. Time's a wastin'." Savannah marched in the direction of a large, weathered barn about 50 yards away from the ranch house.

Tex eyeballed me and jerked his head towards his wife. I nodded and followed behind her.

We passed what I assumed were other outsiders. One of them smiled courteously and the other politely nodded. I returned the salutations in kind. It was more of a reflex than anything else.

"I don't want to seem rude, but no one has ever really explained what's going on—why I'm here or who you all are. Or what any of this is," I said to Savannah as she led the way. "That seems like something I should know."

"Well, then, let's get to taking care of that." She reached the barn and grabbed a handle of an enormous barn door. Then she put her weight into it and slid the huge thing open. Evening sunbeams streamed into the darkened interior and lit up streams of dust, animal stalls, bales of hay, and old tools. Odors of animal crap and mustiness flowed out and slammed into me, forcing me to take a step back. Did everyone and everything stink out here? *This is unbelievable*, I thought.

Savannah stepped into the barn and a small shove from Tex got me going forward again. He hit a switch on the wall and overhead lights burst on with surprising quickness and brilliance. It was like one minute I was gazing into an old barn that had been locked up for decades, and the next I was standing in some sort of museum mocked up to look like an old barn. Well, aside from the powerful smells. Off to the side, I noticed a door with a rather sophisticated locking mechanism on it.

"Alright, Avery, how about we head up to the nest," Savannah said. "I'll tell you exactly what is going on up there."

"The 'nest'?" I repeated.

She reached for the wall and flipped open a small panel I hadn't noticed. Inside was a small, black, square glass with a red light on its left upper side. She placed her thumb in the middle of the glass. It emitted a beep and the red light turned green. The locking mechanism on the door off to the side clicked loudly and the entryway edged open.

Savannah went to the now unlocked door and this time I didn't wait for Tex to tell me to follow her. Once it was fully open, I saw there was only one thing inside: a ladder that went up through a hatch in the ceiling. Without hesitating, Savannah started climbing and put her thumb on another scanner on the wall below the hatch. It clicked and she pushed it open.

I glanced over my shoulder. Tex grinned and motioned upwards with his thumb. With a sigh, I put my right foot on the bottom rung and waited as Savannah ascended. Even with the lead she had, I figured it was polite to give her more space. After all, I was about to have no choice but to look up at her backside. Somehow Tex had missed my faux pas at the porch, but I didn't want to press my luck a second time.

"Just go, Squirrely." Tex nudged me with the strength of a gorilla. "You already seen the headlights, might as well check out the caboose."

Who ARE these people? I mentally screamed.

I took a breath, grabbed the ladder sides, and away I went. Again, it was almost impossible not to look up as I ascended the ladder. With as much time as I had already given Savannah, I figured she would've been at the top by then. I was wrong. As I looked up, there was her jean-covered butt just finishing the climb. It was, of course, magnificent. How could it not be?

I whipped my head away and my eyes ended up staring straight into Tex's. I swallowed hard. "She seems like a very nice person."

"She is. And I love her to death. Now go on. Git."

He waved me on. I hurried up the ladder and reached the top in record time. And I was greeted with yet another surprise.

The nest, as it turned out, was not like the rustic barn below. Not even close. Well, it did have a typical door for loading hay and whatever else barns load. But that's where the similarities ended.

Instead, it was as if I was standing in a high-tech office. A massive worktable took up the middle of the room. Desktop computers, laptops, filing cabinets, and large monitors on the walls filled the rest of it. Taken together, all of it almost screamed that it was a villain's lair from a bad movie.

"This here is the heart of the Crazy Death Ranch." Savannah switched on one of the laptops. The monitor behind her blipped to life.

Tex closed the hatch to the ladder, trapping us all in the nest.

Savannah opened a small refrigerator nearby and started rummaging. "You want a drink? Lemonade? I should've offered you something earlier. Don't know where my manners were. It's just been one of those days, I guess. I'm all outta sorts." She grabbed a can and closed the fridge.

I cleared my throat. "Heh, heh. I know the feeling."

"I bet you do!" Her laugh was light and airy. "Have a seat and we'll get started. We got plenty to do and not enough time to do it." She popped the top on the can of cold lemonade and handed it to me.

As thirsty as I was, I fought the impulse to take a big drink. I thought it might seem rude. Instead, I just sat down in an old office chair next to me. Savannah hadn't been silent for more than a few seconds and yet it felt like an eternity.

She plopped down in front of a laptop and started typing. Her giant, cowboy husband made his way towards the fridge.

"Hope you're looking for lemonade in there 'cause there ain't no beer up here." Savannah said sternly as she clacked away on the keyboard. "I saw you take the cooler in ol' Davy. Don't try to say you didn't either, 'cause I seen it. And take a shower, baby! You smell like something died and rolled around on ya! It's disgusting!"

Tex didn't flinch at her mini outburst. He tugged open the refrigerator door and grabbed a can of lemonade, taking a slow draw before sighing and smiling.

In the midst of all the craziness, these two struck me as odd— the whole situation was odd, but these people were very, very, different. If Sharyl ever yelled at me like that, I'd be ready for a massive four-hour lecture on my failures as a human being. But Tex just grinned, and everything seemed okay.

"I smell like I been working," he told his wife. "Because that's what I been doing. And don't get your panties in a twist. I was planning on taking a shower before we went to bed. And this here lemonade? Just fine with me. It's what I wanted, which is why I'm drinking it. Now tell Squirrely what we do and stop shouting. You're scaring him. Look at the guy."

"You scared?" Savannah asked me.

I squirmed. "I am concerned . . . mildly troubled. Maybe extremely concerned. Is that alright?"

"Sorry about that. You'll get used to it. We're loud people." She finished clacking on the keyboard, stood up, and headed to the giant monitor behind her. It displayed a large map of North America.

"Okay," she continued. "Here's us." She tapped the screen and the image zoomed in on Texas. Another tap and she highlighted a small area on the northwest edge of the state. "As you can see, the CDR—the Crazy Death Ranch—isn't on any official map, and we need to keep it that way. Now, we are part of a much bigger organization, and that's as big of a secret as we are. This whole ranch is just a way station; a stopover for people like yourself—people in trouble, and people looking for a chance to start all over. You with me so far?"

"I think so . . . you help people on the run from the law?"

"Yes. Well, yes and no. We help people on the run from the government. If you're in trouble with them, you're in trouble with the law. And these days they are both out of control. You see, Avery, we're in the freedom business."

"So . . . you're terrorists?" I tried not sounding judgmental, because I figured terrorists wouldn't like it if I sounded like I was judging them. My palms started sweating.

Tex let out a belly laugh. "Hell, no! We ain't terrorists. Freedom fighters! Freedom fighters that don't even fight. We're more like freedom travel agents. All we do is move folks around. Keep 'em out of reeducation camps, prison, and whatnot. People like yourself who get in trouble for doing the right thing.

Savannah tapped the screen again and my mugshot popped up. "You defended yourself from a home invasion and they arrested you for it."

"Yeah, but I did use a gun . . . well, I tried to use a gun." As soon as the words left my mouth, I couldn't figure out why I said something that sounded like I was defending the cops.

Savannah's expression transformed into something close to pity. "Sweetheart, that's not supposed to be a bad thing. You were defending yourself and your girlfriend from a criminal who meant you harm."

"Ex-girlfriend," I corrected.

"Yeah, she left him, baby," Tex chimed in. "You seen the show. Those girls are pissed. Bounty hunters and everything. She don't like him one little bit."

"Never mind all that." She aggressively waved her hand. "My point is this: we used to have a Constitution. The government was supposed to protect people and not harass them. You're probably too young to remember, but it wasn't always like this. Forty years ago, people had the right to bear arms—to protect themselves. We had freedom of speech. Government served the people. Now they lock you up for saying the wrong thing or having the wrong opinion. This ain't right." She gestured in a big circle indicating everything. "This isn't how it's supposed to be and we're helping to fix it."

"And you're not terrorists."

"No. We are not. Government says we are, but we're not." Tex crushed his empty can with one swift squeeze.

"Sooo . . . what do you do? And how do I fit into all this?"

Savannah smiled and tapped the screen again. An image of a tree popped up. It looked like some kind of logo. "We plant seeds. Seeds of Liberty. And we hope they grow. The government has AI watching and listening to everybody, and when they detect a threat—someone like yourself who shows signs of *independent* thinking, they scoop 'em up. Sometimes they send 'em to a camp to get their brain washed. Most of the time, though, as in cases like yours, they just figure out a way to lock people up. The group we work for scoops up such people before the government can."

"We try to, at least," said Tex.

"Right. We *try* to," Savannah agreed. "We take 'em and get 'em out of the system. But we keep 'em in society. Help 'em start over. 'Cause we need more of 'em. We need tons more people out in the middle of things, spreading that *independent* thinking. Making little differences all over. They're little seeds of Liberty and they're gonna grow."

"So, you're just going to help me start a new life? That's it?" I asked.

"Yes and no," Tex replied.

"C'mon, just give me a straight answer for once," I begged.

He held up a hand. "You gotta do us a favor and we'll do you a favor. Good ol' capitalism. You got something we want, and we got something you want. So, let's trade."

"Wait. Kate brings me here against my will and now you tell me *I* have to give *you* something?"

Tex shrugged.

What could I possibly have that they would want?

Savannah chimed in. "If you could start all over—clean slate—where would you want to go? Where would you be happy?"

"Mars." It just popped out of my mouth, like it was a reflex. "I mean, I think I would be happy there. On Mars. It seems great."

"Deal." She slapped her hand on the table. "You help us, and we'll get you to Mars."

"See, Squirrely? Now we're horse trading," Tex barked.

"Wait. What do I have to do?" My heart raced and I waited for whatever horrible thing they were about to say.

Savannah gestured at the screen. "Hide this ranch from a satellite."

"Um . . . how am I supposed to do that, exactly?"

She tapped the screen. It zoomed out and showed the entire globe. Little white lines encircled it. "These are all satellites. Watching, listening, communicating, and tracking. Lots of tracking. You're gonna use your skills to trick this brand new one into thinking we're not here."

"Skills? I was a toilet paper cop. I counted sheets of toilet paper. You really think my skills are going to be able to help you?"

"Don't sell yourself short, son," Tex answered. "You hacked into a government system and taught it to count wrong. We want you to do the same thing."

Savannah indicated a specific white line on the monitor. "Just tell this satellite to count three people on the ranch instead of how many we really got here. It's easy. You can do it."

I vigorously shook my head. "No, it's not. I'm sorry, but it's not. That is a government satellite. Even if I wanted to, I don't think I could do it."

"It's the same software," Savannah claimed.

"How would you know that?"

"This is the government we're talking about. Big, fat, and lazy," she insisted. "This satellite counts things. In this case, people. In your case, sheets of TP. But in the mind of a bureaucrat, counting is counting, so they use the same damn software and charge the taxpayer through the nose."

"I cannot hack into the system." I was more forceful than I had intended.

"We'll get you in. We got people for that. Passwords and everything," Tex said.

"All you gotta do is teach it to count. Like sheets of TP," said Savannah.

I put my head in my hands for a moment and then slowly raised it. "That's it? And you'll get me to Mars? With a new identity?"

"Yep."

"Just change the count?" I asked again.

"Yep."

My head fell into my hands again.

Savannah gently pressed me. "Up to you, Avery. Do you want to go it alone and end up in jail? Or do you want a clean start on Mars? I hear they have big ol' forests of pine trees now."

I took a breath. "I'll do it."

CHAPTER EIGHTEEN

Instant regret swept over me. But Tex and Savannah were overjoyed. He grabbed my shoulders and squeezed right between my collar bones over and over. Thankfully he didn't break any bones with his giant bear hands.

"That's what I'm talking about, Squirrely. You saved the day, son. You got yourself a deal."

"So, when am I supposed to do my thing?" I motioned at a nearby laptop.

Savannah started shutting down the equipment. "Tomorrow night. We'll get you and a small team to the base. You'll meet your contact who'll have the passcodes and then you get to hacking. After that, we'll get you on your way." She winked at me.

"I'm sorry, base? Did you say *base*? What kind of base?" I inquired.

"Military base." Tex gave me a wicked smile. "Don't worry none. You just gotta be close enough to access the router, or the cables, or something. I don't know what it is. It's all mumbo-jumbo to me. But I don't think you gotta break in or nothing."

"Whoa, whoa, whoa. No one mentioned a base," I protested.

Tex lost his smile. "We shook on it. We have a deal. Right, Squirrely?"

"Don't scare him, baby. He said he'd do it, he's gonna do it!" Savannah was almost shouting. She smiled sweetly at me. "Don't worry. I believe he's right. I sincerely think you don't have to break in. Almost one hundred percent."

With everything finally powered down, she returned to

the hatch. She lifted it and made her way down to the ground floor.

Meeting adjourned. Tex slapped my back. Hard. His hand was so huge it felt like it covered my entire spine, from my tailbone to my neck. Another draft of his unique body odor followed and nearly overwhelmed me.

"I'll get you set up in the bunkhouse. You can meet the rest of the folks. Better get some sleep tonight, though. You're gonna wanna be sharp tomorrow. Tip top. Know what I'm saying?"

I nodded and pretended I did. I hustled down the ladder and Tex quickly followed.

Savannah used the thumb reader to lock the room and then led us outside. Tex tightly closed the barn door.

Outside, my regret about what I just agreed to grew like an unstoppable monster. Why did I say yes? How could I back out? What could I say that wouldn't upset them? I'd have to avoid Tex and try think of a way to get Savannah to understand. Then again, could they really get me to Mars? That was the endgame of my long-term plans before San Josisco jacked up my entire life. But they made it sound so easy—like they were going to get me box seats at a ballgame through some connections they had. Why should I trust them?

Off in the distance, a little striped bird landed on a fence post and chirped happily. For some reason I just stared at the little thing. Lucky bastard. It didn't have a care in the world. Another merry chirp and it flew off. I should've been a bird.

"Let's get you to the bunkhouse." Savannah's voice broke me out of my sparrow jealousy. "Get you straightened away. You hungry?"

"Uh, yes. Thanks. Yeah, I think I could eat." The wind blew another wave of Tex's giant funk my way and I pretended not to notice, but I'm pretty sure I winced a little.

"Damn, baby, you really do stink. You gotta go wash up, like now," said Savannah.

"I told you, I'm a working man. This ain't all lilacs and roses." Tex grinned and proudly gestured at himself.

"Well, if it's not lilacs and roses soon, you can forget about getting any tonight. So, you might wanna scrub-a-dub-dub," she teased.

"Alright, then. Squirrely, damn glad you're onboard. But you heard the lady, I'm gonna go get my shower on." He clapped me on the back, almost injuring at least 25 vertebrae, and strode off towards the ranch house. "You wanna scrub my back, darlin'?" he yelled back.

"Scrub your own damn back, ya stinky jackass!" she returned.

He waved to me without turning around and lumbered on.

"He's crazy but I do love him," she sighed. "Sorry about the stink. He just works so hard. Makes him sweat a lot. You know?"

"Oh, sure. Big time. I know. Been there, done that. I'm a sweater too," I rambled.

Savannah nodded her agreement but the look on her face told me she didn't believe me. Hell, I didn't believe me. Thankfully, she started walking away from the barn and towards the fence line. I stuffed my hands into my pockets and followed her.

She didn't stop until she reached the fence. I stopped right beside and gazed over the gently rolling hills.

"Beautiful. Isn't it?" she said.

"Sure is."

She reached into the top of her jeans and pulled out a pistol. She held it out to me.

"What are you doing?" I asked.

"I wanna know if you can shoot," she replied. "Police report says you never fired your gun. You can shoot, though. Right?"

"I can. But don't we need a gun range or something? And why do you care if I know how to shoot? Why would I *need* to shoot? I thought you all were nonviolent," I returned.

"We're nonviolent in that we don't start violence, but we do defend ourselves. We're not idiots. Now, shoot at something."

She pointed at the remains of a tree trunk about 20 feet away. "See if you can hit that." She pushed the gun closer to me.

I grabbed its warm handle. Warm, I supposed, either from the oppressive heat or from being in her pants. The gun looked rather normal while she held it. But in my hands? It felt like a small cannon. I did my best to try to look natural with it. With both hands on the pistol, I raised it and squinted at the tree trunk. I closed one eye and looked down the sights and lined them up with the tree. And then I slowly squeezed the trigger.

Nothing happened.

The trigger didn't even move. Maybe it was a test to see if I'd really try to shoot. I guessed I passed. *Take that*, I mentally said.

"Safety's on," Savannah murmured.

"Yes, it is," I quickly covered.

So, it was a test. Just a different kind than I thought. I searched in vain for the safety.

"Right there." She pointed to a tiny switch on the side and gave me a quizzical look. "I guess we know why you didn't shoot the guy who broke into your house."

"That was a different scenario and a different weapon," I argued. "There was a lock on it. Plus, the safety was in a horrible spot. They should have a standard place for the safety on a gun. That's just common sense. I would actually support that legislation."

Her gaze didn't break away from me.

I turned back to the trunk, flicked the safety off, aimed, and slowly pulled the trigger, half watching the hammer inch backwards until it fell.

BOOM!

The gun seriously attempted to leap out of my hand but I thankfully held on. My left ear rang. I tried acting naturally and checked out the trunk to see if I'd hit it.

"Okay, you can't shoot worth a damn. We'll work on it. Come with me." She held out her hand, palm upward.

My face reddened and I carefully returned the gun to her,

and she led us away. This time she headed towards a smaller outbuilding with a large porch. I, of course, followed her without saying a word. After about 50 feet, I realized I was just like a dog she was leading around on a leash.

"Quick question." I squeezed my hands into fists and stood up straighter. "How are you all going to get me to Mars? I don't see any spaceships out here, and if I don't have assurances . . . maybe I should rethink my decision."

Savannah turned around to face me and walked backwards towards the outbuilding. "You don't see spaceships 'cause this ain't a spaceport." The friendliness remained, but the way she said it was also very businesslike. "We'll get you to one. Don't you worry." She turned back around.

"Wait. You guys have a spaceport?"

"We have access," she corrected me. "We can get people almost anywhere. We got cells all over the place."

"How many?" I asked.

"Well, Tex and I only know specifics on two. The less everyone knows, the better. That way we can't rat everybody else out. You'll be headed to our Chicagoland house after this, and they'll get you to your next stop and ultimately Mars."

"What about assurances? How do I know I'll actually get there?" I continued. "This could all be a con. Right?"

That stopped her in her tracks, and she spun and stared me square in the eyes. "This isn't a con. It's serious as all shit. Nobody is tricking you. Okay? You help us and we will help you. I give you my word. Hell, we already saved your ass once. Now you're practically calling me a liar? You gotta lotta nerve, Squirrely. And I was starting to like you too."

"I'm sorry," I blurted. "I'm not calling anyone anything. I've just never done anything like this before. I've never even been to sleep-away camp. This is all new to me and I don't want to be taken advantage of. I'm sorry."

Her smiled returned. "Don't feel bad. You had a question and you asked. You'd be stupid if you didn't. But nobody's lying to you. You hear?"

"I hear. I do."

Savannah softly chuckled and shook her head. "You are kinda squirrely. That one might stick. But I do kinda like ya. I think you're going to be alright."

"Can I try to get a new nickname? Is there a form or something?" I inquired.

She snorted a small laugh. "No. There ain't no form. Tex does the nicknames. He's good at it and they stick." She waved towards the building we had been marching towards before I had interrupted our trip. "That's the bunkhouse. It's air conditioned in there. We got some clothes that should fit just fine. There's a shower and sundries, and whatnot. Help yourself. Pick out a bed. Should be plenty of room. Just going to be you, a couple others, and Gill in there."

"Gil? As in *Gilbert*? Who's Gil?"

"The only other fella like you in there. Out-of-towner. City fella. You'll figure it out. And it's not *Gil* as in *Gilbert*. He looks kinda like a fish. Ergo . . ."

"*Gill*. Got it."

She started off towards the main house. "I better go check on Tex. Dinner will be served al fresco. We ring a bell. First come, first served."

At first, I didn't move. I just watched her walk away and hoped maybe she was going to stop and give me more information. But instead, she kept on going and disappeared into the ranch house. My face dropped. After another moment of just standing there like a dope, I headed to the bunkhouse. My sandals making their familiar flapping noise the whole way. I was used to the sound now. That didn't take long, I thought. Moments later I was on the shaded porch and slumped into a wooden rocking chair.

No sooner had my butt hit the seat when the bunkhouse door flew open and out came an early thirties, redheaded guy in a pair of shorts and sandals. An extra-large polo shirt provided room for his spacious stomach. He held an open, foaming beer bottle and looked at me with a pair of bulging eyes. I instantly thought of a fish.

"Hey, there!" he exclaimed. "My name's Gill. Or that's what Tex nicknamed me, at least. By the looks of it, you must be doing the same thing I'm doing here."

I arose from the chair and shook his hand. "Good to me you, Gill. I'm Avery."

Gill shuffled to the rocking chair next to mine. "Larkin's the last name, by the way."

We sat down together. "I'm Avery Davies-Plo—. Davies. Just Avery Davies."

"What nickname did Tex give you?"

"Uh, he didn't give me one. At least not that I heard," I lied.

"Weird. He told me he gives everyone a nickname. Oh, well. I guess it doesn't matter. Just like our real names aren't going to matter for much longer. Right? We're getting set up with new identities. Right? Ha!"

Gill actually said *ha*. Who does that? But he was correct. We were getting new identities. How much longer would I be me? That thought landed like a lead balloon.

"Man, it's hot out here." Gill chugged some beer and a healthy amount of it dribbled down his chin and onto his shirt.

This guy had to be a salesman or something. He was completely on his own track.

"I mean, it's warm, but I don't know if I'd call it hot. I actually kind of like it." And it really was growing on me.

Gill slurped more beer. "I don't know what you're talking about. It's hot. Give me air conditioning any day. Can't understand how people used to live without air conditioning."

"It's air conditioned inside," I replied. "That's what Savannah said. And you just came out from there. Maybe you're an inside kind of guy. You can go back in. I'm just going to sit here for a bit. Just got here."

He grunted. "There's a couple people in there that are zero fun to be around. And I could see some of them giving me a look. You know what I mean. Right? I hope I don't get paired up with any of them."

"Paired up?"

"Yeah. Didn't anyone tell you? When they send us out to our waypoint or whatever, they put us in teams. That way we don't feel like we're on our own, and so we have someone to help us." He ran a sweaty hand through his sweaty hair.

"I see," I said. "I can see why you wouldn't want to be paired up with someone who's not compatible with you."

He burped long and loud.

"It would make for quite a trying time to be with someone for a long—"

Another burp.

"—and arduous endeavor."

"Yeah, tell me about it." He reached into his mouth, way in there, and worked at something until he dislodged it from his teeth. "Just think how much worse it would be if I have to do all the work too. Man, I'll flip out if I get someone incompetent. It's going to be hard enough sneaking around like some ninja. It'll be even harder if I have to babysit someone. I hate it when stuff like that happens. Not that I can't do it, of course. I mean, I don't know how many times I've had to pick up the slack of other people at work, but it's been a lot. And it's never any fun. Just makes things more difficult for those of us who are competent. So, it better not happen here."

"Yes, it would be quite the tragedy if that happened." And yet I knew the universe was going to pair me up with this guy Gill. The rude fishman. Tex was better. But what did that say about me—*Squirelly*?

Gill put the beer bottle to his lips for a third time, raising it higher and higher. He gulped every last drop from it. Without missing a beat, he jumped out of the rocking chair and on its back swing it nearly hit the side of the house. "I'm going to get another brewski." He examined the bottle. "Man, these are the small ones. Can't believe these guys are so cheap."

"Hospitality isn't what it used to be," I told him.

Gill nodded and went back inside. I sat in the wooden rocking chair, looked at my prison shower shoes and contemplated my horrible life choices. My gaze went back to the fence post where I had seen the bird. It was long gone. Lucky guy.

CHAPTER NINETEEN

My thoughts circled back to the same place they had been since I arrived at the Crazy Death Ranch. How could I get out of this? That's all I could think. I had to get out of this deranged plan and away from these people. Unless they *could* get me to Mars. They talked like they could, that was for sure, but talk was cheap. What if they couldn't? Where could I go then? I'd end up on the road and get caught, then sent to prison. So... how was I going to get out of it?

It was hard to believe that two days ago my life was genuinely easier. Two days ago, I was just some guy from San Josisco on the run from the authorities, his girlfriend and group of bloodthirsty bounty hunters from a reality show. Now, I had somehow made things worse. I was at some insane ranch with a bunch of insane people who wanted me to go on some insane mission with them to a military installation where I'd be part of a team that was going to hack a government network. You know, like a bunch of highly trained commandos would do. And I definitely wasn't a highly trained commando. Pretty sure no one else around here was either.

So, I had to get out of it. Once again, I ended up at the beginning of my thought process. I was caught in a loop.

Dinner on the ranch was mostly a blur. Rows of picnic tables lined up end to end outside. I counted about eighteen people. Mostly ranch hand types from the looks of their clothing. Only a few normies like myself and Gill. That guy could eat. He didn't do that like a fish. In the food department he was more of a bear or large dog. Whatever animal he was, he was a hungry one. Not that I could really blame him. The meal was delicious.

Grilled beef, roasted potatoes, and cornbread with real butter. I ate my fill and kept to myself. Just tried to listen and think.

Tex and Savannah seemed relaxed for the most part. Most of their talk was about the day-to-day operations of the ranch. Feeding these animals, cleaning up after those animals, fixing fences. They didn't sound like terrorists. They laughed way too much for that. Not evil laughs either. Just loud laughter from happy people. It was so strange.

Kate was still gone, though. She must still be out doing whatever it was she did. The whole thing was unsettling, so I kept to myself and thought. I had to figure a way out.

After dinner I helped clean up. Seemed to be the right thing to do. Everyone else pitched in as well. Every once in a while I could feel Savannah or Tex looking at me, but for the most part they left me alone.

Back in the bunk house I found a shelf of travel sized toiletries, soap, toothpaste, brushes, deodorant, and everything like that. That felt like a small victory. I took a shower and got cleaned up. I almost managed to feel halfway human again. There was another shelf with clothing that seemed like it was up for grabs. After a few tries I found some jeans that fit, along with an old work shirt and some work shoes. I slipped my oversized prison shower sandals under the bed. Somehow it felt wrong to throw them away. Besides, they helped get me out of San Josisco. I decided to hang on to them and my hard-fought-for frozen pizza jacket. They were like strange trophies in a way. And who knew? Maybe I would need them again.

Looking in the mirror I was shocked to see not the reflection of Avery the toilet paper cop. I looked more like a ranch hand. An extremely pale ranch hand. The whole look and feeling was very, very odd.

Gill came barging in. No knock. No nothing. Just blew in like he owned the place. Somewhere he'd found another beer.

"Whoa! Look at the new duds! You're fitting in my man!" Good lord the guy was loud.

"Thanks. I guess," I muttered as I made my way back out

to the porch. Everything felt better outside. I could look around at the landscape. It at least felt like I wasn't as trapped as I really was.

So, I sat there and watched the ranch and the gently rolling hills of Texas. I watched the lights go out in main house. I sat and listened to noises I'd never heard before as darkness settled in. Strange barks off in the distance. Coyotes? Were there coyotes out here? Could they get in the compound? Of course, they could. I listened more to try to figure out if they were getting closer, wondering if I should go inside. I didn't want to go back in the bunkhouse though. I liked it on the porch.

Then I looked up at the sky. It was easily the most stars I had ever seen in my life. It was wondrous. Just spectacular. Way better than the field trip to the planetarium we took in sixth grade. I wondered where all those kids were now. Probably all grown up with families of their own. Living normal lives in regular apartment pods. Not on the run from the law with a team of bounty hunters from a reality show chasing them.

The weight of my failure pressed down on me. There was no denying it. I messed up on a massive level. There are consequences for screwing up as badly as I did, and I was in the middle of them and wasn't even smart enough to figure a way out.

So, I sat and I listened to the night, and I watched a million stars and felt small.

Hours went by.

Then the gentle noises were interrupted by the distant rumble of a motor. And it was getting closer. I quietly got up from my seat and saw a pair of headlights creeping over the hilltop on the road leading down into the ranch.

I got off the porch as fast I could and ducked into the shadows along the side of the bunkhouse. My instincts were screaming for me to hide, and I was all about listening to my instincts now. Something had to be wrong. It's the middle of the night and a vehicle is rolling in? No way was I not going to hide. I was also prepared to run if I had to.

The headlights got closer. They were attached to a truck. Was that Kate's truck? Hard to tell. Security lights came on as the vehicle pulled up in front of the main house. They must be hooked up to motion detectors, I thought. Good to know. I'll have to avoid those if I decide to scamper off into the night. Just then a coyote yipped in the distance. Okay. Avoid the motion detectors and hungry wild animals. Could anything be easy now? Anything?!

The driver side door of the truck opened and thankfully Kate stepped out and not a team of bounty hunters. She seemed okay. Maybe a little tired. Where was she coming from in the middle of the night? Savannah came outside wrapped in a robe and welcomed Kate with a friendly hug. They were talking but I was too far away to hear anything. After a minute they both went inside.

Who the hell are these people? I waited for few minutes. No lights came on in the house. A few minutes more and still no lights. They had probably gone to bed.

I thought about stealing the truck and trying to make a break for it. That seemed stupid. Once I hit the main road, I wouldn't even know whether to turn left or right. I had no idea where to go. Plus, how was I going to get gas?

Crap.

I snuck across the porch and quietly made my way inside the bunkhouse. Gill's snoring covered any slight sound I might have made. Gill's snoring would also have covered the sound of a small plane. Of course he snored. Of course. It was only fitting that the big, loud fishman would snore.

I laid back onto my bed and stared at the ceiling, knowing for a fact, sleep wouldn't be happening. It was impossible. My mind was racing a mile a minute.

*****

Waking up was interesting. Puffing and squeaking broke through my slumber and my eyes slowly opened. Blackness. Was it still night? I reached for my phone but of course it wasn't there. My sight eventually found the red digits on the ancient radio alarm clock next to my bed. 4:30 in the morning. More puffing and squeaking noises.

Motion off to the left caught my attention. A big blob of darkness was waving around. I kept up the illusion that I was still asleep and opened my eyes just enough to try and figure out the mystery. What was that? Was that Gill? He was standing near the foot of his bed doing . . . windmills? He was doing windmills. The guy was exercising. Hands out to the side, bending over and touching his left foot with his right hand, then back to standing, then right foot with left hand, and so forth. He puffed in rhythm and the wooden floorboards beneath him squeaked. So not a murderer creeping up on me. Good. Now that I knew I was going to live, I was irate.

"What are you *doing*?" I pushed up onto my elbows.

"Hey, roomie. Good morning. Wanna exercise with me?" he said at full volume. Regular voice. Nothing close to a, "Sorry did I wake you?" was remotely in his tone.

"It's 4:30."

"Yep. Like I said, good morning."

"The sun isn't even up. What are you doing?"

"Already asked, and already answered," said Gill.

My head hit the pillow. I grabbed it and shoved it over my face. *Man, I have to get out of this*, I told myself.

CHAPTER TWENTY

Breakfast was over before sunrise. I watched the sun start to come up as I stood on the porch of the mess hall drinking what had to be the strongest cup of coffee ever made. No cream. No sugar. Just a bitter, black, hot, lava blast of caffeine. It was horrible. I had three cups. Kate arrived soon after.

"Kate? You're back?" I said, trying to act surprised.

She sauntered up to Gill and myself, and I checked the corners of my mouth to ensure no breakfast leftovers were hanging on. That would be embarrassing.

Gill belched loudly. The hot air hit the side of my head. As I stood there in shock, he wiped the entire lower half of his face with his forearm as if that were the problem.

I slowly closed my eyes and opened them again.

"Look at you, Avery. You're still alive." Kate patted my side.

I smiled. "Yeah. For now, anyway. So, where'd you go?"

"Nowhere special," she said with a nonchalant little grin.

I shrugged. "Okay. Anyway, listen, we need to talk. I think I've made a big mistake. You see—"

"Well, good mornin'. Y'all ready to get started?" Tex appeared out of nowhere. Savannah was on his left. They walked with purpose towards us. Tex gave his jeans a mighty hitch.

"Well, you see—" I started again to Kate.

"How 'bout you, miss Kate?" Tex boomed.

"Let's do it." She nodded. Confident.

"Wait?" I said with more than a little surprise. "You're supposed to go on this mission thing too?"

"Yep."

"Great! Since there are no objections, let's head to the

barn." Tex's voice was way too loud, especially for this hour of the morning.

He didn't wait for any further input and started off. Savannah swaggered next to him. Kate and Gill didn't hesitate in following either. I hurried to catch up.

Getting up the barn ladder into the nest was uneventful this time and minutes later we were standing and listening to Savannah give us a briefing on what we were about to do. Or, at least, what we were supposed to do. I needed to pick the perfect time to let them know I was out. With something like this, timing was everything. I'm not certain when I decided I wasn't going. Maybe it was on the walk over to the barn. I don't know. But I was certain I couldn't go on any mission and just had to let them down at the most opportune time.

"As soon as the sun goes down, you'll be headed out in two aircars," Savannah announced. "Kate and Tex will pilot. Avery, you're going with her. Gill, you'll be with Tex."

"Sweet," Gill said.

"When you get to the rendezvous point, you'll link up with our contact," she continued. "And from there, he'll lead you to your objective where Avery will complete the mission for us."

"What's Gill going to be doing?" I blurted out. As if I was still onboard with this mass psychosis.

"I'm the muscle," he snorted.

Savannah offered a polite smile. "Gill has skills that helped us modify the aircars to the specs we needed, which included taking out all the tracking devices the authorities just love so damned much."

Gill proudly grinned. "I'm a systems engineer, and I'm really good with working on mechanical stuff too. They put five different trackers on an aircar. But they only list two. So in a sense, I kind of already saved the day."

"Are you serious?" I asked.

"Hard time believing your ol' pal Gill is so smart?" he replied.

"We just met, Gill. We're not pals." I tried to sound polite.

He snorted again. "We will be. Trust me, Avery. You won't be able to resist. I grow on people. It's a gift." He grinned like an idiot fish.

I rolled my eyes.

"So, does everyone understand the basic concept of the operation so far?" Savannah asked.

That snapped me back to reality. "No! I mean, I do. But I've changed my mind. I can't do this." Shit. Not sure it was the right moment but here we go.

"Say again, Squirrely?" Tex said.

"Look, you people don't understand. This isn't me. Any of this." I quickly spread my arms to indicate the "any of this" part and almost whacked Kate, who bent sideways just in time. "I'm not an outlaw. You are. And you seem very good at it. But I don't want to make my situation any worse. Right? You get that. So, thanks for everything you've done, I really appreciate it but, uh, I need to leave here. The sooner the better. Oh! And I swear to never tell anyone about any of this. Your secrets are safe with me. And I mean that. For real."

"What happened to Mars, Squirrely?" asked Tex. "Don't wanna do that either? 'Cause this here's a package deal."

"Yeah, I thought about that. And I'm not calling anyone a liar. But I'm not a hundred percent sure you guys can get me there. Again. Not calling anyone a liar."

The room got very still. Tex stared me straight in the eyes. Gill breathed heavily. That was probably his usual breathing, but it was all I could hear.

"Savannah?" Tex asked. His gaze never leaving mine. "How many people have we been responsible for getting off planet to that little red ball of freedom known as Mars?"

"Sixty-two," she replied flatly. She was staring at me too. I could feel it.

"Sixty-two!" boomed Tex. "More than a damn deck of playing cards! Have they all made it? Did we EVER have a problem, sweetcheeks?"

"Not till now."

Again, the awkward stillness. Everyone was waiting for me to talk.

"That's a very impressive track record." I started. "I just—"

Tex didn't let me finish.

"Yes, it is. One we are extremely proud of." He was still staring right at me. "Savannah, will you explain the situation to Squirrely here?" He drew out the syllables of my nickname. Not a good sign. I've never been in a gang before but that was definitely not good at all.

Savannah chimed in. Calm and cool. "There's no backing out now, sweetheart. We had an agreement last night. We gave you our word and you gave us yours. Now, there is a satellite launch this afternoon and that thing's gonna be operational later on tonight. So, you're gonna hack it for us or we're all screwed six ways to Sunday. I don't wanna have to pull up stakes and set up a new outpost. We are staying put right here. We all like it here and this place is ours. It's home. So, suck it up, buttercup, and get used to doing things that you might not be too comfortable with. We had a deal and now we're counting on you. As much as I don't like it, we need you. And if you still want to go to Mars, well then you need us too. So, just hack the stupid satellite, all right?"

Again . . .everyone was waiting for me to talk. This was happening way too much.

"Fine. I'll do it." What else could I say?

Savannah wasn't finished with me. "Now after this is all done and you want us to take you somewhere else, you need to speak up. We can make that happen too. But right now, the wheels are in motion to get you and Gill to Mars. Lots of people are working to make that happen. Brave people. Not a single one of them deserves to have their lives endangered or their time wasted. So, you have till tonight to let us know. After that, no deal. Understand?"

"I do. Completely"

"Good. Don't worry so damn much. Tonight's gonna be easy peasy, lemon squeezy." Finally, she smiled. The tension left the room.

"Now let's go have some fun and pick out some guns for your little field trip!" she added happily.

"Guns?"

Tex grinned. "Don't worry. I'll teach ya."

With that, everyone made their way towards the ladder and outside. As if everything was totally normal.

We made our way across the compound to another old building. Tex said they used to use it for chickens. Must have been a lot of chickens. The place was the size of a small barn.

He came out grinning, carrying a large footlocker. It had to be full of guns.

"Alright, let's get you boys and girls some weapons."

I knew it. Crap.

The giant cowboy opened the case to reveal a small armory. Rifles, handguns, shotguns, you name it. They had it all.

"Squirrely, you and Gill can grab a handgun. Kate and I will take the big stuff."

Kate walked over and grabbed some kind of rifle and handled it with the casual confidence of someone who's done this kind of thing a million times. Even Gill wasted no time in sauntering over and selecting a handgun. What a piece of work, that guy. He even spun the barrel and checked the sights!

I slowly made my way over and pretended to know what I was looking at. Tex waited patiently. I tilted my head as if I were really weighing my options.

Tex chuckled and handed me a smaller-sized grey pistol.

"Good choice," I said with slight nod.

"Yes, is it. That there's a Glock. Great gun. One hell of gun. Now let's teach you how to shoot it."

The next hour was dedicated to weapons training. Tex and Savannah made sure we were all confident handling the weapons. Now when I say "we all," I mean me.

Kate operated at some kind of assassin level. Calmly hitting every target she aimed at. Tex and Savannah had a series of metal plates attached to posts at various distances. Kate and her auto rifle hit all of them with ease. She didn't miss.

Gill was next. Savannah handed him some ammo and the guy actually knew what he was doing. He loaded his gun, took aim and the ping, ping, ping of bullets hitting steel plates reverberated across the ranch.

My turn. This was going to be embarrassing. After Tex repeated everything he just told me about weapons and safety for the third time, making me repeat it to make sure I understood, he handed me a clip. The big guy was actually a good teacher. Had to hand it to him. He had done his job and I wasn't terrified of the gun.

I took the clip and slapped into the grip. Almost. Something was wrong. It hadn't gone all the way in.

"Backwards," Kate muttered under her breath. She gave me a little wink.

Okay, so off to great start. I quickly turned the clip around and loaded the Glock. Much easier this way with the bullets pointed in the right direction.

I assumed the stance that Tex had shown me and rolled my shoulder to loosen up.

"Just aim at that that one, honey," Savannah said as she pointed to the closest target, twenty feet away.

I took a breath. Pulled the trigger and missed. Gill snorted, stifling a laugh. I quietly took aim again and missed. No ping. Not good. I was about to give up when Kate intervened.

She came up right behind me and put her hands on top of mine.

"Relax," she said. "Just think of it as an extra part of your hand. Look at what you want to hit. Line up your sites and squeeze." Her breath as she spoke in my ear took my mind off everything else. Also feeling her breasts against my back was quite nice. I don't think I've ever felt breasts against my back. I immediately decided I liked it.

"Now shoot," she said quietly.

I aimed at the steel plate and pulled the trigger. Ping! I hit it. I shot the thing I was trying to shoot. That was shocking. Kate stepped back. I aimed and pulled the trigger again. Ping. Again, on purpose and not a fluke.

Tex chuckled. "Watch out now. Looks like Squirrely's a shooter. How about you aim at that next one down a ways."

I squeezed the trigger. Missed.

The colossal cowboy clapped me on the back. "Well, you can hit the close ones and you ain't gonna shoot anybody on accident. That's an improvement. That's all we need for today. Improvement."

He collected the guns and class was over. I went over to Kate.

"Thanks. For, uh, jumping in just now. That was a big help."

"You're welcome. Glad to do it," she said as she squinted in the bright sunshine. She even squinted cool.

A hand wrapped around my waist and pulled me away. Savannah.

"Let's get to it. You and I need to look at the tech you'll be using tonight. These three need to go double check the cars. Make sure they're good to go." She said as she led us back towards the barn.

"I said they'd be ready. They'll be ready," barked Tex.

"How much charge to they have?!" Savannah shouted back.

"I don't know. I've been here with you!" boomed Tex.

"That's why I want you to check, you idiot! Nothing goes wrong tonight!"

"Hey, woman!"

"What?!"

"I love you," Tex said with a smile.

Savannah smiled but didn't turn around. "Love you too, you horny old goat. Now go make sure those cars are ready!" She turned to me. "I do love him. But I swear it's just like talking to a brick wall sometimes."

We walked into the barn and headed up to the nest.

She opened up a small, locked cabinet and handed me an

ancient looking laptop computer. I hadn't seen one of these since grade school. My surprise must have shown.

"It'll work. It's old as shit, but it'll get you on the internet. All the software's up to date. Now listen up, do not turn that thing on until you get to the location, and you've met up with Wifi. He'll let you know the rest."

"Wait . . . Wifi?"

"He's your contact. That's his codename. He knows how to get you into the military systems."

"But he get's a codename like Wifi and I'm Squirrely?"

"Yes, he does. First impressions are everything."

"Okay. Well, as long as codename Wifi knows what he's doing, and you guys trust him. This whole thing makes me extremely nervous. Are you sure there's no other way?"

"There isn't. I'm sorry, honey. Try not to worry so much. You got a good team. And I'm sure Wifi knows what he's doing. At least he says he does." Then she added. "He better or we're all gonna have a bad night."

She locked the laptop back in the cabinet and we headed down the ladder to the warm Texas afternoon.

CHAPTER TWENTY-ONE

The sun was getting dangerously close to the horizon as I sat on the porch with my plate of food. I didn't have much of an appetite. My heart seemed to beat faster with every passing moment. Every time I looked up the sun seemed to have drifted even lower. I knew as soon as it was dark, we would head out on our "mission." This was madness. My stomach did flip flops as it twisted itself into a series of small knots.

"Hey, you want some ice cream?" Kate's voice interrupted my anxiety death spiral. I looked up and there she was, holding two ice cream cones. Like everything was even close to normal. She handed one to me as she eased into the chair next to mine.

"Wow . . . uh . . .thanks," I stammered.

"No problem," she said.

The silence stretched on. I had to say something. But what? She was so at ease. *Do I tell her how much I'm secretly flipping out? Or do I just say something even if it sounds stupid? Just the first thing that pops into my mind.*

"How can they afford this?" I guess my brain went with stupid.

She casually licked her ice cream from the side to correct for a drip.

"They make it." She looked at me a bit quizzically.

"Oh. That never occurred to me. You can do that." I took a lick of my cone. I wasn't really in the mood for ice cream but I sure as hell didn't want to offend the one person I almost felt

I could trust. The cold vanilla hit my tongue. Easily the best ice cream I'd ever had. Holy crap!

"Good, right?"

"This is incredible. I feel like I've never eaten ice cream before." I was truly astonished.

"You probably haven't. I mean, not homemade. Made with real milk. Not processed and beaten to death with chemical and additives. No, the real thing is so much better." She took another lick.

"Well, thanks . . . again. For the ice cream and the shooting lesson earlier."

"No problem. You're welcome. Looked like you could use some help. That goes for both the ice cream and the gun," she said with just a hint of a laugh. Not making fun of me. Just a good-natured little mini tease. It felt great. I smiled back and had another lick of cold vanilla heaven.

"I think I may be better with the ice cream cone than the gun. Also, there's a much smaller chance I'll kill someone with one of these. Although there is still some chance. I can't say zero. I wish I could. But if someone tries to take this deliciousness from me now? Boom. Dead. I kill them. Sad but true."

"Right?" She said with a laugh. "Totally justified."

We sat there for bit with our ice cream cones. The moment maybe lasted thirty seconds, but it was wonderful. I was just guy eating an ice cream sitting on porch next to a beautiful girl who seemed to enjoy my company.

"Kate, can I ask you something?"

"That depends. What do you want to know?"

"Everything. I mean, you. This place. These people. Who are they? How does all this work? What is going on here? And are we going to live through tonight?"

"That was like seven questions."

"I'm needy. And I can't count. It felt like one."

She smiled, took a breath and began. "Okay, I'll tell you what I can—"

"Whoa! How good was that food?" Gill barked as he

approached. This guy was really starting to bug me. "Savannah and Tex say it's time to get ready. So, let's do this. Wooo!" He added a little fist pump flourish at the end. If it was false bravado, it was a good act. How could he even pretend to be excited?

I took a quick look around. The sun had sunk behind the hills on the horizon. It would be full dark soon. Shit.

Kate stood up and turned to me.

"Try not to worry too much. Relax. We can talk later, okay? Right now, we need to focus."

"Sure. Good call. Focus."

She headed off towards the main house. Gill and I watched her go.

"My man. You two looked like you were having a serious convo! What's up with that?" Gill nodded at me. He looked amazingly like a fish when he did it. A rude, loud fish.

I shook my head and headed inside to change into the mission clothes Savannah gave to us.

Minutes later I stepped into the aircar. Both were parked just outside an outbuilding. I was decked out in black jeans and a black hooded sweatshirt. Kate was dressed similarly, but she looked completely natural. The laptop, spare batteries, and my loaded gun were in a backpack that I carried. I sweated profusely.

Kate sat in the pilot's seat and fired up the engine. The six rotors came to life and the car rose a good foot off the ground. Even though my door was still open it was incredibly quiet. Just a mild, slight hum. The rotors cutting through the air were probably the loudest part.

Savannah hurried over. I could see Tex and Gill in their aircar as it hovered nearby. They were ready. Savannah leaned in my side, reached over, and handed Kate a small piece of paper.

"There ya go, sweetheart. Those are the coordinates. Wifi is standing by. He says we're good to go. Squirrely, you can do this. All you're doing is teaching that satellite to count toilet paper wrong. Okay?"

"I don't know."

She acted like I hadn't said a word and just kept going. Then she spoke to Kate.

"Now it's a military base so be careful. Hopefully, everything goes smooth as silk, but if it don't and something goes wrong, get the hell out of there at meet back at the Triple R. Fly low, fly quiet, and fly safe. See ya back here in a jiffy."

She turned and looked to me with a big grin.

"Just like counting toilet paper." She winked and closed the door before I could say a word.

Kate took us up about fifty feet, turned off the headlights and stopped.

"What are we doing? Are we calling it off? Good idea. Thank you. We should figure out a Plan B."

She looked at the paper and started punching numbers into what I guess was a navigation program on the dashboard.

"Nope. We're still going. Just need to know where," she stated softly. Almost a whisper, really. "Now we're going to be super quiet, okay? We need to fly low. Under the radar. I need a second for my eyes to adjust to the dark, so we don't hit a tree or worse."

"Hit a tree? How low are we going?"

Kate looked around to indicate this was it. This was as high as we'd be flying. She was an insane person evidently.

"Are you trying to kill us? We can't do this!"

"Shhhh. Whisper. If you need to say something, whisper. No loud noises," she snapped.

"Why?" I whispered.

"Because the military doesn't just have radar. There are AI listening posts among other things. Loud noises are a dead giveaway. Don't worry about how low we are. It's a good thing. The closer we are to the ground, the less noise we make. And the harder we are to spot. I've done this before. Don't worry. We'll *cricket* most of the way."

"Don't worry?! What's a cricket? What does that even mean? How can you expect me not to worry when you say things like that?"

"It's a kind of sonar. You know how bats navigate? Every couple of seconds, we'll let out a little electronic chirp and it'll ping back here. Let us know what's what. Now shush." She pointed to the nav screen on the dash. It was black.

"It's broken!" I whisper shouted.

Kate pressed another button, and the faintest chirping noise came from the front of the car. Sounded just like a real cricket chirp. Before my surprise could register, a green outline of the ground appeared on screen.

"See? It's not broken." She whispered back. As another chirp sounded, Kate piloted us forward. I looked outside and the other aircar with Tex and Gill were right behind us.

She accelerated. Faster and faster. The only noise was the chirp every few seconds. As soon as the digital outline of the terrain faded another chirp would sound.

It was a lengthy experiment in terror. Each time the image died I was sure the system had failed, and we'd end up slamming into something. Then, another tiny cricket chirp, the image would come back, and we were allowed to live. At least until the next chirp.

Hills and ridges appeared, and Kate would guide us smoothly over them. She was the epitome of calm determination. Her eyes constantly scanning the horizon and the readouts of the aircar. I wanted to know how fast we were flying but thought it would be better not to look. Kate seemed to be in complete control. Tex somehow managed to keep up. Every time I looked back, there was the other aircar. Just as dark and quiet as ours.

Like two strange giant beetles, we flew across the Texas night.

It went on like this for an eternity. As soon as I would even start to whisper something, Kate would give me serious nod that said, *Not now*. The electronic cricket would chirp. The motor would hum, I would remain terrified, and I couldn't even talk about it!

Then it finally happened. After the chirp, the screen just

showed green static. What the hell? I looked to Kate who was in deep concentration. The chirp sounded again. Now the screen showed nothing but an odd irregular line across the top of the display. I did the only thing I could think of. I tapped it. A repeating panic induced a series of taps. What was that line? Another chirp. The weird line showed up again. This time a bit lower on the screen. Then it dawned on me; that line wasn't a glitch. It was the top of hills!

"Shit." I just said it. Screw whispering. We were about to slam into a hillside, I was allowed to curse now.

My stomach nosedived into my small intestines and said hello to my sphincter as Kate pulled the aircar almost vertical. My back pressed against the seat as my field of vision filled with nothing but a starry Texas sky. We hadn't hit yet. Still, we climbed. I braced for impact.

The cricket chirped again. Now the stupid line was at the bottom of the screen. What the hell? Oh, no. If that line was the top of the hill, now we had to go down the other side. I looked to Kate, pleading.

"Please don't."

She didn't listen. We just went rocketing down the other side. I held onto the roof as my stomach and colon decided to go pay my throat a visit. Now it was indeed just a matter of time before we slammed into the ground. Through my panic and gritted teeth, I turned my head to Kate.

"I said please."

Just before the earth rammed through the windshield—I could see it all quite clearly, even the Texas dirt with an insane amount of detail; other people got to re-live their lives in their last moments; see loved ones again; I got high-definition, slow-motion soil and rocks; (just my luck) Kate pulled us out of the dive and we leveled off.

I slowly peeled my hand off the roof as I realized we were alive. We flew on in silence.

After a minute, Kate whispered to me. "You okay? That part's always a little hairy."

"I can't talk to you right now," I whispered back. "Because my stomach's in my throat and my intestines are still unraveling. And I'm pretty sure my butthole is in my armpit. They haven't seen each other in awhile."

She just smiled and stifled a laugh.

"Guess what?" she whispered.

"What?"

"We get to do it again on the way back." She grinned as if it was a great joke.

"IF we get back," I whisper shouted. "IF. And it's a big *if*. We might die on this mission. We might not get another try at death mountain back there."

"Good point." She nodded.

We flew on in the strange quiet. Me desperately wanting her to say something that contradicted my "we might die" theory. But she didn't.

After about another hour, Kate suddenly slowed down the aircar, her eyes scanning our surroundings.

"What's wrong?

"Just looking for a landmark," she calmly stated. "And I just found it."

She took us down and we gently landed near a rock the size of a small car. Tex and Gill parked their aircar nearby. I saw them both getting out.

"What are we doing?" I whispered to Kate as I followed her outside. She was walking over to the rock.

"Supplies," she whispered back.

Kate squatted down and reached underneath the boulder. Was she looking for something?

A giant meaty hand clapped me on the shoulder. Tex.

"How you doing, Squirrely? You hangin' in there?" Even his whispers were loud.

"Not a fan of the near-death experience. Not at all."

Gill approached. For once he wasn't being a loudmouth braggart. Maybe the reality of the evening's insanity had finally hit him. He nodded a greeting to me, and I nodded back. Seemed like the polite thing to do.

Tex made his way over to Kate who still had her hands in the dirt under the large rock.

"Got it," she softly said to Tex and then she lifted the boulder up from one side as easily as a person opening the lid to a dumpster. I couldn't believe what I was seeing. That thing had to weigh tons. Tons! Gill and I rushed over.

"Holy shit!" I exclaimed. "How did you do that?"

"Once I found the latch, I just opened it," Kate said quietly as she brushed dirt from her hands. Under the rock was a large pit full of what looked like various-sized boxes all covered with tarps.

"Looks real, doesn't it?" she said as she lightly tapped on the rock with her knuckles. It was plastic. The "boulder" was an empty shell. "These things are great. Pretty convincing in the daytime too," she added.

Tex had already stepped down into the hole and was grabbing items and putting them aside.

"This here's a little supply depo, boys" the big man said as he handed up items to Gill and me. "We got these all over. Never know when you'll need extra gas or batteries and whatnot."

He handed me a heavy five-gallon container of gasoline and I set it aside.

"Why would we need extra? I thought we had plenty to get us there and back," I asked.

"In case something goes wrong and we have to make a run for it. We can't go back to the ranch. We just might have to get out of there and go. Every man for himself." Gill stated it so matter of fact it made my face hurt. I winced. I actually looked at him and winced.

"Bingo. Gill gets it," Tex rumbled.

I looked at Kate. She just shrugged as if to say, *What else can I say?* My face was stuck on full wince.

"Wait . . . every man for himself? Shouldn't we have some kind of rendezvous point or something?" My whisper was just regular talking now. Whispers could wait. This was some bullshit.

Kate chimed in. "If something goes wrong, just stay by me or Tex. We know where the nearest safehouses are."

"Maybe you should let us know too. Just as a back-up," I said, indicating me and Gill.

"Nope." Tex lowered the fake rock back down. "The more people who know locations just make it worse for everyone else. Nobody knows more than two at any given time. That way if somebody gets nabbed, they can't rat out the whole operation. It's for everybody's safety. You can't talk about stuff you don't know. It's pretty standard operating procedure for any kinda secret society. Now let's get moving. We're making pretty good time. We should be meeting up with Wifi in the next half hour. Let's top off the gas tanks, switch out the batteries on the aircars, and get going. If you need to pee, now's the time."

Ten minutes later, we were headed out again. I turned to Kate as she flew.

"Okay. This might be matter-of-fact, standard operating procedure for you guys, but it isn't for me. Is there anything else I need to know?"

"Just focus on your job. You do the hacking. Leave everything else to me, Tex, Gill and Wifi."

"Yeah, what about this Wifi person? What's his job? Who is he anyway? Do we trust Wifi? Because honestly, I'm having major trust issues right about now. I've struggled with those for years and tonight isn't helping. My social sensitivity coach would call it a major setback."

"Don't worry about Wifi. He's good people. He's worked on this base for years. Just be glad he's also brave enough to do what's right. He's a vigilante, just like me. I wish we had more Wifi's in this world."

I gave up. It was no use. I was flying across Texas in an aircar piloted by a self-described vigilante. Part of a secret society of armed "freedom fighters" on our way to hack a satellite from a military base with the help of another vigilante who went by the code name Wifi. It was all so surreal. I just sat and stared out the front window as the weight of that thought settled over me like a lead blanket.

Kate whispered to me. "I just hope we don't have to shoot anybody."

I turned to her. Hoping to see a smile or some indication of a joke. Nope. She was serious.

"Thanks for saying that. That hadn't occurred to me. I hope so too." The lead blanket just got heavier.

I decided to go back to staring out the window.

The distant lights of the military base peeked out over the horizon. Maybe a mile away? Kate slowed us down and stopped the aircar, hovering low. A mere three feet above the ground. She double checked the nav points on the car's display. I looked to see Tex and Gill's car hovering nearby.

"Alright, Wifi. Where are you?" Kate uttered.

"He's not here. We should go. Abort. Abort, right?"

She looked at me, trying to figure out if I was joking. I tried forcing a smile to pretend I was.

"These are the coordinates. He'll be here," she said with a slight nod.

"How long do we wait? For real."

A small red dot appeared on Kate's shoulder. Almost like a laser pointer. The dot shimmered and enlarged to the size of a pinky fingernail.

"Kate." I tried to stay calm, but panic was rising. I pointed to the dot. Which shimmered again and transformed from a red circle into a smiley face.

She just grinned. "There he is." Her eyes tracked the source of the beam. It was coming from a nearby hillside. Kate lowered the car to the ground and killed the engine.

"Showtime, Squirrely," she said with a mischievous smirk and opened her door to step out. "Don't forget the bag," she added.

I grabbed the backback with the laptop and gun and got out of the car.

Tex and Gill were hurrying over. They each had their guns

out. Not a good sign as far as I was concerned. But who knows? That could be basic standard operating procedure.

I followed Kate's lead as we all hustled to the hill where the smiley face beam originated.

Halfway up the incline, we heard a voice softly call out: "Subway."

"Eat fresh," Kate responded.

"That's the password? *Subway. Eat fresh*?" I was incredulous.

"It worked," said Kate, casually.

"And didn't they go out of business years ago for selling fake mealworms?"

She ignored me as a pudgy man wearing a skintight black outfit appeared as if from nowhere. He pulled off a knit mask to reveal a face belonging to a man in his mid-fifties. He needed a shave.

"You made it. Just in time," he said.

"Wouldn't miss it," Kate replied.

"Wifi, this is Squirrely. He's our hacker," she continued.

He shook my hand. "Nice to meet you."

"Yeah, same," I lied.

Tex and Gill caught up.

"What's the play? How's it looking?" said Tex, a bit out of breath. Gill was sucking wind a bit too.

My ears started ringing. As soon as this idiot launched into some plan about cutting through fences and sneaking onto a military base, I was sure I was going to faint. That was just a fact. Out cold.

Wifi took a breath and began.

"As long as your guy knows what he's doing, we're good to go from here." He reached down and produced a small, hard-shelled case. "This transmitter should come in handy." Wifi said with a grin as he opened the container, revealing a signal boosting kit.

I wanted to shout with joy. "He has a signal kit! This guy has a signal kit! We can do this from here! I love this guy!" I scream whispered.

"*Wifi*," the paunchy man said, now deadly serious. "'This guy is called *Wifi*."

"Yes, you are, and I apologize. But you can get me on the base networks with that, right?"

He nodded the affirmative. I scrambled to get out my laptop.

Tex grabbed me by the shoulder. "Relax, Squirrely, you got plenty of time. You and Wifi work your magic and the three of us will be on lookout." He nodded towards Kate and Gill. "You just teach that satellite how to count the way we want it too."

He and the others headed off to take up their lookout positions. Wifi and I got busy.

The guy hadn't lied. He knew what he was doing. I hooked up the laptop to Wifi's machine and he had us hooked into the right military network in no time at all. Then he simply input his codes that authorized our little visit to the secure site. After that we just scrolled through our choices of satellites! They were all listed as if they were on a menu at a coffee shop!

I selected the one we were looking for and clicked it. This was insanely easy. I looked at Wifi. "There is no way it's this simple. This code looks like it hasn't been updated in decades!"

He looked at me and smirked.

"It hasn't. Welcome to the wonderful world of antiquated, overpriced, big government tech. It's laughable."

I couldn't help but smile.

He nodded back at the laptop, reminding me to get on with it. I did. The sub-program I needed to hack was easy enough to find. Click. And it was so close to the program that counted sheets of toilet paper, they could have been written by the same person. They might have been. I launched into my counting hack. Click. Just like my old job as a toilet paper cop. Click. Now to teach the program to count the way Savannah and Tex wanted. Click. I pressed enter and we were done. Wifi had me download the satellite info so we could double check later that my hack worked. That took another couple of minutes and then we were finished.

I packed up my laptop and Wifi closed the case to his equipment.

"Good job, Squirrely. It would've taken me hours trying to figure out what you just did. Nice work."

"Thank you, Wifi. Good job yourself." We smiled and shook hands, then quickly made our way down the hill where we were joined by the others.

"How'd we do, Squirrely?" whispered Tex.

"All set!" I gladly whispered back.

Then it was a series of handshakes and pats on the back all the way around. Gill was all smiles as well. We said our goodbye to Wifi, who then made his way back into the Texas night.

"Anybody else want to get out of here and go home for a cold beer?" Kate asked with a grin.

"Yes, please," I answered.

We all got back in our aircars and headed off for the ranch. We flew low. The sound of the soft electronic chirping reverberating through the vehicle, which was fine with me. I couldn't stop smiling. Finally, something had gone right. It was great. For the first time in a long time, I felt truly happy.

Kate whispered over to me. "Want me to go little slower when we come up on that big hill that scared the shit out of you?"

"That would be great. Thank you," I replied, genuinely pleased.

"Will do." She smiled.

And we quietly flew on through the Texas night. Two happy vigilantes.

CHAPTER TWENTY-TWO

Kate gently landed the aircar inside the outbuilding where they were kept and shut off the engine with a press of a button.

"Well, look at that, we made it," she said to me with slight tilt of her head.

"Yes, we did," I replied with a smile, imitating her head move. Her forehead creased in puzzlement as it took her a moment to realize I was only teasing. Then a grin crept over her face.

"Oh, now you're gonna get cocky?" she asked.

"I'm just happy, that's all. Happy I'm not getting shot. Happy I'm not headed to prison. Right now, it's all good."

"Mmm-hmm." She did the head tilt thing again. "So, I guess you're headed to Mars, right?"

The realization slowly dawned on me. "Yeah . . . I guess I am." This just made my smile all the bigger.

"Alright! Let's get this gear stowed!" shouted Tex as he and Gill got out of their aircar parked behind us. I grabbed the backpack with the laptop. Kate took the guns, and we made our way towards the barn, following Tex and Gill. Tex whistled a little tune as he went and I could tell he was a happy giant. There was a palpable sense of relief all the way around.

Savannah ran over to meet us, her substantial breasts bouncing beneath her white tee shirt with each step. Kate elbowed me. Damn, did I just get busted again? I looked over at Kate, who oddly enough was also admiring Savannah's assets.

"They're great, aren't they?" she asked. This had to be a trap.

"Hmmm? I don't know what you're taking about." I tried to look sincere.

She laughed. "Okay. Good for you. I was talking about her shoes, by the way."

"Oh . . . yeah. Very nice."

"Also, her boobs. Savannah has a great rack. I'm a little jealous." Kate added, knowingly. Now she was just messing with me.

"I hadn't noticed . . . her boobs . . ." I stammered. "Or anyone's boobs for that matter," I quickly added. Kate gave a little laugh.

Savannah gave Tex a kiss and wrapped her arm around the cowboy's waist, which was quite the accomplishment considering their size difference, and we all headed toward the barn. She updated us as we went.

"I guess everything went smooth out there. I been monitoring communications and I haven't heard anything. Nothing from the police, sheriff, the base, nobody. It's just been regular chatter. That's good. That's what we want."

"Smooth as silk, darlin'." Tex gave her another kiss and a mischievous wink as we walked inside.

"Mission accomplished. Am I right?" a cocky Gill blurted out. This guy was too much. "Hey, is it too late to grab some chow or something to drink? I'm starving," he added.

"Now just hold your horses, sweetheart," Savannah said as she made her way up the ladder followed by Tex, who smacked her on the backside. "Dammit, baby. Don't do that right now," she chided him. Then for everyone else's benefit she added, "We just got to get word from Wifi that everything's looking good on that satellite. It'll make its first pass in just a bit. Baby, if you touch my ass again, I'm gonna kick you in the head. Just wait. Now Gill, once we get word that we're in the clear we can all officially relax, and we'll rustle up something for you. How's that sound?"

"Good times. Much obliged," Gill replied with a nod of his fishlike head. *"Much obliged?"* I thought. *Did he just say "much obliged?" Gill needs to dial down his suck up factor by about one hundred.*

Once upstairs in the nest, we locked up the guns. I left the backpack with the laptop in it on the table. Then we went back down the ladder and waited for Savannah who stayed up in the nest, waiting for a signal from Wifi. I had no idea how that would be accomplished. Just add that to the list of things I didn't need to know, I guessed.

Moments later Savannah came scurrying down the ladder and practically leapt into Tex's arms.

"We're all good! Wifi says it worked. He just confirmed the count from the department's systems test. We don't have to move! We can stay!" She showered Tex with kisses. Gill, Kate and I just looked on happily. I knew it worked. I did it. Still a gigantic relief to get the official word, though.

Savannah broke away from her husband long enough to give me a big hug as well.

"You did good, Squirrely." She planted a kiss on my cheek. "You did your part, now let's get you off to Mars, if that's what you still want. Last chance to change your mind."

"Yes. Mars. Please. Let's do it."

"We'll go over all the details in the morning, but right now, I think we need to party. Just a little bit. Y'all earned it."

So, that's what we did.

*****

I sat on the porch of the bunkhouse drinking a cold beer as country music played from a speaker across the way. Tex said it was a guy named Hank Williams singing. Never heard of him before. He had a high-pitched, warbly voice, but I kind of liked it. The ranch hands and everyone else seemed to be milling around, enjoying themselves, chatting happily over by the main house. I was perfectly content with my spot on the porch. It was awfully close to being relaxing.

Savannah strolled over, a beer in each hand, looking like

she was feeling good about everything too. "You ready for another cold one?" she asked as she approached.

I saluted her with my beer bottle. "I'm good, thanks. Still working on this one."

"Suit yourself." She sat down in the chair next to mine. For a second, we just looked out into the night. I still couldn't get over how far off you could see, just by the light of the stars. Savannah reached out and pointed to a particularly bright one, flickering in the night sky.

"There's your new home. That one's Mars." She said it like she was showing me a shirt on a website. So casual. "This time next week, you'll be sitting up there having drinks and looking back down here at us."

That thought had never occurred to me. In all my years of dreaming about going to Mars it all just never seemed real, but now I guess it was. If this group Savannah and Tex worked for could, in fact, get me there.

"How does this work, exactly? How do I actually get there?" I had to ask. She reached into her back pocket and produced a folded white envelope and handed it to me. As I went to open it, she stopped me.

"In there is all the info for your next contact. It'll be another safehouse and they'll set you up with everything you need: ID, passport, all that shit. Then they'll send you on to the next. That'll probably be a spaceport that they got some people working for and then you'll get on a rocket and . . . whoooosh, off you go to Mars and freedom." She ended her explanation by pointing her beer bottle towards the star she said was Mars, then turned back towards me.

"And you trust these people?" I gestured to the envelope.

"Absolutely."

"When can I open this?"

"As soon as I'm not around. I don't wanna know any more than I have to. And don't go telling anyone else where you're headed. This whole thing works on people being able to keep secrets. Less people know, the better, for everyone's sake." She took a sip of her beer and added, "I'm just glad Tex and I don't have to pull up stakes and leave. Tex! You're getting laid tonight!" she yelled to the giant over by the main house then turned back to me nonchalant. "You can stay too, you know. We need people with your skills. We could get you set up with another cell somewhere in North America. You could be a freedom fighter just like us. That'd be easy as falling off a log."

"I think I'll stick with the Mars plan. It's just been my dream for such a long time. Besides, I don't think I could ever relax down here anymore knowing I'm a wanted man. And I'm not cut out for stuff like this. Missions and guns in the middle of the night. That's for crazy people. No offense. You know what I mean. You aren't crazy . . . you and Tex and Kate are just . . . different. In a good way." I quickly added.

She gave me a little wink and a knowing nod then got up. "No worries. Mars it is. Just hang on to that envelope. We'll get you on your way manana."

I smiled and nodded back. She patted me on the shoulder and headed back to the party and the group. I sat there, holding my ticket to a new life in my hand and took a deep breath. It was all so unreal. My gaze drifted across the ranch and all the people, looking for Kate. She was nowhere to be seen.

Bits of people's conversations and laughter drifted across the ranch. They all seemed so happy. I looked back up at Mars, shining in the night, and tucked the envelope into my back pocket.

The Hank Williams guy on the music player was singing a song about a whippoorwill and being so lonesome he could cry.

As I took a sip of my beer my eyes were drawn to a nearby hillside. Something was on top of it. A dog? If it was a dog, it was a huge one. Then the light hit it just right. I could tell then; it was a wolf. An actual wolf. Like in a zoo, but outside. It was just standing there on the hill, watching us. The creature was magnificent. I'd never seen anything like it. A real, wild animal. It almost felt like it was looking at me. I looked back at him. Hank Williams kept singing about being lonely. It was a great song. Just perfect. Then it ended and the wolf in the distance slowly trotted away into the dark and the moment was over.

"Canis lupus," a voice whispered from my right. It was Kate. Sitting in the chair next me. How did she do that? I never even heard her. That was an unsettling little trick, but I was glad to see her.

"Did you see that thing?" I asked.

"I did. Very cool." She looked off towards the hill where the wild animal had just been. "They used to be all over Texas, then they got killed or chased out. Somehow they survived and started coming back a few years ago."

"I wonder why?"

"Guess they wanted it."

"Guess so," I added.

The sound of one of Gill's loud, barkish laughs erupted from the group over by the main house. I was glad he was over there. Happy to have a moment that was just me and Kate. No insane levels of stress over secret missions or getting shot. Just my usual heart-pounding anxiety over a situation like this. Kate and I on a porch, having a beer. And me with a million things I wanted to know about her. I didn't know where to start.

"Savannah give you your envelope?" she asked.

"She did. Guess I'm all set." I took a breath. "Can I ask you a question?"

"Shoot."

"How did you end up here? With these people? How did you get this life?"

"That was three."

"Oh. I'm a horrible counter. I thought you knew. Don't tell Tex or Savannah; they'll be super pissed about the satellite thing," I said with grin.

Kate grinned back and took a swig from her beer. "Well, long story short, a few years ago I started seeing some things I didn't like. Not really seeing but noticing. I was going to school, studying history like a good little college person."

"Ah, history major. Nice. I like it."

"Thank you. Well, that's what the high school placement test said, so I was kind of locked into that one. I made the mistake of studying American history. Anyway, a good friend of mine worked at the library and had access to everything, including all kinds of banned books. None of these were allowed on the shelves. The university had 'em under lock and key. I had no idea there were so many! But there were tons and I started reading and, you know, taking it all in. Fiction, non-fiction, historical stuff mostly. And then it started to dawn on me: this place, this country wasn't always like it is now. People used to be free. It sounded wonderful. No giant government running your life. You could make your own decisions. Go where you wanted. Say what you wanted. This place used to be amazing. The more I read, and the more I learned, the more changes I noticed. We'd lost the idea of what made us different and incredible, and it pissed me off. Then I started acting out, getting in trouble. A lot of trouble." She had a far-off look in her eyes.

"What happened?"

"Someone got hurt. Someone I cared about. Someone who didn't deserve any of it."

"I'm sorry about that."

Well, we both got in trouble. Big time. The authorities were less than pleased with my . . . activities. My friend ended up making a deal to testify against me and I got sentenced to a re-education camp. Four years. But . . . before I got transferred, that beautiful lady over there swooped in and got me out." She pointed to Savannah who was locked in a conversation with Gill, poor soul.

"Wow. So, Savannah got you? Like you got me."

"Yup, been with her and Tex and the rest of the outfit ever since. That was . . . eight years ago? Funny thing is, if big brother hadn't made me study to be a history teacher, I never would've ended up here fighting big brother. I didn't even want to be a history teacher.

"What did you want to be?"

She took a moment to consider. "I wanted to own a

motorcycle shop."

"They don't even make those things anymore. Too many people got hurt."

"That's what they tell me. But isn't it my decision if I want a motorcycle? It should be. It used to be."

"Good point. I bet you'd be great on a motorcycle. You sure can fly the hell out of an aircar." I meant it. She could do whatever she wanted. Kate had that confidence.

She looked at me and smiled. It dawned on me then that I probably wouldn't see her again after tomorrow. This would be it. I'd only known her for a couple days, but I didn't want it to end. There just wasn't enough time.

The cowboy on the speakers was singing another song I'd never heard before. It was a slow one about how there wouldn't be any teardrops tonight. My heart practically beat out the same rhythm as I looked at Kate. I desperately wanted to at least just ask her to dance, but I was terrified. I looked back to where the wolf had been. He was long gone. Then something just clicked. Screw it, I told myself. This is your only chance.

Hank Williams kept singing and I stood up. I looked at Kate as the music played. I could tell she knew what I was about to do. She looked up at me as a mischievous grin started to lift the corners of her perfect mouth.

"Kate?"

"Avery."

Just ask her to dance idiot. It's now or never. What happens if she says no? It will just be incredibly embarrassing and soul crushing. It's not the end of the world.

"Would you like to—"

A flash of blueish light in the distance, accompanied by a sound like the end of the world, interrupted me. A loud, low boom washed over the ranch.

CHAPTER TWENTY-THREE

Kate leapt up from her chair. She had seen it too. What was I saying? I think half of Texas saw it and if they hadn't seen the flash, they definitely heard the gigantic boom. Everyone at the camp stopped in their tracks, listening. Someone finally turned off the music. An eerie hush settled over the ranch.

"What was that?" I whispered to Kate. I don't know why I was whispering but it seemed like the right thing to do. "Was that some kind of lightning?"

Her eyes scanned the horizon. "No, I don't think so. That wasn't like any lightning I've ever seen."

Another flash of blue light just on the other side of the nearby hills. Followed by another low boom.

Alarms blared at the ranch. A female AI voice came over a loudspeaker. "Warning. Perimeter breach. There is activity in zones five, seven, and nine." The message repeated. Savannah shouted to be heard over the warning.

"Hang tight, people! Nobody panics! Everyone, get to your stations and stand by! You know what to do!

I looked at Kate. I had no idea what to do. Another flash. This one was far off to our right, followed by another boom. This one was louder. Closer sounding.

Savannah and Tex ran to the barn. Followed quickly by Kate and myself. No way was I going to be left alone. Screw that. We all rushed up the ladder and into the little command center. Savannah and Tex hurried to bring all the electronics to life. Gill scrambled up too. Sweaty and out of breath. He had the wide-eyed look of disbelief usually worn by idiots. So, it fit.

"What the hell's going on?" he asked between gulps of air.

Tex shot back. "That's what we're trying to figure out. We must've been tracked or ol' Squirrely here tripped an alarm when he was hackin'."

"We weren't tracked, Tex," Kate said with authority.

"And I didn't set anything off," I added as a deep, almost thunderclap, reverberated.

Gill chimed in. "Then what the hell is that?!"

"Everybody shut up," Savannah barked. "We got eyes out there." She typed in a code to her computer and the monitor screen on the wall came to life. It showed several smaller screens, each being a different area around the perimeter of the greater ranch property. We all huddled around to get a better look, making sure that Tex and Savannah had the best vantage points. In one screen you could see the image of some kind of machine on the ground. It was tough to make out due to the darkness.

"Military drone?" asked Tex to no one in particular.

Savannah answered. "That ain't military . . . maybe it's local law enforcement. . . ."

"Well, what are we going to do? What the hell do we do!?" a panicky Gill asked.

"Shut up and stand by," said Tex.

Gill's mouth hung open. He was about to say something else and clearly thought better of it.

My heart was hammering in my chest. I looked over at Kate who was still all business. That helped. A little. Knowing she wasn't flipping out.

Another flash of light on the screen. It overwhelmed the camera. The image was a blur of white and blue. Savannah rushed back to her computer and typed in a series of commands. Another deep boom rumbled through the camp.

"Our defenses are up and running. Some of those are our flashbangs. But it's not the military trying to get in . . . it's a damn TV show." Savannah hit a keystroke and one of the boxes on screen now showed an all too familiar smiling face. Kira. Kira's reality show was broadcasting live from the highway just outside the Crazy Death Ranch. Shit.

Savannah grabbed the remote and increased the volume so we could all hear. Kira stood by the side of road, microphone in hand, a smug look on her face as she spoke.

"—the pervert who's been on the run for days. This gun-running psychopath. This impotent maniac will finally come to justice . . . tonight. We're just moments away from an all-out assault on the compound of death that this scum now calls home. We're doing this for you, America. We're doing this for the poor woman who suffered at his hand."

The camera pulled back to reveal Sharyl, her crocodile tears flowing freely but with a look of what she must've thought would be perceived as determination on her face. She looked more like she was really constipated. And the tears just made it weird. Like she was *so* backed up it was making her sad.

Kira continued. "We're doing this with these fierce warriors." The camera showed a quick series of shots of the bounty hunters. All seated in their individual tricked-out attack drones. They took turns mugging for the camera.

The video switched to a wide shot. An aerial view. A small army of security bots were positioned as far as the eye could see. Attack drones hovered nearby. Too many to count. Who brings that much stuff to capture me?!

The TV returned to Kira. "And we're doing it all LIVE. Right after this quick word from our sponsors. Stay tuned . . . for justice."

The screen went to a commercial for Aunt Hank's Spicey Protein Sauce. *"The sauce so good, it'll change your mind about bug sauce . . . and your gender! Aunt Hank's Protein Sauce. Preferred pronoun? His, hers, YOURS!"*

Savannah leapt into action.

"That's it. We're leaving. Everyone goes now! We got about thirty seconds till all hell breaks loose."

Tex looked at me and practically growled, "Avery, you still got that envelope? I nodded that I did. "Good. You need that. Kate, get 'em out with an aircar. Just wait for the signal." With that he threw open the hatch and launched himself down the ladder.

Kate turned to Savannah. She was worried. "What about you and Tex? We're not going to leave you behind."

Savannah was busy activating programs on her computer. She didn't even look up. "We'll be fine. Just got to give 'em something to slow 'em down while everyone gets out. Dammit. I was really starting to like this place."

Gill was making his way down the ladder. I wasn't too far behind him, but I wasn't going anywhere without Kate.

On the screen the commercial was over. Kira had an odd smile on her face. She ignited a road flare and waved it over her head in a red smokey circle. Then with a maniacal grin she looked into the lens and shouted, "Now! Justice!" and pointed the billowing flare towards the ranch. The giant line of security bots and drones started forward towards the ranch. It was surreal.

Savannah typed in a command on her laptop. "How about this, ya little pricks?" she said through gritted teeth. A series of small greenish pulses exploded across the distant fence line where the spider-like bots were approaching. The robots near the pulse were instantly crippled. There were just so many more coming.

"That's right, we got EMP's! How you like that?! Savannah shouted at the screen with more than a touch of glee in her voice. "What are you all still doing here? Go!" she shouted at us.

I watched three large drones coming in fast. They were flying high enough to avoid the EMP's. I figured those were the bounty hunters. Their ships were bristling with weapons.

Kira came back on screen. "You all saw that. Looks like our wanted criminal wants to play. Well, we're ready for him. And Avery, if you're listening, your days of bullying and pushing people around are over. There's someone here who wants to say something. Something personal." She handed the mic to Sharyl who was doing her best to look "fierce." Someone stood next to her. A guy. I could only make out his shoulder and arm. Was that Red? The cameraman changed his angle and now I could clearly see. It was Red! He was here too? What the hell?

Sharyl started into her speech. I knew I should be headed down the ladder, but I also had to know what she was going to say.

"Avery, for years you tried to make me doubt myself. You tried to erase who I really was. You tried to deny me my identity because you were afraid of who I would become if I blossomed. Fear and threats of violence and so many micro-aggressions I lost count. So many. I tried to count them the other day. I really did. And I couldn't. That's a lot." She choked back some fake tears. "Well, today it all ends. You're going to jail and I'm going to blossom."

Red sidled up next to her, his face practically pressing against hers. Sharyl leaned on him. Red looked deeply into her eyes. "That was beautiful. You're blossoming right now. Don't stop."

Was he crying too? It was beyond belief for me. Then my former best friend turned and looked directly into the camera.

"You suck, Avery! You hear me, you sick twisted freak? You're going down. You're toxic, bro! We're stronger than you. Love conquers hate and we're gonna throw you in jail for the rest of your life, you worthless disgusting piece of shit. You make me sick! You're a monster." He ended his tirade by kissing Sharyl on the forehead. She sobbed. Red comforted her. I tried my best to process what I just witnessed.

I just didn't have time. One of the bounty hunter's drones picked that exact moment to launch a missile into the ranch house. The explosion knocked us to the floor. I got to my feet and looked out the window. The house was gone. Just flaming piles of debris strewn everywhere. Tex was picking himself up of the ground. He didn't look hurt. The giant cowboy was dazed, though.

Savannah could barely control her rage. "You dirty

bitches. You damned, dirty bitches blew up my house!"

She pushed Kate and I towards the ladder. We scrambled down as fast as we could. I could hear the whine of drones overhead. It sounded like they were everywhere. Tex was waiting just outside the barn. A beer in each hand.

"You see the house?" he calmly asked Savannah.

"I did."

"I'm pretty pissed off." He was almost emotionless. "I say we roll out the thunder. Let these people know who they're messing with." He handed Savannah a beer.

"I agree. You blow up a person's house, there's hell to pay."

The two of them were sheer, grim determination. They popped the tops and took a long drink.

Then Savannah gazed up at her giant cowboy husband. "Start the music. It's showtime."

The two headed off towards the large shed next to the shooting range.

Tex yelled back towards me and Kate. "Get in the aircar and wait for the signal! Head south then get to those coordinates in Squirrely's pocket."

"What about you?" Kate shouted back.

Savannah stopped and looked at Kate. The strange look of calm still on her face. "Don't worry about us. We'll be right behind you. Now go!"

A massive drone swooped overhead and fired a small missile into an outbuilding. The explosion was huge. The fireball cast eerie shadows across the property. Ranch hands were scrambling in every direction, following whatever directions they had been given. It was a mad dash to escape. If that was still possible.

Kate grabbed me by the shoulder and looked me square in the eyes. "I have to get something out of my truck. Go start the aircar. I'll be there in a second."

"I'll go with you!" Another explosion.

"There's no time. Just start the car and hover. I'll be right there."

I took too long to answer. She must've thought I was okay with being left alone because she just nodded once and ran off through the flames and rubble.

"Hurry!" was all I could think to yell. I cautiously made my way towards where we had parked the aircars earlier, looking back for Kate almost constantly.

Small security robots were now on the property. I could see them crawling in the distance like metallic spiders moving closer. A ranch hand went running by me on his way to I don't know where. Quickly followed by the familiar whir of a small security drone as it tracked him from overhead. The flying bot shot a dart and hit the poor guy in the back of the neck as he ran. He reached back to pull out the dart but whatever toxin they used worked fast. His body hit the ground before he was able to take another two steps. Just an unconscious heap in the dirt.

I immediately grabbed a hunk of lumber off the ground to protect myself with. Probably stupid but it seemed like the right thing to do. I tried to stay low and crept along the sides of buildings, my eyes on the lookout for more needle shooting drones. Their numbers were increasing by the minute. Another explosion across the compound. All I could think of was Kate. She was counting on me to get the aircar started. Why did she have to go back to her stupid truck? I didn't know what to do. Go find Kate or go start the aircar. I froze with indecision. Huddled in the shadow of a building. I didn't know what to do.

Then the music started. Loud music. So loud it drowned out the sound of the swarming drones overhead. Electric guitars. Drums. All blaring from speakers around the ranch, an up-tempo song from decades ago. As crazy as it was, I think I actually knew this one. I had heard it when I was a kid. It was by a band my dad used to listen to before they were banned, Lynyrd Skynyrd. The man on the record started singing:

Call me the breeze
I keep blowin' down the road
Well now, they call me the breeze
I keep blowin' down the road

I ain't got me nobody
I don't carry me no load
Ain't no change in the weather
Ain't no changes in me
Well, there ain't no change in the weather
Ain't no changes in me
And I ain't hidin' from nobody
Nobody's hidin' from me.

It broke me out of my stupor. I knew what to do. Get to the aircar. Get it started and go look for Kate. I just hoped I could make it in time. Staying as close as I could to the sides of buildings, I crept to where we had parked the air cars.

Drones were still swooping down, looking for targets. Luckily, none had found me. One more corner and I should be right where I needed to be. So close.

A security drone blew up in mid-flight. Then another. Someone was shooting back, and they were good. I peeked around the corner to see and off in the distance were Tex and Savannah, shooting some kind of missiles at the swarming attackers. They looked like they were having the time of their lives.

Savannah was perched in an office chair behind what looked like a giant crossbow. She was laughing maniacally with each successful shot as Tex loaded the weapon for her. Arrows a yard long with plastic explosives on the tip. *Thoooom.* Savannah let loose with a shout. Then a drone would be blasted into bits and Tex would reload, roaring his encouragement the whole time.

The music played. Fiery explosions and crazy laughter. It was a madhouse. A madhouse quickly being overrun. Spider security drones were getting closer. It was way past time to leave.

Just as I was about to make a mad dash to the car in the distance, I saw Gill's body lying in the dirt. Shit. Did that guy get himself killed? Maybe he just got hit with a dart. As much as the dope annoyed me I had to help if I could, so I stayed low and ran over to him.

He wasn't dead. The tranquilizer dart was still in his back. I pulled it out and threw it as far as I could. That's what saved me. When I turned to make my throw, I saw the security drone targeting me. I heaved Gill's body and used him as a shield. It was a reflex really. Gill took another dart. This one to his groin. Good thing he was already out.

Thooom. The sound of the giant crossbow. The drone targeting me blew up.

Savannah yelled at me. "Get going, Squirrely! When you see the signal, go!"

I struggled with Gill's unconscious body. He was a big guy and one hundred percent dead weight. Somehow, I managed to drag him to the aircar. Getting him inside was a whole different challenge, but somehow, after several failed attempts, I was able to get him behind the passenger seat. His head might have hit every possible piece of the car on the way, but I got him in. Now I just had to fly the thing and find Kate.

Starting the aircar was easier than I imagined. With just the press of a button the engines and rotors fired up. Seconds later we were hovering a foot off the ground. I did it! I figured it out. That was good. Remembering what I had witnessed as Kate piloted the craft earlier, I did my best to replicate what she had done. The thing was pretty simple, just like an old-fashioned car, but if you pulled the wheel towards you, the car went up. Push it away and the car went down. Okay. That was good. I could fly an aircar now. Kind of.

The battle for the ranch raged in the rearview mirror as I slowly spun the car around so I could try and get a look at what was going on. It would also give me a better chance of success for the next part of my plan: finding Kate. The second aircar, still empty and parked, crept into view as I completed my slow turn. Now I could even see Savannah and Tex as they continued to gleefully launch missile after missile at attacking drones. Where the hell was Kate?

The side door flew open, and she leapt in the aircar,

carrying a large duffle bag.

"I was just about to go look for you."

"I told you to wait."

"I'm sorry. I was worried."

"Don't be sorry. It's okay." She was out of breath. I was thrilled to see her.

Suddenly Kate reached across the seat and pushed the controls down. The aircar slammed to the ground.

"What the—" I started to say and then I saw it. One of the large bounty hunter ships had zoomed in and launched a rocket right at us. Kate's quick action saved our lives. The missile slammed into the other aircar behind us and it exploded into a giant fireball.

That was the car for Tex and Savannah's escape. Now what? I looked over to where the two outlaws were still manning their weapon. Savannah gave me a knowing nod and Tex waved his hat as if to say goodbye. The hulking cowboy threw down the crossbow bolt he was about to load and picked up a much larger one instead. It was enormous.

The music still blared. Kate started to open the door on her side of the car, but Savannah shook her head and waved her off. Tex got the giant missile loaded and tapped his wife on the shoulder. This was it.

Security robots crawled like insects across the compound with zero resistance. Anyone left had already been darted. Smaller drones seemed to be hovering or flying everywhere. The three large bounty hunter ships approached overhead, flying in formation. They were showing off. Precision flying. Any second now and they would fire their rockets and that would be that. The end.

Savannah and Tex launched theirs first, though. The busty freedom fighter shot her gigantic bolt almost straight up. What an odd thing to do.

Then the massive explosion. A large, blue ball of pure energy erupted in the middle of the sky. The shock wave made every building left standing shake all the way to the foundations. That had to be the signal.

I pulled up on the controls and we were airborne again. The bounty hunters' ships were falling to the ground. Whatever that blue ball of energy was must've kicked their asses. My happiness was short lived, though. One of the ships managed to get off one last shot. The missile aimed directly at the ranch's last defense—Savannah, Tex, and the oversized crossbow.

The blast from the explosion knocked the aircar into the side of what was left of the small wooden outbuilding next to us, but we were still hovering somehow. Kate let out a gasp of shock. Neither of us could believe what we just saw. It was too much.

The music stopped. Drones were dropping all around the compound, including the last remaining craft piloted by the bounty hunter. I was frozen in shock at the violence.

Kate stifled a small sob and pulled up on the controls, taking us up.

"We have to go," she said, choking back tears.

I tried to get some semblance of composure myself and put both hands on the controls.

Kate pointed off into the distance.

"That way. Fast," she said.

I put my foot on the accelerator and we flew off. The wreckage of the Crazy Death Ranch behind us.

CHAPTER TWENTY-FOUR

I did my best to operate the aircar like Kate had on our satellite hacking mission. I wasn't nearly as close to the ground as she had flown, but I guess I was doing an okay job. We were still in the air. That was something. Honestly, I couldn't believe I was behind the wheel. I couldn't process any of what just happened. The attack on the ranch. The violence. It was all too much. That's why I was thankful to be flying the aircar. The sheer terror of that task gave me something to concentrate on. The idea of taking any kind of inventory of my life was just too daunting. It was much simpler to just concentrate on keeping us in the air. Flying across the dark landscape in a barely controlled panic mixed with fear. Occasionally looking at the screen that displayed the view of the rear-facing cameras, expecting to see the flashing lights of everyone who was trying to catch me. It seemed inevitable.

So, I tried to concentrate on the job at hand. My eyes constantly darting from the landscape below to the rear cameras then to the dashboard information: fuel, altitude, engine heat, and all that stuff. Then back to the landscape and the cycle would start all over again. This was enough stress. *Just do this and don't mess it up*, I told myself. Don't think about anything else. Don't think about all the people who were probably dead right now. Don't think about Tex and Savannah. Don't think about any of it.

I stole a glance over at Kate in the passenger seat. She

was staring out the side window at the darkness. Whatever emotions that had been threatening to overwhelm her as we took off were gone. She looked . . . blank. Gill snored softly in the backseat. Hopefully he'd be okay. It was Kate I worried about. She had been so close to everyone at that crazy ranch, especially Savannah and Tex. I couldn't imagine what she was going through. She just sat there, stone-faced, looking out the window.

"Hey," I whispered. "You okay?"

She took a deep breath and continued to stare into the night. "No. I'm not."

"That's what I'm worried about," I said. "You, not being okay. Should we talk about it? I feel like we should talk about it. 'Cause I'm not okay either."

"Just keep flying."

"That's another thing. Where are we going? I'm just kind of headed in a general direction. Don't we need a plan or something?"

She finally looked at me. Still with the same lifeless expression.

"They, uh, they gave you an envelope, right? Instructions?"

"Yeah, Savannah did." I dug in my back pocket and handed the folded envelope to Kate. She had her hand out, so I gave it to her. She opened it. Inside was a single sheet of paper with small row of numbers and some writing.

"What is it?" I asked.

"Coordinates," Kate said, punching in a series of numbers into the aircar's navigation system. The car slightly veered to the right. It was startling, but we were still in the air. The car just had a direction now. She shoved the paper back into the envelope and handed it to me. I returned it to my back pocket.

"Where are we headed?"

"Fuel," Kate said quietly. "It's an old hybrid engine. Batteries only get us so far. We still need fuel." She went back to staring out the window. Gill snored in the backseat.

"Can you tell me anything else, beyond fuel?" I gently

asked.

"No, Avery. I cannot. I can't talk about anything else, okay?" She snapped back, looking at me. I could see tears beginning to well up in her eyes. "Just keep us in the air." She turned away, blinked back the tears and went back to staring out the window.

"I'm sorry. I'll get us to the fuel."

A few hours later the sky in the east started taking on a purple tone as the sun threatened to rise yet again. An indicator light came to life on the instrument panel. It took me a second to figure it out, but it seemed to be the nav system telling me we were close to where we were supposed to be.

Even with the soft glow on the horizon, I couldn't see much. We'd been going without any kind of running lights since we took off. All I knew is we were in the middle of nowhere. Flying over fields and empty landscapes all night as far as I could tell. Nothing but the occasional stand of trees or small forest to break up the monotony. The monotony being me being terrified of crashing in the dark as Kate stared off into the distance and Gill slept the sleep of a large man who had been darted like a wild animal. My eyes strained to see some kind of a landmark as I slowed the aircar. We were getting low on fuel, and I didn't want to miss it.

Kate seemed to come to life as well as she readjusted her body to get a better look around. I slowed the vehicle even more. Then, off towards the corner of an old cornfield, on the edge of a forest I spotted what appeared to be a familiar looking large rock, almost a boulder next to the tree line. I pointed at it.

"It that a "rock" rock, or is that one of yours?"

Kate nodded. "That's it. Put us down as close as you can."

The lack of any kind of serious winds made the landing only mildly panic inducing, but somehow, I managed not to wreck as I set down the craft with a thud in the middle of what looked to be last year's corn. The brown stalks still tall enough to hide our location from any drones. That's what I hoped anyway.

Kate and I headed toward the boulder. Gill was still fast

asleep.

She slipped her hand under the plastic rock and undid the hidden fastener in silence. It opened just like the one in Texas. Underneath was a large hole with spare batteries, containers of fuel and several backpacks. Kate handed me everything we needed, including two of the backpacks. She kept one for herself. Not a word was spoken.

Kate changed the batteries on the aircar, and I refilled the tank. We went back to the boulder to hide the empty containers and close it back up. The silence was killing me.

"So . . . what do we do now?" I ventured.

"We don't do anything," she said flatly. "I get you to Chicagoland. You meet your contact, then I get you and Gill on your way to Mars." She squatted down and started rifling through the contents of her backpack.

"Come with me . . .to Mars." I said it before I thought about it. It just popped out. She paused from her backpack inventory and looked up at me, a pained expression on her face. She was trying to hide it, but it was there, in her eyes.

"No. That won't be happening."

"Why not? Why not leave? You saw what just happened back at the ranch."

She stood up suddenly, an intensity in her eyes I had never seen before.

"You think I didn't see what happened? You think I didn't watch my friends die? You think I missed that? Well, I didn't. I saw it all. I'm sick of it. I am sick of watching people I care about get hurt. I'm not doing it anymore." Her eyes glistened with the threat of fresh tears. She kept going, though. Her body getting close enough to mine that I could feel her warm breath as she spoke. "So, no. I'm done caring. I'm done making mistakes. I do one thing really well and that's all I'm going to do from here on out. I fight. When I get close to people, they die, so I'm going to fight and that's it. I made a mistake with Savannah and Tex and I'm not doing it again. You hear me?"

"Listen, I'm sorry. I just think—"

She cut me off. "Stop! Stop thinking. Stop caring. That's a good way to get hurt. I'm getting you where you need to go, and I'm done!"

We looked at each other for a moment. She was so upset. I had no idea what to say. My mind was racing. Why did I bring up her coming with me to Mars? I already knew the answer to that one. Because I wanted her to say yes. I was falling in love with her. How could I say that now, though? Kate stared at me, a fierce look on her face, almost daring me to say something else. I had to, though. I had to say something.

"You guys, okay? Where the hell are we?" Gill's unannounced arrival ended that notion. He stood there like a big dope. Just as I was about to tell him he was interrupting, the guy started up again.

"Is there water or something? My head is killing me." He took in our surroundings, his matted hair sticking up wildly, dried drool on his chin. "Where are we?" the moron asked again.

Kate threw him a backpack, "Bottles of water in there. Some protein bars too." She headed off towards the aircar. I watched her go as Gill opened his bag and grabbed a water. He drank it down greedily. Even the way he drank was annoying. He let loose a belch as he finished the water and wiped his chin.

"Anybody want to tell me what's going on?"

"Tex and Savannah are dead. It's just the three of us now. We're on our way to Chicagoland." I didn't even try to sugarcoat it. Didn't have the energy to deal with Gill right now, but I knew enough to give Kate her space.

"Holy shit," he said as the reality of the situation set in. "I should be dead too. How'd I get here?"

"I found you in the dirt, out cold and somehow managed to get you in the car," I told him as I pulled a bottle of water out of my bag.

Gill was in disbelief. "You got me out?" He seemed so puzzled by the idea. "Thanks, I guess. I don't remember much." He scratched his head.

"What do you remember?"

His brows knitted as he strained his tiny fishlike brain. "I remember that reality show showing up with those bounty hunters, a shit ton of drones, and your old girlfriend. She's mean, man."

"You have no idea," I replied dryly.

Kate thought it would be best if we waited a few hours before heading off for Chicagoland. She said she put a new set of fake QR codes on the aircar, that way if we got scanned by security drones we'd come up as legal. Other than that, she didn't talk much. She wanted to be left alone, even Gill could tell. He managed to go through both protein bars in his backpack in a matter of minutes.

The only other contents of the bags were light jackets with hoods, some cash, a couple books of matches, a bandana, and a thin reflective foil blanket. Whoever left the backpacks under the rock must've just left them for whoever needed them in case of an emergency. I'm glad they did. This was certainly an emergency.

Just past four in the afternoon we were off again. A stoic Kate behind the controls. Gill tried a couple times to start some kind of conversation but neither Kate nor I would join in. After a while it finally dawned on him to just give up.

I sat and wrestled with the idea of how to talk with Kate about everything. It all just seemed overwhelming. We had both been through a lot. It felt like we were just doing our best not to buckle under the pressure. I knew I was barely hanging on. Anything I said now seemed like it would only make things worse. My thoughts kept going back to the bum in the park who warned me about my string breaking and being either a stick or an arrow. Well, I was a certainly more of a stick, I knew that now, and Kate was definitely an arrow. Both of our strings felt like they were ready to snap, though, and that was the last thing I wanted.

Exhaustion started to catch up with me. I had been awake and on edge for day after day. My body ached and my eyes felt like they had become a mixture of fire and dust. I closed them just for a second. Just a little bit of rest. When I awoke, it was night again and Kate was landing the car on the flat rooftop of a building. We had made it to Chicagoland.

The city could've been San Josisco. The structures and pods looked alike. All it was missing were the hills. Everything else was eerily similar. The urban sprawl was just as immense. It just went on as far as you could see. Buildings of every size. Each just as bland as the ones I'd left behind in San Josisco. The same drones buzzed overhead on their way to who knows where. The same noises: sirens, traffic, and the occasional scream or gunshot off in the distance. Even the wind felt the same as it whipped across the rooftop.

"You still have that envelope?" Kate said, snapping me out of my drifting thoughts.

"Here you go." I fished the folded envelope out of my pocket and hand it to her. She took a look at the paper and punched a set of numbers into the onboard computer.

A name and address popped up on the display. Emmet Hanson, 124 East Granite Street, 2B.

"Who's Emmet Hanson?" I asked.

"Emmet is your contact. He's going to tell you what's next so you two can get to Mars."

I looked around the surrounding cityscape.

"I'm a little fuzzy," I said, rubbing the sleep out of my eyes. "I've never been here before. Do we just wander around Chicagoland and ask directions or . . . ?"

"Memorize the name and address," she flatly stated.

"Got it!" Gill cartoonishly chose to tap his temple, the universal sign for *locked in my brain*.

I couldn't believe this guy. No way did he memorize that so fast. I covered the onboard display with my hand.

"Where are we going again?" I asked smugly.

"Emmet Hanson, 124 East Granite Street, 2B," Gill deadpanned, with a big, fish-like blink at the end. Holy crap, he did have it.

"Well good for Gill," I said with a knowing look. "But

Granite Street could be anywhere."

Kate tapped the screen again and a map popped up with a highlighted area off to the upper right-hand corner.

"He's four blocks away. This is as close as we could get with the aircar," she said, unimpressed.

Gill chimed in. "Wow. You guys are brilliant! A context coding system. Same set of numbers but the information changes based on distance! Really cool stuff."

"What does that even mean?" I said, looking at Kate.

Gil answered for her. "You have a set on numbers. That's your ID. When you put it in the system you get a location, like the city. Once you get in the city, the system knows the context, like how close you are, and gives you more information. It's super smart." He grinned the grin of a well-meaning idiot.

"Okay . . . that's good. So, let's go meet Emmet and get what we need and get out of here." I opened the door. Gill slid past me from the back seat and stepped out onto the roof, pushing onto my shoulder in the process. Kate didn't move.

"You coming?" Suddenly I was worried. More than my normal worry. She stayed behind the controls. I realized she hadn't shut off the engine. Kate didn't even glance at me.

"We have other cells, outposts in the area. I have to tell them what happened. Warn them."

"So, let's do that. Together. Right after the three of us talk to Emmet. We zip in, talk to this guy, get what we need and zip out. We can warn the others then."

"It's not that simple. These places are secret. Not everyone can know where they are. If they do, that just puts everybody in more danger. No one else is going to get hurt because of me."

"Kate, none of this is your fault. It's me. If anything, I'm the one responsible. I can't stop thinking about it. I wish I could go back and change all it. Everything. Never hack the stupid counter on that toilet paper dispenser. None of this would have happened. But then it hits me: if I don't do that then I don't meet you." I meant it. For the first time in a long time, I spoke from my heart. Just rolled the dice.

The quiet hung in the aircar. Kate should have said something by now. Finally, she did. She looked at me with a pained expression.

"Avery, I can't do this. What you want, I can't do. I can't be. You go meet your contact. He'll help you. You'll be fine."

"No, I won't. Kate, I won't be fine. Nowhere near fine. I won't be able to see fine from where I am. This," I said, indicating her and I, "this is the only thing close to fine. And to be honest, I think we're worth a shot. So don't go. Please."

She took a deep breath and tried to force a small smile. "I tell you what, I'll go warn the others and then I'll come back, okay? Meet me back here at midnight."

"Kate—"

"Just let me do what I need to do, and I'll come back for you. Get you to Mars. Be here at midnight, okay?"

"Right here . . . midnight. You're coming back."

"Yes. This rooftop. Trust me."

I thought about it for a second, but I really didn't have a choice. Ultimately it was about trust. Everything was. I thought I'd run out of it completely, but I guess I had a little left. If anyone was worth it, it was Kate.

"Okay, I'll see you back here in a couple hours."

She looked sad all of a sudden. "Yes, Avery. Now go."

I looked at her one last time and got out of the aircar. As I stepped back, it slowly rose into the night sky and joined the other traffic high above. I watched her fly away.

Gill put his hand on my shoulder reassuringly. "That chick is never coming back."

What a dick this guy was.

CHAPTER
TWENTY-FIVE

Gill and I stepped out onto the sidewalk of a windy Chicagoland night. I turned around and looked back at the building where Kate had dropped us off. I couldn't afford to forget it, so I tried to burn it into my brain. It was a basic four-story warehouse-looking thing. Brownish grey like almost all the buildings in the area. Nothing special about it, other than it was the place I was hoping Kate would be at midnight.

"What's up, Squirrely?"

"Trying to remember this building so we can find it later. Would it be too much to have people put numbers over the door?" I said, still looking for some kind if distinguishing feature.

"I hear ya," said Gill, picking up a brick from the trash strewn sidewalk.

Even the streets had the same garbage as San Josisco.

Gill hurled the brick through a window on the second floor. The pane of glass shattered with a loud crash. A couple of nearby homeless people cheered. I looked at Gill in disbelief.

"There you go. It's the one with the broken window on the second floor. C'mon, let's go meet Emmet Hanson at 124 Granite Street, 2B," he said with a nod of his head towards the corner in the distance.

"Okay, yeah," I mumbled, a little startled. I couldn't believe he just did that. I turned and looked at what I thought would be Granite Street. Lots of people. More than I thought would still be out this late. We started walking, avoiding the garbage and debris that seemed to be everywhere.

"Coming back here at midnight is a waste of time. She's gonna be a no show. We should just ask this Emmet guy to line up another ride," Gill said nonchalantly like he was discussing the weather.

"She'll be back." I tried to say it with confidence but even I didn't believe me.

We were almost at the corner now. Thankfully at least one street sign had managed to survive. We had found Granite Street. No drone taxis. No traffic. Just a mass of people wearing hoodies and masks. Most wearing backpacks and all walking the same direction. They were chanting something, but I couldn't make it out.

"We're gonna fit right in," said Gill as he tied his bandana around his neck and pulled it up to cover his face. I did the same. We both pulled our hoods up and made our way to join the throng of people.

Drones zoomed by overhead. I never really liked those things before and after what happened at the ranch, they really made me nervous. I had to fight the instinct to flinch every time I heard one.

"I know. Me too," said Gill has he patted me on the back and acknowledged my obvious skittishness. "Home stretch," he added as we made the corner of Granite.

I could make out what the crowd was chanting now as they marched. "Ho-ho hey-hey! Just eight days is a big mistake!" Someone was banging a plastic bucket as a drum to keep time. Others were blowing whistles and waving road flares, but almost everyone who was along the sidewalk or marching down the street was joining in the refrain of: "Ho-ho hey-hey! Just eight days is a big mistake!"

I looked to Gill, confused as to what to do. "Should we go around?" I shouted to be heard above the din.

"No, this is our street. Let's just join in. I think they're going the direction we need to go anyway."

I glanced around, nervous, not liking this situation at all. But I also wasn't thrilled with getting off the street we needed to get us to our contact. It was only a couple blocks. Worth the risk. I nodded my agreement to Gill, and we stepped into the rally or march or whatever it was. I tapped Gill on the shoulder to get his attention. The crowd kept up the chant as we slowly moved along. A light rain started to fall.

"Just be cool. Let's keep our heads down and keep a low profile. We should stick to the edge, too. Just to be on the safe side. We don't know who these people are or what they're mad about." I waited for Gill to nod in agreement. He didn't.

"I'll find out!" He shouted at me like an idiot.

Before I could stop him, he approached the person walking next to him. Some absolute stranger wearing a black hoodie and a mask that read: "If you can read this, you're too close, Nazi."

Gill interrupted the person mid-chant, which in my mind was kind of rude. "What's up bud? Why we marching?"

The crowd slowed to a stop. Something must've happened up ahead. The kid just looked at Gill and tilted his head as if he were looking at a crazy person.

"Why are we marching?!" The kid yelled. "Why . . . are . . . we . . . marching?!"

We weren't moving at all now. Several people around us turned to see the confrontation between the angry kid and the human fish named Gill who just did some stupid shit without thinking.

"WHY? ARE? WE? MARCHING?!"

Could this kid be more dramatic? What the hell? And why weren't we moving? Why was everyone just standing around?

Lightning in the distance. Might have been fireworks from the crowd up ahead. The rain stopped. A pocket of quiet descended on the area around us. Dramatic kid stared at Gill. A wildness in his eyes. He was waiting for Gill to answer. Gill just stood there.

I did the only thing I could think of. I took up drama kid's question as if it were a chant.

"Why are we marching?!" I yelled halfheartedly. Drama kid shifted his focus from Gill to me. I shouted it again. "Why are we marching?!" I gave Gil a nudge.

"Why are we marching?" he shouted.

This could work. We just needed a few more people to chime in with us. I waved my arms in a let's-get-loud fashion, like a cheerleader at a pep rally. "Why are we marching?!" A few people were following my lead! It was catching on!

Dramatic boy wasn't having it. He got up in Gill's face, practically screaming. "We are demanding the University of Chicagoland increase the paid holiday celebrating the birth of Michelle Obama to two weeks instead of one, and those racist, Nazis think eight days is enough! Eight days is a joke! And everyone knows that eight days is a thinly veiled reference to the white supremacist group from England in the 1940's, The Beatles!"

The surrounding crowd gave a cheer of acknowledgment. As if this guy had said something that made sense. He wasn't done.

"The Beatles racist rallying cry "Eight Days a Week" is a dog whistle for how long the Third Reich would last. And just how far fascists will go to keep people of color under their thumb! Which is another racist song from the white supremacy group The Rolling Stones. Why don't you read a book before you take to the streets, dumbass?"

Another murmur of approval from the people around us. Drama boy was giving them a little show and they were into it.

Now, I don't know much about music history, but I knew this kid was insane. I struggled to put his logic together. I remember being taught about the best president in history, Obama, when I was a kid, and I knew that the anniversary of his birth was a week-long national holiday with pay. And I know we also celebrate the birth of his wife Michelle because it would be sexist not to, so that's a holiday as well. And I know that twenty years ago the Vatican was attacked and churches were burned when Pope Jeffery the First refused to give both Obamas sainthood. But the last bit about the music groups had me confused. I tried to work it out.

"So, we're marching because we want two weeks paid vacation for Michelle Obama Day and the university is only offering eight days . . . which is a reference to The Beatles' song "Eight Days a Week" and that's a racist dog whistle," I offered up.

Drama boy just looked at me as if I had just stated the obvious and said the sky was blue. I nodded my head like I finally understood, which I didn't. World War II was over a hundred years ago but even I knew The Beatles weren't Nazis. I also knew it was bad form to correct an insane person in the middle of a march. So, I agreed with him.

"Those sons of bitches," I said, with an emphatic shake of my head. "Those dirty sons of bitches!"

A small cheer went up around us. "We're not going to take it!" I added, shoving my fist in the air. "Let's go!" A bigger cheer.

I pushed Gill and we started forward through the still standing crowd. Almost everyone behind us followed. We were now a mass of people trying to make our way through an even bigger mass in front of us. I could hear drama boy screaming his approval from just behind us.

"Go!" His shrill voice cut through the din.

The crowd picked up the cue. "Go! Go! Go!" they yelled as we bullied our way into a solid wall of fellow protesters.

We could hear the group in front yell as they thought they we're being attacked. I couldn't blame them. One second they're standing in the street and out of nowhere, a throng of people screaming "Go! Go! Go!" are shoving through your ranks. It could've been greater Chicagoland security for all they knew.

Turns out, the idea of being overrun by Chicagoland security didn't appeal to them. At all. That's when the projectiles started flying.

From out in front of us several bottles and rocks were thrown back towards the *attackers*. Gill and I instinctively ducked as various hunks of rubble flew overhead and hit random people behind us. Drones hovered nearby, catching all the action as the people in the back of the mob went on offense against the front. Hurling bottles, cans, and anything else that they thought would draw blood.

Things escalated quickly. The air above the crowd filled with every kind of debris as both sides went to war against each other.

I held onto Gill's jacket as we dodged and pushed our way forward. I tried to keep one eye on potential threats in the air and one eye on building numbers. We had to be close.

120! A building still had its street number painted above the doorway. Two buildings down would be 124 and Emmet Hanson. Gill must've seen it too because he redoubled his efforts to slip between the now quite angry and violent mob.

Fireworks lit up the sky all around us. The sounds of breaking windows, and the screams of furious marchers and the injured echoed down the block. Gill and I were on the sidewalk now. I still had his jacket in a death grip.

122! One more building. More objects being thrown. Now people on rooftops joined the melee, tossing whatever they could find at the people below. The word pandemonium came to mind. We hopped over the shell of a deceased garbage robot and kept our heads down. Rocks, bottles, and pieces of building filled the air.

"We made it!" Gill proudly declared and we ducked in front of the entrance of 124 Granite Street. He went to open the door, his back now turned to the battle. Big mistake.

A hunk of cinder block came hurtling from the mob, arcing through the air and straight towards Gill's head.

I used my grip on his jacket to pull him to the side just in the nick of time. The block missed him by inches and smashed into the building with a sickening crack.

Gill looked at me in amazement. The realization of what just happened dawning on him. "Good eye, Squirrely. Holy shit," he said, still shocked at his close call.

"No problem," I said as I motioned towards the entrance.

"We should go inside now."

Miraculously, the door was unlocked. We hurried in, leaving the war on the street in full bloom. I locked the door behind us and we made our way to the stairwell. Gill's hand quivered a bit as he grabbed the handrail. He must've been shaken from the near miss. I couldn't blame him. I'd be shaking too if a melon-sized hunk of concrete almost hit me in the head. He covered it as well as he could, though, as we made it to the second floor.

CHAPTER
TWENTY-SIX

2B was easy enough to find. It was the only office with the lights still on. The placard by the door read: *Professor Emmet Hanson.* I checked the knob with a tentative twist. Unlocked. I slowly opened the door.

"Hello? Anybody here?" I said to the empty reception area.

"One second. Be right with you!" came a man's voice from the adjoining room.

We could still hear the muffled noise of the brawl going on down in the street. A few sirens had joined the chorus.

"Can I help you?" said the man as he saw Gill and myself standing in the waiting area. He was thin, looked to be in his forties, and he had a neatly trimmed beard. He wore jeans and a blazer with patches on the elbows. The kind that every college must insist its professors own before being allowed to teach.

"Emmet Hanson?" I asked, secretly wondering who else it could possibly be.

"That's me." He replied with a slight raise of the eyebrows. "And you are?"

It hit me that no one had given us any kind of codeword or signal. There was a pause as I tried to navigate the moment.

"I'm Gill and this is Avery. Tex and Savannah sent us. From Texas," he just blurted out.

"Good," he replied with a small smile. "I was hoping it was you. Glad you made it. Maybe something good can come of all this. I heard what happened at the Texas site, but we can't dwell on that now. Now is a time for action. We can grieve later. Let's get you two on your way to Mars. That'll be a small victory. It's not much, but sadly it's all we have at the moment."

"Yeah," I chimed in. "So, um . . . how does this work exactly?"

"It's much easier than you think," said the professor as he motioned to the door. "Come with me. Everything we need is in my studio."

"Your studio? I asked.

"Art studio. I'm a professor of art history at University of Chicagoland, the one the students are so upset with. I'm not allowed to paint on campus due the hazards of accidental triggers. The college can't afford the insurance for all the possible emotional damage, so I keep a small studio here. My little secret," he said as we stepped out into the hall. The professor locked the office door and took the lead as we followed him down the corridor.

Lights automatically came on as we walked, illuminating our way. Framed paintings hung along the hallway. Each one appearing to be a blank canvas of a different size. Framed and hung with care. And each had nothing on it. Completely blank.

"So . . . you teach art," I said as we walked, and I looked at yet another blank canvas.

"These aren't mine." He turned and we stopped. "These are student pieces. The only art we can show or sanction as a college."

"They're blank," I offered meekly, unsure of what was really going on here.

"Not blank. Art," he said as he pulled out a set of keys and unlocked a door. "As I said, it's the only form of art the college can approve. In their infinite wisdom the students and the college board both came to the conclusion that any depiction of an object, animal, or person in the form of art is cruel due to the objectifying nature of being the subject of art. Also, it is inherently sexist and/or racist. And that cannot be condoned by free thinking individuals of higher learning."

"I'm so confused," I said to myself, but Emmet must've heard me.

"It's simple really, if you look at it from the triggered point of view. All art that is made by people is selfish and flawed as it was made by a person who is selfish and flawed. Every human being cannot be fully cleansed of some form of horrible *woke* sin, and if there is even the tiniest bit of sexism or racism even suspected to still exist in the artist, then to celebrate their art would be equal to celebrating the *ism*. The idea is too much for them. So, now art has been reduced to blank canvases as to better reflect the idea of art. The theory being, only the absence of a thing is a true artistic idea of the thing that isn't there."

"So, who makes these? The students?" said Gill.

"No. Again, if a male student hangs a blank canvas, that's a form of ownership and incredibly sexist and offensive at the same time. And if a female student creates art, it's only a reaffirmation of the patriarchy. So, these were actually created several years ago by a trans orangutan who we think was liberated from the Chicagoland Zoo. She showed up one morning in a sundress on campus and displayed a knack for putting squares of paper on walls with tape. It was incredible. We all agreed to call it art even though the squares of paper were white, which was considered so racist that two English literature professors quit and a third attempted suicide. It was the first time we had publicly displayed 'art' without a riot in four years. Emily the orangutan would wander around campus with a stack of paper and scotch tape, putting her art wherever she pleased, occasionally shitting in her hand and throwing it or lifting her dress and waving her penis at passersby, but everyone was appreciative of her art. We all loved her and for time she seemed happy."

"What happened?" I asked.

"One morning Emily had just finished urinating on the heads of several students and there was a bit of a commotion. Unfortunately, during the confusion, someone left half a hot dog unattended, and Emily found it at ate it. Several vegan students witnessed the event and were so traumatized they wanted Emily put down and the majority of students agreed."

"That's crazy," I said.

"Quite. Fortunately, I was able to save Emily's life and get her relocated to a sanctuary in the Amazon, but I was almost fired for insubordination and being dismissive of the emotions of the student body. It was shortly after that, that I joined out group of merry misfits trying to set things right."

We walked into the studio and the professor turned on the lights. The room was large and mostly empty. Easels, paints, and various old-school art supplies littered the space.

"Now, let's get you two to Mars," he said with a mischievous grin.

The plan was much simpler than I thought it could be. Emmet explained how the organization had a large presence of operatives at all the spaceports on the continent. Gill and I would be leaving out of Florida tomorrow afternoon. Arrangements had been made for us to meet a man named Moses Adams. Moses is the head of security at the Jacksonville Port. He would simply walk us up to the check in desk, past security, and then make sure we got on the ship and that would be that.

Emmet also presented us with our *magic tickets*. The magic was that the codes on the tickets weren't attached to any real person. They were linked to two QR codes. The QR codes were digital dummies assigned to people who never existed. Just scan the QR code and the system automatically gets the green light and you're good to go.

The only thing we couldn't lose, Emmet explained, was the phone number for Moses (who was expecting us) and the QR code stickers. Two tiny stickers we needed to put on a hat or a pair of glasses so that as we walked through the spaceport the passive facial recognition cameras would get the same digital information and be convinced we weren't two criminals.

Everything was in a nice little plastic packet that also included two burner phones so we could call Moses. They even included a couple credit cards so we could buy snacks when we woke up from cryo-sleep. I held on to the packet like it was Gill's jacket in the middle of an angry mob.

Somehow, though, it all seemed too easy. I double-checked the contents of the packet. Everything was in there. I handed a phone and a credit card to Gill. He looked a little pensive as well. It was the first time I'd ever seen him appear to be thinking. It was strange.

"You okay?" I asked.

He covered quickly, snapping back to his usual fish-person self. "Oh yeah. All good. Let's do this."

I looked at Emmet. "So, if this doesn't work, and we get caught . . ."

Emmet nodded and smiled knowingly. "It will work. It's worked thousands of times. That's how I'm still here and not in jail or a re-education center. Everyone who's come through here always has the same look on their face. Like you're about to jump off a cliff. And in a way you are, but you'll be landing on a free planet soon and not in prison. Your days of worry are at an end. A contact will pick you up on the same rooftop you arrived on and get you to Jacksonville. All you do then is call Moses and you're done." Again, the knowing smile. If he was a liar, he was one of the best I'd ever seen.

"I, um . . . I think Kate is coming back for us . . . " I stammered.

Emmet looked taken aback. "That wasn't the arrangement that was made. I have an operative coming in just over an hour," he said, glancing at his watch. "I have no idea about Kate or her plans."

Gill gave me a pat on the back. Not sure if it was meant to be reassuring or an I-told-you-so. Either way it hurt a little.

"Now you two had better be off. It's getting late. May I suggest leaving through the back and avoiding the *peaceful* protest out front?"

The sounds of fighting had quieted down somewhat but I could still hear plenty of sirens and yelling. Leaving through the back exit sounded like a very good idea.

"We'll do that."

"Off we go then," Emmet said, as made to lead us out. Then he stopped. "Can I show you something first?"

"Sure," I said after a quick glance at Gill.

"Good, good. I only get to show people this as they sneak through out little pipeline to freedom. It's a bit of a treat for me."

Emmet went to the side of the room and reached behind a series of blank canvases, pulling out one from the back that actually had a painted image on it. It was a picture of a bird at the top of a tree, surrounded by fog. The bird looked as if it was just unfolding it wings. The moment right before it took flight.

"That's beautiful," I said. "You painted that?"

"Finished it this morning. I'll burn it later tonight. Just wanted someone to see it before it goes."

I could tell it pained him, but Emmet forced a smile and then put the painting back into its hiding place.

He led us to the back stairway and down to the alley. There wasn't a soul around other than us three. "Off you go then," he said. "Your ride will arrive soon. Better get a move on."

"Yeah, I think I know where we're going now," I said with a quick look around. "Thank you, Emmet. For all your help. I don't know what else to say other than thank you and take care of yourself."

"Yeah, thanks," Gill chimed in.

"It's my pleasure. Now go. You don't want to be late for Mars!" Emmet said with a twinkle in his eye.

I liked this guy. His students were lucky to have him, even if he wasn't allowed to teach anything about art. I shook his hand. "Goodbye, Professor." I paused. "I really liked your painting. You shouldn't burn it."

"Have to. Can't afford to get in trouble," he said with a wink. "Safe travels to you both." With that, he turned and went back inside.

CHAPTER TWENTY-SEVEN

The walk back to the warehouse was uneventful. Garbage, old needles, debris of various kinds, and the usual city street trash with the occasional robot part made me feel right at home. Gill was unusually quiet. I thought he'd be more talkative now that we were on the homestretch. All I could think about was Kate. It had to be close to midnight and I really wanted to see her come flying back. She had to. She said she would.

I knew I was probably fooling myself. I saw the look on her face. That was the look of someone saying the thing they thought you wanted to hear. It was the look I'd given Sharyl for almost our entire relationship. If you could call what we had a relationship. Well, now Kate had given me the look and it sucked, because I knew what it meant. I practically invented it. I just couldn't imagine her not coming back, so I decided to hold on to hope a little longer.

We made it back to the building with the busted window on the second floor. After scooting around to the back, we sneaked inside and climbed the stairs and stepped out onto the darkened warehouse rooftop. We had made it. Now all Gill and I had to do was wait. We stayed in the shadows, not wanting to draw attention to ourselves. We didn't talk, we just listened to the city. The sounds from the street and the nearby apartment pods or the occasional drone overhead. Each alone with our thoughts.

The rain clouds from earlier were breaking up. Stars

peeked out from behind the gloom. A chill breeze blew across the rooftops. Chicagoland was cold. We waited. And I hoped for Kate to come back.

"Alright, screw it. Screw all of it." Gill startled me with his sudden outburst.

"You okay?"

"No, Squirrely, I'm not. I'm not okay. But screw it, here we go."

Gill had an intense look on his face. I'd never seen him like this before. It wasn't fish-like at all. If he was about to say something stupid, he was going to say it with intensity. He gathered himself for a moment, took a deep breath, then launched in.

"I'm a cop. I'm an undercover cop."

"Okay, you can shut up now. Not funny," I said.

"I'm not joking, Avery. I work for the government. United National Security. We used to be part of Homeland Security but too many people were triggered by the name, so they made us our own bureaucracy. But that doesn't matter now. What matters is a lot of people are about to go to jail for a long time and I don't want you to be one of them."

"What are you talking about?" There was no way what Gill was saying could be true. I refused to believe it.

"We've been working on this case for years and I finally managed to get on the inside. These *freedom fighter vigilante* groups are popping up everywhere and the government is pissed. They want arrests. It doesn't matter if it's twenty people or two as long as we get 'em off the streets. I was sent in to gather as much intel as I could. And after that? Everyone involved is going away. Like forever."

Shit. He was telling the truth. I could tell. Gill kept on talking. Just letting it all spill out.

"You saved my life at least once, maybe twice, and I can't stop thinking about it. I owe you, Squirrely. I owe you big time. I'm not dead on the sidewalk or on some ranch because of you. So, I'm gonna make you an offer and I sincerely hope you take it. Come in with me, turn state's evidence, agree to testify against these people, and I'll make all your problems disappear. I promise you right here and right now that you'll walk away from all this. It's the least I can do."

"I . . . um . . . I don't know what to say. What about Kate?" I stammered.

"Avery. Why are you even thinking about her? You need to stop. She's not coming back. Get her out of your head. You need to think about you now. I can get you your life back. Just do what I'm telling you and you're a free man with a clean slate. No more running. Heck, I bet we can even get you your old job back."

I'd be lying if I said that didn't sound a bit appealing. Not the old job part. The clean slate and no more running. Gill must have been able to tell I was thinking about it. He stood there, waiting, letting his offer soak in.

"What about Mars? Could I still go?" I asked.

"Sorry, pal. Mars and all their freedoms and elections bullshit are going to be off limits soon. The government has plans to shut down all flights off planet before the end of the year. We're losing too many people to their old-fashioned ways. The state wants everybody here on earth. Competition is bad for business."

So, no Kate and no Mars. Just back to my old life. But the running would stop. I could start over.

"Can I think about it? Take some time to mull it over?"

"Sorry, Squirrelly. I can't give you any more time. I'm done. I almost took a brick to the head today. I'm out. And when I'm gone the offer goes too. I've got two tracking devices implanted and when they activate the cavalry is going to swoop in and get me out of here. They can take you too."

"Wait . . . you have tracking devices in your body?"

"Yeah. My left nut was removed and replaced with a tracker. If I squeeze it or I'm frisked it sends out a signal to my location. I also have one in my colon. All I have to do is squeeze my ass cheeks together twice and it activates too. It's a fail-safe. For my safety."

"So, don't activate it," I said.

"I think it's too late. I may have accidentally squeezed a couple times as we were coming up the stairs. That doesn't matter, though. Once our ride to Florida arrives, I'm grabbing my nut and I'm done. We've got plenty of arrests to make already. The professor, any stragglers from Texas, and now all the info on spaceport traitors. We'll be heroes. It's a good offer, Squirrelly. I'm throwing you a lifeline. Really suggest you take it."

It was too much to think about. My head was swimming. Why couldn't anything be easy? Just once.

"What about Sharyl and Kira and her show?"

"That's easy. Probably be great press. When people find out you were working undercover? It'll be great for ratings. Everyone from that show will thank you."

I had to think this through. It *was* a great offer. Going with Gill and starting over had a huge appeal. I could just go back. All would be forgiven. My old life. But was I happy then? I stood there and thought about my happiest moments. It amazed me how many involved Texas and Kate. The way it felt just being able to be myself when I was around her. Somehow, I thought I'd caught a glimpse of another me being around her. An Avery that could've been. I just didn't think there'd be a future for that guy. The freedom fighter Avery who got the girl of his dreams. Besides, Kate was nowhere to be seen. I was all alone again. Time to make the smart move and look out for myself. Do the safe thing. It wasn't sexy but it was safe.

Once again, my thoughts went back to the crazy bum I met in San Josisco. He asked me if I was a stick. He told me I had to choose if I would be a stick or an arrow. Maybe the universe had chosen for me. Maybe I was a stick. Was that so bad?

"Avery—"

Gill's voice brought me back to reality. I turned and looked at him. He had the strangest expression on his face, like he couldn't understand something. Then he collapsed in a heap on the rooftop. A dart sticking out of the back of his neck.

CHAPTER TWENTY-EIGHT

Renée the bounty hunter, her blonde ponytail swaying in the breeze, stood on roof of the building next door, reloading her dart gun. A wicked grin on her face.

"Well, hello, hello, hello, Avery! Where do you think you're going?" Kira's voice boomed across the neighborhood. She was broadcasting live from her drone that slowly rose above the building across from me. Her face appeared on the digital billboard on the rooftop.

More drones hovered into view. Several small security models and another larger passenger style. I could only imagine who was in that one.

"We are live, people! Tonight, we will finally witness a criminal meet the justice he deserves! We're all here for this, so you be here for us!" Kira's face took up the entire billboard and cast strange, surreal shadows across the roof. She went on. "He's trapped like the rat that he is! Tonight's capture of this selfish animal is dedicated to everyone who's ever been lied to. Everyone who's ever been hurt. And everyone who wants justice for the people!"

A cheer went up from the street and nearby buildings. People must've been watching, not only on the billboard but on their phones as well. Kira still wasn't done with her speech.

"And who did Avery hurt the most? The only woman strong enough to fight back, the woman who turned him in . . . Sharyl!"

A large drone landed on the roof and Sharyl stepped out, a small camera drone capturing the moment for the show. Sharyl's incredibly fake look of determination filled the screen. Another cheer from the neighbors.

"You're going down this time, asshole. I'm stronger than you." she told me. She had the audacity to smile at the camera.

Then Red stepped out of the passenger side with a raised fist in the air. The cheer was even louder for him. He looked into the camera and winked. Then he pointed at me and shook his head in disappointment. "I hate you man! You used my friendship for evil!"

"What!?" I screamed. "You used my friendship for reward money! And I had to beg you just to borrow a stupid shirt!" Red looked at me, deadly serious. "It wasn't a stupid shirt. It was cool. And you can keep it. I don't want anything from a sick, twisted, scumbag like you." The crowd howled with approval.

A small camera drone drifted over to me. Evidently, they wanted more of my reaction on camera. I looked back at the door to the stairwell Gill and I had used to get to the roof. It was guarded by a security robot. The way was blocked. I was trapped on this shit-show.

Kira must've seen my desperation. "Ah, ah, ahhhh," she chided. "No chance to escape that way, little man. You won't be going anywhere tonight but jail where you belong." The crowd voiced their approval. "You don't have your outlaw friends this time. It's just you against us and the best team of women bounty hunters the world has ever seen!"

The camera revealed the bounty hunters now standing in a hero pose, Tasers and dart guns out, next to Sharyl and Red.

"And it's all happening live!" Kira's billboard sized face shouted. The crowd went wild. The bounty hunters slowly started towards me.

"Wait!" I yelled. "Everybody just wait a second!" The image on the billboard changed to a live shot of me. "This isn't right. None of this is right."

Boos from the neighborhood audience. Kira shut that

down quickly.

"What's the matter, Avery, are you scared?" That got a laugh from the crowd.

The bounty hunters stopped their advance. The laughter quieted down. I looked at Gill lying face down, then around the rooftop and the spectacle of it all as I gathered my thoughts.

"Yeah. I am scared." A small ripple of laughter from the crowd. "And not just now. I've been scared my whole life. Scared of doing the wrong thing. Scared of thinking the wrong thought. Scared of what people would think of me if acted like myself and not what they said I should be. For the longest time I didn't even know it. I didn't know I was afraid. I just thought I didn't fit in. Maybe another class could fix me. Maybe another pill or treatment would help. Maybe if I ate what you ate and acted like you, I'd finally fit in somewhere—anywhere! So, yes, I'm scared. Scared that everything got this far. Scared of what this world has been twisted into where up is down and wrong is right!

"What's my crime? I helped a fellow human being get a couple squares of toilet paper so she could have some dignity! Yes. I'm guilty! I tried to protect the woman I thought I cared for from harm when an attacker broke into our home! I'm guilty!"

A small cheer could be heard on that one. Thank God. I was wearing my heart on my sleeve and the words just poured out of me.

"I'm also guilty of knowing the truth. We're not supposed to live like this. Eating bugs and living in pods with our eyes glued to our phones. Being fed a constant string of lies. We're supposed to think for ourselves. Live how we want. We can be free! We spend our lives letting other people make decisions for us. Letting strangers convince us they know best and that without the giant machine of government and big tech our lives will unravel. None of that is true! I've seen it with my own two eyes. I've seen freedom. Only for a few days but I saw it! Freedom is real and it's good, but you have to want it. We deserve a chance to stand up and make our own choices. To live how we want to live! Don't let anybody tell you that you aren't good enough.

You are! Don't let them keep freedom from you! They know that when you taste it, you'll want more! That's what scares them! Good! Let them be afraid! They should be! All it takes is one spark of freedom and we can all have it! We can all be free!"

My words hung in the air. My pleading face on the billboard.

Then the crowd let loose a thunderous boo.

"Get him girls," Kira barked. The bounty hunters started toward me. I didn't know what to do. This was it. The end.

The aircar came out of nowhere. Slamming into two of the bounty hunters and Sharyl's passenger drone as it skidded to a stop on the rooftop. The driver's door opened, and a figure leapt out. I thought it must be Kate, but this was a vigilante dressed all in dark blue. A skintight body suit with a vest of tactical gear. Where had I seen her before? Then it hit me: this was the same woman from the street in San Josisco, Rabbit Girl!

She moved with the same grace and determination I had seen before. The crowd went wild!

Kira yelled in defiance and the figure in blue took a device off her vest and aimed it at Kira's drone. She pulled the trigger and a small projectile launched, landing on the vehicle. The now familiar blueish light of an electro-magnetic pulse lit up the area and the drone with Kira inside came crashing down on the top of the building across the street.

Rabbit Girl then turned her attention to the enemies on our roof. I couldn't see her face as it was covered with the same mask she wore before, but she walked with a quiet calm. The bounty hunters Renée and Denise blocked her way So did Red. Lydia, the third bounty hunter, hurried towards me.

I turned to run and immediately tripped over Gill's unconscious form. As I got up, I was met with a fist to the face. The loud crack set me right back down on my ass. The pain was blinding. Stars filled my vision. I shook my head and blinked hard, hoping it would clear things up. *Whack!* A sudden shooting pain in my ribs. That had to be a kick. It knocked the air from my lungs. I did my best to crawl away like an animal. I could hear

Lydia laugh.

My vision started to clear a bit as I struggled to my feet. I guess this lady was going to let me get up before she did more damage.

Behind her I could see Rabbit Girl dispatching any threat with an almost effortless ease. Her spinning kick took out Red, almost sending him off the edge of the building. The crowd roared its approval. Renée and Denise circled her, trying to get the advantage by forcing her to split her focus. The figure in blue wasted no time and went on the attack. Kicking the knee of Denise and breaking it with an audible crack.

Lydia started in on me again. Ready to dish out more pain. I pointed over her shoulder.

"You better watch out! That girl's a badass," I said in a hopeless attempt to buy time. She actually turned to look! I couldn't believe it. It worked!

We both watched as the figure in blue took on Renée. She launched a quick series of punches and acrobatic kicks. It was all over in moments.

Lydia was the last one left. Now it was just the blue vigilante against her. They approached one another. Squaring off for the final confrontation.

Lydia launched her attack without warning and with all the fury she could muster. The figure in blue countered every blow. Blocking with lightning speed. Then it was blue's turn. Letting lose with a flurry of kicks and punches that were more like a violent dance. With one spinning backhand punch she connected with Lydia's jaw. I heard the crunch from where I stood. Lydia was no longer a threat. She was out cold. Hell, I thought she might've been dead. The crowd reacted with an audible, "Oooohhhh!"

I stood there as the masked figure walked towards me. The carnage of downed drones, an aircar and several bodies behind her. I just stood still as she approached.

She stopped just in front of me and pulled off her mask. Kate. It was Kate. I'd never been so shocked or happy to see someone. Of course, it was her. Who else could it have been?

"Am I late?" she asked with that little smirk of hers that was simply perfect.

"Right on time I think." I smiled back.

"Good." Then her eyes went wide.

Kate had that same look on her face that Gill wore a few moments before. That I-just-heard-something-I-can't-understand look. Her knees buckled and I just managed to catch her before she fell. I laid her down as easy as I could. She had the all too familiar dart in her back. Sharyl stood behind her, a few feet away, holding the dart gun, a grin of victory on her face.

"Not this time, asshole," she said through clenched teeth. The crowd roared. Somehow, we were still broadcasting. The digital billboard keeping up with all the action as Sharyl approached me.

"Sharyl, don't," I pleaded.

"Shut up!" she screamed. "You are a horrible person! You're a piece of shit! You ruined my life! And when you do that to someone, there are consequences!"

Big cheer of approval from the crowd. Huge.

"Sharyl, I just want to go. I don't want to yell. I don't want to argue. Please, just let me leave. Okay? Can we just let it go? Please?"

More loud boos from the crowd. I certainly wasn't the fan favorite.

I watched Sharyl as she slowly made a fist, but I knew she wouldn't hit me. Sharyl had a code. Violence was never the solution. Ever.

Her punch landed with a crack in the exact same spot as Lydia's had. Right on the nose. Pain shot through my face and the stars were back. Holy crap, that hurt. That had to be broken.

The crowd roared. Yep, I was definitely the villain.

My eyes watered from the pain as I looked at Sharyl, a hideous grin of satisfaction on her face. She balled up her fist again.

"Don't," I said as calmly as I could. "I've had enough. I've been framed, vilified, chased, shot at, and beat up twice tonight. I've had enough. You can only push people so far. So, I'm telling you now, think about this. If you hit me again, I will hit you back. And you won't like it."

"Ohhhhhh," the crowd responded in mock surprise.

Sharyl reached back and hit me again. Right in the face. As hard as she could. It hurt. It hurt a lot. My vision went in and out of focus. After a moment, it cleared and I looked at Sharyl, disappointed. I guess this was it.

I punched her. Right in the face. Not as hard as I could, but hard. Her knees wobbled and she fell right on her ass, then kind of slowly laid down.

"OHHHHHHHHH!!" The audience was horrified.

I rushed to her side. Terrified that I'd killed her. Thankfully, she let out a slight moan. That was a relief; she was alive. So, I wasn't a murderer.

The sounds of sirens whooped in the distance. Sirens that were quickly getting closer. Panic started to rise. *What should I do now?* I asked myself. Kate was unconscious. Gill was out cold. *Should I run for it? But how do I run without Kate?* I couldn't do that. Maybe I could get her to her aircar. It looked like it would still fly. But would she just leave me again when she woke up? And then there was Gill's offer to think about. I could get my life back. Never be on the run again. If I could get Gill in the air car, we could sort it all out later.

Shit! I hated all the decisions. *What should I do?*

I closed my eyes and took a deep breath. By the time I exhaled, I knew exactly what choice I needed to make. It was easy. When I took a moment and thought about everything without panic, it was very easy.

CHAPTER TWENTY-NINE

The sky in the east took on the pinkish glow that signaled the coming sunrise. I had flown the aircar all night, exhausted and beaten, but somehow, I had made it. Florida and a chance to get to a new life on Mars. It was hard to believe but here it was.

The spaceport glimmered in the distance. The rockets shining on the horizon like silver arrowheads. I set down as gently as I could. This was only my second time landing one of these things. *Not too bad*, I thought as the vehicle touched down with a slight thud.

I looked over at the passenger seat and Kate lying there, her eyes still closed.

She had slept the whole flight. Six hours. I had flown as low as I dared after I got us out of Chicagoland proper. Occasionally looking over at Kate just to make sure she was still breathing. She had looked so peaceful. It felt good to be looking out for her for once.

The fact that it had been her who had saved me back in San Josisco and again on the rooftop of Chicagoland didn't really come as shock. It all made a weird kind of sense. I still had plenty of questions, but I figured now we would have time for all of that.

Popping the rear hatch, I reached in and gathered everything we would need. Kate's duffle bag, and the backpacks with everything Emmet had given to Gill and me for our escape to Mars.

I didn't feel bad about leaving Gill on the roof. He could go back to his old life now. That wasn't an option for me anymore. My path was clear. It was an amazing feeling.

Quietly, I opened the passenger door. It was time to wake Kate up and get going.

Her fist connected with my stomach with lightning speed, doubling me over. The air came out of my lungs with a whoosh as I keeled over backwards, landing in the dirt.

"What the . . ." I tried to say, but it just came out as groan with a question mark. Did not expect to get punched. Not at all.

Kate leapt out of the car and rushed to my aid, a look of horror on her face. "Shit! Avery! I'm so sorry! I woke up and didn't see anybody, so I pretended to be asleep when the door opened. You never know. You could've been anyone!"

I was finally able to suck in some air. "It's okay . . . I'm okay," I wheezed out. Waving my hand with a classic give-me-a-second gesture.

She reached down and helped me up. "Avery . . . what happened? Where are we?"

"Let me get you caught up. Gill's an undercover officer. He was playing everyone this whole time. Just gathering intel on your operation."

"That son of a bitch," she said with disgust.

"He told me on the roof. Offered me a way out. Clean slate." I smiled mischievously. "That didn't work out. Then, long story short, Sharyl shot you with a tranq dart. She punched me a couple times. Then I punched her back."

"Good for you," Kate chimed in.

"Thank you . . . I guess . . . yeah. Thank you! Anyway, at the end of it all it was just me on the roof. The cops were coming, and I had to make a choice: escape with Gill and go back to my old life or escape with you and start something new." I waited for her to interrupt me. She didn't. She just looked at me and smiled.

"Thanks for coming back for me by the way," I added.

"You're welcome."

She threw her arms around my neck, and we kissed. A

deep soulful kiss. She tasted like strawberries, and it was simply the best kiss of my life. I didn't want it to end but of course it did.

We both smiled like two idiots. I can't be sure, but I think there's a chance I may have levitated.

"Wow. Thank you again," I said with a grin.

"You're welcome again," she grinned back. "So, where are we?"

"That's the best part. We're at the Florida spaceport and I've got everything we need to get to Mars. The two of us. It'll be easy. Emmet says all we need are these QR code things and your guy, Moses, at the port can take care of the rest. We can get out of here. Get off this crazy rock and start over, just you and me."

Her smiled faltered and she slowly let go of me. Not a good sign.

"What's wrong with that plan?" I asked. "That's a really good plan. I talked to Emmet about it last night on the phone in the aircar. I had to warn him about Gill being a cop, and he said Moses could get us both out before he went underground. It's a solid plan and it's the only plan. Kate, we have to go. Like now."

A sadness crept over her face. "I can't."

"What do you mean you can't? You have to. There's nothing left for you here. Mars is everything! It's the dream!"

"It's your dream. Mars sounds great but I can't go. Somebody has to stay here and fight for these people and freedom. And encourage others to stand up. This place used to be great, and I can't give up on it. I have to show others the way. Leaving would be easy. But it's not the answer. If everyone leaves the misery just grows."

She meant it. I could tell. There wasn't going to be any talking her out of it.

"Mars has been everything to me for as long as I remember. I don't think I'm cut out for life down here. I don't think I can live like you. Do what you do . . . I don't know anything anymore."

"Then you should go. You should go to Mars, Avery. I want you to be happy with no regrets." She forced a smile then kissed me again. A kiss goodbye. Definitely not a good as the first one. "Goodbye, Avery. Take care of yourself."

"Yeah. I'll try. Goodbye, Kate." I took a long look at her. Trying to lock in everything about her. I didn't even have a picture. This memory of her standing there next to the aircar would have to last.

My heart felt like a stone as I shouldered my backpack and slowly walked away. I promised myself I wouldn't turn around. *Just keep putting one foot in front of the other*, I told myself. *Some people are sticks and some people are arrows. Turns out I am a stick after all.*

I heard the door to the aircar close as Kate got in. Then the sound of the engine firing up.

One foot in front of the other.

I didn't hear the aircar lift off. She was still back there. All I had to do was turn around. One more step and I'd being going to Mars, but if I stopped . . . I'd stay here. But with Kate and a chance to make a difference. And to be happy.

I stopped. I wasn't an idiot.

Kate opened the door to aircar and stepped out as I walked up. A knowing smile on my face.

"You came back," she said, clearly delighted with my choice.

"Yeah. I got the wrong backpack. Mine is the other one, right over there."

"Oh." She was crestfallen.

"You know I'm lying, right? It's a joke. If this relationship is going to work, you're going to have to know when I'm joking. You're also going to need to teach me to fight. If we're going to save people and get 'em fired up, you're going to have to teach me a lot. A whole lot," I said with a grin.

"Deal." She practically beamed with joy.

In that instant I was certain I had just made the best decision of my life. As long as I lived, I'd never forget her look of complete happiness. It was fantastic. I wasn't a worthless stick anymore. She made me feel like an arrow.

Then she threw her arms around my neck and I held her close. We kissed. She tasted like strawberries. It was perfect. *This* was the first day of the rest of my life.

EPILOGUE

The wind swept across the burned-out remnants of a ranch in Texas. The stars twinkled in the night sky. A full moon cast strange shadows across the landscape. A patch of dirt next to the remains of an old wooden fence trembled as a trap door slowly opened.

An extremely large, dirty hand pushed it free. A hand that belonged to a giant cowboy named Tex.

"They finally gone?" whispered Savannah from the darkness of the hidden underground bunker.

Tex looked around at the desolation. A large wolf watched them from a nearby hillside then slowly trotted off. The giant watched it go.

"Yup. Looks like," he said.

"Then let's get started," said his wife.

And they did.

THE END

ACKNOWLEDGEMENTS

Some may call it an "Acknowledgements" page or a "Special Thanks" page. I have decided to refer to mine as a "Without These People There Is No Book" page. It's that simple really.

Right out of the gate? My friend Paul Hair. Without him, we wouldn't be here. Paul had the insane idea for a novel in the first place. It started with a very funny phone call and a suggestion that we write a book. Insanity! Several conversations later, an outline or two, and me going rogue on a draft or three. It had become real. From one phone call and a couple of grown men laughing like hyenas over an idea, a book had somehow occurred. Paul Hair, ladies and gentlemen. A fine hombre. Can't thank you enough.

Finally, another special thanks to my family—those who have passed, who I miss every day, and those that are still here. Lord knows I don't make it easy. I'm so very thankful you're around.

ABOUT THE AUTHOR

Michael Loftus

Michael Loftus is the byproduct of a childhood full of books, no cable television, and a family who believed in what therapists would describe as healthy mockery. Who gets ridiculed for reading The Lord of the Rings when they're twelve? The author. That's who. He's certainly not holding a grudge. Just saying it out loud.

The mocking paid off, though. A career as a writer on several hit television shows, performing his stand up all over the world, and now a novelist.

Michael resides in North America with his family and his beloved dog Jack at his side. They have deep discussions on squirrels, treats, and the plight of humanity in a post-World War 2 geopolitical reality. It's a good life.

Made in the USA
Las Vegas, NV
17 June 2024

91170380R00157